It was said that Stalingrad had been burning since August, since the dropping of the first German bombs.

There was not much joy in looking ahead: there was nothing lying in wait for us there but death or destruction. There was no joy at all in looking back: what had passed was a nightmare best forgotten. So we stared down instead towards the far-off river, the silver ribbon of the Volga, where the dancing rays of the autumn sun made shining rings on the water. And for a short while we were almost hypnotised into believing that the present could last for ever, and the past could be wiped out and the future avoided . . .

Also by SVEN HASSEL

and published by CORGI BOOKS

Sven Hassel

S.S. General

Translated from the French by
Jean Ure

CORGI BOOKS

S.S. GENERAL

A CORGI BOOK 0 552 08874 9

First publication in Great Britain

PRINTING HISTORY
Corgi edition published 1972
Corgi edition reprinted 1972 (twice)
Corgi edition reprinted 1973 (twice)
Corgi edition reprinted 1974
Corgi edition reprinted 1975
Corgi edition reprinted 1976 (twice)
Corgi edition reprinted 1977
Corgi edition reprinted 1978
Corgi edition reprinted 1979
Corgi edition reprinted 1980
Corgi edition reprinted 1981
Corgi edition reprinted 1982
Corgi edition reprinted 1984
Corgi edition reprinted 1985
Corgi edition reprinted 1986
Corgi edition reprinted 1987

This book is set in 9/10½ pt. Plantin

Corgi Books are published by Transworld Publishers Ltd.,
61–63 Uxbridge Road, Ealing, London W5 5SA,
in Australia by Transworld Publishers (Aust.) Pty. Ltd.,
15–23 Helles Avenue, Moorebank, NSW 2170, and in New
Zealand by Transworld Publishers (N.Z.) Ltd., Cnr. Moselle
and Waipareira Avenues, Henderson, Auckland.

Reproduced, printed and bound in Great Britain by
Hazell Watson & Viney Limited,
Member of the BPCC Group,
Aylesbury, Bucks

S.S. GENERAL

Germany has had the good fortune to find a leader capable of bringing together the forces of the entire country to work as a collective body for the common prosperity.

Daily Mail, London
10th October 1933

Sunday, 30th June 1934, was one of the hottest days Berlin had ever known, but it has gone down in history as one of the bloodiest. Long before sunrise on that day the city had been surrounded by an unbroken cordon of troops. All roads leading in and out were closed, guarded by the men who served under General Goering and Reichsführer SS Himmler.

At five o'clock on the morning of 30th June, a large black Mercedes, with the inscription 'SA Brigadenstandarte' on the windscreen, was stopped on the road between Lübeck and Berlin. Its important occupant, a Brigadier-General, was ordered out at gun-point and thrown into the back of a police wagon. The driver, SA Truppenführer Horst Ackermann, was bluntly advised to move himself, which he did at top speed. He regained Lübeck and made his report to the Head of Police, who at first refused to attach any credence whatsoever to the story. Upon the Truppenführer's insisting, the man could think of nothing more constructive to do than pick up the telephone and seek help and advice from his old friend the Head of the Criminal Police. Both of them had been members of the SA, the old guard of the National Socialist assault troops, but the previous year, along with all the other police officers in the Third Reich, they had been transferred to the SS.

'So what do you think?'

There was an uneasy silence from the telephone. The Head of Police tried a new tack.

'Grünert? Are you still there? It's hardly likely they'd dare lay hands on one of the SA's best-known officers, is it?'

Another silence.

'Is it?' he repeated, nervously.

This time, there was a cynical laugh from the other end of the line.

'You think not? In that case, I suggest you leave the telephone a moment and take a quick look through the window . . . You're behind the times, my friend! I've known this was

7

coming for the past few months and more. All the signs were there, for anyone who kept their eyes and ears open ... Eicke's been far too active for far too long, something had to break ... Not only that, they cleared the camp at Borgemoor a while ago, and you're not trying to tell me they'd let a place like that stay empty for very long? Not on your life! It's been taken over by Eicke's SS boys and they're already prepared for full-scale murder down there ...'

The Brigadier-General, Paul Hatzke, found himself shut up in a cell at the former cadet-training school of Gross Lichterfeld, now used as a barracks for Adolf Hitler's personal troops. He sat on a pile of bricks and calmly smoked a cigarette, his legs in their long black cavalry boots stretched out before him, his back against the wall. He was put out at his unceremonious treatment, but he saw no reason to fear for his personal safety. He was, after all, a brigadier-general and commanded fifty thousand troops of the SA. He was also an ex-captain of His Majesty the Emperor's own personal guards. He was far too big a man for anyone to touch.

Outside the tranquillity of his cell, the world seemed to be in temporary uproar. Men shouted, doors banged, footsteps thudded impatiently along passages and up and down staircases. The SS men who had arrested the Brigadier-General had muttered something about a revolt.

'Nonsense! No such thing!' Hatzke had retorted, with angry contempt. 'Any talk of a revolt and I should most certainly have had word of it. It's all a ridiculous mistake.'

'Of course, of course,' they had murmured, soothingly. 'That's all it is ... a ridiculous mistake ...'

Hatzke tore open his fourth packet of cigarettes and raised his eyes to the small barred window high up in the wall.

A revolt! Arrant nonsense! He smiled to himself. All other considerations apart, the SA didn't possess sufficient arms to attempt a revolt. On this point at least he was well briefed.

On the other hand, as far as the 1933 revolution was concerned, it was only to be expected that the two million members of the SA should not be altogether satisfied with the treatment they had received. Not one of the pre-revolution promises made to them had been kept; not even the most basic promise to find them work. Some, indeed, had been given positions in the police force, but their ranks were inferior and their wages were lower than the unemployment benefit paid in the times of the Weimar Republic. But while it was certainly true that the men were disgruntled and bitter, from there to an open declaration of war was a gap too great to be bridged. Particularly war against the Führer. If the SA ever were going to rise up, it would sooner be against the Army of the Reich, the number one enemy of the workers.

Hatzke suddenly stubbed out his cigarette and held his head to one side, listening. Was that the sound of gunfire he had just heard? A lorry started up somewhere outside, its engine coughing; a motor-cycle screamed past; a car backfired ... Or was it a rifle shot? He could not be sure, but the idea unnerved him. Gunfire in Berlin on this hot summer's day? It made no sense. Men were going on leave, preparing to meet their girls, lying in the sun ...

The palms of Hatzke's hands grew damp. He clenched his fists. This time there could be no mistake. He could not indefinitely pretend that the sharp crack of rifles was the backfiring of a car. And there it went again ... and again ... Outside, the lorry was still trying to pull away. It had been joined now by a recalcitrant motor-cycle. The thought crossed Hatzke's mind that they could have been planted there deliberately, in an attempt to mask the sounds of gunfire ... A shudder of anticipation shook his body. What was Himmler's band of thugs up to this time? You couldn't shoot men on mere suspicion. Not in Germany. Amongst the savages of South America, perhaps, one expected that sort of brutality. But not even amongst the barbaric Russians—and certainly not in Germany.

Another salvo of shots. Hatzke leaped to his feet, his upper lip awash with perspiration. What the devil was going on out there? They surely weren't conducting exercises in this weather?

He took an agitated turn about his cell. Could there after all be some truth in this absurd story of an SA uprising? But God in heaven, it was sheer madness!

He tried to arrange his pile of bricks so that he could stand on them and see through the window, but there were not enough for a double row and they collapsed as soon as he put his foot on them.

The firing went on. It was regular and deliberate, meeting with no opposition. It was obvious, now, that this was no exercise. It sounded to Hatzke suspiciously like a firing squad ...

He leaned back against the wall, wondering, not for the first time, what evil lay behind the gathering forces of the SS. That sick dwarf, Himmler, for example; vain, irritable and highly

9

dangerous; reputedly a homosexual ... Why did the Führer tolerate him? What plans had he made for him? What dark and unsuspected purpose was the man going to serve?

Hatzke turned to face the door as he heard footsteps along the passage. They came to a halt outside his cell. The key turned in the lock. He found himself confronted by an SS Untersturmführer and four soldiers, their steel helmets glinting in the gloom of the passage. They were all members of Eicke's division, the only division in the SS to wear brown uniforms instead of the familiar black and not to carry the letters 'SS' on their collars.

'About time, too!' Hatzke faced them, furiously. 'Someone's going to be in trouble for this day's work, and so I tell you! When General Röhm gets to hear about it——'

The Untersturmführer said nothing; merely cut across Hatzke's words by yanking him out of the cell and pushing him up the passage, flanked on either side by soldiers. He himself strode behind, his spurs clinking and his leather boots creaking. He was a mere boy, scarcely twenty years old. His hair was thick and honey-coloured; his eyes were blue, fringed with long blond lashes. He had the face of an angel, with soft childlike contours and a chin that was baby-smooth. But hatred stared naked from the beautiful blue eyes and the wide mouth was set as hard as granite. They were like that, in the SS: the flower of German youth systematically turned into efficient killing machines.

The great grey buildings of the barracks were washed by brilliant sunshine. Hatzke and his escort marched across the hot paving stones of the courtyard, where not long since children of eight years old had been accustomed to drill. In these same barracks, for years past, children whose destiny was war had been prepared to take their places as uncomplaining cannon fodder in the Army of Imperial Germany. In all the best families of the Reich were to be seen fading sepia photographs of boys of seventeen, dressed up in their heroes' uniforms and departing in all their false and glittering glory for death in the trenches of First World War France. They died as they had lived, according to the rule book. And who knew but that death might not indeed have been welcome after eight years of training and torture in the courtyards of Gross Lichterfeld?

Hatzke marched on past the stables, now filled not with horses but with weapons. The sound of revving engines was very close. He stopped and turned to his escort.

'Where are you taking me?'

10

'To see SS Standartenführer Eicke.' The man curled his top lip, derisively. 'I shouldn't try anything on, if I were you. It won't get you anywhere.'

The Brigadier-General grunted and walked on. Time to see about the lack of respect later. For the moment it was sufficient to reflect that for whatever reason they had arrested him, he would at least be guaranteed a fair trial. Men were not shot without a fair trial in Germany. That was what the regulations laid down, and Germany was a country that lived according to the rules. The Führer himself had declared that henceforth there was to be an end to democratic disorder and the start of strict regimentation. Every man should know his rights, and those who attempted to sabotage those rights would pay dearly for it.

They left the stables behind them and went through to a small courtyard, enclosed by high walls. In former days it had been reserved for cadets under arrest. Inside this courtyard were the lorry and the motor-cycle responsible for the distracting noises. The lorry was a large Krupp, a diesel, and the brown-clad SS driver was sitting smoking behind the wheel. He stared without interest as Hatzke and his escort appeared.

In the centre of the courtyard was a group of officers. At the far end was a platoon of twelve men, in two rows of six. The first row were on their knees, their rifles held at the ready; behind them stood the second row, rifles at their sides. Not far off stood a couple more platoons, patiently awaiting their turn in the slaughter. Twenty executions only, and then you were relieved. That was the regulation. Twenty executions ... Hatzke tried to turn his eyes away, but the scene held his attention in spite of himself. He had to look back again.

A man in the uniform of the SA was lying face downwards on the damp, red sand. On his shoulder was the gold epaulette of an Obergruppenführer. His body was just sufficiently twisted for Hatzke to glimpse the lapel of his jacket. It was red: the red lapel of a general. Hatzke found himself trembling. He turned his head away and wiped a hand across his brow. It was cold and clammy.

An SS Hauptsturmführer, a sheaf of papers in his hand, walked up to Hatzke. He did not trouble himself with any preliminary courtesies. He merely consulted his papers and barked out the one word:

'Name?'

'SA Brigadenführer Paul Egon Hatzke.'

11

He was ticked off the list. He stood watching as down at the far end of the courtyard two SS men picked up the dead general and slung his body into a cart.

The Hauptsturmführer tucked his papers under his arm.

'Right. Down to the far end and up against the wall. No shilly-shallying, please, we've got a lot to get through.'

Until that moment, Hatzke still had not believed it could be true; and had certainly not believed it could ever happen to him. He turned on the man in sudden, abject terror.

'I want to see Standartenführer Eicke! I'm not going anywhere until I've seen him! If you think——'

He stopped short as he felt the hard butt of a pistol being dug into his kidneys.

'That's quite enough of that. I'm not here to talk, I'm here to carry out my orders. Besides, shouting will get you nowhere.'

Hatzke jerked his head round, seeking somewhere—somehow, from someone—a grain of hope or pity. But the faces he saw beneath the steel helmets were merciless in their very indifference. And the wall at the far end of the courtyard was splashed with blood, and the sand was crimson and a thin red stream was gurgling along the gutter and into the drain.

'I'm warning you,' said the Hauptsturmführer. 'I've got a schedule to keep to.'

Someone slapped Hatzke hard across the face and tore open half his cheek with the sharp edge of a ring. As he stood there, the blood splashed down on to his collar and his gold epaulettes, and he knew with a clarity that amazed him that this was indeed the end. His own end, and the end of a vision that had dreamed up a socialist state where the word justice should at last have some meaning. Heydrich and Goering had gained the upper hand and Germany was lost.

Very calm, very dignified, Brigadier-General Paul Egon Hatzke walked across the courtyard and took up his position against the blood-splashed wall. With arms crossed and head held high in defiance, he awaited his death.

The firing squad raised their rifles. Hatzke looked across at them with neither fear nor hatred, but a kind of patient resignation. He felt himself to be a martyr in a great cause. As the rifles fired in unison, he shouted out his final words on earth: 'Long live Germany and Adolf Hitler!' and crumpled up into the warm, welcoming sand.

The next SA officer was already being brought into the courtyard. The slaughter continued throughout the day and well into the night. Word was sent to Eicke that the men who were dying, the men who had been his former comrades, were one and all expressing a wish to speak with him. He waved his hands impatiently. He was a man with a mission, he had no time to indulge in sentimental farewells.

'Get rid of them! Just check their names and get it over with! They're there to be shot, and the quicker the better.'

The furies and follies of that day were not quickly forgotten in Germany. It was those massacres of 30th June which accelerated the rise to power of a trio of men: Himmler, vain as any peacock and hitherto a totally unknown bureaucrat; Heydrich, a disgraced naval officer; and Theodore Eicke, a publican from Alsace.

Fifteen days later, the soldiers who had formed the firing squads, together with all but four officers, were thrown out of the SS—a total of six thousand men. Before the year was out, three thousand five hundred of them had been executed under various trumped-up charges. It was an idea of Eicke's, a final clean sweep, as it were, and it was loudly applauded by an appreciative Goering. Those who survived were packed off to the waiting camp at Borgemoor, where for the most part they were simply left to rot. According to Goebbels, Minister of Propaganda, they had met their death while quelling the SA revolt, and Rudolph Hess even went so far as to hold them up before the public as brave men and martyrs.

The Führer, of course, had known all along of the plans for the massacre. He had taken care to remove himself to more pleasant surroundings on that hot summer's day, and even as the murders were being carried out, Adolf Hitler was enjoying himself as a guest at a wedding party at Gauleiter Terboven's house in Essen ...

ONE

THE BRIDGE

Somewhere on the road before us lay Stalingrad, and we stopped the tank and stepped out into the open air to have a look. We recognised the town in the distance, by the thick clouds of smoke that still hung overhead, the thin wisps that still curled upwards into the mists. It was said that Stalingrad had been burning since August, since the dropping of the first German bombs.

There was not much joy in looking ahead: there was nothing lying in wait for us there but death and destruction. There was no joy at all in looking back: what had passed was a nightmare best forgotten. So we stared down instead towards the far-off river, the silver ribbon of the Volga, where the dancing rays of the autumn sun made shining rings on the water. And for a short while we were almost hypnotised into believing that the present could last for ever, and the past could be wiped out and the future avoided ...

But the tank that had borne us through the past was a solid reality at our sides, waiting to carry us on into the inevitable future, and there could be no escape. For four months we had lived in that tank—slept in it and eaten in it, fought our battles in it, both with each other and with the enemy—until we had become as much dependent on it as a tortoise on its shell. The only times we had ever come to a halt were to take on more fuel or more ammunition, and even then the supplies had been brought to the doorstep while we sat and waited in our steel burrow. Small wonder we had long ago begun to hate each other more than we hated the Russians! Within the four walls of the tank there were perpetual warring factions, feuds and blood-baths and petty squabbles which ended in a man half dead or at the least disfigured for life. The latest victim was Heide. He and Tiny had come to blows over a missing hunk of stale black bread, and when the rest of us had lost patience with two bodies crashing into us and kicking us and raining stray blows upon our heads, we intervened in the matter ourselves and passed judgement against Heide, with the result that he was condemned to travel the next hundred kilometres lashed to the outside of the rear door. It was not until he dropped unconscious, saturated in carbon dioxide, that we remembered his presence and hauled him back to safety.

All day long the tank rumbled on towards the Volga. Shortly after sunset we made out the shape of another tank, stationary at the edge of a wood. A man was sitting on the turret, calmly smoking a cigarette and contemplating the smoke as it rose into the dusk. Both he and the tank seemed marvellously at peace with the world.

'Must have caught up with the rest of the Company at long last,' said Barcelona.

'Thank God for that.' The Old Man shook his head, wonderingly. 'I'd begun to wonder where the bastards had got to. These Russian maps are bloody well impossible, they all seem to be at least a hundred years out of date.'

We moved slowly up to the edge of the wood and Porta pulled to a halt a few metres from the other tank. Joyfully we pushed open the observation slits and allowed the fresh night air to penetrate the sweaty hell of our prison. The Old Man hoisted himself out into the open and called across to the unsuspecting smoker.

'Hi, there! I thought we'd never make it, we've been looking for you all over the place. What the hell have you been up to?'

He was about to jump down to the ground when the other man tossed away his cigarette, made a dive for the hatch and disappeared inside the tank like a fox going to ground.

'It's the Russians!' yelled the Old Man.

As he fell back amongst us, we prepared for combat. We were lucky: the enemy, lulled no doubt by the calm of their surroundings, must have taken the opportunity for a nap. Even before they had managed to swing their cannon round to face us we had sent an S grenade, super-explosive, straight into their turret. At that range, we could hardly miss. The tank was transformed instantly into an active volcano, throwing up great chunks of mutilated men and machinery and belching black smoke and yellow flames into the dusky sky.

Carefully now, with observation slits closed and ears and eyes on the alert, we nosed our way forward in a wide detour.

'Enemy tanks ahead!'

Porta pulled to a halt once again. Several metres ahead, tucked away at the side of the road, were nine T34s. They looked peaceful enough, expecting no trouble, but their guns were all turned in our direction. The Old Man hesitated. The Russians had obviously not spotted us yet, but they were almost certain to do so if we turned about and retraced our path.

'OK.' The Old Man nodded at Porta. 'Start her up again, full steam ahead. We'll just have to try and bluff our way through.'

He opened the hatch and peered out. In the gloom of the approaching night his helmet looked not unlike its Russian counterpart. He was gambling on the chance that the enemy were not expecting any German tanks to be in the vicinity.

As we moved forward, it occurred to me that none but a complete cretin could fail to notice the difference between the

15

sound of our engine and that of a T34, but possibly the Russian crews were tone-deaf. At all events, they made no hostile gestures, merely waving at us and giving us the thumbs-up as we passed. The Old Man responded graciously, while we sat and sweated inside.

An hour later and we appeared to be approaching civilisation. Isolated houses, and then little knots of them, and finally long straggling rows, and we knew we were coming to a town. We drove past a station, where a goods train stood roaring and puffing. We drove through to the town centre. The place was crawling with enemy tanks and soldiers, but in the darkness and the general confusion we passed unnoticed. As we slowly emerged on the far side a policeman waved us down and yelled at us to give way to an armoured car containing some general in a hurry. We obediently fell back and allowed him to pass.

Not far out of town we found ourselves tagging on to the end of a column of Russian tanks. Under their protection we moved past a battery of anti-tank guns and parted company, quite reluctantly on our part, when we came to a crossroads, the Russians going straight on while we turned off for Stalingrad.

The roads were full of traffic. We had not gone far before we had once again to run the gauntlet, passing along the length of a column of stationary T34s. They let us go by without comment, and we guessed that their crews were snatching what sleep they could before being pushed once more into battle.

After the tanks, an infantry battalion, footslogging it along the road. They resentfully parted to make way for us, but our passage was punctuated by oaths of such vehemence and vulgarity that they might almost have known us for the enemy we were.

Another detour, to avoid taking the road through a forest, and we were at last on the way back to our own lines.

Three days later, the Company had reached the banks of the Volga, twenty-five miles north of Stalingrad, and there was an uncontrolled scramble down the slopes to fill our water-cans. It seemed that everybody wanted to claim the privilege of being the first man to taste the Volga.

It was, at this point, about fifteen miles across from bank to bank. The scene looked peaceful and pleasant enough, with a small tug-boat pulling a string of barges behind it and not a tank or a soldier in sight, apart from ourselves. Suddenly, as we splashed about on the bank, a battery of 75s went into action. Great spouts of water rose into the air and the unfortunate tug began a frenzied zigzag in an effort to avoid the worst of the onslaught. She might as well have saved her energy, she stood no chance whatsoever. Shells fell fore and aft, to right and to left of her, and finally, and inevitably, one landed amidships and the little tug snapped in two like a matchstick. The barges floated erratically onwards, a flock of silly sheep without their leader, and the 75s picked them off at will. Ten minutes later and the river was peaceful once again. Had it not been for the wreckage still floating on the surface, the little tug and her charges might never have existed.

Stalingrad was still burning. From where we were, the pungent odour of roasting flesh and cinders, of brick dust and ash, was carried to our nostrils and made us retch. It was a smell that clung to our hair, to our clothes, to our very skin, and it was to be with us for months afterwards.

We had seen many cities burn, but never a city that burned like that one. The sight and the smell of Stalingrad, voraciously devouring itself as it roared headlong towards its own death, was something that etched itself deep into our memories, and none who experienced it could ever forget.

The Company dug itself in opposite the hills of Mamajev, where an entire Russian staff was entrenched in a network of old grottos. During the night our heavy mortars bombarded the face of these hills, keeping up a constant barrage, hour after hour. Whenever they fired short, the blast of their high-explosive grenades almost tore us bodily from the trenches. Tanks went into action, but without any success. The bombardment renewed its fury and the 14th Panzer Division was finally sent in and managed to push ahead through the grottos and sweep them clean with flame-throwers, assisted by small-arms fire. No prisoners were taken. Any men captured were killed outright. Any who attempted to surrender were slaughtered before they had time to speak. It was the sort of bloodbath the SS might have enjoyed, but for most of us it was a sickening and degrading exercise in murder, forced upon us by one of those uncompromising orders from the top, which made wild beasts out of human beings and merely incited the Russians to return outrage for outrage and swear to fight until death rather than give in.

Summer had given way to autumn, and autumn was now giving way to winter. Slowly, at first, so that we scarcely noticed the creeping cold and only complained bitterly of the incessant rain which fell in torrents from the grey skies and turned the ground into one vast, squelching bog that sucked at our boots as we marched through it. It rained for three weeks without stopping. Men and uniforms began to acquire a greenish tinge. We smelt of mould, and clumps of furry white mildew sprang up overnight. We were given a special powder, which we ritually sprinkled over ourselves and our equipment, but it had no noticeable effect.

After the rain came the cold, and the first of the nightly frosts. We were still forbidden to wear greatcoats, but in any case hardly anyone had a greatcoat left to wear. They had either been lost during the course of a battle or deliberately discarded back in the summer, when we had been fighting on the steppes in temperatures of 100° + in the shade. Deliveries of winter uniforms were promised regularly from day to day, but they never came. Instead, they sent us some more troops, lorry loads of reservists older than God and probably unfit even to run for a bus, or raw recruits with beardless faces and innocently shining eyes. They came to us to fight in the hell of Stalingrad, fresh from their training colleges and barracks. They had no idea of what war was about, but they had been pumped full of propaganda and a determination to die for a useless cause. They flung themselves straight away into the fighting, into the gaping mouths of the Russian guns. There was nothing to be done in the face of such ignorant heroics. Their misplaced zeal took us all unawares and we could only stand back and listen to them die, as they lay limbless and moaning on the ground or hung screaming in the barbed wire and were used for enemy target practice.

That first mad suicidal gesture was enough to knock all the spirit from the few who survived. Propaganda was thrown back where it belonged, on the rubbish dump, and reality took over. They walked about with glazed eyes and defensively hunched shoulders, treating the enemy with the respect they deserved and placing the value of their own lives far higher than any spectacular death for Adolf Hitler and the Fatherland. Nevertheless, they made no complaints, these babes in arms and old men who had been forced to volunteer for active service. They were still Germans, and Germans were too proud to whine. They suffered the discomforts of the battle in silence, and they went on dying in vast numbers.

We had been promised one day of leave for every twenty recruits we managed to salvage from the field of slaughter, but it was a dangerous game and for the most part we resisted the temptation. More men were lost as they squelched through the mud in search of survivors, slipping on pieces of raw human flesh and tripping over mildewed bodies, than were ever recovered. The Russians were on the look-out for such rescue attempts and they had an unnerving tendency to release a barrage of fire at the least sound. Seven of our own men were lost in that way, and from that moment on we turned our backs on the lure of extra leave and let others chase after the mirage if they would.

The net slowly tightened round Stalingrad, where three Russian armies were said to be trapped. 'The greatest victory of all time!' screamed the propaganda machine, but we no longer cared for victory. All we wanted was to save our own skins and see out the end of the war. Only Heide showed any signs of enthusiasm.

'You just wait!' he told us, with a fanatical excitement that left us totally unmoved. 'After Stalingrad—Moscow! We'll be there, you see if we're not!'

'Sod Moscow,' grumbled Porta. 'Moscow can go and get stuffed for all I bleeding well care.'

I think Porta probably spoke for all of us. Heide was something of an exception, and his views could never be taken as representative of any but the lunatic fringe.

The Italian Eighth Army had requested of the German High Command that they be allowed the privilege of being the first to enter Stalingrad, and this was fine by all of us. Whether the Italian troops were so pleased is, of course, a different matter, but as far as we were concerned, the Spaghettis were welcome to all the honour and glory they liked. Strangely enough, the Rumanians also stepped in and demanded pride of place, and we sat back smugly and waited for them to fight it out between them.

'Who the hell cares?' said Porta. 'Who the hell cares WHO takes the flaming place so long as it's not us?'

'It's odd, though,' mused Barcelona. 'The Spaghettis don't usually go in for the death-and-glory stuff...'

The countryside for miles about became suddenly thick with Italian and Rumanian troops. We used to watch from our trenches as long columns of men swung past, singing as they marched to Stalingrad.

One day, while we were still waiting for news of victory, we were given a mission behind the Russian lines. It was a little matter of blowing up a bridge; a bridge that was essential to the enemy supply line and so well camouflaged that our planes could not spot it from the air. We were casually informed that although it would be the devil's own job planting the explosives, owing to the bridge being guarded day and night with as much loving care as if it were the Kremlin itself, the stickiest part of the mission would be to reach the thing in the first place.

'We've only got to crawl across a bog,' said the Old Man, sourly. 'Miles and miles of bleeding bog on our hands and knees...'

I thought he was exaggerating. I thought the bog would probably turn out to be a mud patch the size of a large duck-pond set in an area of general fens and marshes. No such luck. It took us several days to cross it, and I discovered that a Russian bog is one of the most treacherous bastards you could ever wish to meet.

To begin with, we weren't helped by the fact that each of us had to carry forty-five pounds of dynamite in a container on his chest. This in itself was enough to make life a sheer misery. In addition, we travelled by night and spent the day shivering miserably in the bushes, and after the first forty-eight hours we were up to our knees in mud and water. All round us were inviting tussocks of coarse grass, but these were treacherous and we stuck to the pathway: a trail of tree-trunks, just wide enough for one man, sunk a foot and a half beneath the surface. We had to feel our way blindly, and God help anyone who slipped. The bog was waiting on either side, thick and brown and evil, ever greedy for prey. And not only the bog but a variety of man-made traps strewn along our path by the thoughtful enemy. Push an overhanging branch to one side, and the ground suddenly opened up beneath your feet; pull on it an you found youself split in two by a concealed bayonet. Catch hold of an innocent-looking creeper to help maintain your balance and the chances were you'd set off a whole flight of arrows, sufficient to kill an entire column of men. One particularly nasty trick was to plant poisoned bayonets along the side of the tree-trunk path at one of its narrowest points. These were bayonets that had been dipped into a dripping mass of putrefying flesh, and one scratch while you concentrated on trying to pass safely by and at the same time remain on the path was enough to give a man tetanus.

No wonder our nerves were on edge. No wonder Gregor went berserk and hurled a grenade at an impudent frog that leaped croaking hideously from the reeds and gave us all the fright of our lives...

The sound of the explosion rang across the marshes. Terrified, we crouched down and waited for something to happen. A matter of seconds and we heard voices, a motor being started up, the grinding of tank tracks.

Porta, who was in the lead, turned and whispered.

'Ivan's spotted us . . .'

'Let's get the hell out!' urged Gregor.

We looked at him pityingly. Out where? Out into the bottomless marshes that lay all round us? Straight on along the path towards the waiting Russians?

The olive green nose of a T34 appeared, questing and sinister amongst the trees. The cannon swung round and pointed out over the marshes, over our heads. They fired three shells, and then very slowly, very quietly, with the minimum amount of fuss, the heavy vehicle began to roll down the banks towards the edge of the bog. We watched, horrified but thankful, as it slipped ever nearer the waiting brown waters. For a moment it rallied and we thought it might hold firm, and then in a final burst it performed a mad elephantine zigzag, turned turtle and disappeared. Seconds before, there had been an enemy tank: now there was only a thick sucking and thubbing as the contented bog smacked its lips together.

Some figures in brown appeared amongst the trees. They crept cautiously down the bank in search of their lost companions, exclaiming and pointing. Barcelona turned his submachine-gun on them and we sat hunched up in the reeds awaiting developments. A few moments' silence, and then a sergeant appeared, a short stocky brute who remained in the shelter of the trees and called out to the men behind him.

'Dawaï, dawaï!' (Quickly, quickly!)

They came tumbling out and Barcelona opened fire. The first to fall was the sergeant. For the rest, some ran back into the trees and others crumpled up and lay still. After it was over we lay still ourselves, crouching in the stinking brown waters, not daring to show our heads.

An hour passed. Another hour began. The boredom and the discomfort were growing intolerable, but at last the enemy tired of waiting and struck blindly into the heart of the marshes. A second tank was sent to investigate. Ponderously it positioned itself amongst the trees; slowly and silently it pointed its flamethrower in what was roughly our direction. A fierce tongue of fire shot out and looped across the marshes. It just missed us, but the heat was intense. They had two more tries. The marshes were ablaze all round us and we sunk ourselves deeper and deeper into the muddy waters, catching our breath and trying not to cough. Surely if they made a fourth attempt they would hardly be able to miss us?

There was a pause. Porta cautiously peered out through the reeds. A brown-helmeted figure had hoisted itself out of the turret and was staring out across the marshes, screwing up his eyes to see what damage had been done.

Porta raised his flame-thrower. Those of us who could see what he was doing could scarcely bear to watch, for if he missed his target and gave away our position we should all be done for.

I held my breath and kept my hands over my eyes until the shattering sound of an explosion forced me to look up. It was the tank. Porta's shot had found its mark and the entire vehicle was in flames.

We picked ourselves up, cramped and stiff, and continued on our way. Porta was in the lead, testing every inch of the path before him, Tiny one pace behind with his heavy revolver at the ready, on the watch for snipers. We knew from experience that no one could touch the Russians in the art of camouflage, and some of their men had apparently endless patience and powers of endurance. A Siberian we had once encountered had been capable of remaining at his post at the top of a tree for twenty-four hours at a stretch, becoming so much a part of his hiding-place that even the birds had accepted him and had gone to roost on his shoulders.

Suddenly, without any warning, Porta dropped to his knees in the water. Only his head was showing. He signalled to the rest of us and we dived in an instant, pulling out our respirator tubes and putting them into our mouths. Our camouflaged helmets were all that remained visible. For ten long minutes, which seemed more like ten long hours when you're submerged in filthy water, we remained hidden. Nothing happened. It was either a false alarm or the danger had passed by. Either way, such incidents were trying on the nerves.

Another mile or so, and before our eyes appeared the most curious and wonderful bird. Green and yellow, perched on a rotten branch, it performed a little dance of welcome, intended no doubt to intrigue and invite. It wagged its tail from side to side like a dog, laid its head on the ground and its rump in the air like a courting pigeon, whistled a tune and rolled its bright button eyes at us. That bird was there for a purpose. A trap for the unwary. But we were too long in the tooth to take beautiful performing birds at their face value. We knew that somewhere near by the enemy was in hiding, waiting for us to take the fatal step.

Porta, still in the lead, ducked down beneath the water and slowly waded forward. Only the faintest of ripples betrayed his presence. The little Legionnaire dived after him, his knife clenched tight between his teeth. The rest of us sank down and watched.

Porta reached the bird and gently surfaced. A quick look round, a hand stretched out ... Instantly, two shadows rose up. Two shadows dressed in green uniforms ... But before they could carry out their task, Porta had turned his gun on the one and the Legionnaire had planted his knife in the other. The bird, released from its role of decoy, rose squeaking into the air and flapped off towards the nearest trees.

'Christ almighty!' said the Old Man, straightening up. 'What a life!'

He took a step forward, his foot slipped and he swayed sideways. As he did so, he instinctively threw out a hand to save himself, clutching at the nearest clump of vegetation.

'Watch it!' screamed Barcelona.

He caught the Old Man just in time and they lurched back together on the path. Trembling, Barcelona pointed to the bushes at the side. We saw a couple of wires disappearing snake-like into the water and curling under the tree-trunks. We could only guess at the explosive that was packed away down there

'Jesus, what a life!' repeated the Old Man, wiping the sweat off his forehead. 'What a sodding awful life!'

A few hours later we softly approached a hut made of branches and balanced on one of the firmer areas of the marsh. We had spotted it from a distance and kept careful watch, and there was no sign of enemy activity. Inside the hut we discovered five of the partisans, three men and two women, who made their bases in the marshland and who dressed themselves up in hideous green masks whenever they went on operations. These particular five were in no state to offer any resistance. The vodka bottle had obviously been circulating and they were lying in a heap with their arms round one another and their mouths wide open. We disposed of them quickly and callously threw their bodies into the marsh, then spent the night in the hut disposing of the remains of their vodka and a case of dried fish we found there.

The following day we arrived at our objective: the bridge that we were to blow up. It was the biggest, heaviest, most imposing bridge I had ever seen. The prospect of destroying it was really quite daunting, and I began to wonder whether our journey might have been a waste of time.

Half-way across, snug in his box, stood the sentry. He was leaning back smoking, and his rifle was propped negligently at his side. As far as we could see, the reports had been wrong and the bridge was guarded by only the one man. On the other hand, it was strong enough to defeat the most determined of sabotage efforts and it was so well camouflaged that it would certainly have been invisible from the air.

As we watched, a column of tanks and light trucks rolled across. The sentry stubbed out his cigarette, snatched up his rifle and stood to attention until they had passed, when he at once relapsed into his daydreams. He lit another cigarette and the air became alive with the sharp smell of the machorka and its pungent Russian tobacco. I guessed that, like us, this man was quite indifferent to the outcome of the war if only he could be left in peace to follow his own life. He was not young. They had probably dragged him away from his farm or his village to come and strut and pose on their ridiculous bridge night after night, and he made a sad figure, with his drooping Chinese-style moustache, his fur bonnet, his long crumpled boots and his thin summer tunic.

'Look at that,' whispered Tiny, gleefully. 'Fancy wearing a thing like that in this weather ... he's either bleeding barmy or else they're just as badly off as what we are ... you can have boots or a coat, but not both. Sorry, mate, but you'll just have to take your choice.'

We crawled along in the darkness, underneath the bridge, fixing up the explosives. It was a long and tedious job and the Legionnaire did more than anyone. He seemed able to see perfectly well in the dark, and he swung like a monkey from one arch to the next. We finally withdrew to a safe spot and listened to Tiny and Porta arguing as to which of them should be allowed the privilege of pressing the plunger.

Another column of lorries came across the bridge. They were preceded by a jeep flying a red flag, and Porta looked at them longingly.

'Ammo trucks! Let's blow 'em up along with the bridge!'

He looked appealingly at the Old Man. 'Think of the show it would make! Come on, don't be a miserable sod! I'm game if

24

you are——'

'Shut up and sit down,' said the Old Man, curtly. 'I have no wish to be blown to kingdom come for the sake of a pretty firework display, thank you very much.'

We waited until the bridge was clear, and then crept away to the shelter of some rocks. Dawn was drifting across the sky in feathery pink trails and I felt sorry about the unsuspecting chap in the sentry box. Tiny and Porta were still having words on the question of precedence. I don't know which of them finally set the thing off, but the noise was shattering. Seconds later my eardrums were still ringing, the sound still banging from side to side of my head. I picked myself up and looked towards the bridge ... and then looked again ... The damned thing was still there! The main supports had been blown clean away and the metal superstructure was a twisted heap, but the bridge itself, the actual span of the bridge, had been dropped bodily into the water and now lay only a few feet below the surface. It was a ruined bridge, certainly; but still, at a pinch, a very usable bridge.

Gregor let out a shrill hoot of laughter and went running across it, with the rest of us following, singing and shouting and splashing like a crowd of punch-drunk loonies.

'We've sunk the bridge, we've sunk the bridge!' chanted Gregor.

At no point did the water rise above our knees!

'So what the fuck do we do now?' demanded Porta.

'We pull ourselves together and get the hell out,' said the Old Man, grimly. 'I've got a feeling this place is going to attract a lot of attention any minute now.'

Even as he spoke we heard the sound of men's voices, and we dived of one accord into the cover of the trees. At least we were going back by forest and not by marsh, which was a comfort—but only a scanty one, because in a matter of hours we were hopelessly lost. We trailed up and down, in and out of the trees, across streams and along little twisting paths that came to dead ends. In all that time we met no one, and when at last we came to a clearing and saw an old fellow chopping wood outside a hut we were in no mood to bother with evasive action. Instead, we pushed Porta forward as our best interpreter, and he gave the old boy an amiable one-toothed grin of unparalleled villainy and addressed him in Russian.

'Good day, tovaritch!'

The little old tovaritch slowly lifted his head. He was so old it almost hurt to look at him. His skin was parched, the wrinkles scored so deeply they were like gaping ravines, but his eyes were a bright, clear blue and they looked Porta wonderingly up and down.

'Ah, it's you, is it?' he said, letting fall his axe. 'And where have you been all these months?'

Porta is fortunately a natural liar. He doesn't have to stop and think about it, he marches right in with both feet.

'I've been away at the war, haven't I?' he said, very cocky and sure of himself. 'And where've you been hiding, Grandad? The Jerries are back again, didn't you know that?'

'Ah yes!' The blue eyes flickered thoughtfully over the rest of us and back at Porta. 'How's your mother getting on?'

'The old lady's fine,' said Porta.

'Good, good ... I like to hear of old friends ... Have you killed many Germans?'

'A fair amount,' said Porta, modestly, and he held out a packet of machorkas.

The old man shook his head.

'Army tobacco,' he said, deprecatingly.

He picked up his axe and turned back to his wood without another word. Porta hunched his shoulders and we went on our way, tramping blindly through the pine trees.

A couple of hours later we found ourselves back at the bridge, which was now a noisy hive of activity.

'This is bloody futile,' declared the Old Man. 'To hell with playing ring-a-ring-of-roses in the woods, I'm going to take a chance and follow the river.'

There was a very real risk of bumping into Russian troops, but by that time we were all past caring. We had half suffocated in the stinking marshes, risked our lives crawling about underneath a bridge that refused to die, walked our legs to stumps amongst the pine trees, and wanted only to return to the comparative safety and comfort of our own lines.

Two days later, under the protection of whatever blessed saint it is who looks after those who have come to the end of their tether, we staggered home again and the Old Man made his report—'Mission accomplished'—without either batting an eyelid or troubling anyone with tedious explanations. As he said, he didn't want to upset them. And besides, we had blown up the bridge as we had been told, and it certainly wasn't our fault if it had come down again—in one piece.

And now the winter was really closing in, and we experienced the first blizzards of the season. We still had no overcoats, and we had to pad our uniforms with newspaper and pieces of cardboard and other junk to keep out the worst of the razor-sharp winds. Rations were dropped to us by parachute. No new troops arrived and orders came through that we were on no account to waste ammunition. Food was cut down daily. Men were starving and freezing, and the first cases of frostbite were already being reported—some induced deliberately, in a final, despairing attempt to be relieved from the hell of the Russian front. Two men in our own company were found to be sleeping in wet socks and were summarily executed in the forest of Tatare.

Not even Heide spoke now of the Great Victory of Stalingrad, and the propaganda machine had been ominously silent for some weeks ...

*

The SS Standartenführer, with a pleasure that he did not trouble to conceal, tossed the top-secret telegram on to the table and nodded at SS Sturmbannführer Lippert.

'Take a look at that, Michel . . . What do you reckon?'

Lippert picked up the telegram. A smile curved slowly upwards on his face.

'I reckon it means we're in business at last!'

'Dead right we are.' Eicke picked it up again and re-read it. 'Well, those bastards in the Army have had it coming to them, it was only a question of time. The Führer's a reasonable man, but he can't be expected to tolerate traitors in his midst . . .'

The large Porshe bearing Eicke's standard pulled slowly out of Dachau and turned off towards Munich, with Eicke and Lippert lolling in the back seat. They stopped on the way to pick up Haupsturmführer Schmausser, and at 1500 hours exactly the three SS officers arrived at the central prison of Munich. They were taken at once to the office of the Governor, Herr Koch, and without troubling themselves with any tiresome preliminaries demanded that the prisoner General Röhm be delivered up to them.

Koch regarded the three men distastefully. It was plain to him that they had been drinking, and he was not at all sure how to deal with them. He began uncompromisingly by ignoring their demand for Röhm, banging his fist so hard on his desk that his inkwell overturned, and ordering them to leave his office and his prison forthwith, unless they themselves wished to be detained in one of his cells. He then sat back to await developments.

For the next few minutes the ball was tossed back and forth over the net—Eicke demanding Röhm, Koch refusing Röhm—with neither side gaining any advantage. Finally, to settle matters, Koch picked up the telephone and rang straight through to the Minister of Justice. The Minister of Justice heard the story with a sense of mounting indignation and personal outrage, until he could actually be heard to grow purple in the face and seemed on the verge of an apoplectic fit, at which point Eicke leaned across the desk and snatched the receiver away from the unsuspecting Koch.

'I may as well inform you straight away, Minister,' he snarled into the telephone, 'that I am here on the personal orders of the Führer. I have no time to waste bandying words with petty

28

officialdom, and if I meet with any more attempts to sabotage the Führer's instructions I don't need to remind you that there are always plenty of free places waiting to be filled at Dachau!'

He thrust the receiver back into Koch's still outstretched hand. There was a long, trembling pause before the Minister spoke. Koch nodded, his face white and furrowed. He dialled another number, and without a word to Eicke he gave instructions to the prison staff to allow the three SS officers access to Röhm.

Cell 474. SA Stabschef Ernst Röhm was sitting on a low wooden bench staring into space. He was naked from the waist up, but it was airless in the tiny cell and he was perspiring heavily. Eicke smiled at him in friendly fashion and held out his hand.

'How goes it, Ernst?'

Röhm hunched an indifferent shoulder.

'Not so good,' he said. 'Not so good ...'

Eicke sat down beside him on the bench.

'Warm in here, isn't it?' He jerked a thumb up towards the window. Through the small pane of speckled glass could be seen the blue cloudless skies of that hot July of 1934. 'Even worse out there,' he said, with a grin. 'Half the birds are going about without their knickers on ... you walk up the stairs behind them, it gets you in a muck sweat!'

Röhm attempted a smile. He patted his face with a torn and dirty handkerchief.

'Have you come for me, Theo? Has the Führer heard I've been arrested?' He looked searchingly at his old friend. 'I don't even know what I'm supposed to have done. Some of the guards have been talking about a revolution, I can't make head or tail of it ... What revolution? Has there really been any revolution? Has the Army gone and done something stupid?'

Eicke pulled a face. He removed his helmet, carefully wiped it, put it back on again. The death's-head insignia stared straight up at the ceiling.

'I shouldn't worry yourself with prison gossip,' he advised. 'You've more important things to think about right now.'

'I just want to know what I'm doing here!' snapped Röhm. 'I want to know if the Führer's heard about it——'

'Oh, he's heard all right,' said Eicke, soothingly. 'It was the Führer who told me to come along and see you. He told me to give you this ...' He pulled out his revolver and laid it carefully on the bench between them. 'One thing nobody can deny about the Führer, he's always loyal to his old friends. Even when they're in trouble, like you are, Ernst ... Especially when they're in trouble like you are ... You know what I mean?' He patted the revolver. 'He's giving you a way out, Ernst. Be best if you took it.'

Röhm stared uncomprehendingly at Eicke. Without refocusing, his eyes slipped away from his friend and down to the revolver. A big black revolver glistening with grease ... Slowly it grew clear to him; it swam into focus ...

'But that's madness!' he said. His eyes snapped back to Eicke. 'That's madness, Theo, and you know it! I've always been one of the Führer's loyallest followers ... I've put the Party above everything, above my wife, above my children, above myself ... I've sacrificed everything I've got for the Party ...' He suddenly caught hold of Eicke's shoulders and began shaking him. 'Didn't I save the Führer on two occasions when the revolution looked like crushing us? Didn't I? Didn't I save him at Stuttgart? When you and all the others ran off and left him, and Wollweber and his Communists were having it all their own way ... wasn't it me who stayed behind and rescued him?'

'Yes, yes,' said Eicke, soothingly. He removed the prisoner's frenzied hands from his shoulders and stood up. 'Unfortunately, my poor Ernst, you have a tendency to live in the past. The Führer is concerned only with the present ... All I know is that you've been expelled from the Party and are no longer regarded as—ah—one of the faithful, as it were.' He smiled and smoothed down his uniform. 'Out of deference, I shall now retire and leave the final arrangements to you. All I ask is that you don't make things more difficult than you have to ... We are, after all, old friends, are we not? And I can promise you that this really is the best way out. Look—you can see for yourself the way the wind is blowing.'

From his pocket he pulled out a page of the *Völkischer Beobachter* and handed it to Röhm. In the largest capital letters the printer could provide were the words: STABSCHEF ROHM ARRESTED. FULL-SCALE PURGE OF SA ON ORDERS OF FUEHRER: ALL TRAITORS MUST DIE!

Röhm looked across as Eicke, his face white and his eyes blank with disbelief.

'If this is true——' He waved a despairing hand and for a moment he faltered and seemed unable to go on. 'If this is true, then it means the man's nothing but a murderer ... it means you're all insane ... it means it's all been for nothing ...'

30

'Oh, I wouldn't say that,' returned Eicke, cheerfully. 'Don't be naïve, Ernst. You know as well as I that you risk your neck when you start playing politics. You today, me tomorrow ... who knows? As far as I'm concerned, we're all playing our luck, and yours has just happened to run out a bit sooner than mine...'

He raised his hand in farewell and went out to the corridor, where Lippert and Schmausser were waiting for him.

'Well?' said Lippert.

Eicke shrugged.

'Give him time. The idea's hardly sunk in yet.'

They gave him fifteen minutes, but not a sound was heard. It was cheerless and stuffy in the prison corridor and the three SS men began to lose patience. Eicke went back into the cell and frowned with annoyance: Röhm was still sitting on his bench, and the revolver was still lying untouched by his side.

'All right,' said Eicke. 'You don't feel like co-operating, so we'll have to do it the hard way. It makes no difference to me: I just thought you might prefer to die with dignity.' He picked up the revolver and gestured at the prisoner. 'Come on, on your feet, let's get it over with.'

A little unsteady, Röhm staggered upright. He placed himself against the wall, directly beneath the window with its dirty pane of glass and its mocking glimpse of the free blue sky. Eicke raised his arm and coldly took aim. At the last moment, Röhm cried out.

'Mein Führer! Mein Führer!'

Eicke watched dispassionately as his old friend and colleague sank slowly to the floor, his back leaving a damp mark as it slid down the wall of the cell. He walked forward to look at him. Röhm was not quite dead. Three months ago he had been one of the most powerful men in Germany, and now he lay twisting and moaning on the filthy floor of a Munich prison cell. Eicke turned him over with the toe of his boot. Agonised eyes stared up at him. Calmly he pointed his revolver at the man's temple and blew half his head away.

Stabschef Ernst Röhm, who had once been Adolf Hitler's closest friend and who died with the name of the Führer still on his lips, was assassinated in Munich prison at six o'clock on 1st July 1934. At the same hour, in Potsdam, they were preparing for a grand banquet, the like of which had not been seen since the reign of William II. Adolf Hitler had invited all the best families in Germany to be present at the occasion, and all

31

the best families duly turned up and drank a toast to the rebirth of Justice, while Stabschef Ernst Röhm lay murdered in his prison cell ...

TWO

JOURNEY BY SLEDGE

For the last few days life at the front had settled into a routine which, for the old hands, was at least tolerable if not particularly luxurious. For the newcomers, of course, it probably seemed like a hell upon earth, but they either learned quickly or not at all. When the enemy machine-guns started up, you got down and you stayed down, a simple fact of life with which we were so well acquainted that we did it as a reflex action, without being consciously aware that we were under fire. We had even grown accustomed to heavy shelling and accepted it as a matter of course. We could hear the shells as they were fired and had almost learnt to predict with accuracy where they would land. The new boys thought we were mad, and we watched pityingly as they either frightened themselves into hysteria or got their heads blown off.

All night long we used to play pontoon, in a stable where Porta and Tiny were serving a rather futile prison sentence. We were not officially allowed in, of course, but the whole place was falling apart and it was easy enough to bash a hole in the rotting wood and climb through one at a time when the guard was not looking. They had lashed the two prisoners to one of the feeding troughs, to stop them escaping—a notion which gave us all the biggest laugh we had had in years. The idea of anyone in their position wishing to escape seemed to us a joke of the highest order. Nothing to do but sleep all day and play cards all night—what more could a soldier want? Mind you, it was only very recently that they had begun to treat prisoners with such civility. Until a short while ago a man was stood against a tree-trunk, his hands tied together, for twelve hours at a stretch. Three hours off, twelve hours against the tree-trunk, and this in all weathers, in all conditions, for a total of two hundred hours. You took good care not to get caught in those days.

Tiny and Porta were undergoing punishment for having

come to blows with one of the baggage masters, and they were now bemoaning the fact that they were due to be released the following day.

'Should've bust him up good and proper,' said Tiny, ten times a night. 'That way they'd have given us at least three months.'

'Don't worry,' said Porta. 'I'm working on it ... Next time we'll make bloody sure of it.'

'Yeah, we'll make a good job of it next time ...'

'You bet we will! It only beats me why everyone else don't try it on ...'

'Perhaps we ought to make out a roster?' I suggested. 'Take it in turns, so we can all have a bit of a rest?'

The two prisoners at once closed the ranks and stared at me with intense dislike and suspicion.

'You want a rest?' said Porta. 'So it's up to you to go and get it. This is our pigeon. You keep your nose out of it.'

'They'd smell a rat,' said Tiny, jealously. 'You go and poach on someone else's ground.'

'All right,' I said. 'Don't get your knickers twisted. It's not my fault if I do something wrong by mistake and they nab me for it, I suppose?'

They went on looking at me, their eyes narrowed.

'You watch it,' said Porta, at last. 'You just watch it, boy!'

There came the sound of footsteps outside the stable. The Old Man glanced through the dust-covered windows.

'Changing the guard,' he said. 'It's time we were off.' He gave me a dig in the ribs. 'How about some coffee, then?'

It was always me. Because I was the youngest, it was always me who had to go and fetch their stinking coffee for them from the field kitchen. I was not only the youngest, I was also a student officer, but that made no difference, I still had to do all the fetching and carrying and be cursed by the cook, who lived in a permanent rage and had a particular hatred of anyone who was likely to better himself.

On the way back, I tripped over an unexploded bomb and spilt most of the coffee. That meant I was reviled by Heide as well as the cook.

'What's this?' he shouted. 'Half a bleeding cup? Where's the rest gone, then? Down your greedy gullet, I'll bet!'

'Piss off!' I said. 'Go and get your own lousy coffee if you don't like the way I do it! People leave bloody great bombs lying about all over the place, what am I supposed to do?'

At that, they all turned on me, shaking their fists and their half-empty mugs of coffee. I trailed back to the kitchen, where the cook threw a spoon at me and told me, in totally unrepeatable language, to go and get knotted. I finally had to bribe his assistant before I could get a refill, and even then there wasn't enough to go round and I was the one who had to suffer. Naturally. Being the youngest. There weren't any privileges attached to being young in the Army . . .

The next day saw not only Tiny and Porta's ejection from prison but also the order to prepare the motorised sledges to take a new contingent to the front line. In addition we had some post, but the Old Man was the only one of our group to receive a letter. It was from his wife, who drove a number twelve tram in Berlin, and as soon as the Old Man had finished it we passed it round amongst ourselves.

'Dear Willi:

'Why don't you write to us more often? No news for eight weeks and we're all so worried about you. Not a day goes by but you hear someone else you knew is dead, there are now *five pages* in the paper, all deaths columns. Everyone on edge all the time, and last week I had an accident. Am going to see if I can't change jobs to be a conductor, driving make me so tired now we have to do twelve hours at a stretch. They can't get the labour is the trouble, there's such a shortage of people. No men anywhere, only ones that aren't fit, all the rest are gone. Hans Hilmert was killed at Kharkov. Two men from the Party came and told Anna, when she fainted they had to take her to the hospital. They've got the children in care. All of us in the block wanted to look after them but it's the Party decides everything these days. You remember the Sockes who came to live next door? He was badly wounded in Greece, they've told Trude as soon as he's a bit better they'll send him home to Berlin. I don't know, though, I wonder? Jochem is doing very well at school, his old one was bombed and now he's at a new one. The whole building went and half the children were killed. They were digging all night long, I was nearly crazy, but thank God Jochem was OK. The ones that were left, they have to go to the school at Grünewald. It means I have to get up an hour earlier, but Gerda Ilse and me are taking it in turns. They have to change three times and it's very confusing at Schlesigher so they can't manage it alone. I told you about the girl who disappeared back in

34

September? They've now found her body in the grounds of the zoo but not yet her murderer. I have had your snap done larger and in colour so now you are with us all the time. When will you get some leave? I haven't seen you for more than a year. Where are you? It's awful not knowing, that's the worst. Everyone is talking about Stalingrad, I hope you're not there, it sounds like hell. Hohne, the boy on the fourth floor that is, came home on leave but after two days he had a telegram saying to go back to his regiment. He'd only just left and the police came for him, his wife is half mad not knowing what's happened. She spent a whole day at the Kommandantur trying to find out but nobody will tell her. This war is cruel, it's so hard on everybody, men fighting and the women not knowing and even the children getting killed. They've just cut down the rations again. Last week I heard they were selling horse meat under the counter in Tauenzienstrasse, but I got there too late, it had all gone. Tomorrow I'm going to try at Moritz Platz, see if I can get some without using coupons. The children need meat, it's not for myself, I wouldn't care for it. Willi please look after yourself, because what would we do without you if you never came back? The sirens have just gone again, it'll be the English, they always come between five and eight. We've had three days without them but I knew they'd be back. Can't leave us alone it seems. Please write to me soon, we all send our love,

Liselotte.'

'P.S. Don't worry about us here, we're quite all right, only we wonder where you are.'

We read Willi's letter lingeringly and lovingly. Mail was scarce in our part of the world and we shared it in much the same way as we shared cigarettes. A letter to one of us was a letter to all. And besides, the burden of a letter from home was almost too much for one man to bear by himself. We were all greedy for news, yet whenever it came it unsettled us.

We prepared the sledges and moved out as darkness fell. An icy wind was cutting across our faces and whipping the frozen snow into great peaks. We heard the guns boom out at Jersowska, where they were bombarding Stalingrad. Rumour had it that an entire Russian division was pinned down in Rynok, and that a factory on the Isle of Barricady had been destroyed. Rumour also had it that the 100th Infantry Division and the Rumanian 1st Tank Division had been destroyed. For the most part we stolidly disbelieved everything we heard, whether good or bad. It was, however, a fact that the 2nd Rumanian Infantry Division had bumped into the Russians a few days back, and in their panic-stricken retreat down the banks of the Volga the majority of them had been shot by advancing German troops and their bodies left where they fell, to discourage any more such displays. Their commanding officer had been hanged by his feet outside the Spartakos factory and was still rotting there for all to see.

Tired and irritable, and so cold we felt our very blood had frozen, we moved ahead with the sledges. We had to be at the front with the reinforcements by eleven o'clock, before the Russian artillery started up. The bastards were so regular you could set your watch by them. We knew eleven o'clock was the deadline, but it was hard going across Selwanoff and Serafimowitsch and you had to be constantly on the alert that you weren't heading into the Russian lines at sixty miles per hour and not able to stop until you were well and truly in their midst.

We travelled thirty-five men to each sledge. The one carrying the ammunition was third in line in the column, that being the least vulnerable position for the most vulnerable of the sledges. Lieutenant Wenck was travelling with the ammunition. He was an officer, but we regarded him with more respect and less scorn than most of his kind. In fact we almost paid him the compliment of treating him as one of ourselves, he had been at the front so long.

Porta was in the lead. He was as good as a mine detector any day, he seemed almost to sense the presence of those little surprise packets the partisans were in the habit of leaving for us everywhere they went. Tiny sat by his side on the front seat, manning the machine-gun, a pile of grenades near to hand. Gregor and I were crouching behind Porta, the MG pointing skywards, ready for any attack that might be launched by Russian infantrymen in the area.

It was no joyride, being in a motorised sledge driven by Porta. The thing weighed three tons and he flung it up and down, from side to side, with the same recklessness as if he were on a car at a funfair. We shot up hills like fire-balls from the cannon's mouth and fell straight down the other side, landing with a spine-jarring crash on the ground. Porta laughed so much that he several times lost all control and we tore through the snow at seventy or eighty miles per hour, the wind cutting across our faces as we clutched the sides of the sledge and prayed, our faces green with suppressed vomit.

'Wheeee!' shouted Porta, as the sledge launched itself into space from the summit of a fairly steep hill.

We held our breath and closed our eyes as we waited for the crash. Tiny and Porta roared with exhilaration and the sledge hit the hard-packed snow and bounced up again.

'This is the last time I ever travel with you, you stupid brainless bastard!' sobbed Heide, almost choking himself with rage and panic.

Porta merely flung back his head and laughed. Even as I watched, he took both hands off the wheel and gave his attention to a bottle of vodka he had with him. I turned in despair to Gregor.

'He's drunk,' I said. 'We shall all be killed.'

Gregor was hanging on to the MG for dear life.

'I'd rather be killed than suffer this much longer,' he muttered, through clenched teeth.

Porta laughed again, rather wildly, and had another swig from his bottle. We had all been given supplementary rations of vodka, half a litre each, before we left, but Porta, in his usual manner, had ended up with three times more than anyone else.

'Where exactly are we going?' inquired a young and rather superior NCO, who had recently joined us and was fresh out of training.

'To the war, my young friend, to the war!'

The Legionnaire, who was the only one apart from Tiny and Porta who seemed unmoved by the crazy cavortings of the sledge, patted the boy condescendingly on the back.

'You shall see action at last,' he promised him. 'You shall see men risk their lives and their sanity for little bits of tin to hang on their breasts ... only most of them will end up instead with little bits of wood to stick into their graves.'

'Yes, yes, I know all that!' said the boy, frowning with impatience. 'But where are we going?'

'You'll see soon enough. Don't be so eager. Wait till you get there, you'll probably wish you'd never come.'

'What do you mean by that remark? I'm not scared of a load of lousy Communists!'

The boy turned on the Legionnaire, his blue eyes narrowed. He was a model of National Socialist soldiery. Mad keen to come to grips with the wicked Communist bogy men and quite

37

unable to picture the degrading butchery that it entailed.

The Legionnaire looked at him and slowly shook his head.

'You may not be scared now, lad, but you'd bloody well better be later on ... because that's the only way you're likely to survive. Don't under-estimate the enemy, they're not quite the little paper dolls they made them out to be at home.'

Contemptuously, the boy turned his back on the Legionnaire. I sat watching him and wondering how long he was likely to last.

It took us four hours of Porta's switchback driving to reach the rear positions. The temperature was way below freezing point, and although we were packed with newspaper we still shivered in our thin capes.

There was no fresh snow on the track here, it was a river of ice and the sledges zipped along the surface that was exhilarating on level ground and heart-stopping on slopes or sharp corners. We tore down the side of a steep hill, narrowly missing a boulder which would have chopped us into pieces, and found ourselves approaching a hairpin bend at almost a hundred miles per hour. Below us lay the charred remains of the stricken village of Dobrinka. The slightest error of judgement from Porta and we should be thrown hurtling into space towards the jagged brick ruins which waited for us on either side of the track like so many open mouths.

'Hold tight!' yelled Porta. 'This could be it, lads!'

It was only too plain that the thick-headed idiot was enjoying himself. The sledge shot screaming round the bend, rising vertically into the air as it did so. Men were flung about like skittles, and a young recruit lost his grip and was tossed out into the road, where the following sledge ran over him. By the time we regained the horizontal and sorted ourselves out, the incident was over and forgotten. It seemed a silly way to go, to meet your death falling out of a sledge, but probably no more pointless than treading on a land-mine or running into the face of an enemy machine-gun.

Porta was singing a song, seemingly indifferent to the dangers all about us. We had survived the hairpin bend but we were now running down into the village and the track was full of twists and turns. Just the spot for a few well-placed mines, and we had already passed a couple of burnt-out lorries ...

The heavy sledge went bucking and rearing on its way. It needed only one small hidden obstruction and we should all be blown sky high. Everyone except Tiny, nursing his machine-gun in the front seat, curled into a protective ball, head between knees, arms round legs, prepared for a crash-landing.

The last bend brought us into the village. A sudden movement caught Tiny's attention. A fugitive figure in white had slipped out of one of the ruined huts. It raised its arm in a throwing action ... and at the same moment Tiny's machine-gun opened up. The figure was tossed legs flying and arms waving into the air. The grenade intended for us missed its mark and exploded harmlessly by the side of the track. Porta took his foot off the brake and the sledge bounded forward again. Gregor and I exchanged haggard glances, and I wiped the perspiration from my forehead.

'Jesus, it's cold,' whined Gregor. 'It's enough to freeze the balls off a brass monkey. I've never been so cold in all my bleeding life. I don't know how they can expect——'

'Ah, shuddup moaning!' snapped Tiny. 'What fool invented these perishing coffins on skates, anyway?'

'A German colonel,' said Heide, always very well informed on such matters.

'Yeah, it would be,' said Tiny, in disgust. 'Trust a sodding stupid colonel!'

'I bet he's never had to travel in one,' added Gregor, vindictively. 'Not in the freezing perishing cold without so much as a——'

'Mine!' roared Porta.

We spun round, eyes wide and staring. There it was, some way ahead of us, an innocent white hump in the middle of the track, the size and shape of an inverted meat pie. Some way ahead, but we were gaining on it fast ... Porta slammed on the brakes and the sledge reared up and almost did a backward somersault. It crashed down to earth, veered sideways and shot back into the path of the mine. It should have stopped by now, but instead it raced straight on: the hydraulics had evidently given way, and we tore onwards towards the mine at manic speed.

'God almighty!'

The Old Man stared ahead at approaching death, his hands clutching tightly at the guard-rail. Gregor and I clung to the MG as if it were a life-raft. Behind us, the new recruits sat white-faced and uncomprehending. We knew what those mines could do, we had seen them rip the bottom of a sixty-ton Tiger, but what did the partisans and their constant booby-traps mean to new troops, fresh out from Germany? They had not yet seen the twisted broken bodies of men who had been blown up.

'Jump!' yelled Porta, over his shoulder.

We flexed our muscles, preparing for the last moment, when we should have to take the plunge. Better to risk multiple fractures than sit tight and wait for the world to explode.

I stared hypnotically at the inverted meat pie as we rushed down upon it. It was a favourite trick of the partisans to steal out at night, dig a hole in the ice, deposit a mine and pour in some water, which soon froze over, leaving scarcely any trace of what lay beneath. To anyone else, it might have been a stone; only a cunning old fox like Porta was able to spot it in time and know it for the death-trap it was.

'Jump!' he now screamed again, and without taking his eyes off the track he reached out with one hand and gave a tremendous push at the nearest recruit, who fell overboard with a shrill yell of fear. Heide dived headfirst into a snowdrift. Tiny turned round, picked up two terrified boys by the scruff of their necks and hurled them bodily into space, then threw himself after them. The rest of the recruits clung anxiously to the hand-rail, not fully understanding the danger that was now only seconds away from them, but understanding only too well the kind of accident that could befall anyone fool enough to jump off a vehicle moving along at sixty miles per hour.

'Enemy aircraft!' shouted the Old Man, as he hurtled over the side.

By some miracle, it worked. It seemed that they could understand enemy aircraft. Probably it had been part of their training. At any rate, they jumped!

Gregor and I abandoned our precious MG and disappeared together into the snow. I landed like a bullet only inches away from a telegraph pole. I sat up, feeling sick. Another fraction to the right and my head would have been crushed like an egg shell. A helmet would have saved me, but for the most part we had given up wearing them, finding that the advantage of having a protective layer of steel on top of your head was more than outweighed by the disadvantage of impaired sight and hearing.

Porta made one final attempt to brake by using the clutch but it had no perceptible effect. The sledge was now almost on top of the mine. At the very last second Porta gave a despairing wrench at the wheel and the sledge slewed away in the opposite direction, but we had no time to sit back and applaud, nor to mop our brows with relief, nor to check our casualties, for the second sledge was approaching fast. We rushed into the road, waving our arms and screaming at Barcelona, who was driving.

'Mine! There's a mine!'

Too late. They were too close on our tail and hadn't a chance of pulling up. Barcelona applied the brakes with all his force, but the sledge merely upended and burst into flames as the mine exploded beneath it.

The third sledge, the one carrying the ammunition, was taking desperate avoiding action, but it was out of control and the wreckage of the second sledge was scattered in its path. It went ploughing through it, through the flames and across the writhing screaming bodies, turned two clumsy somersaults and then itself exploded. Lieutenant Wenck was propelled up into the air like a human torch. We ran to the spot, but the body that fell back into the snow was a twisted, grinning parody of a human being, and it died before we could reach it.

Slowly, the noise of the explosions died away; slowly, the whirling debris came to rest. Pieces of broken machinery and torn chunks of human flesh sank down into the melting snow. We found Barcelona lying some way off, where he had been thrown by the first explosion. He was alive but unconscious, with his uniform in ribbons and a huge hole in the side of his chest. We patched him up as best we could and carried him carefully back to the road, where a medical orderly had already set up a first-aid post. As we laid Barcelona gently in the snow, our eyes were drawn to a sight that was almost too horrible to contemplate. And yet at the same time it compelled you to look ... You looked until you felt sick with disgust and torn apart with horror, and still your eyes refused to turn away from the mangled mess that lay trapped beneath an overturned sledge. A young soldier, half crushed, half destroyed, yet incredibly and horribly still breathing ...

'Oh my God,' muttered the Old Man, putting a hand over his eyes. 'Oh God, let him die ...'

Appalled as I had never been before, I stood with the rest staring down at the infinitely pathetic, infinitely repulsive thing that only seconds ago had been a human being. It lay with its lower half beneath the sledge, the crushed remnants of its chest still heaving as some sort of life struggled on within it. Where the face had been was now only a patchwork of blood and skin and black, gaping holes. Empty eye-sockets, and a cavity for a nose; mouth and chin both blown away; tongue torn out, one eye hanging from a strip of loose flesh ...

To turn one's head away and vomit seemed an act of dis-

41

loyalty to a fallen comrade. To walk away and forget seemed a desertion. So I remained, staring, at my post, willing the man's heart to stop its senseless beating and thus relieve me from my self-imposed task of watching over another's agony.

I became slowly aware that Gregor had pulled out his revolver. I wished I had pulled mine first and that we had finished the job.

'Don't,' said the Old Man. 'Don't do it.'

He shook his head and gently removed the gun from Gregor's hand.

'But we can't let him go in that state ... he'll die anyway ... and even if he lives,' babbled Gregor, clutching at the Old Man's arm, 'he won't look like a human being again ...'

'Never say that,' said the orderly, bending down by the man's side and beginning patiently on the task of reassembling all the scattered components. 'Everyone has a right to live. He'll pull through, if he's got the will.'

'But his face ...' whispered Gregor.

The orderly took out his syringe.

'They'll patch it up. There's a special hospital near Baden-Baden ... just outside the town. Plastic surgery, they call it. They can put him together again.'

Gregor looked disbelievingly at the pitiful mess that had been a human face. The orderly bit his lip as he gave the injection.

'Well ... perhaps not quite the same as before,' he admitted. 'But at least they're alive ... and they keep them all together, see? Don't let them go out of the grounds or anything like that ... It's better for morale.'

There was a silence.

'Whose morale?' I said. I jerked my head at the mutilated man. 'His? Or everyone else's?'

'Don't ask me,' muttered the orderly. 'It's a top secret establishment, that's all I know.'

The Old Man glanced across at some of the recruits, who were huddled in a terrified bunch, surveying the scene.

'Go on, you take a good look,' he told them, bitterly. 'That was a man, lying down there. Did they ever tell you that was how it was going to be? Did they ever tell you that was the sort of sacrifice they expected of you? Not a good quick death, but something you have to suffer for the rest of your life ... So if any of you survive the slaughter, you just make damn sure you tell your sons, when you have any, that that's what war is all about ... human beings like lumps of raw flesh on the butcher's

42

shelf . . .'

We piled the wounded on to the remaining sledges and set off once more towards the front line. Barcelona had regained consciousness and was muttering feverishly and occasionlly crying out as he lay at the bottom of the sledge. We did our best for him but already the blood had soaked through the bandages. We had only just pulled out of the village when the Russian artillery started up. The Legionnaire glanced at his watch.

'Eleven o'clock. Just like always. What should we do without them?'

As soon as we arrived, we carried Barcelona to the field hispital and bribed one of the doctors to take particular care of him. We visited him the next day. He was lying in bed with a face greyer than the coarse grey sheets, he had a drain in his chest and he was feeling rather sorry for himself. By his bed lay his food rations, which he had not the strength to eat: an egg, some sausage and an orange . . . Tiny's eyes went back time and again to the plate, until finally he could contain himself no longer.

'Aren't you hungry?' he said.

Barcelona shook his head weakly from side to side.

'Well, in that case——' Tiny stretched out a great greedy claw and snatched up the food. 'It's silly to leave it for some other bastard to pinch.'

'That's all right,' whispered Barcelona, as the sausage disappeared into Tiny's mouth. 'You can have it . . . And the orange,' he added, as Tiny began ripping off the skin with his teeth.

'What about your reefer coat?' Tiny wanted to know, cramming pieces of orange into his mouth.

He looked at it longingly. He himself had only his thin camouflage jacket over his normal tunic, and we all knew that if Barcelona should die one of the medical orderlies would certainly appropriate his coat. A good thick reefer like that was worth more than its weight in gold.

'What about it?' said Tiny. 'You don't need it while you're in here. Why can't I just borrow it?'

'No!'

Barcelona was far too weak to shout, but the intended vehemence of his protest was obvious. He turned his eyes so imploringly upon us that the Old Man gave Tiny a sharp kick in the leg and told him to shut up.

As we left, we had a quick whip round and made Barcelona a present of all our opium cigarettes and two litres of vodka. If he was going to pull through, he would need something to sustain him. We pushed them safely under his pillow when no one else was looking and waved him goodbye.

When we went back the following day we were told that Barcelona had been transferred to a hospital in Stalingrad.

'Sod it!' shouted Tiny. 'Now they've both gone ... him and his jacket! What a couple of shits!'

All that we have hoped for, all that we have worked for, has now become reality. We have not only a well-ordered state but also, in Adolf Hitler, a leader we will follow to the very end.

Pastor Steinemann
5th August 1933

SS Reichsführer Henrich Himmler, seated behind his desk, stared thoughtfully across at Standartenführer Theodor Eicke, who was sprawled in an armchair and seemed unaware of his gaze.

After a moment, Himmler pushed back his chair and stood up. Shoes creaking, he walked across to the window and looked out upon the white wastes of Prinz Albrecht Strasse, where the first snow of the winter was still untrodden. He frowned, cleared his throat, placed his hands behind his back and turned to face Eicke.

'I hope for your own sake, my dear fellow...' He paused, and gave a grim, warning smile. 'I hope for your own sake that what you've just told me is true.'

'Reichsführer!' Eicke's exclamation of protest rang out almost mockingly. He seemed very sure of himself. 'The old bitch quite definitely had Jewish blood in her ... and more than a few drops, too. At least a quarter Yid, I should say. I've suspected it for a long time, I just never had the proof until now ... But in any case, you've only got to look at the family hooter, it sticks out a mile!'

He flung back his head in a great burst of laughter. Himmler, nostrils pinched and eyes closed, took a deep breath and counted to ten. This man Eicke irritated him every time he opened his mouth. His language was coarse and his sense of humour bordered on the moronic.

'Very well. I shall have to take your word for it. You have nothing else to report? In that case, I shall wish you a very good day ... Heil Hitler!'

The minute Eicke had left the room, Himmler seated himself once more at his desk and picked up the telephone. He drummed his fingers impatiently on the papers Eicke had left with him.

'Send Obergruppenführer Heydrich to me ... at once!'

Heydrich arrived a few seconds later, padding silently into the room. He was more wild beast than man, with the elegance and the cunning and the cruelty of a lynx. Himmler watched as he crossed the room, and Heydrich, ever on the alert for danger, returned his gaze out of hooded eyes that gave away no secrets.

'Take a seat, Obergruppenführer.'

Heydrich inclined his head and seated himself in the chair that was still warm from Eicke's presence. His blue eyes were deep and chill and his light grey uniform, pressed to knife-edge precision, gave off a faint odour of horses. Every morning, from five o'clock to seven, Heydrich was in the habit of taking a ride with his mortal enemy, Admiral Canaris.

Himmler removed his pince-nez, polished the lenses, rubbed the bridge of his nose. The two men looked at each other across the desk, and it was Himmler who broke first, under the pretext of replacing his pince-nez. He settled them back on his nose and began leafing through Eicke's papers. He spoke without looking up.

'Tell me, Obergruppenführer ... what exactly was it that was written on your grandmother's tombstone?'

Almost imperceptibly, Heydrich stiffened. And then laughed. His lips parted in amusement, but the chill blue eyes narrowed to slits.

'Her name, for one thing,' he said. 'Her name was Sarah ...'

Himmler looked across at him.

'I'm told you went to some lengths to have the tombstone removed?'

'Removed?' echoed Heydrich, raising his eyebrows. 'Why should I do such a thing, Reichsführer? It cost a great deal of money.'

'Which is doubtless why you have now had it replaced ... but without the name of Sarah, curiously enough.'

There was a silence.

'This name ... this Sarah,' suggested Heydrich. 'Has it ever appeared on the tombstone of my great grandmother, Reichsführer?'

Himmler stared across the table at him. Heydrich sat calmly in his chair, an expression of alert curiosity on his face, and it slowly came to Himmler that this, his most competent of generals, was also his most dangerous. He decided, for the moment, to let the matter drop.

'All right, Heydrich. You can go. We'll forget it for now.'

Heydrich smiled an inward smile of triumph and trod silently over to the door. He also had his weapons, but they were not yet for public display. The time was not ripe...

THREE

PORTA'S BREAKFAST

Sergeant Lutz kicked open the door so hard I thought an earthquake had hit us. We were wakened every morning by his lousy shouting voice.

'Wake up, you lazy load of gits! Rise and shine, out of bed, put some vim into it!'

This morning, it was even worse than usual. For one thing, it wasn't so much the morning as the middle of the night; and for another, he had a special message for Porta, myself and Tiny, which he relayed in a gloating bellow.

'You—you—and you! Report immediatly to the CO! And when I say immediately, I mean immediately ... for special duties, no less, aren't you the lucky ones?'

'Go and get bleeding knotted!' was the only reply to be heard, from the depths of Porta's blankets.

'I'm warning you!' barked Lutz. 'Any more of that and I'll have you up on a charge!'

Tiny shot up the bed and regarded Lutz with one frenzied, red-rimmed eye.

'What the hell's the matter with you? You got a flea up your bum or something? Can't you see we're trying to flaming sleep?'

Porta let loose one of his celebrated, reverberating farts and lay in bed sniggering.

'Wrap that one up and take it to the CO with my compliments!'

Lutz breathed very deeply.

'I'm not telling you again,' he said, nastily. 'But you'd better get a move on ... You'd just better get a move on, or I'm warning you ... you'll be up on a charge of refusing to obey orders.'

He slammed out again, happy at the havoc he had wrought. The air was full of obscenity, but we reluctantly wriggled out of our warm blankets into the freezing blasts of the extreme early

47

morning. Lutz was a bastard and as good as his word, and being had up on a charge of refusing to obey orders could well prove to be worse than the orders themselves.

Porta sat up, cursing, and deftly picked off a flea that was crawling over his thin chicken chest in a vain search for blood. He crushed it between finger- and thumb-nail and shot it across the room.

'Sod the lot of 'em!' he declared. 'I can't do nothing without my breakfast.'

'You'll be lucky,' I said. 'Breakfast at this hour of the perishing night?'

'Don't you worry!' Porta jumped out of bed and into his uniform in one perfected movement. He advanced towards the door, doing up his buttons. 'Don't you worry, I'll get some breakfast out of the buggers if it's the last thing I do.'

Tiny and I hurried after him, half dressed and anxious, pulling on boots and jackets, determined not to miss our share. At our own field kitchen there was nothing doing. Porta stood and bawled his head off, with no result.

'Bloody swine! You call that co-operation, do you? You call that co-operation? Let your mates go off into the freezing bloody cold without so much as a cup of coffee? Well, God rot the balls off the lot of you, that's all I can say!'

Actually, he said a great deal more, accompanied by much spitting and a variety of oaths, until the happy notion struck him that the Third Company's cook owed him some money, and we trotted off behind him to batter the unfortunate man into wakefulness. We were stopped on the way by Lieutenant Welz, who seemed to think we were reporting for duty.

'There you are!' he said, tersely. 'And about time, too!'

'Ah, give it a rest, Ulrich!' Porta pushed the lieutenant in the chest and moved him contemptuously to one side. 'Just because you've gone up in the world you think you can shove your old mates around, eh? We know you don't mean it, we know it's all show, so don't try it on, there's a good lad.'

'Obergefreiter Porta, this isn't the first time I've had to tell you that under Paragraph 165——'

'All right, don't blow a gasket,' said Porta, peaceably. 'You'll wear yourself out before you reach puberty, the way you're carrying on.' He put a hand over the other's mouth. 'You forgotten that day I pulled you out of a shell hole, have you? You forgotten I risked my life for you? Your lousy bones'd still be rotting there if it weren't for me, wouldn't they?'

The lieutenant jerked his head away.

'I've repaid you for it.'

'What? Slipped me a few stinking marks now and again? You call that repayment? I call it more like bribery and corruption ... Ah, come off it, Ulrich, I can run circles round you and you know it!'

We walked on towards the Third Company, with Lieutenant Welz in our midst. Porta dragged a sleep-ridden but meekly unprotesting cook from his blankets and we gathered round to watch as he brewed us up some coffee on a spirit stove. Even Welz, temporarily forgetting his rank and the particular circumstances, accepted a cup and found the time to put away a thick ham sandwich. The cook, meanwhile, had succeeded in negotiating another loan from Porta, at quite phenomenal rates of interest.

Half an hour later, we reported for duty. Colonel Hinka was waiting for us.

'So! You've deigned to put in an appearance, have you? Very good of you, I must say. I was beginning to think I should have to come and fetch you myself ... All right, all right, Obergefreiter, don't waste time with fanciful explanations, I've a job for you to do. Gather round and take a look.'

He spread a map across his table and we jostled at his elbows with a show of great eagerness, trying to atone for our unpunctuality.

'Now look, the thing is this ... It's essential we know exactly what the enemy are up to. We already have information about a tank unit up here at point X. What I want to know is what they've got hidden away between point X and Jersowka, down here. In other words, I want you three men to take a good look at the enemy build-up between those two points. Got the idea?'

He turned and smiled enchantingly at us. I smiled back and wondered sourly why he had chosen us for the task. Porta scratched his chest.

'Blimey, it's a good thing that coffee was strong,' he muttered.

Hinka ignored Porta and turned back to the map.

'I've already warned our infantry. You can cross at this point here.' He jabbed a finger on the map, and we all peered anxiously towards it. 'Now, I suggest you check your watches. The time is exactly 0145. I want you back here again within six hours, reporting to me by 0800 at the latest.' He smiled again. 'All right? If you're delayed by more than half an hour,' he said, pleasantly, 'it'll be a court martial for each of you ... Any questions?'

'Yes, sir.' Porta stopped scratching his chest and stood to attention. 'I should like to ask how far the enemy lines extend. According to the Führer they go all the way from the Black Sea up to the north coast. Well, it seems to me we couldn't possibly get up to the north coast and back in six hours and then——'

Hinka held up a hand.

'Don't push your luck, Obergefreiter! Do you never listen to a word I say?'

'Yes, sir, but——'

'Between point X and Jersowka. No more than three miles at the most. There's no question of going all the way to the Black Sea. Don't be futile, man!'

The night was black and moonless and it was beginning to snow. We were all three agreed that a rest was required before we set out, and we accordingly crept into the shelter of a thick clump of bushes and passed round a bottle of French cognac I had recently picked up.

'Where'd you get it?' demanded Porta, jealously.

I shrugged.

'General HQ. You'd be amazed the stuff old Paulus has stashed away there.'

'Not really,' said Porta, who never allowed himself to be amazed by anything. 'That's the way it goes, ain't it? The higher you are, the more you get away with. I reckon it's always been like that ... You know that war they had in China?'

'What war?' demanded Tiny, at once.

Porta wrinkled his forehead.

'What's it matter? Some lousy war. Some lousy rebellion. Half the flaming world had to go and stick their noses in and send their troops over there——'.

'The Boxer Rebellion,' I suggested.

'That's it,' agreed Porta. 'That's what I said ... Well, anyway, they were fighting all over the bleeding desert, weren't they? And it seems like the Chinese desert ain't too well provided with luxuries—know what I mean? No booze, no nosh, no birds—right? So, one day they comes across this perishing great colonel feeding his face off the fat of the land—sodding great chunks of roast meat, lashings of the stuff, and the best cuts and all ... Know what it was? When they took it off him and looked at it, you know what it was?'

'No,' said Tiny. 'What was it?'

50

'Camel?' I said, vaguely.

'Camel!' Porta gave a scornful laugh. 'Bird, that was what it was ... roast bird. Human bird ... Chinese human bird. Seeems he'd taken her along for the ride, lost one sort of appetite and found another ... So he cuts her up and pops her in the stewpot. Easy!'

'I'd like to see you in that situation,' I said. 'You'd go raving potty, wouldn't you? Trying to eat it and stuff it at one and the same time——'

Porta grinned, evilly. Tiny snatched the cognac away from me.

'All this gab ... I haven't had my eight hours' kip. I don't work so good without I get my eight hours.' He downed a few mouthfuls of cognac and wiped his mouth on his sleeve. 'Why couldn't the stupid bastard ask for volunteers, eh? There's always a gaggle of 'em lusting after iron crosses. Why pick on us? What have we done to get in his hair?'

'Ah, stop bellyaching!' said Porta. 'It's an honour, that's what it is. You ought to be proud of it——'

'Yeah, big talk!' jeered Tiny. 'Only right at this moment I got gooseflesh, and it ain't just because I'm cold ... You know they got the bleeding Siberians out there somewhere? You fancy being nailed on to a tree and used for target practice like they done to that patrol from the Second Tank Regiment?'

'Stuff it,' said Porta, curtly. 'What's the time?'

I looked at my watch.

'Quarter past one.'

'OK, come on. Let's get cracking.'

Tiny moaned and clutched protectively at the empty cognac bottle.

'Why can't we spent the night here and make up some codswallop to satisfy him?'

Porta turned and hissed in his ear.

'Because when the sods found out we'd been lying we'd be for the flaming high jump, that's why! Now get off your great fat arse and get a bleeding move on!'

Yawning and muttering, Tiny staggered to his feet. We left our own lines and crept forward into no-man's-land. It was fortunate the night was so dark. Even Tiny's vast bulk merged into the background, while Porta, flitting a few paces ahead of us, might not have been there at all. Nevertheless, we used what cover there was, slinking along by the side of bushes, taking care to make no sound.

As we approached the Russian lines, I became aware of a faint, unidentifiable clicking somewhere to our right. I stood still, straining my ears. The sound came again. It was rather like a gas-mask case knocking against a rifle. Porta turned and moved a few paces towards me. He waved his hand in an imperative motion, get down and stay down, and I relayed it to Tiny, a few feet behind me. We sank into the snow and waited. I saw Porta crouch behind a bush and raise his sub-machine-gun. Tiny's hand gripped my arm.

'What's the stupid sod doing that for?'

'Christ knows,' I muttered.

'He fires that and we'll all be done for——'

From a few yards away, five solid black shapes emerged from the shelter of a coppice and began treading single file through the snow. They were Russians, but too big and bulky in build for the dreaded Siberians. They passed very close to us. I could hear the thud of their boots and the swish of the snow. I held my breath, wondering if they would notice our tracks, but thank God it was too dark. They moved on, straight across our path, and I felt Tiny relax at my side.

As we rose to our feet, Porta farted. A sharp crack like a gunshot. The sound travelled far and fast through the still night air, and Tiny and I were back on the ground in an instant.

'For crying out loud!' I protested. 'Another one like that and we'll have the whole of the Red Army on the look-out for us!'

'I can't help it,' said Porta, with dignity. 'It's the way I'm constituted. I've always been like it. The least bit of excitement and it goes to my bowels.'

'Well, just try and control it!' I snapped, in no mood to humour his physiological weaknesses. 'It's like a bloody cannon going off!'

'Stick a cork up your bum,' suggested Tiny.

'Germany's secret weapon,' I said, sourly. 'The human champagne bottle ... Turns his back to the enemy and kills off whole regiments at a fart ...'

'Ah, give your arse a chance!' snarled Porta.

We crept on towards the river. We were almost on top of the Russian trenches now and had to crawl on our hands and knees. We could see the enemy machine-guns looming up before us, and Porta became hooked on some barbed wire and exercised his physiological weakness so long and so loud as we tried to rescue him that Tiny lost his nerve and threatened to cut his throat if he didn't stop. It was as much as I could do to prevent full-scale combat on the spot, and I whispered myself hoarse telling them to keep their raucous voices down.

We yanked him free at last, only to stumble almost immediately upon an enemy battery, where a sentry demanded to know the password. We froze into horrified silence. Finally, for want of anything better, Porta shouted back an obscenity. The sentry promptly replied in kind. We stood there, waiting to be shot, but nothing happened. Either the Russians were in the habit of using pornographic passwords, or else the sentry had been so insulted he could no longer be bothered with us. At all events, after a few more seconds' hesitation we moved on into the darkness and were allowed through with no more questions asked.

Another ten minutes and we were nestling together in a deep, dark shell hole, Tiny shading the torch with one hand while I held the map and Porta licked the end of a pencil stub and laboriously marked in all the Russian positions between point X and Jersowka. Our mission was completed. It was now only a question of returning safely to our own lines.

We stayed in our shell hole a while, sharing our last cigarette amongst the three of us, huddling into our coats and listening to the silence. Occasionally it was broken by the distant sound of gunfire, but for the most part the night was still and untroubled. The snow had stopped falling and the sky was crisscrossed with searchlights. We were reluctant to leave the comfort of our nest, but the colonel had given us six hours and we had in any case to beat the dawn if we wanted to survive.

We moved off again into the treacherous night. With the velvet-black sky above, and the thick untrodden snow beneath, deadening all sound, we could run into an enemy patrol at any moment and never even know what had hit us. We came at last to a point where the trail forked. After a short discussion we turned to the right, but about a mile further on I drew to a halt and looked reluctantly about me.

'What's up?' said Porta, impatiently.

I shook my head.

'I'm not sure ... it's just a feeling, I may be wrong, but I don't reckon this is the right direction.'

'Oh balls!' said Porta. 'We looked at the map, didn't we?'

'Sure we looked at the map——'

'So what is it, then?'

'I don't know,' I repeated. 'It just doesn't FEEL right ...'

Tiny shuffled his feet in some anxiety.

'All bleeding roads are all the bleeding same, they all lead to

53

the bleeding graveyard in the end, so let's get a move on and shut up talking about it.'

We got a move on. We proceeded uncertainly for perhaps another hundred yards, and this time it was Porta who stopped. He stood rubbing his eyes and staring ahead.

'Hallo, hallo, hallo!' he said. 'Either I'm seeing things or that map's been rigged ... Keep calm, lads, don't hang on my skirts like that, it'll all come right in the end ...'

'What are you on about?' grumbled Tiny.

'Take no notice,' said Porta. 'I'm losing my marbles ...' He grabbed Tiny's arm. 'You see that bleeding great wood over there——'

Tiny and I both looked in the direction he was pointing. The wood was unmistakable. Tiny nodded.

'Yeah, so what? I seen one before.'

'Not one like that you haven't ... that's a wood that ain't there. Not marked on the map, see? Don't exist ... a sort of mirage, like.'

'Hang on,' I said. 'Let's have a gander.'

We spread the map out and shone the torch over it.

'It's there, all right,' I told them. 'See? We've taken the wrong flaming path. We should've have gone left back at that fork. If we'd have gone left, we'd have come to this little river here ... takes us straight back to our own lines.'

'So what happens now?' Tiny wanted to know.

'Search me,' I said, folding the map. 'We're well and truly in the shit.'

'You mean we're lost?' demanded Tiny.

'That's about the size of it,' I said.

Tiny turned to stare incredulously at Porta.

'You've lost us!' he said. 'You stupid great sod, you've gone and lost us!'

'I knew we were on the wrong road,' I said. 'I told you it felt wrong.'

'Lost in the middle of bleeding nowhere,' said Tiny. 'You'd lose your bleeding head given half a chance, wouldn't you? You'd lose your balls if they weren't in a bag. You'd lose your——'

'Shut up moaning!' hissed Porta. 'You had your opportunity for looking at the map the same as what the rest of us did.'

'What d'you reckon it's best to do?' I said. 'We can either go back to the fork and start again or try to get back this way.'

Leaving Tiny to drone on to himself in a disgruntled and

disgusted monotone, Porta and I put our heads together and studied the map. We opted in the end for the wood: time was running out, and the trees at least offered a refuge should we still be wandering round at dawn.

'Good thing you lads got me with you,' said Porta, in his usual self-satisfied way. 'You never know what interesting information we might unearth in this here wood. Just imagine old Hinka's face if we managed to——'

'Give it a rest!' I said, urgently. 'I've got the feeling we're not alone in here.'

A few yards ahead, through the trees, could be seen a faint light.

'Russians!' whispered Tiny. 'What'll we do? Go and have a dekko or steer clear of 'em?'

'Best take a look,' said Porta. 'See how many there. Hinka might be interested.'

'Sod Hinka,' muttered Tiny.

Porta ignored him. He gave me a slight push.

'Sven, you take the right. Tiny, the left. I'll carry straight on. See you back here in fifteen minutes.'

It was Porta who returned with the news.

'It's OK, we can manage 'em. Far as I can see, they're all sleeping their heads off. Bit further on there's a half-track armoured personnel carrier. Looks to me like they're using it as a sub-radar station.'

'You're not suggesting we go in and mop them up?' I looked at him, horrified. 'If that's a bloody wireless vehicle, you can bet your sweet life there'll be a staff HQ somewhere round about. And where there's staff, there's sentries. And where there's sentries, there's trouble. And——'

'So what?' said Porta. 'All I'm interested in is getting my hands on that truck——'

'Take the truck?'

'Why not? Take the truck and scarper with it.'

'Which way?'

'Way we come. We got transport and we got all the time in the world.'

'And how about that battery we had to pass? We fooled 'em once, it's not going to work a second time.'

'Why not? Who's to know? You see one of your own trucks going by, you don't stop and wonder if the enemy's inside it.'

That, at least, was true. We separated once again and went off on another reconnaissance trip. Twenty minutes later, we reassembled to exchange reports.

'Nothing,' said Tiny. 'I've combed the whole eastern section. Notting there.'

Porta looked at him, suspiciously.

'You sure?'

'Course I'm sure! What do you take me for?'

'The biggest con in the whole bleeding company!' snapped Porta. He turned to me. 'How about you, then?'

'Well, apart from nearly tripping over four lads having a kip by the side of the truck, I didn't see a thing.'

'That's not so bad,' said Porta. 'I found a couple snoring their heads off inside a tent, and four more in a pill-box tucking into some nosh.'

'That makes ten of 'em altogether,' I said. 'And what's the betting the rest of the battalion's not far away?'

'All right, no need to shit yourself,' said Porta, equably. 'We've been in worse holes than this before now. And I'm not letting that truck slip through my fingers ... Slog home on foot when we could go back in style? You must be joking!'

'Come on, let's get started,' agitated Tiny. 'I'll clobber the pair in the tent.'

We split up yet again and crept back into the trees. As I crawled towards the half-track radio car, one of the men in the pill-box stuck his head out and shouted to the four who were asleep on the ground. All hell at once broke loose. The four men picked themselves up and made a dive for the radio. Before they could reach it, Porta had hurled a clutch of grenades across the clearing and the ground exploded beneath their feet. Seconds later, and I heard the angry chattering of a machine-gun somewhere amongst the trees behind us. A few grenades lobbed in that direction and the gun was silenced. I saw Tiny advance upon the tent. From the pill-box came the crackling of an MPI. I tore the pin out of a grenade and hurled it across the clearing. The tent went up in flames. Porta advanced upon the pill-box. The grenade exploded and two of the occupants were killed outright. The other two survived uninjured and came stumbling out with their arms held high above their heads. Tiny and I had them trussed up in an instant, while Porta shouted triumphantly at us from the truck.

'What did I tell you? A piece of piss! One private car and two prisoners ... What more could you want?'

It suddenly occurred to him what more, in fact, was to be had. He left the truck and dived down into the pill-box, yelling at us to follow. We pushed the prisoners before us and found Porta already tucking in to the remains of a hearty meal. Tiny and I eagerly helped him clear the plates and finish off a bottle of vodka, while the prisoners looked on sullenly.

'Here, what's all this gubbins?' asked Tiny, picking up a document case. He pulled out a sheaf of papers and studied them upside down with illiterate interest. 'What's it all about, then?'

Porta took the papers from him and glanced through them.

'Letters,' he announced, importantly. 'Despatches ... secret documents ... This here one's a note from a general. Sent to another general.' He frowned. 'The one what sent it must be quite a big noise. I reckon the other's just a little fellow.'

'How do you make that out?' I demanded.

'Easy. Read what it says . . "My dear Steicker, I suggest that as a matter of urgency you select one of your most capable staff officers and have him transported to Berlin to let the Führer know at first hand the impossible position in which we find ourselves after the Russian breakthrough at Kaltsch. Yours very sincerely, Schmidt!"' He looked at me, triumphantly. 'Get it?'

'Yeah ... Yeah, I see what you mean,' I agreed.

'I don't,' said Tiny, at once.

We tried to explain to him. A really big noise—a field-marshal, for instance—could well address an inferior as 'my dear Steicker' and sign himself 'yours very sincerely' ... but just let the inferior try the same tactics with the field-marshal and his name would soon be mud! Tiny scratched in his hair and said he supposed so, but something still seeemed to be bothering him and I hardly felt that he was convinced.

'It's a matter of psychology,' explained Porta, earnestly.

'Yeah, but——'

'Listen to this one,' I said. 'This couple weren't exactly in love, were they?'

I read it out:

'TOP SECRET. Golumbiskaya, 16.11.42. To: Gen. Seydlitz.

'Reorganisation of the following is urgently required: 16th and 24th Panzer Divisions; 3rd Infantry Division; 100th Artillery; 76th, 113th and 384th Infantry Divisions. Kindly attend and expedite matter.

'Heil Hitler!'

'Very cold,' said Porta, drawing in his breath. 'Very nasty atmosphere. Cut it with a knife.'

'Listen,' said Tiny, 'I don't understand. Why's he going on about the 16th? Eh?' He looked at us, round-eyed. 'That's us, that is. That's us what he's talking about.'

'Blimey, he's right!' said Porta, gathering all the papers together. 'What's Ivan doing with our letters?' He shook his fist at the silent prisoners. 'What're you doing with other people's mail?'

'No wonder we don't get no post,' grumbled Tiny. 'The bastards must've knocked off a whole sackful.'

Porta looked across at the prisoners with a gleam in his eye.

'I reckon we could make 'em talk easy enough. How about it? Just give me five minutes alone with 'em...'

'Sod that,' I said, making for the exit. 'Let's concentrate on getting back home. Take the letters with us. Hinka can have himself a ball with 'em.'

We pushed our prisoners into the truck, closed all the observation slits and nosed our way out of the woods, back towards the fork where we had gone wrong. There was more activity on the road now. We passed several Russan convoys, but no one attempted to stop us. On the other hand, the Germans gave us a very hot reception as we attempted to cross back into our own lines.

'Stupid sodding bastards!' cried Tiny, already agitating the cannon. 'They're asking for trouble, carrying on like that!'

'We're the ones that's asking for trouble!' I retorted, holding on tight as the truck bucked and swerved. 'We'll be lucky if we get back in one piece.'

Porta somehow managed to plough through unscathed. With a magnificent flourish, he pulled up directly outside the command post, literally at Colonel Hinka's feet. He jumped down and saluted.

'Obergefreiter Joseph Porta presenting his report, sir! Mission accomplished successfully.'

Hinka stared past him open-mouthed at the truck.

'Where the devil did this thing come from?' He waved a hand at the rest star on the turret. 'What's been going on?'

'Nothing, sir.' Porta turned his puzzled gaze from Hinka to our vehicle. 'You mean the truck, sir?' He shrugged. 'We were running a bit behind schedule. We needed it to get back in time.'

'But where in heaven's name did you get it from?'

'Well, it was like this, sir.'

Porta tried unsuccessfully to stand to attention and dig a finger between the cheeks of his bottom at the same moment. Hinka clicked his tongue impatiently.

'Well? I'm waiting!'

'Well—it was a sort of accident, really, sir. We was in this wood, you see. You know what Russian woods are like, they go on for perishing miles, and like I said, we were running behind schedule.' He looked vaguely at the truck. 'We just sort of bumped into it. It seemed like a good idea ... oh, and incidentally,' he added, turning back again, 'we've brought along a couple of prisoners with us, sir. And a stack of mail.'

'Mail?' barked Hinka. 'What mail?'

'German mail, sir. We reckon they must've nicked it from us. The prisoners, I mean.'

Hinka frowned.

'Are you serious, Obergefreiter?'

'Oh yes, sir.' Porta jerked his head at Tiny. 'Fetch 'em out and let the colonel have a gander at them.'

The prisoners were hauled into the open by Tiny and deposited before Hinka. A gaping lieutenant came forward to untie their hands.

'Good God!' said Hinka.

He stood staring at them, his eyes straining forward in their sockets. Porta looked the prisoners up and down with an air of pride. He nodded, approvingly.

'They're your actual genuine thing, sir.'

Hinka passed a hand across his eyes. The strain of such prolonged staring was obviously beginning to tell. I found myself wondering if the man had actually ever seen a Russian before. Porta seemed also to be experiencing doubts.

'Your actual genuine native,' he said, earnestly. 'Your real actual——'

'Yes, yes,' said Hinka. He took a last look at the prisoners and dragged his eyes reluctantly away to regard Porta instead. 'Tell me, Obergefreiter, are you aware of the rank of these men?'

'They're your actual genuine Russians,' began Porta, in a defensive bleat. He glared repressively at the prisoners. 'They had this bag of mail, sir. OUR mail ... GERMAN mail ... When we was in Torgau, that was a very serious offence, that was. Nicking mail. I mean, you could——'

'Obergefreiter!'

Hinka's voice thundered out. Porta looked up at him in surprise.

'Yes, sir?'

'These—gentlemen—whom you have captured ... You are obviously not aware that one is a lieutenant-general and the other a colonel!'

There was a moment's uneasy silence. I saw Porta's Adam's apple move slowly up his scrawny throat and fall back with a bang. As one in a dream, he turned on his heel and saluted.

Tiny stood watching him with his mouth gaping open. He looked wonderingly at the prisoners—at the lieutenant-general he had kicked in the shins, and the colonel he had punched in the stomach—and slowly he, too, saluted.

As for me ... Well, I hadn't actually used physical violence on either of them. I hadn't actually abused them. I'd only tied their hands up and threatened to shoot them and shoved them about a bit ...

Quietly, I sunk my neck into my shoulders and slipped away unnoticed.

We swear to you, Adolf Hitler, that we shall keep faith.

August Wilhelm
Prince of Prussia, 1933

SS Obergruppenführer Reinhard Heydrich, head of the RSHA,* stormed angrily through the corridors of number 8 Prinz Albrecht Strasse, abusing all those who had the temerity to cross his path. He reached his own office, kicked open the door, strode past his astonished adjutant and snatched up the telephone.

'Schellenberg! I want to see you up here immediately!'

Without waiting for a reply, he slammed down the receiver again.

'Sir——' began the adjutant.

Heydrich ignored him. He pressed a button on his desk, next door to the telephone. The response not being instantaneous, he then pressed again, keeping his finger on the buzzer. The loud-speaker crackled and a coarse, grating voice filled the room.

'Gruppenführer Müller, Gestapo——'

'Müller! What's the matter with you? Wake your ideas up! I want to see you in my office straight away.'

The adjutant bit his lip and slunk silently from the room. Heydrich threw himself into the depths of a leather armchair, crossed his legs and began drumming his fingers on his thigh. There was a rap at the door. An ordnance officer announced the arrival of SS Gruppenführer Müller of the Gestapo and SS Brigadenführer Schellenberg of the Security Service.

Schellenberg was the first to enter. He was, as usual, dressed in civilian clothes, in a discreet grey suit. Gestapo Müller bustled behind, eager and anxious, his big red face on its thick neck bobbing awkwardly above his uniform. The ex-postman from Munich had never yet learnt how to wear his clothes with the elegance required of a German officer.

Schellenberg, relaxed and smiling, saluted easily. Müller rather more clumsily followed suit.

'So very nice to see you both,' said Heydrich, from the depths of his armchair. 'I trust you had a good night's sleep? It's a luxury that's denied to some of us, but I'm glad you manage to make the most of it, gentlemen...' He narrowed his eyes and looked across at the two officers. 'You!' He suddenly shot out a

* Bureau of State Security.

61

hand and pointed at Müller. 'While you were snoring under your great stuffed quilt this morning, *I* was at the receiving end of a complaining telephone call from the Führer. Not very pleasant, as you can possibly imagine. It delayed my morning ride for over half an hour.' He breathed deeply. 'The Führer was very angry, Müller. And he vented his anger on me ... me, you understand! It seems I am to be held personally responsible for your prolonged sleeping habits! You choose to stay like a pig in bed, while I am abused by the Führer because of it ... Tell me, Müller, at what hour did you put in an appearance this morning?'

Müller swallowed noisily.

'At half past eight, Obergruppenführer.'

'Half past eight! You're in the Gestapo now, Müller, you're not still delivering post in the streets of Munich. What do you think this war is? A joyride? We can't afford to carry passengers, Müller. Anyone who chooses to sleep while the rest of the world is working is a highly dispensible commodity ... There are many other postmen, both in and out of Munich, who would be only too pleased to walk into your shoes.'

Müller's fat red face seemed on the point of bursting in two like an overripe tomato. It crossed his fuddled mind that life had really been far simpler and happier in Munich. Heydrich's voice barked on.

'The Army Secret Service has intercepted a telegram that was sent by the Belgian ambassador in Rome to his Minister for Foreign Affairs. In that telegram, Müller, were set out our entire plans for the invasion of Belgium and Holland. What do you have to say about that?'

At this point, Schellenberg suavely interrupted.

'Pardon me, Obergruppenführer, but we have known for some time of the existence of that telegram. In fact, as I recall, it was first brought to our attention on the very day our troops crossed the Dutch border.'

Heydrich inclined his head in Schellenberg's direction.

'Thank you, Brigadenführer. I was aware. However, if you will allow me to say so, there is all the difference in the world between your department knowing of it and the Führer coming to hear of it ... You understand me?'

Schellenberg smiled.

'Perfectly, Obergruppenführer. Forgive the interruption.' He hesitated a moment. 'May one ask what the Führer intends to do about it?'

Heydrich hunched an indifferent shoulder.

'Who can tell? Everything is always ultra top secret at that end of the line, as you very well know. Doubtless the Führer lays his plans much as we lay ours.' Heydrich turned back savagely to his attack on Müller. 'Well? How about you, Herr Sherlock Holmes? What information do you have on our little nest of traitors? Admiral Canaris—Ambassdor Ulrich von Hassel—Oberburgermeister Goedler—Generalmajor Oster—General Beck ... to name but a few. What can you tell me about them?'

'Obergruppenführer——'

Müller shifted heavily from foot to foot, washing his hands in the air and sweating all over.

'For God's sake try to keep still!' snapped Heydrich.

The Head of the Gestapo obediently rooted himself to the spot.

'I can assure you, Obergruppenführer, that all these traitors are followed night and day by my men.'

'All of them?'

'All of them, Obergruppenführer.'

'Mm-hm ...' Heydrich gazed down a moment at his fingernails. 'And Sturmbannführer Axter from your division 111/2? Is he one of those on watchdog duty?'

'Oh yes,' said Müller, anxiously. 'Oh yes, he is, indeed! All my men are trained—they are all told—I make quite sure——'

'Precisely,' agreed Heydrich. 'But to return to this man Axter. You doubtless receive daily reports from him?'

'Er—yes,' allowed Müller, rather more cautiously. 'Yes, that is so. All my men are instructed——'

'You will therefore have heard from him within the last twenty-four hours?'

'Er—no.' Müller shook his head, miserably, and began washing his hands again. 'No, as a matter of fact I haven't, Obergruppenführer. But the man shall be punished for it! I shall see to it personally. Such behaviour is most unusual, my men are always most punctual, most efficient, most——'

'I'm sure they are,' agreed Heydrich. 'But I fear the miscreant Axter is beyond reach of all punishment. He was killed last night in the Morellenschlucht and his body has been disposed of.'

'But——'

'The man was a spy,' said Heydrich, curtly. 'Did you never check up on his background? Did it never occur to you that anyone who had served two years on the Führer's staff and suddenly switched his loyalties to the Gestapo might bear a little investigation on your part?'

'I always check on all my men, Obergruppenführer——'

'Evidently not well enough. I suggest in future you do your own homework. I cannot always be expected to play nursemaid ... In the meanwhile, I leave it to you to answer any awkward questions that may be raised regarding the man's death. Do you suppose you could at least be trusted with that?'

'Oh yes, Obergruppenführer, you leave it to me, I'll deal with it all right for you.'

'Let us hope so ... And now, about this business in Rome. Tell me what you know of it. As Head of the Gestapo you presumably have up-to-date information?

'Ah yes. Well——' Müller put a hand to his mouth and closed his teeth over his index finger while he sought for words. 'Yes. Well, we knew, of course, about the telegram. And we knew the agent who sold the information to the Belgians——'

'Really?' said Heydrich, pleasantly. 'I congratulate you, Müller! What did you do about it?'

'Well—unfortunately—we weren't able to discover very much until it was too late. But the agent's out of the way now, all right. You needn't worry about that, Obergruppenführer. Indeed, no!'

'Your men took care of him? Brought him in for questioning?'

'N-no ... not exactly ... The fact is,' said Müller, in a burst of confidence, 'the man was killed in a motor accident on the Via Veneto!'

'I see.'

'We did what we could. It was hardly our fault if he walked across the road without looking——'

'One moment.' Heydrich held up a slim shapely hand. 'You say you have dealt with the agent. But have you yet dealt with the agent's contact, I wonder?'

Müller opened his mouth to speak, but Heydrich cut in.

'Obviously not. Do I have to think of everything round here?' He stared piercingly at the unhappy Müller, then turned to regard Schellenberg, who had been listening to the scene with a whimsical smile on his lips. 'I think from now on it might be as well to keep a particular eye on our friend Admiral Canaris. I heard this morning that the Führer has entrusted to him the task of discovering the traitor in our midst ... the man who

64

sold the agent the information in the first place...'

'Ludicrous!' muttered Schellenberg.

'It does strike one,' agreed Heydrich, 'as being dangerously close to appointing a wolf to look after one's sheep, but there you have it, gentlemen ... Let us make what use of the opportunity we can.'

He gave a narrow-lipped smile. Schellenberg shook his head.

'Canaris!' he repeated, as even now he could not believe it.

'Canaris,' confirmed Heydrich. 'Of all people ... It did occur to me, Brigadenführer, that since you are on good terms with the Admiral, it might be as well if you—ah—flung him a few choice scraps to pass on to the Führer? Perhaps we might even furnish him, very discreetly, with one or two assistants from your department? For instance, you have a secretary in Section IV/2/B ... married to an officer, with a brother in England. She might do rather well ... You take my meaning?'

Schellenberg gravely nodded.

'At the same time,' continued Heydrich, 'we must naturally do all we can to help the admiral lay his hands on the traitor. That is your pigeon, Müller. And any more incompetence from your department and you can prepare to pick up your postbag and start tramping the streets of Munich once again ... Do I make myself clear?'

FOUR

THE BATTLE OF KRASNIJ OKJABRE

Several days later we arrived at a position to the north-east of Stalingrad, before the large naval steelworks factory called Krasnij Okjabre.* For some months past, this area had been the scenes of many clashes between German and Russian troops. Two enemy regiments were holding out in the steelworks and had so far refused to be dislodged. The factory itself was now a tangled mass of twisted girders and fallen brickwork. Repeated bombardments from German artillery had blown huge holes in the walls, and the smell of death and demolition was everywhere in the air; a mixture of brick dust and charred human flesh. The ruins were full of rats. They had grown big and bold, they were the size of large tomcats and they were scared of no man.

* 'Red October.'

We, on the other hand, were absolutely terrified of them. According to Heide, it was only a question of time before we had an outbreak of the plague, and we now hurled grenades into their midst every time we saw any of the loathsome creatures. To hell with their demands that we save ammunition: plague-carrying rats were worse than Russians any day!

We had been there for almost a week when one morning the Old Man was called to see the Company Commander, Captain Schwan. He was away for some time and we sat grumbling and speculating while he was gone.

'Just take a little trip round the enemy lines and see how it goes, old boy!' Porta turned and spat in disgust. 'Always bleeding well us, ain't it?'

'It oughta be someone else's turn,' said Gregor, piously. 'It's time they picked on someone else.'

'Who are you kidding?' I demanded. 'Who had to go sodding off last time to see what the flaming Russians were up to? Not you, as I recall!'

'Yeah, and who came back with a pissing general tucked under his arm?' jeered Gregor.

At this point the Old Man returned. He beckoned grimly to Heide, and the rest of us fell silent as they moved away together.

By straining our ears and quite unashamedly eavesdropping, we could just make out what was being said.

'Tell us the worst,' invited Heide. 'They want us to press on alone and take Moscow single-handed?'

'Almost as bad,' agreed the Old Man. 'It's that dirty great bunker in front of the steelworks. The one that's been causing all the trouble.'

'What about it?'

'It's got to go.'

Heide paused.

'What do you mean, it's got to go? You mean we've got to get rid of it?'

'That's about the size of it,' said the Old Man, almost apologetically.

Porta pulled a face of hideous rage and gloom and turned to the rest of us.

'What did I bleeding tell you?' he hissed.

'How?' Heide was coldly demanding. 'How in hell are we supposed to get rid of a filthy great bunker?'

'You're to take your group up to it while we cover you with

machine-gun fire. As soon as you reach the foot of the bunker, stuff as many grenades as possible through the loopholes, sit back and wait for it to go bang ... You'll also have five magnetic charges for the doors. OK?'

From the look on Heide's face, we gathered that it was far from OK. We were inclined to agree with him.

'The doors?' he repeated, stiffly.

'Yes, the doors ... things that open and shut ... All right?'

'No,' said Heide, 'Frankly not.' He looked frostily at the Old Man. 'I never heard such a flaming stupid idea in all my life! How the hell are we supposed to stuff grenades through the bleeding loopholes when they're about six feet above our heads? Give us some step-ladders and we might have a bash, but we're not bloody acrobats!'

'Well, that's your problem,' said the Old Man. 'How you do it is entirely up to you. I'm just passing on the orders: get out there and blow that bunker up.'

For a moment the two men stood glaring at each other, then Heide swore briefly, turned on his heel and came back to the rest of us. We knew there was nothing he could do, just as he knew that the Old Man would already have protested on our behalf at the futility of such an order.

'All right, 2nd Group fall in behind me!'

Heide shouldered his machine-gun, jerked his head and set off without a backward glance, his lips pressed tight together. We snatched up our weapons and hurried after him along a track that had once been a road and was now a macabre hotchpotch of derelict houses, the burnt-out wreckage of motor vehicles and tanks, shell craters, piles of rubble and human remains. The corpses that lay everywhere were those of civilians, not soldiers. All were horribly mutilated. In a bucket of water floated the severed head of a child. The eyes still stared in sightless stupefaction towards heaven. I found myself stumbling on through the ruins with the image of that head bouncing before me, until I put a foot straight into the putrefying remains of a human torso and found other things to think about.

A few yards ahead of me, Porta suddenly stopped and shouted to Heide.

'Hey! I've found the ideal spot!'

Heide looked round.

'What the hell are you babbling about?'

I caught up with Porta and saw that he had discovered a shell hole partially covered with fallen timber and concrete.

'I can set up the machine-gun,' declared Porta, promptly doing so. 'Just the right place for giving you the maximum cover.'

'Sod that!' screamed Heide, wheeling across to us. 'Pick the bloody thing up again and get a move on! I'm the one that's in charge! You stop when I say, and not before——'

At that moment, they caught sight of us from the bunker and opened fire. Heide was blown on top of us as the blast caught him, and we fell into Porta's shell hole together.

'See what I mean?' said Porta. 'It's the ideal spot.'

Heide pulled himself up and straightened his battledress.

'Two seconds to get out,' he told Porta, curtly. 'You're not out by then and I report you.'

'Do what you like,' said Porta, cheerfully. 'I'm staying put.'

'Sergeant!'

It was Captain Schwan's voice. We peered out and saw him running towards us through the rising dust. Heide and I scrambled from the shell hole. Porta turned back to his machine-gun.

'What are you waiting for?' panted Schwan.

Heide threw a black look towards Porta and opened his mouth to complain, but he wasn't fast enough: Porta leapt in first. He saluted smartly and gestured at the machine-gun.

'All set up, sir, ready to give cover.'

'Good man.' Schwan nodded approvingly at Porta and turned to Heide. 'Off you go, then, Sergeant!'

Heide had no option. With rage and hatred in his eyes, he sprinted up the track, stumbling furiously over the rubble, too angry even to notice the screaming shells and bullets raining down upon us from the bunker.

And since Heide had gone, we in our turn had no option but to follow. I shot after him with Gregor and Ponz running unhappily at my side. Ponz was a naval gunner who had recently joined the Company after a disastrous episode on the Don, when he was sole survivor from his ship. He rolled his eyes despairingly at me as we raced along, with the shells falling all round us.

It was a question of reaching the bunker before they found their length. I tripped over a pile of bricks, picked myself up, rushed onwards, fell again, stumbled to my feet. I felt as if all the breath had been squeezed out of my body. I had a sudden cramp in my side, needle-sharp pains plunged down my left lung, my heart battered desperately against my ribs and the blood pounded and thundered in my ears. I fell for the third time and lay sobbing in the snow, fighting for breath. We were almost at the bunker now. Just that final leap across ... A boot came crashing into my ribs. Mercilessly, again and again. A manic voice yelled in my ear.

'Get to your feet, you snivelling rat! Get up or I'll shoot you!'

'Leave me alone, I can't!'

It was my own voice, screaming hysterically. I hardly recognised it. Heide thrust the butt of his sub-machine-gun against my ear.

'Get up and jump or I'll kill you on the spot!'

Porta's machine-gun went into action and the bullets sprayed out over the surface of the bunker, embedding themselves in the walls. Porta was great with a machine-gun. You could rely on Porta.

I crouched, ready to spring. I didn't want to jump, I was scared rigid, I knew I'd never make it, the air was awash with bullets between us and the bunker. The only trouble was, I was even more scared of Heide. Heide was a fanatic, and a sadistic bastard into the bargain, and when he said he'd shoot he meant it. On the other hand——

'Get going!'

He jabbed me in the kidneys with his sub. Sobbing with fear, I bunched my muscles together and launched myself into the bullet-ridden air. I was the first man over the ditch, but almost the second I landed the others were with me. Ponz was by my side, with the pouch of grenades. He was making an odd snuffling noise. I glanced at him, my nerve suddenly restored, and discovered that he was now in the state I had been in on the other side of the ditch.

'Do what you flaming like!' he whimpered at Heide. 'My war's coming to an end right here in this ditch! Sod the Führer and sod the Fatherland and sod the pissing Reich!'

'And sod the Navy, too!' roared Heide.

In a sea of bullets, the rattling of machine-gun fire and the bursting of shells, they stood and glared at each other. I stared up at the shattered walls of the steelworks and realised slowly what it would mean if the factory fell. That place was Stalin's pride and joy. When Red October had gone, what would he have left?

I became suddenly aware that Heide had abandoned Ponz and gone bounding up the slope towards the bunker. This was perhaps the most dangerous moment yet. The slope was steep and snow-covered and criss-crossed in enemy fire. I watched Heide spring to safety at the foot of the bunker and crouch there exultantly. One of us, at least, had made it. I turned to the shivering sailor.

'You coming, or not?'

'Sod that for a laugh!'

It was all he would say. I shrugged my shoulders and threw myself at the slope. Bullets zipped across my path and buried themselves all round me in the snow. I rolled panting into the shadow of the great bunker. Its massive concrete walls rose menacingly above us. Those inside must feel so safe, while we skirmishing figures outside were so tiny and unprotected, so relatively powerless . . .

I pressed myself hard against the foot, seeking some shelter from the storm.

'What's the matter with you?' jeered Heide. 'Got the wind up, have you?'

'I'm not the only one,' I muttered. 'Harebrained bloody idea this was!'

Heide held out his hand.

'Never mind that. Where are the grenades?'

'I don't know,' I said. 'It's not my job to carry them. I'm not a bleeding packhorse.'

'Who the hell's got them, then?'

I suddenly remembered.

'He has.' I pointed back down the slope, to where Ponz was still cowering in the ditch. 'He's got them.'

Heide looked aghast.

'You mean you came up here without any flaming grenades?'

'You mean you did?' I retorted.

'It's not my job to carry grenades!'

'And it's not mine, either! They were given to him, it's up to him to bring them!'

'Fuck that!' shouted Heide, in a frenzy. He grabbed me by the collar and shook me. 'You go right back down there and get them! What the hell are we supposed to do up here without any grenades?'

I tore myself away.

'Let someone else get the sodding things!'

'I said you!' bellowed Heide. 'You're the best man we've got with a grenade, and I'm ordering you to go down there and get them!'

70

'And I'm telling you to go and get stuffed!' I bellowed back. I waved a hand in the direction of the terrified sailor. 'Why can't he bring them up here? I'm not risking my neck going all the way down there and back again. You must be flaming joking!'

Heide gave me a look of maniacal dislike, then turned abruptly and shouted down at Ponz.

'Hey! You there! Ponce, or whatever your name is ... Get a move on out of that hole!'

As the sailor simply withdrew further into the protection of his ditch, Heide opened fire. The effect was instantaneous. With one bound, the man was up the hill and by our side. Without the grenades ... In his anguish, he had abandoned them in the ditch. With a howl of rage, Heide lashed out with his foot and sent the man rolling back down the slope.

'You get those grenades up here quick sharp!'

Ponz lay whining and grizzling in the ditch.

'You fired at me! You could have killed me——'

'That was my intention! I'm sorry I missed, I'll try again ...'

Gregor and the Legionnaire had now crept round to join us. Ponz gave a wild shriek as Heide opened fire and came skittering up the hill with tears rolling down his cheeks and the pouch of grenades bumping at his side. We snatched them from him and began feverishly to concoct our own brand of home-made bombs: a clutch of four grenades secured to a bottle filled with petrol.

'OK, Sven.' Heide pointed to the nearest loophole, which looked to be about five miles above my head. 'I'll cover you while you chuck it in.'

'What, me?' I said, aghast.

Heide looked at me.

'I said you, didn't I?'

'Yes, but how the hell can I?'

'Don't ask me,' said Heide, indifferently. 'I didn't think up the idea, I only have to make sure it's carried out.'

I stared up at the loophole. A good ten or eleven feet above the ground.

'You're the expert,' said Gregor. 'You've always been a cracker with grenades.'

I gave him a look of hatred. Heide jerked his head at me, and unwillingly I moved out into the open. A machine-gunner posted high up behind one of the factory walls at once began plastering me with bullets. The air all round me buzzed like a swarm of lusting wasps. I took aim, opening my chest wide to their fire, drew back my arm and flung the grenades up towards the loophole ... There was not sufficient strength behind my arm. The angle was wrong. The bomb crashed into the wall a couple of feet below the loophole and bounced down to the ground at out feet. I was scarcely aware of Heide hurling himself at me, knocking me off balance and into safety as the thing exploded. My arm was wrenched almost off my body by the force of the blast. I was quite hopeful for a moment, but when I felt it it appeared still to be attached.

'Bloody idiot!' snarled Heide. 'They've spotted us now!'

I sat resentfully on the ground, massaging my shoulder. Heide kicked at me with his boot.

'Up!' He gestured at me. 'Only one thing for it. You'll have to stand on my shoulders and stuff the thing through the hole that way.'

I stared up at him, horrified. Heide was mad. Stark mad. I had always half suspected it.

'Come on!' He snapped his fingers at me as if I were a well-trained dog. 'Let's get the thing over with.'

Behind the shadow of the bunker wall the fury was still raging. Despite Porta's ceaselessly accurate machine-gun fire the Russian guns were still in action.

'Look,' I said, trying to be reasonable with the demonic Heide, 'I think someone else ought to have a go. My arm's been almost torn off my body, and I don't——'

'Liar!'

Heide gripped me by my injured shoulder and hauled me to my feet. Tongues of red-hot fire raced down the right side of my body. Heide slapped me backwards and forwards across the face until I felt dizzy, and then he stepped back and clasped his hands together.

'Right! Shove your foot in there and get up.'

I had no alternative. There never was any alternative in this bloody war. Heide was far stronger than I, he would kill me without a moment's hesitation if I again refused to obey his idiotic orders. And no one would blame him. I looked round hopelessly at the others. Ponz was snivelling against the wall. Gregor was glaring aggressively at me. Only the Legionnaire gave me a faint encouraging grin and a wink.

I swallowed some bitter-tasting liquid that had come into my mouth, placed my foot in Heide's hands and swung myself up on to his shoulders. Gregor passed up the grenades. Heide took a few paces backwards into the enemy fire and I stretched up towards the loophole. But as I stuffed the grenades inside, the butt of a rifle appeared and bolted them out again ... I lost my balance, grabbed at Heide's head, collapsed completely and brought him down with me. Together we rolled, in a flurry of snow, back down the slope to the ditch.

'You did that on purpose!' screamed Heide. 'You lousy filthy coward, I'll have you shot for this!'

I jerked my head round and saw his eyes, red-rimmed, burning with the desire to kill. I saw his lips, drawn back over his sharp white teeth, I saw a speck of foam at the corners of his mouth. I saw the gleam of metal in his hand and I didn't stop to plead with him. I leapt out of the ditch and bounded back up that cursed slope with Heide howling like a wolf behind me. I flung myself gasping between Gregor and the Legionnaire, just as Heide's knife rebounded off the wall above my head. Heide stopped dead in the middle of the gunfire, half-way up the slope, with bullets shaving the very stubble off his cheeks. He raised a clenched and threatening fist towards the impregnable bunker.

'You just wait, you bastards! I'll get you yet!'

He made a sudden dive at the wall and succeeded in running half-way up it in his rage. He fell panting on to his back in the snow, picked himself up and made a second furious assault. By some miracle, he found a foothold. a brick that had moved position very slightly and projected perhaps an inch beyond its companions. It was enough for the maddened Heide. He clawed upwards with both hands and gripped on to the barrel of the gun that was sticking out of the loophole. Round his neck, attached by a lanyard, he was carrying a mine. If he were to slip and accidentally wrench out the fuse mechanism, he would be blown to pieces.

'The man's mad,' declared Gregor, shortly.

'He's a bloody Nazi!' I retorted.

The Legionnaire stared upwards, shaking his head in reluctant admiration.

'Both mad and a Nazi,' he agreed, 'but a bloody good soldier for all that.'

Heide freed one arm and pulled the lanyard over his head. With his other hand he gripped the rifle, bending his body underneath him so that his boots pressed against the wall. Very calmly and coldly he pushed the heavy mine through the loophole. Next moment, he was back on the ground at our feet, springing up instantly and setting off at a run, yelling at us to follow him.

We took the opposite direction and had scarcely turned the corner of the bunker when the door swung open and a blood-stained figure stumbled out. In one swift movement the Legionnaire smashed his sub-machine-gun in the man's face, rammed his knee into his guts, tossed him to one side and rushed through into the bunker with Gregor and I behind him. We crouched down in the corner, surrounded by boxes of ammunition. Somewhere up above, on another floor, we heard the ceaseless pounding of the heavy guns.

'Hey, you!' Gregor beckoned at Ponz, who was hovering at the entrance. 'Go and find Heide and tell him we're in! And make it snappy or he'll start chucking more mines about the place ... God knows, he's bloody mad enough!'

'Oh, all right, if I must.'

Ponz turned unhappily away, took one step forward and walked straight into Heide. He gave a horrified yelp and tried to side step. Heide pushed him inside to join the rest of us.

'What's going on? Why aren't you upstairs killing Russians?' He glared round, and his glance singled me out for special castigation. 'Sitting down here with your thumb up your bum and your brains in neutral! That's not going to get you anywhere, is it?' He jabbed his finger into my chest. 'You want to be an officer! All right: show us what you're made of. Get up that bleeding ladder and have a look round!'

This time, I didn't protest. I went up the ladder like a spring lamb, eased open the trap a few inches and peered through. I was surrounded on all sides by sleeping Russians. On their helmets I could see the dreaded letters NKVD. That was more than enough for me. I closed the trap and scuttled back down the ladder. Heide was waiting for me, his hands on his hips.

'Well? I didn't hear any shooting. What happened? You just said hallo and came straight back again, did you?'

I pointed wild-eyed up the ladder.

'NKVD,' I hissed. 'Thousands of 'em!'

Heide frowned. He snatched up a handful of grenades, pulled out the pins, pushed me to one side and went tearing up the ladder. The trap was thrown back with a clatter, the grenades went in and Heide flung himself down again even faster than he'd gone up. Seconds later, there was a series of shattering explosions. We waited for them to subside, then Heide moved forward.

'Right-oh, let's get up there.'

This time, it was the Legionnaire who led the way. As a matter of precaution he sprayed the whole area with bullets before we stepped through the trap, but there seemed no sign of life. Heide's grenades had done their work. It looked like a butcher's shop up there, all blood and carcases.

As we stood on the threshold I became aware of a cautious movement away to my left. I spun round in time to see a Russian lieutenant crouched down and aiming his heavy revolver. I jumped aside and the bullet scraped the edge of my helmet, and at the same time Gregor opened fire and the man fell back with his face a red pulpy mass with no features. Somewhere else an arm was raised to fling a grenade, but the Legionnaire moved in with his bayonet. These men were wounded, but we had to wade through the blood searching for signs of life and extinguishing it wherever we found it. A Siberian will fight to the death. We had once watched one of our own men get his head blown off as he bent down to offer water to a wounded Siberian. Since that day, we had taken no chances.

As I led the way up the ladder to the next floor, the trap above my head was cautiously eased back and an enormous Mongoloid face thrust itself forward. I froze in horror to the spot, pressing myself against the wall. The face remained where it was, the slit eyes narrowing in terrified amazement as they saw what was coming up the ladder. For perhaps a couple of seconds we did nothing but stare at each other, and then my right arm shot out, apparently of its own volition, my fingers plunged deep into the man's flared nostrils and I hooked him forward, over the edge of the trap. He crashed to the floor below, where Heide stood waiting for him.

There was no time, now, for a slow and careful ascent. There were sounds of frenzied activity above us, and I hurled a couple of grenades through the trap and flung myself back down the ladder. They exploded before I could reach the bottom, and the force of the blast lifted me high into the air and tossed me across the floor in a limp heap.

For a few moments I lay semi-conscious in a pool of someone else's blood. By the time I found the willpower to sit up and look about me, the dust was beginning to settle and the great bunker was silent. Gregor was drinking from a flask he had taken from a dead Russian gunner. The Legionnaire was sitting on the floor, smoking. Ponz was leaning against the wall looking dazed and vacant. And Heide—Heide was solemnly washing himself in a bucket of icy water! Scrubbing the grime from his hands and face, sponging down his uniform, cleaning his nails, combing his hair, polishing his equipment ... Five minutes' hard labour and he was restored to his normal model self, the perfect Prussian soldier with every last hair in place and even his toe-nails clean and shining.

The Third Company were called up to hold the bunker. In peace-time it had been used as a place of work for prisoners, and down in the cellars, beneath the foundations, we found a large number of bodies. Some had green circles sewn on to their uniforms, indicating that they had been political detainees; others had black, for various criminal offences. All had been shot in the back of the head.

Before the Third Company arrived, we combed every inch of that bunker in search of booby-traps. The Siberian NKVD were possessed of a fanaticism that made even Heide seem a placid and peaceable soul, and we came cross several lethal packages planted above doorways and beneath floorboards. We were terrified of the Siberians. They gave no quarter to anyone, not even to their own side, and were rarely content to dispose of their prisoners by shooting: they more generally tortured them to death. If you were unfortunate enough to fall into their hands alive the most lenient treatment you could expect was to be hung naked out of a window, attached by wire cords round the ankle. It took a man six hours to die that way, and that was comparatively easy ...

Now that we had taken the bunker, the next step was to move on to the steelworks themselves. A light artillery company moved up and were soon settled in with their howitzers. When twenty-four of those things went off in unison it sounded like the end of the world.

Our first few attacks were strongly repulsed. The Siberians came out and fought us with everything they had; we kicked and clawed each other in nightmare hand-to-hand combat, we twisted bayonets in each other's guts, we blew each other up with grenades and shells, the white snow became crimson with spilt blood and men fought ankle deep in the mush of human flesh. And still the Siberians held firm. After each attack we had to fall back again, with the loss of a few more hundred men.

On the ninth day, we intercepted one of their radio messages:

'Krasnij Okjabre, Krasnij Okjabre ... calling base. We are still under attack and food supplies are exhausted. Can't hold out much longer. Request permission to surrender.'

We found this news most encouraging. If the dreadnought Siberians were willing to talk of giving in, we knew they must be in an even worse state than we ourselves. Needless to say, the reply they received was categorical: in no circumstances were they to surrender, now or ever; they were to carry on the fight like the good Soviet soldiers they were and rise above the animal demands of their bellies for food.

Another five days of futile fighting, another few hundred lives thrown away, and still the starving Siberians kept us from the door. But their radio appeals were growing ever more desperate: they had now run out of water as well as food and many of their men had killed themselves rather than go on. Back came the answer, uncompromising as before:

'Russian soldiers, the time has come to prove yourselves! Show yourselves worthy to be members of the great Red Army! Have faith and fight on, Stalin has not forgotten you! ON NO ACCOUNT ABANDON YOUR POSITIONS.'

They held out for another three days. Even with the psychological advantage of knowing their plight, we still could not break them. And then came their last radio message: no more ammunition, request permission to surrender. And the canting reply as before:

'Comrades, the Soviets salute you! The workers are in your debt! Fight on! Permission to surrender is refused. A RUSSIAN SOLDIER NEVER SURRENDERS.'

Shortly before midnight, they came for us. Rushing towards us in a final futile fling, bayonets fixed to their useless rifles. Wave upon wave of them were butchered by our machine-gun fire. Those that managed to break through fought like wild beasts, with a strength and a fury that our own men could not match. The Siberians were starving, half mad with thirst, certain to die one way or another. They had nothing to lose any more, they had already lost it, and the first ferocious horde that ran through the machine-gun fire and fell upon us with their bayonets took us by surprise. A Russian officer came at me from the side. I swung round to face him, lashed out in a panic, kicked him to the ground and stuck my bayonet deep into his abdomen. Still he found the strength to lunge at me. I looked down at the glittering eyes in the gaunt face, and the naked hatred unnerved me. With a savage cry of fear, I tore out my bayonet and slashed at his face until the features were obliterated and the light had gone from the glittering eyes. Afterwards I felt ashamed, but when we finally broke through into the great hall of the factory and saw numbers of our own men hanging naked by their ankles I felt a vicious glow of satisfaction for my revenge.

Under the great silent machines of the steelworks Russian soldiers lay dead or dying. We shot all those who were still breathing. They watched as we came, and made no attempt to plead with us. They knew it was useless. One or two, still able to crawl or to drag themselves about the floor, committed suicide before we could reach them. They flung themselves from the windows or down the lift shafts.

By evening time, the battle was over and the vast factory of Krasnij Okjabre was conquered. And yet it seemed a sour victory. Much as we hated and feared them, the Siberians had earned our respect and in the final analysis they had been beaten not so much by superior forces as by circumstance. From then until the end of the war their heroic resistance was to be held up as an example to encourage those in difficulties: 'Remember Krasnij Okjabre! If they can do it, so can you . . .'

Afterwards, relaxing in the sudden anticlimax, we lay about on the factory floor, stretched out on benches or leaning against machines. Porta was listlessly thumbing through a news-sheet.

'What's happening in the rest of the world, then?' demanded the Old Man, clamping his teeth on his empty pipe.

It was always difficult, after a few weeks of intensive fighting, to drag your mind back to the realities of the general situation and remember that your little section of the war was only one piece of the jigsaw; that other fronts did exist, men were fighting in other countries, and your particular victory did not mean an end to the hostilities.

'So what's going on?' said the Old Man.

'Sweet bugger all.' Porta screwed the news-sheet into a ball and threw it at him. 'Same as always. The Navy's sunk practically every enemy ship on the high seas and England's had it.'

Gregor frowned.

'I don't get it,' he complained. 'Month after month they tell

78

you that. Ever since Poland they've been saying it ... England's had it ... England's washed up ... England's on her knees ... So why the hell can't the stupid sods throw in the sponge and put an end to it all?'

'Just what I say,' chimed in Tiny, eagerly. 'What's the point of carrying on? They haven't got no ships left, have they? Their ports have all been bombed to buggery, their planes are all out of date and they're running short of manpower, so what's the POINT of carrying on?'

'I reckon they're only doing it out of pig-headedness,' said Gregor, sagely.

'Just bloody-minded,' agreed Tiny.

The Legionnaire twisted his lips in a sardonic grin.

'I wonder how it is,' he murmured, 'that the RAF can keep on bombing German towns night after night in their out-of-date planes with their shortage of manpower?'

'Don't ask awkward questions,' said the Old Man. 'Listen, here's a bit might interest you.' He had straightened out the news-sheet and spread it before him across a work-bench. ' "At Stalingrad, our lads are fighting valiantly. The men of the Sixth Army will go down in history as true heroes of the Fatherland. God is with us! The boys of Stalingrad are fighting with faith in their hearts and bibles in their hands ..." '

He was cut short by Gregor making vomiting noises and Tiny shouting out an obscene protest. The Old Man shrugged his shoulders.

'I just thought it might amuse you,' he said, mildly.

We were not left long in peace. Captain Schwan soon called all the section leaders together and gave them new sets of orders, and minutes later we were being turned out once again into the cold.

For us, it was a question of mounting guard on the monstrously ugly and sinister GPU building, where General Paulus and his staff were playing war games in the safety of the cellars. While the rest of us fought and suffered and died, they sat smoking and drinking and sticking coloured pins in maps of Russia. Those pins represented us; they represented men who were weary and wounded, half starved, suffering from frostbite, appalled by the constant slaughter, living in a state of unrelenting terror. But to Paulus and his staff we were just so many pins stuck in a map, and as they sat smug in their shelters and juggled with our lives, we struggled onward through the bitter Russian night, hurrying on our way to keep guard over them.

We moved single file along the Street of the Revolution, where most of the houses were still standing. There were gaps here and there, a few walls blown down, a few windows smashed, but on the whole the street had been spared the worst excesses of.war. There had been no heavy bombardment, only a few stray shells, and the people had continued to live in their homes, although there was now a straggling line of refugees carrying away their household goods and transporting their wounded on mattresses and in carts. Now and again a child would appear and sidle up to us begging for food. God knows we had little enough for ourselves, but we generally managed to find a spare crust of bread for them. A small boy suddenly darted out of a ruined building and ran straight up to Tiny, snatching at his hand and staring up appealingly.

'Gospodin soldier! Will you be my father?'

Tiny looked down at the child in some perplexity, and the child looked gravely back, hopping and skipping by his side to keep up with Tiny's giant paces. His head was half hidden beneath a German infantry helmet, and in one hand he was clutching a Russian sabre. Tiny bent down and swung the boy up on to his shoulder.

'OK, chum, if that's what you want...' He and the child grinned amiably at each other. 'How old are you, anyway?' demanded Tiny. 'I ought to know, didn't I? If I'm going to be your father.'

The boy shook his head.

'I'm quite old,' he said. 'Nobody's ever told me, really, but——' He suddenly hooked an arm round Tiny's neck and looked at him out of large round eyes. 'Gospodin soldier, would you like to be my sister's father, as well?'

'Now that's quite a suggestion!' said Tiny, swinging the boy back to ground level. 'Where is she?'

'I'll go and get her!' cried the boy. 'Just stay here and I'll go and get her!'

He shot off again up the road. At that moment someone threw a grenade. Probably a lone Russian soldier hiding out in one of the ruined buildings. We flung ourselves to the ground and covered our heads and the sound of the explosion roared up the narrow street. When we stood up again, Tiny's newly acquired son was nowhere to be seen. All that was left of him was a Germany infantry helmet and a Russian sabre, side by side at the centre of the blast...

After two days of guard duty at the GPU building, we were transferred to an infantry barracks and Porta was promoted from lance-corporal to corporal.

'Well, I'll be damned!' declared Sergeant Franz Krupka, seeing the additional stripe on Porta's sleeve. 'Going up in the world, aren't we? We'll be a field-marshal before we know where we are ...' He flipped a finger at the new stripe. 'How about a round of drinks, then?'

'That's a bloody bright idea,' said Porta, acidly. 'What do you suggest we drink? Melted snow? I haven't seen a bottle of anything for weeks.'

Krupka glanced over his shoulder and then back at Porta.

'You want to know where to get hold of some?'

Porta looked at him.

'Are you kidding?'

'No, I'm asking you ... You want to know where to get hold of some? Because if you do, I can tell you. Only keep it under your hat if you want to hang on to that nice new stripe.'

'You think I was born yesterday?' jeered Porta.

'I was just warning you. Don't let it go any further ... It's that fat bastard Wilke, he's managed to nick four crates of vodka from somewhere.'

Porta's little glass-bead eyes opened themselves wide in greedy astonishment.

'Four crates? Christ almighty, with one of those inside me I could finish the bleeding war single-handed! How did that turd get hold of 'em?'

Krupka hunched a shoulder.

'Buggered if I know. He didn't tell me, and I didn't ask.'

'Quite right, too.' Porta pulled out a pencil stub and began briskly to make out a list. 'Let's see ... one crate of vodka ... I don't suppose we can hope for more than one, so we don't want to divide it too many ways. Just you and me, and the Old Man and Gregor ... and Tiny and Sven and the Legionnaire ...' He hesitated. 'And Heide, I suppose. I'd just as soon be without him, but what can you do? He'll only get his knickers twisted if we have a binge and don't invite him.'

'That makes eight altogether,' said Krupka. 'I reckon if we can get hold of some beer and mix it in with the vodka, it should be enough to get pissed on.'

'Some of us,' said Porta, 'get pissed more quickly than others ... I'm thinking of Tiny. One drink and he's rolling about like a pig in shit with his legs in the air ... And that reminds me,'

81

he added, obscurely, 'the Legionnaire owes me a packet of fags.'

'Yeah, well you make a note of it and get 'em back quick sharp before we go into action again,' advised Krupka. 'That bastard Pinsky—you know Pinsky? Well, he's dead now. Got himself blown up by a shell a couple of weeks ago. Owed me three packets of grifas,* the swine. I won't never see THEM again, will I?' Krupka shook his head, broodingly. 'I told his section they ought to take over his debts now he's gone, but they weren't having any.'

Porta sucked in his breath.

'It's disgraceful,' he said. 'A man didn't ought to be allowed to go into battle in that condition. Not owing money and such-like, he didn't ... We ought to have accountants out here. I bet if the Jews were here, they'd have accountants.'

'I'll tell you one thing,' said Krupka, darkly. 'I've learnt my lesson. No more lending from now on. I've been too soft-hearted with people, they've taken me for a ride. But no more! Not even if they offer me hundred per cent interest. The game's not worth the candle.'

'Hundred per cent?' said Porta, his eyes at once inflating. 'You mean to tell me there really are mugs what'd be mad enough to give you a hundred per cent?'

'They bloody well ought to give a hundred per cent!' roared Krupka. 'When you think of the risks you have to run—never knowing if you're likely to see colour of their money ... You know what?' he said, incredulously. 'A few months back I helped an officer out of trouble when he was on his beam ends. Now you'd .think you could trust an officer, of all people, to behave like a gentleman, wouldn't you?' He turned and spat. 'Not on your bleeding life! He only goes and throws himself under a T34, doesn't he? On purpose, mind you. He done it on purpose. That's what really gets me. Sod my money, just so long as he could pick up his flaming Iron Cross.'

'What a shit!' said Porta, in disgust.

'Times are very hard,' grumbled Krupka. 'Very hard indeed.'

Porta went off in search of Wilke, the big fat cook with the four precious crates of vodka. He was engrossed in stirring a pot of greasy water, which would later be dished up to us under the guise of soup.

'Hi, Wilke!' Porta bashed him amiably across the shoulders.

* Narcotic cigarettes.

'Heard the latest, have you?'

'Latest what? I'm not interested in the latest. It's all lies, all of it.'

'Have a fag,' said Porta. He pulled out the solid gold cigarette case he had removed from the body of a dead general. 'You'll need one when I've told you the news.'

'Bugger the news! I'd rather stand here and stir my soup and think of my hotel. The news can get on by itself.'

'What hotel's that, then?'

'The one I'm going to build after the war. I'm planning it. It's got——'

Porta laughed.

'You'll be lucky! You'll be six foot under ground by then, along with the rest of us ... New top secret orders came through yesterday. I managed to have a dekko at them—never mind how, that's my business. But you know what they said? The German Army's going to fight to the last man and the last bullet ... That's as true as I stand here. Top secret instructions from the Führer himself.'

Wilke spat into his stewpot and stirred vigorously.

'It's all lies,' he muttered.

'You reckon?' Porta looked at him thoughtfully, then moved close and hissed into his ear. 'As a matter of interest, what would you say to the chance of getting out of it? Eh? Out of Russia? Out of the war? Back home in an aeroplane, to a nice cushy job...'

Wilke turned to look at Porta.

'What would YOU say?' he retorted.

'I'd say, lead me to it! Seriously, though, and don't let it go no further ... I was with the CO yesterday, and while I was there I heard a very interesting bit of news——'

'He told you himself?' jeered Wilke. 'Takes you into his confidence, does he?'

Porta shook his head, with a smile of superior amusement.

'You'd be surprised the contacts I have ... you get to meet people when you're a corporal, you know ... Anyway, to tell you the truth, I didn't take too much notice at first. I mean, you don't, do you, when you don't stand to gain nothing personally? It was only afterwards I got thinking. I thought of all the pals I've got what are cooks. All the cooks what are here in Stalingrad. It's them it concerns.'

'What are you on about?' demanded Wilke.

'Don't believe me if you don't want to,' said Porta, generously. 'But I've heard they're looking for a really good cook, with war experience and all, like what you've got, to take over the catering section at the Military Training School in Stettin.'

Wilke's flabby jaw dropped open. His double chin trebled. He stole a cowlike glance at Porta, then turned back to his ruminative stirring.

'You was one of the first I thought of,' continued Porta. 'I mean, you and me have been through a lot together, one way or another. You remember that time at Paderborn?' he said, affectionately. 'When I found out you was cheating us on the rations? You remember how I covered up for you? Well, it was the least I could do for an old pal. I couldn't stand by and watch them drag you off to Torgau, could I?'

Wilke suddenly banged down his spoon.

'Ah, for God's sake don't bring that up again! As if I haven't repaid you over and over!' He snorted. 'Old pal, my arse! You're nothing but a blackmailing Jew!'

'I've been called worse,' said Porta, equably. 'So anyway, how about going back to Stettin to be a teacher, eh? Better than this hell-hole, ain't it?'

Wilke licked his puffy lips. Everyone knew Porta for a thief and a cheat and a liar. It was absurd to believe even a quarter of what he said. And yet, there was always a first time . . .

'Look,' he said, earnestly, 'you know I'm a married man with two kids, I can't afford to take risks . . . Is it true or isn't it, this story about them wanting a cook from Stalingrad?'

'It's as true as I stand here,' said Porta, solemnly. 'I only wish to God I was a cook . . . but as I'm not, I had a word with a pal of mine in Personnel and took the liberty of giving him your name. If anyone can fiddle it so you get the job, it's him.'

Wilke stood gaping.

'You gave him my name? Just like that? For free?'

'Nothing's for free in this horrible world,' said Porta. 'You know that as well as I do. But he didn't ask much, only a crate of vodka. As far as I'm concerned, it's just a friendly gesture. I don't want nothing for it. Not for putting in a good word on behalf of an old mate. Wouldn't be reasonable, would it?'

Wilke chewed frenziedly at his thumb-nail. Already he could hear the throbbing engine of a JU 52, waiting to take him home . . .

'Only thing is,' went on Porta, opening the lid of a saucepan and peering inside, 'don't say a word to no one or you'll knacker the whole thing. It's top secret, see? Morale's pretty low back

84

home and old Adolf's suddenly realised the way to win the war is to keep men's bellies filled. So now there's this great panic on to start training more cooks.'

'But why come all the way to Stalingrad?' protested Wilke, with a final fling of common sense. 'There must be a thousand cooks in Stettin.'

'Ah yes,' said Porta. 'But how many will have had your experience? It's not many cooks what can survive in a place like Stalingrad ... Anyway, I just thought I'd mention it. If you're not interested I'll offer it to someone else. Old Richter, for example. He'd be willing to pay a bomb for a nice safe billet like that.'

'Willing to pay?' repeated Wilke. 'I thought you said you were doing it for nothing?'

'I am,' agreed Porta. 'It's my friend in Personnel what demands payment ... well, you can't blame him, really. He's one of the few men round this place really knows what's going on, and believe you me, things are getting pretty desperate ... You know what else he told me? On account of we've lost so many men, there's not going to be no more going sick nor nothing of that sort. Don't matter if you got both your legs blown off, they're going to send you right back into the front line. The way they look at it, a man with no legs is just another mouth to feed, so he might as well go and get himself killed by the enemy and save someone more useful getting a bullet through the brain. It makes sense, I suppose.' He pulled a face. 'What we've been through so far ain't nothing to what's going to come.'

Wilke passed a trembling fat hand over his head, which was bald and perspiring. It was said in the company that his hair had fallen out through constant worry as to how he could best cheat the men out of their rations. Wilke was known as the meanest, fattest and most dishonest cook in the whole of the German Army.

'I'll tell you something else,' said Porta, putting a consoling arm round him. 'Even cooks are going to have to fight from now on ... God's truth! No more messing about with the stewpots, you'll find yourself running along in the mud with the rest of us ... except it'll be even worse for you, being a sergeant. They'll probably put you in charge of a machine-gun section ... Anyway, that's enough of that. I can't stand gossiping with you all day, I've got other things to do. They keep a man very busy when he's a corporal.' He patted Wilke on the

85

shoulder and walked off, turning back again as he reached the door. 'So I'll tell my friend in Personnel you're not interested, then?'

'No!' Wilke hurried across to him, all his fleshy folds flouncing up and down as he moved. 'Of course I'm interested, I'd be a fool not to be!'

'Well, that's what I thought,' agreed Porta. 'I thought anyone who'd stay on to fight Russians when he could be cooking in Stettin was a bit of a mug.'

'So what happens?' demanded Wilke, breathlessly.

'I'll have a word with my friend in Personnel and he'll see to it you get the job ... oh, and I'd better take him his crate of vodka, or the shit's likely to rat on us.'

Wilke moved back a pace.

'Vodka?' he said. 'Where would I get vodka from?'

'Search me,' said Porta, frankly. 'I was rather curious about that myself, to tell the honest truth, but I won't stick my nose in, I'll just take the one case and keep my mouth shut.'

'You must be mad!' gasped Wilke, indignantly. 'I can't lay my hands on a crate of vodka just like that!'

'I see.'

Porta raised a cold eyebrow. He paused a second, then turned on his heel and left the room. He walked singing down the steps.

> 'There's a bullet that's coming this way ...
> For me—or for you—
> I couldn't say ...'

Behind him, he heard the patter of agitated footsteps.

'Don't be so hasty!' cried Wilke. 'Come back a moment and let's discuss terms.'

'Not discussible,' said Porta. 'I already told you what they are. Just say yes or no and stop wasting my time.'

'Yes!' screamed Wilke. His puffy fingers pawed at Porta's arm. 'I'll give it to you straight away.'

He had hidden the vodka beneath an old tarpaulin. Porta regarded the crate suspiciously and took out every single bottle and held it up to the light before he was satisfied.

'Take it and go,' said Wilke, pulling back the tarpaulin. 'And make sure it's my name and no one else's you give to your friend.'

'You bet,' said Porta.

86

He humped the crate on to his shoulder and strode back to our quarters with it.

'Feast your eyes on that!' he told the astounded Krupka.

'You got it?' said Krupka. 'You actually got it? I've been trying to lay my hands on some of that stuff for the past two months.' He looked wonderingly at Porta. 'How'd you manage it?'

'Trade secret,' said Porta, tapping the side of his nose. 'Bit of the old psychological warfare stuff. It always gets 'em.'

That evening, we drank ourselves silly. Krupka was the first to go under, followed quickly by Gregor. Tiny staggered about on top of the table, minus his boots and most of his uniform, flapping his arms in the air and making buzzing noises. He seemed to be under the impression he was an aeroplane.

'Shout for help!' he called down to us. 'Shout for help and I'll come and rescue you!'

We all shouted for help at the tops of our voices, not quite sure what game we were playing but interested to see what would happen. Tiny leapt off the table with a wild scream.

'Hold on, I'm coming!'

He bounced off the Legionnaire and crash-landed on the floor. We all turned to look at him.

'Why didn't anyone tell me the water was frozen solid?' he complained, sitting up and holding his head. 'I could have had a nasty accident.'

Shortly afterwards, he passed out.

Meanwhile, those of us that still survived went on steadily drinking. Porta sat cross-legged on the floor and solemnly raised his rifle to his lips. The barrel was filled with a revolting cocktail mixed from vodka, oil, powder and beer. The idea was that he should swallow it without bringing it straight back up again. If he could keep it down for as long as five minutes, we reckoned it as a victory. I never discovered whether he did or he didn't, because I almost immediately felt a sympathetic urge in myself to go to the window and spew.

When I returned, I saw the Old Man running round the room with a hatchet, making wild chopping motions in the air. Heide was kneeling on the floor, embracing one of the table legs.

'You're my friend,' he was whispering to it. 'My one and only friend . . .'

Porta had taken off his tunic and was slobbering over his new stripe. The Legionnaire was holding a conversation with himself in French. For my part, I felt far better now that I had vomited. I felt happier than I had in a long time. The last thing I remember was laughing so hard that I fell over...

The only living creature not to get drunk was Porta's cat. It was a big fat black creature, suspiciously sleek and well fed, and it had taken up residence with Porta the first day we had arrived at the barracks. It now sat on its broad bottom in the middle of the room, swishing the tip of its tail and regarding us all out of scornful green eyes. Porta threw a bottle at it, but the cat just sneered and began genteelly to groom itself.

'I hate that cat,' said Porta, between clenched teeth. 'God how I hate that cat...'

Obergruppenführer Heydrich, in response to a summons, knocked at the door of Himmler's office and had entered even before the thin voice of the Reichsführer had said, 'Come in.'

'Obergruppenführer,' began Himmler, without preamble, 'I am told that you have a file containing the personal details of every single man in the Party, in the SS and in the Army. Is this true?'

'Certainly, Reichsführer. In so far as I am responsible for both the internal and external security of our country, I feel it to be no less than my duty.'

'Quite so.' Himmler gave him a frozen smile, which Heydrich graciously acknowledged with a slight dip of the head. 'I wonder if by any chance you have a file containing my personal details, also?'

'It's more than likely, Reischsführer, but of course I couldn't say for certain without checking. You'll understand, I don't have the time to read through every file for myself. I see a person's details only when it becomes necessary that I should do so ... if a person draws attention to himself in any way.'

'Of course.'

Heydrich leaned back comfortably in his chair.

'As a matter of fact, it was my opposite number in Moscow who gave me the idea of a comprehensive filing system. I must say it seems to work admirably.'

'I'm sure it does,' agreed Himmler.

The two men smiled at each other. There was a pause.

'So tell me,' said Himmler, 'what news from the Vatican?'

Heydrich lightly hunched a shoulder.

'I'm surprised you should ask me, Reichsführer. I imagined you would be far better informed on the Vatican than I am.'

'Oh? And how should that be?'

Heydrich allowed a fleeting frown of puzzlement to brush across his forehead.

'General Bocchini ... the Italian Chief of Police ... you'll pardon me, Reichsführer, but I understood he was a close friend of yours?'

Under the desk, Himmler tapped a foot with annoyance. His relationship with Bocchini was not one that he wished to broad-cast.

'So! Your comprehensive filing system from Moscow really does work. I congratulate you.'

'Thank you, Reichsführer. But one point I confess has puzzled me: I am most curious to know why you should have sent the general that piece of old wood three weeks ago?'

'Old wood?' Himmler's eyebrows went up, one after the other. 'That was not old wood, Obergruppenführer, that was a log from Wotan's oak tree. I've had experts searching all over the place for it, it took them the better part of a year to find it for me. I sent it to the general as a sign of our friendship.'

'I see...' Heydrich nodded, pensively. 'In that case—I fear you won't be best pleased when I tell you that the general was very much put out by your gesture. To him it was none other than a piece of firewood. He was strongly inclined to believe you were insulting him.'

'The man's a fool!' said Himmler, sharply. 'I hope to Christ he didn't throw it away?'

'Oh, worse than that,' murmured Heydrich. 'He put it on the fire and set light to it ...'

Under the table, Himmler's foot tapped itself into a frenzy. His top half breathed heavily and leaned across towards Heydrich.

'Tell me, Obergruppenführer, do you by any chance have a file on Bocchini?'

'I have a file on everyone,' said Heydrich, simply.

'Good. In that case, I want you to make arrangements for Bocchini's details to be brought to the Duce's notice. Very discreetly, of course. He mustn't suspect where it's come from ... I take it there is plenty of—ah—incriminating evidence against our Italian friend?'

'Oh, plenty,' said Heydrich, with a smile. 'More than sufficient for your purposes, Reichsführer.'

FIVE

THE YOUNG LIEUTENANT

Porta and I were servicing the machine-gun. We had had two days of comparative calm and were waiting uneasily for the storm to break again.

'I'd like to know what the hell they're brewing down there.' The Old Man jerked his head in the direction of the Russian lines. 'Something's going on, you can bet your sweet life.' He turned back to Porta and me. 'How much ammunition have you got left for that thing?'

'Five thousand rounds and that's your lot.'

The Old Man shrugged his shoulders fatalistically.

'Well, I suppose it'll keep us going for a bit.'

'So long as the Russians don't suddenly run mad,' I said.

Gregor looked across, frowning.

'What about those reinforcements they were supposed to be sending us? Where have they got to? They should have been here days ago.'

'Reinforcements!' Porta gave a cynical, snorting laugh. 'That's a bleeding myth if ever there was one!'

'You mean there aren't going to be any reinforcements?'

'Of course there bleeding well ain't! That was just a load of bull to keep us quiet for a bit.'

'So what happens?' faltered Gregor.

'We either get out of this stinking hole by our own efforts or else we commit mass suicide. It's as simple as that. But it's no bloody good sitting on our backsides waiting for something that ain't never going to turn up.'

Gregor looked at him blankly.

'You're mad,' he muttered. 'We haven't a hope in hell of getting out of here by ourselves ... Besides, they wouldn't sacrifice a whole army just like that——'

'Who says they wouldn't?' jeered Porta.

'It stands to reason,' protested Gregor. 'A million men! They couldn't afford it. Hitler would have to be a raving nut——'

Porta said nothing: just raised an eyebrow. Gregor broke off in confusion.

'In any case,' I said, 'it's not a million men any more. Not by a long chalk, it isn't. Only a few hundred thousand.'

'Yeah, and what's a few hundred thousand more or less?' said Porta. 'The Sixth Army's a dead duck and Hitler knows it. He might just as well make a present of us to the enemy and get on with something more profitable elsewhere. Paulus won't do nothing about it, he always was a feeble bastard.'

'I don't believe you,' said Gregor, stubbornly.

'All right, have it your own way.' Porta turned back to the machine-gun. 'But I'm telling you, they've turned us into bloody Wagner heroes whether we like it or not. They've made a balls-up, see, and it's us what's got to pay for it. It'll look good in the history books, won't it? In fifty years' time, when they can turn round and talk about a million men in the Sixth Army laying down their lives for the flaming Führer ... yeah, I can see it all now,' said Porta, bitterly. 'Filthy great books with gold leaf all round the edges and pictures of Hitler's heroes lying about in the snow with their guts hanging out——'

'Give it a rest,' said the Old Man. 'I think something's going on down there.'

We turned to look in the direction of the enemy lines.

'Seems the same as usual to me,' said Porta, indifferently.

The Old Man shook his head.

'They're up to something. I don't know what it is, but I can smell trouble.'

It was true that the Old Man had an instinct in such matters. I turned back to the machine-gun and began frantically reassembling it. The Old Man jerked his head at Gregor.

'Go and tell Captain Schwan I think the enemy's preparing to attack.'

'OK.'

Gregor loped off, and Porta calmly sat back and lit a cigarette.

'What's the rush? Nothing's happened yet.'

'It will,' said the Old Man.

Porta glanced at his watch.

'Ten-thirty? Not on your life!'

At 1300 hours on the dot, the Russian batteries opened up in earnest. The ground began quaking beneath our feet and Gregor dived in a panic into the nearest bunker.

'This is it!' he yelled. 'They're coming over!'

Porta and I remained in the trench with the machine-gun. I knew we were just as safe down there as in the bunker, yet it never felt as safe and I always yearned for a protective layer of concrete above my head. Porta gave me an encouraging grin, and the black cat appeared from nowhere in a great hurry and came running up to us with its tongue sticking out of its mouth.

The first heavy Haubitz shell landed just in front of the trench, covering us in a spray of earth and shrapnel.

'Here comes the next one!' shouted Porta.

Captain Schwan snatched up the field telephone and began speaking rapidly to Colonel Hinka, explaining that we were under heavy fire and that he expected the enemy to launch a full-scale attack at any moment. He requested artillery support, but as usual Hinka refused to be impressed by the urgency of the situation.

'All right, all right, Captain, let's not lose our heads over a few stray shells. Wait and see how it goes. They'll probably quieten down again in a minute.'

'But if they don't, sir——'

'If they don't,' said Hinka, calmly, 'we shall review the situation. If it gets any worse I can let you have a section of light artillery.'

'But——'

The line went dead. Schwan slammed the telephone down and swore. He snatched up his revolver, stuck his knife down the side of his boot and ran off along the communication trench.

Inside the bunker, men sat and waited for the enemy to come. This was the worst part of all. Waiting. Not knowing what to expect, nor when to expect it. Whether it would be five minutes or five hours. Tiny was playing his mouth-organ, as he always did at such moments. His large, booted foot tapped out the measure, but no one listened to him. The Old Man leaned against the wall, sucking on his empty pipe. The Legionnaire was chewing a matchstick. Gregor was gnawing a mutilated finger-nail.

When the attack came, it came suddenly, unexpectedly, just as it always did. No matter how long you sat and waited, it always took you by surprise. There was a loud explosion and the solid bunker shuddered. Another, somewhere outside. Then a whole series of explosions, some very nearly direct hits. Inside the bunker there were pockets of calm and occasional bursts of panic, when men fought to get out and had to be restrained.

Very suddenly, the bombardment ceased and the silence seemed sinister and unnatural, so that men held their breath and wondered what new horrors were about to be launched upon them. The Old Man pushed his pipe into his pocket, helped himself to some hand-grenades, picked up his sub-machine-gun and called to the Second Section to follow him.

Out in the trenches it was like a lunar battlefield. The scene was stark and desolate, the ground torn into craters, the snow grey and dirty and the sky bleak. We dug ourselves in as best we could and settled down for yet another waiting period.

They came at us suddenly, in waves, one after another, endless and inevitable as the tides washing up the beaches. To us, in our ruined trenches, they were a vision from hell. An invincible sea of soldiery, howling as they plunged forward behind their gleaming bayonets.

I heard Captain Schwan's whistle, followed instantly by the

massed chorus of our machine-guns. The first wave of Siberians fell beneath the onslaught, but the second and third waves rushed onwards, pitilessly trampling their torn and bleeding comrades into the snow. They used the corpses for throwing on to the barbed wire, massing them up until they formed a bridge.

A smell of sulphur wafted into the trenches, burning men's throats and lungs. We pulled on our gas-masks and turned back to the approaching enemy. Porta was firing the machine-gun like an automaton. From left to right, from right to left, back and forth, back and forth. It was comforting, almost hypnotic in its regularity. I felt that Porta was immortal, that no bullet, no shell, could ever stop him firing that gun.

A hand-grenade came straight for us, heading into the trench. I acted instinctively, plucked it out of the air and hurled it back over the top. But there was no time to congratulate myself, for now the machine-gun was in difficulties. Porta the automaton was still in working order, but the gun itself was not. The breech mechanism was blocked by a bullet, and since the special tool for removing such obstacles had long ago been lost, stolen or sold, we had to dig it out ourselves. It was not until the gun was firing again that I realised it had been red-hot and that I had badly burnt one of my hands on it.

'Watch it,' I told Porta, spitting on the burn and waving my hand in the air. 'There's only another fifteen hundred rounds left.'

'They're there to be used!' he retorted.

I turned and grabbed some grenades, ready for the moment when we should run out of ammunition, but now the Siberians had broken through further along the lines and we had to pick up the machine-gun and make a dash for it. I stumbled along with the tripod on my shoulder and my head directly beneath the muzzle. After a few yards, we threw ourselves to the ground and took up firing positions again, but then for the second time the gun became blocked. We couldn't stop to put it right, we abandoned it on the spot and continued the fight with the first weapons that came to hand. I fitted my bayonet and plunged forward. I had acquired a Russian rifle that was far better than our own outmoded 98. Porta had snatched up a stray shovel and bashed it straight into the face of an oncoming Russian. Near by I caught a glimpse of Tiny. He seemed to have disdained all mechanical aids and to be using only his feet and his fists. As I rushed past him I saw him snatch up two Russians and bang their heads together, but I was unable to stop long enough to see the outcome.

The trenches were awash with blood. Mangled bodies, both Russian and German, lay at the bottom or hung over the sides. The air was full of shouts and cries and screams of agony. All up and down the narrow trenches men were locked together, fighting and killing each other.

The attack lasted some hours and was then quite suddenly brought to a halt. We never knew what lay behind the order, but it gave us a desperately needed respite. The two sides parted company and sat back to lick their wounds and to count their dead, but out in no-man's land men still lay writhing and moaning. The smoke still rose wraithlike into the air, the new silence was still occasionally torn apart by the screams of dying men.

We pulled off our gas-masks and quenched our thirst with great handfuls of snow. The snow was dirty, men had bled in it, spat in it, trampled in it, but our throats were dry as sandpaper and every time you swallowed it was as if you had a razor blade in your gullet.

At the foot of the trench there was a tangled crush of bodies; some dead, some still dying. We threw ourselves amongst them, too exhausted to care. The enemy could attack again at any moment, and in the meantime it was every man for himself and to hell with the weak and the wounded. The Old Man appeared, with his inevitable pipe. Porta produced some opium cigarettes and handed them round. Gregor and Tiny came up from opposite directions, and shortly afterwards we were joined by the Legionnaire. He was covered in blood, yet he seemed unhurt.

'Been sticking pigs?' suggested Gregor.

The Legionnaire gave him a look of withering distaste.

'Some damn-fool officer got a bayonet stuck in his neck. Jesus, what a mess! Like a flaming geyser, blood spouting out all over the place. It went all over me.'

The whole of our group had survived, but Captain Schwan had disappeared. We found him several hours later, lying on his back with his belly ripped open and his intestines torn out. Near by, with half his head gone, was Porta's friend Franz Krupka. We had to bury everyone, Russians and Germans alike, in the same grave. We dug a shallow pit, bundled the bodies in pell-mell, packed them with snow and planted rifles by the side. We had neither the time nor the energy to give them a more elaborate graveyard.

The regiment was withdrawn to be re-formed. In our company alone we had lost sixty-eight men, and at first we thought our fat friend Wilke was amongst their number, because the field kitchen was now being run by someone quite different.

'Hallo, there!' said Porta, surprised. 'Where's Sergeant Wilke gone? Don't tell me a stray shell got him at last?'

'No, he went off this morning in a plane with General Hube.'

'He what?' said Porta.

'Went off in a plane. Back to Germany, the lucky bastard.'

'You're joking!' Porta tossed his head in an attempt at bravado, but we could see that he was shaken. 'Where's he really gone?'

'I told you once,' said the man, irritably. 'What's the matter with you, you deaf or something? I told you, he's gone back home.'

Porta's jaw dropped open and his cigarette fell to the ground. He stooped unsteadily to pick it up. He had the look of a man who has just been punched in the face.

'By the way,' continued the new cook, 'you don't happen to know a bloke called Joseph Porta, do you? Wilke left a parcel for him. Said he was the best pal he'd ever had. I don't know what he was going on about, but I've got the parcel right here. If you meet this Porta chap, you might tell him to come and pick it up.'

Porta staggered away without another word. It was the first time I had ever seen him at a loss. While the rest of us settled down to sleep, Porta walked up and down feverishly muttering to himself, and not until the Legionnaire threatened to put a bullet through him did he come to his senses. He went striding out to see the new cook, and with grunts of relief we closed our eyes and lost consciousness. But scarcely five minutes later, Porta was back again. He banged something down in the middle of the floor, and we were resentfully back into wakefulness.

'What the hell's going on?' snarled the Legionnaire. He shot upright and saw Porta. The great scar down the side of his face glowed bright red with anger. 'It's you again!' He sounded incredulous. 'I told you once, you're asking for trouble!'

He snatched up his revolver, but before he could fire Porta had held up a restraining hand.

'Just take a gander at this little lot,' he suggested.

The Legionnaire peered forward suspiciously.

'What is it?'

A blissful smile painted itself across Porta's face.

96

'Vodka,' he said. 'A whole crate of vodka ...'

There was a stunned silence. The Legionnaire slowly put his revolver away and staggered out of bed.

'Where did it come from?' demanded Tiny, digging his knuckles into his eyes and blinking.

'My friend Wilke,' said Porta, nonchalantly.

'Your friend Wilke?'

'Yeah ... I did him a good turn, didn't I? Got him a ticket back to Germany.'

We looked at him; six pairs of eyes, all disbelieving.

'How?' said the Old Man, bluntly.

'Well, that's the trouble,' confessed Porta, with a frown. 'I don't know how ... I only wish I did, I'd do the same for myself!'

Some time later, when Porta was wandering round inebriated with a bottle in his hand, he bumped into a new lieutenant who had recently joined us. The lieutenant was young and zealous. Newly hatched from his egg and still with some of the yolk behind his ears. He and Porta had not crossed paths before. The lieutenant stood back, evidently awaiting some sign of respect and obeisance from Porta. Porta stared up at him from little glittering eyes that were full of frank condescension.

'You! Corporal! Don't you know what the Führer's orders are?'

Porta opened wide his eyes.

'Sorry, sir. He hasn't been able to give us any orders since the enemy tore him in half yesterday evening. We buried him in one of the trenches.'

The lieutenant stiffened.

'Are you trying to be funny, Corporal? Are you deliberately insulting your Führer?'

Porta clicked his heels together and saluted with the hand that was holding the bottle.

'Certainly not, sir. I wouldn't dream of it, sir.'

'Then what the devil do you mean by saying that you buried the Führer in one of the trenches?'

Porta looked innocently into the tight-lipped face of the lieutenant. His blue eyes slowly cleared.

'Oh, you mean THAT Führer, sir!'

'What did you suppose I meant?'

'I thought you meant OUR Führer, sir. Captain Schwan, what was killed last night. When you said the Führer's orders, I thought you was referring to the captain.' Porta smiled, brightly. 'He was the only one round here ever gave us any orders, sir. We wouldn't have taken them from no one else.'

The lieutenant stretched his neck out of his collar and swallowed in a somewhat strangulated fashion.

'What are your duties in the company, Corporal?'

'Well, a little bit of everything, really. I'm in charge of the third section just at the moment.'

'Then may God preserve us, that's all I can say! Which cretin promoted you to be a section leader?'

'Sir,' said Porta, earnestly, 'it doesn't give me no pleasure to have men ander my command. It's what I call a duty more than a pleasure. But orders is orders and everyone knows that us corporals is the backbone of the German Army. Officers, if you'll forgive the liberty, sir, because I'm only saying what's the truth, but officers is just a sort of icing on the cake ... If you'll pardon the expression,' he added, ingratiatingly. 'Not meaning to be rude, sir, but where'd we be without us lot?'

'I'm warning you, Corporal! You'd better watch what you're saying!'

'But, sir——'

'The Führer himself—the Führer Adolf Hitler——' The lieutenant broke off and glared at Porta. 'Stand to attention when I speak of the Führer!'

'All right, sir. Can I just put this bottle down? It makes it easier when you're not holding bottles in your hand.'

'You have no right to be holding bottles in your hand! You have no right to be gorging yourself on drink! False courage is forbidden!'

'Blimey,' said Porta.

He was an expert in officer-baiting. From a safe distance we sat and drank and watched the fun. The young lieutenant drew himself up very straight and his pale cheeks acquired a hectic purple flush.

'Corporal! It is the solemn bounden duty of every German citizen, man, woman or child, soldier or civilian, to have the strong red blood of pride running through his veins!'

Porta stood blinking. The lieutenant gulped down some air and fell back to a more mundane level of speech.

'From now on,' he said, pettishly, 'I shall be the one to give you orders. You understand? You're under my command now, and I suggest you remember it. I'm a stickler for discipline! The men under me must be as strong as Krupp steel! No slacking, no back-sliding!'

'I couldn't agree more,' said Porta. 'May I go now, sir?'

It was not a good day for the new lieutenant. A couple of hours later he was foolish enough to cross swords with Tiny. The two men were hurrying in opposite directions. Tiny was carrying a bucket of water in either hand, on his way to the field kitchen. He had his head down, and the lieutenant was reading some papers. They jostled each other as they went past. Some of the water slopped over the side of the buckets, and Tiny swore aloud as he went on his way. The lieutenant stopped and looked back, to see what ill-mannered oaf was daring to swear at an officer.

'Hey, you, soldier! Don't you salute your officers in this part of the world?'

Tiny continued stolidly walking with his buckets. This was not the first officer who had joined us fresh out of training school and thought the war could be won by a smart salute and a row of brass buttons.

'You!' screeched the outraged lieutenant. 'It's you I'm talking to! You with the buckets! What's your name?'

Tiny paused. He turned, politely, and regarded the officer. As Porta often remarked, if you wanted to survive in this war you had to play along with them to a certain extent; you had to humour their whims and their odd flights of fancy.

'The name's Creutzfeld,' said Tiny. 'And if I'd realised it was me you was shouting at, I'd have stopped straight away, sir.'

'Well, now that you do know, you might care to answer my question.'

'What was that, sir?'

'I asked you whether you didn't salute your officers in this part of the world!'

Tiny's forehead puckered in a puzzled frown.

'Salute our officers, sir?' He held out the buckets of water. 'It's just I can't do two things at once, sir. I can't run backwards and forwards carrying water for the cook AND salute every Tom, Dick and Harry that crosses my path. I mean, I'd like to, sir, but it just ain't possible. Specially when this here is water for the officers' soup, sir.'

'Private Creutzfeld, I consider that a gross impertinence! As your commanding officer I do not rank alongside every Tom, Dick and Harry! I resent the implications! Report to me at 1300 hours tomorrow and I shall teach you a few elementary good manners.'

'Sorry, sir,' said Tiny, with a regretful shake of the head. 'I'd love to come, I would, really, but I'm already booked. Got to be with Colonel Hinka at twelve-thirty.' He took a step nearer the lieutenant and spoke confidentially. 'I don't know whether you've met the colonel, sir, but he's not a man I'd care to disappoint. Know what I mean? And after all, a colonel IS higher than a lieutenant, sir. It says so in Regulations.'

'In that case, Private, you can make it eight o'clock tomorrow morning!'

'Yeah, OK,' agreed Tiny. 'I reckon I can manage that, sir.'

As the lieutenant opened his mouth to censure Tiny for this new piece of impudence, a deep, calm voice spoke from behind.

'Good evening, Lieutenant Pirch. Glad to see you're making the acquaintance of the Fifth Company.'

The lieutenant swung round, red-faced. Colonel Hinka smiled blandly at him.

'Everything going all right, then?'

'Oh yes, sir, thank you, sir! Heil Hitler, sir!'

'Heil Hitler,' responded Hinka, amiably. He jerked his head at Tiny. 'Off you go with your water, before the cooks start shouting for it.'

'Yes, sir. Thank you, sir. It's for the officers' soup, sir.'

Tiny put down one of his buckets, gave a brisk salute, picked up the bucket again and hurried off. Lieutenant Pirch stared after him with narrowed eyes.

'Well, then, Lieutenant!' Hinka turned to him, with a pleasant smile. 'You've come to take over the Fifth Company, have you?'

'Sir!'

Pirch stiffened, and Hinka's smile stiffened with him.

'A word of advice, Lieutenant, before you start digging yourself in: we're in Russia now, you know, not Germany. We're in the trenches, not in the barracks. A salute may do wonders for your ego, but it's not going to save a man's life.' He nodded, severely. 'The Fifth Company's a good bunch. Make sure you look after them well, they're worth a hundred lieutenants or colonels.'

'Yes, sir.'

Hinka strolled casually away, leaving Lieutenant Pirch with an uneasy feeling that the war was not all that it had been made out to be.

The Prince of Bentheim Tecklenberg, President of the Association of German Aristocracy, today announced his association's whole-hearted support of National Socialism and its policies on race. In particular, he laid stress on the fact that all the members of the Association could trace their Aryan descent back as far as the year 1750, and in some cases even further.

19.1.1935

A black Mercedes coupé drove slowly past the peaceful villas of Berlin Dahlem. The car pulled up outside one of them and the SS driver leapt smartly from his seat and held open the rear door for Obergruppenführer Reinhard Heydrich. Heydrich stepped elegantly from the car and made his way up the trimly clipped path towards the house.

It was a white, two-storey building, set back some way from the road. Flowers and fruit trees scented the path up to the front door. The garden gate had a grille across it but was not locked, and Heydrich gave a smoothing pat to his immaculate grey uniform and walked straight through.

The owner of the house, Admiral Canaris, Head of the Information Service, was stretched out in the sun on a wickerwork chaise-longue. Near by sat his wife, a pretty, dark-haired woman with bright eyes and an intelligent face.

As Canaris caught sight of his unexpected visitor, he pulled himself into a different position and stared across the lawn, one hand shading his eyes from the sunlight.

'Heydrich!' he muttered. 'What the devil does he want?'

His wife also looked across at the approaching figure.

'A social call?' she suggested.

'That's a man that doesn't pay social calls.'

'Business?'

Canaris shrugged and pulled a face.

'You think it means trouble?'

'It always means trouble when he's around.'

'In that case, we must just make him welcome and hope for the best.'

Creasing her face into a polite smile, Frau Canaris left her chair and walked forward to meet the Obergruppenführer. Her husband, visibly apprehensive, had risen from the chaise-longue and stood watching.

'Herr Obergruppenführer, this is an unexpected surprise!'
Frau Canaris held out her hand and greeted their guest with
every sign of pleasure. 'Do please sit down. May I offer you a
drink? We have some very good cognac.'

'Thank you, that would be most acceptable.'

Heydrich inclined his head and smiled. He shook hands with
Canaris. The two men sat down in the sunshine while Frau
Canaris fetched the cognac. It was very hot on the lawn. The
air was still and stifling, the flowers wilted, the trees drooped
and Canaris perspired. Only Heydrich in his pearl-grey uniform
looked cool and fresh.

'You must find this weather very tiring?' suggested Frau
Canaris, lightly fanning herself with a magazine.

'To tell the truth,' said Heydrich, 'I scarcely ever notice the
weather. Snow or sunshine, it's all the same when one is em-
barked upon a sea of work and troubles.'

He turned his head slightly and looked at Canaris. The
admiral met his gaze squarely.

'I confess I am a martyr to the weather.' Frau Canaris leaned
back in her chair with a charming and apologetic smile. 'Ex-
tremes of heat and cold affect me greatly.'

'It's as well we're not all the same,' said Heydrich, politely.
'For my own part, I am too occupied with tedious affairs such as
this one in Düsseldorf to pay very much attention to the
climate.'

Again he looked at Canaris; again the admiral returned his
gaze.

'You're up to date with the latest developments, of course?'
Heydrich smoothly continued. 'My men were to have arrested a
certain Count Osterburg ... I don't know whether you're
acquainted with him?'

There was a sharp, involuntary intake of breath from the
lady. Heydrich raised an inquiring eyebrow, but she had already
recovered herself and was all poise again.

'And have they not been able to do so?' she asked, with
sympathetic interest.

Heydrich raised a second eyebrow to join the first.

'My men always do what they set out to do, Frau Canaris.'

'Oh, I'm sure ... it was just that I gathered—from the way
you spoke ... "they were to have arrested" ... I thought
perhaps——'

'Quite so. They were and they shall.' Heydrich smiled and
turned back to Canaris. 'The strange part of the story is that the

man has now turned up in Rome. He's been seen there on several occasions in the company of one Angelo Ritano ... Correct me if I'm wrong, Admiral, but is not Ritano a member of your staff?'

Canaris hunched a shoulder.

'He could well be. I don't, of course, know the name of everyone who works for me. But if you wish I can always have inquiries made.'

'Not worth the trouble,' said Heydrich. 'I can do it quicker myself.'

'It would be no trouble, but if you're really in that much of a hurry——'

'I am always in a hurry,' said Heydrich. 'The Führer expects prompt results and a high standard of efficiency. It is as well, I find, to give him what he wants.' He laid aside his glass and stood up. 'Now, if you will excuse me, I have an appointment with the Head of the Gestapo.'

He trod silently down the neat garden path, out through the gate and into the waiting Mercedes. Canaris and his wife looked at each other without speaking.

SIX

FAREWELL TO THE COLONEL

One cold morning, in the middle of a snowstorm, Porta and I were given the task of transporting Colonel Hinka to the aerodrome at Gumrak. The colonel had been the only man to escape from a blazing tank, throwing himself out seconds before it exploded, and he was seriously injured.

When we reached the airfield we found hundreds of other wounded men waiting to be carried out of the hell of Stalingrad and taken back to some sort of sanity. There were three aeroplanes standing by, engines ticking over and crew anxious to be off, but there were many more men than there were places. A medical officer was running dementedly to and fro amongst the snow-covered stretchers, tending to men who were on the point of dying, pointing out those who should be given priority, those who must be left behind, running in ever diminishing circles and frequently contradicting himself. Colonal Hinka was twice designated as a priority case and twice the order was counter-

103

manded, until at length Porta could stand it no longer. He jabbed me in the ribs and jerked his head at our stretcher.

'This is sodding useless. Keep an eye on him, I won't be long.'

'Where are you going?'

Porta closed one eye.

'See a friend of mine ... see if I can't get things moving. We'll be here till the end of the war, otherwise.'

I shrugged my shoulders and squatted on my haunches by the side of the unconscious Colonel Hinka. Porta's friends were legion, and they were all on the fiddle. I guarantee if we had ever been lost in the middle of the Sahara desert Porta would have found an acquaintance peddling black-market water and stolen camels.

Quarter of an hour later he turned up with an Oberfeldwebel wearing flying gear. The Oberfeldwebel was wringing his hands together and seemed unhappy.

'All right, don't keep nagging at me! It'll be OK, I've already told you ... Those papers would be enough to guarantee a safe passage for a china doll, never mind a flaming colonel! Just use them and shut up ... you open your big mouth too wide and it's curtains for both of us ... And don't you forget what I've done for you, either!'

'I won't,' promised Porta. 'But just stop bleating, there's a good lad. You make me nervous, jittering about like that.'

The man moved confidentially closer.

'So when do I get paid, then?'

'As soon as I know these papers are genuine.'

Porta bent down and stowed them away in the colonel's inside pocket. He then changed the number of his division, attaching a new one to the colonel's wrist.

'What's that going to do?' I said.

'Wait and see,' advised Porta. He looked over his shoulder at his nervous friend. 'It had bloody well better do something!' he said, threateningly.

Ten minutes later the manic medical officer came back. He glared down at Hinka, then up at us.

'I told you before, get that man to the dressing station. It's no good hanging about here, he won't be going off today.'

'Excuse me, sir,' said Porta, firmly, 'but it's special orders, sir. The colonel has to be got off.'

'Look here, Corporal, it's no damn use your arguing with me! I don't give a tinker's cuss for your special orders, I'm the one who makes the decisions round here, not even the Führer has any say in it! Now get that man out before I lose my temper.'

'Oh, very well, sir,' said Porta. He bent down and took the colonel's papers from his pocket. 'Could you just tell me what the time is, sir?'

'Ten-thirty, and don't ask damn-fool questions! Just do what you're told and hurry up about it.'

'Yes, sir.' Porta stood stolidly with a pencil in his hand, noting down the time. 'May I just have your name, sir, before you go? Not meaning to be impertinent, sir, but I was specially told to take the name of anyone what sabotaged these special orders. And to write down the time and all. It's not my doing, sir, it's an Army matter, it's nothing to do with me——'

'Show me those wretched orders!'

The MO snatched the papers away from Porta and looked briefly through them. I was astonished to see an immediate change of attitude. He was grudging, but respectful.

'All right.' He handed back the papers. 'Get him on a plane ... but if you've been pulling a fast one, Corporal, God help you! I haven't the time to check up on you now, but I'm warning you ... I never forget a face!'

We picked up the stretcher and marched off at a fast trot to the first aeroplane that was due to leave.

'I don't know what was in those bloody papers,' I panted, 'but if he finds out you've been conning him, there'll be hell to pay.'

'He won't find out,' retorted Porta, scornfully. 'He'll have forgotten all about it this time tomorrow.'

'Don't you be so sure, he had a very funny look in his eye.'

'Balls!' said Porta. 'You can get away with murder if you know how. I once told someone that Heydrich was my mother's uncle ... it went down a fair treat, I got enough free petrol to make me an oil millionaire ...'

'First I heard of it,' I grunted.

We had just stowed the colonel away inside the belly of the plane when a lieutenant-colonel came running up with a slip of paper in his hand. He flung himself at the cockpit with a pitiful bleat. He looked to be in perfect health, and he hadn't a mark on him. Not even a strip of sticky plaster for decency's sake.

'Wait for me! I've got a place on that plane! It's from the Führer himself!'

He thrust his slip of paper into the pilot's face, but the pilot promptly pushed it back again.

'Sorry, sir, we've no room for anyone else. This plane is reserved for the wounded, and my orders are to take off as soon as I've got my quota.'

'But the Führer ... this is from the Führer!'

The pilot looked at him pityingly.

'They're out of date, sir. Those orders were cancelled three days ago. Too many deserters from the combat areas.'

'Deserters! Are you calling me a deserter?'

'You don't look to be wounded, sir ...'

The colonel dropped his piece of paper and made an angry move towards the pilot. Porta at once swept up the paper and read it.

'He's right,' he said. 'This is direct from the Führer.' He looked sternly at the pilot. 'Fancy treating a German officer like that! You ought to be ashamed of yourself. He's probably wounded somewhere it don't show.' He tapped his extra stripe, nodded and winked. 'I can't ignore a thing like this. I wouldn't be doing my duty as a corporal, would I?'

'That is quite correct.' The colonel looked at him, rather stunned. 'You certainly wouldn't.'

'I reckon it's my duty to call in the MPs,' said Porta. 'They'll soon have the matter sorted out.'

'You just do that,' agreed the pilot, with a broad grin. 'I'd be interested to see their reaction.'

I noticed that the colonel's agitation had perceptibly increased. He suddenly caught Porta by the shoulder, leaned forward and whispered urgently to him and the pilot.

'No need to go to the Military Police, you know. No need at all. I don't want to get anyone into trouble. There is a war on, this is a time of stress ...'

'But orders from the Führer!' hissed Porta.

'Never mind the Führer, what about twenty thousand Reichsmark? Twenty thousand for a seat on the plane? How about it?'

'Filthy old goat!'

The pilot stretched out a hand and gave the colonel a shove. He fell back into the arms of Porta, who jerked him away, stuck out a foot and tripped him into a snowdrift.

'Go away and get your head blown off!' shouted the pilot. 'Then come back and try again! You might stand a better chance next time!'

At that point, a couple of Military Police arrived. They at

once clapped heavy hands upon Porta.

'All right, you've cooked your goose, soldier! Attacking an officer?'

They slowly shook their heads, savouring the situation. Porta glared at them.

'Attacking a deserter, more like! That bastard's just offered us twenty thousand marks for a place on the plane ... and not a scratch on him!'

The colonel picked himself out of the snowdrift and gestured arrogantly towards Porta.

'Arrest that man! He used violence on an officer of the Reich!'

'Get stuffed,' said Porta, imperturbable as ever. He held out his piece of paper. 'Take a gander at that. He tried to tell us it was an order from the Führer. We was only doing our duty.'

The two men took one look at the paper and turned scarlet with rage.

'An order from the Führer?' screamed one of them. 'Three days out of date and you're still trying to use it? When you're not even wounded?' He turned to his companion. 'Arrest this officer on a charge of attempted desertion!'

The colonel was led away, grey-faced and stumbling. I shook my head as I watched.

'I don't know that I blame him,' I muttered. 'Who wouldn't give it a try if they thought they stood a chance? He might have got away with it.'

'He might, but he didn't.'

'But at least it was a possibility,' I argued. 'That's more than we've got, stuck here in this hell-hole.' I looked solemnly at Porta. 'We'll never get out alive. You know that, don't you?'

Porta shrugged his shoulders.

'Live for today, lad. Bugger tomorrow. We'll make it yet, if we keep our heads.'

'Like hell!' I said.

The first aeroplane was preparing to take off. A horde of wounded men were milling round it, begging, crying, screaming, some on crutches, some supported by friends, some crawling through the deep snow on hands and knees. It was like some infernal Lourdes, all the sick and the lame praying for help, but God the aeroplane was going off without them. They swarmed round the cockpit, flung themselves at the doors, beat with their fists on the side of the fuselage. A place on the plane meant a chance of survival: to be left behind, a wounded man on the

Russian front, meant almost certain death. The police beat them back with pitiless blows from the butts of their revolvers. There was nothing else they could do. All three planes were filled to overflowing with the torn and bleeding bodies of the most seriously injured. I had seen men mummified in bandages, men with mutilated stumps where their hands and feet should have been, men with no features, men with no arms or legs. There was no room for anyone who still had sufficient strength to drag himself weeping across the airfield. Radio equipment, dressings, ammunition, they had all been jettisoned to make room for a few extra bodies. Any more weight and the planes would be in jeopardy.

The first one was moving ponderously forward along the runway. Porta and I stood watching, praying that it would be able to get off the ground. It gathered speed, reached the end of the path and rose heavily into the air in a cloud of snow. It skimmed low over the hangar, then flew in a wide arc and disappeared into the grey skies.

'They've got no radio,' I said. 'What do they do if they run into trouble?'

'Jesus,' said Porta, 'doesn't anything good ever happen in your dreams?'

The second plane moved along the runway. We watched it rise into the air. Just as it seemed to have taken off successfully it suddenly bucked and reared, dropped like a stone on to its belly and exploded. It was all over within seconds. I looked at Porta.

'I'm not a pessimist,' I said. 'I'm just a realist.'

He turned and walked away without another word. I stayed to watch the third plane just miss crashing into the barbed wire enclosure and then followed him.

He was waiting by the side of the amphi-car in which we had transported the colonel. As he saw me coming, he pointed silently at an inert grey mass in the snow. I stopped to examine it. It was the lieutenant-colonel who had tried to buy a place on the plane.

'My God,' I said, shaken. 'They got rid of him quickly.'

'Justice is pretty swift in this part of the world,' said Porta, wisely.

'So is injustice!' I retorted. I pushed the dead figure out of the way with my boot. 'I wonder exactly how many men they've executed in this zone?'

'Oh, hundreds,' said Porta, casually. 'If not thousands ... a chap I was talking to the other day told me they'd done away with eight hundred and fifty in his company alone.'

'He must have been exaggerating,' I protested.

Porta cocked an eyebrow at me.

'You reckon?'

We got in the car and drove slowly down the rue Litvinov towards the Place Rouge, where some cellars had been turned into a temporary hospital. After seeing the colonel safely on to an aeroplane, our orders were to collect a crate of dressings for the Regiment. In the makeshift hospital there was a repellent stench of blood and excreta, vomit and dirt and rotting human flesh. Men lay in rows on the floor for lack of beds, the dying and the dead cheek by jowl. The only lights were from candle stubs. I had hardly moved two paces forward before I tripped over a corpse and fell on top of a wounded man, who shrieked in agony.

'Get the hell out of here!' roared a Feldwebel, who was lying at my feet with a bandage over one eye. 'We're full up, there's no room for any more.'

'What's the matter? Where are you wounded?'

I picked myself up and saw a doctor regarding us hostilely from beneath his mask.

'Nowhere,' I said, and I felt guilty that I was still in one piece. 'We've come to pick up some dressings.'

'Fourth door to the left. Watch where you put your feet.'

'Yes, sir.'

'And stand to attention when you talk to an officer! We're still at war, you know!'

'Yes, sir.'

Porta and I saluted and hurried along to the fourth door on the left. There were bodies even in the dank stone passages, it was impossible not to tread on them as you pushed your way past. The Sanitätshauptfeldwebel to whom we handed our requisition order read it through with a stony face.

'Bandages?' he said, at last. 'Dressings?' he said. He shrugged his shoulders. 'I can give you a bundle of newsprint, if you like. We don't use dressings any more.'

We looked at him, wonderingly. He tapped a finger on our list.

'Morphine? You're sure you wouldn't like an entire operating theatre while you're about it?'

'Not unless it says so——' began Porta, dubiously.

The man gave a short scream and thrust the requisition at

us.

'Take it and go, and don't come pestering me with any more damn-fool demands! Bandages! Morphine! What do you think I am, a bloody magician? Santa Claus? Christ almighty, you people make me sick! Go back to your regiment and remind them, with my compliments, that we're at Stalingrad. Nobody sends us any dressings or bandages any more. Nobody sends us anything any more. We're on our own from now on.'

'But look here——' said Porta.

'Look my arse! Can't you get it into your great thick skull that as an army we don't exist any more? It's no bloody good coming whining to me for help: I can't give you what I haven't got, can I?'

We knew he was speaking the truth. We had seen those effigies of men lying on the ground, we had smelt the blood and the foulness. We knew there was nothing he could do for us.

We left the hospital and drove on empty-handed from the town. About half a mile out we were stopped by an idiot wearing a white fur coat and waving a rifle. We pulled up and a lieutenant demanded to see our papers.

'We're on out way back to our regiment.' said Porta. 'Just taken our colonel to Gumrak.'

'Right-oh.' He handed back the papers. 'Sorry, but we need you here for the moment. Hide your car under those trees over there and grab yourself some grenades.'

We were hardly in a position to argue. We did as he said and tagged on to the end of a section commanded by a Feldwebel. I turned to a lance-corporal by my side.

'What's going on here?' I demanded.

He pulled a hideous face.

'Court-martial commando. Take a look at that pit behind you.'

I did so: it was full of bodies. I remembered what Porta had said about the eight hundred and fifty executions in one company alone, and I began to wonder if it had been an exaggeration after all.

'Grisly business,' said the lance-corporal, disparagingly. 'And that's only one morning's work. It's no picnic.'

'I believe you,' I muttered.

Minutes later, an infantry battalion arrived, full steam ahead, magnificently equipped qnd very sure of themselves. The maniac with the rifle and the white fur coat stepped into the middle of the road and waved them down, and again the lieutenant moved forward to ask his standard questions.

'Where are you going?'

'We've got orders to reassemble further on along the Don.'

A major stuck his head out of one of the leading cars and spoke impatiently. The lieutenant shook his head.

'Sorry. All orders cancelled. No one to move out of the area. You'll have to stay here with us for the time being.'

'We'll do no such damn thing!' barked the major. 'How do I know the orders are cancelled? No one told me about it.'

'I'm telling you now.' The lieutenant took out his revolver and levelled it at the major. 'You either do as I say or I have you shot as a deserter. The choice is yours.'

The major bit his lip. He climbed slowly from his car, and the lieutenant beckoned to one of his men.

'Helmer, show the major where to go.'

'Yes, sir.'

'Look, I don't know what all this is about,' began the major, 'but I can——'

'It's about desertion.' The lieutenant stared at him, coldly. 'I've already told you, the choice is yours. If you want to stay and argue, by all means do so. If not, I advise you to get out of the road before the Russians come through in their T34s.'

For six hours Porta and I stayed at our posts. During that time there was a steady flow of would-be deserters, all of them held up by the fur-coated gentleman, interrogated by the lieutenant and either persuaded to stay or sent to the firing squad. Rank was no protection and neither were papers nor orders. There was to be no taking the easy road out of the horrors of Stalingrad.

At the end of six hours we were relieved of our duties and were able to proceed on our way—not through any special favours, but simply because it was discovered that we were carrying orders marked with the stamp of the High Command, and even the fanatical lieutenant had come to the conclusion that they must be genuine.

Porta, uncaring as ever, whistled inappropriate songs as the amphi-car bounced along the road to Kuperossnoje. I sat by his side trying to sleep but so cold I kept shivering and waking myself up. It was pouring with snow, and on two occasions the vehicle came to a full stop and we had to dig ourselves out. On either side of the road the drifts were piled higher than the telegraph poles.

When we were still some way off from Kuperossnoje we

overtook a cavalry column. The horses were slipping and dancing on the ice, and Porta and I looked at them in astonishment.

'Where the blazes did they come from?' demanded Porta. 'Walking bloody beefsteaks! What I wouldn't give for a nice bit of horse's arse . . .'

It did seem rather incredible that some men were starving, while others rode round on supplies of food. The horses skidded and whinnied, their breath billowing out into the cold air. We heard the creaking saddles and the tinkling of bits, and we smelt the hot horsey smell of hay and damp leather.

We moved on past the cavalry and drew level with the artillery, coming towards us with the cannons of their field-guns pointing skywards into the falling snow. After the artillery it was the engineers, with their bulldozers and mechanical shovels.

Porta and I exchanged puzzled glances.

'Reinforcements?' I said. 'All that lovely new equipment?'

'Don't seem possible,' said Porta.

There was a silence.

'Rumanians?' I said.

'Could be.'

'Well, what else?'

Porta shrugged his shoulders.

For two hours we drove past the oncoming columns. There must have been at least one division, if not more. We waved amiably to them, and sometimes they waved back. Quite suddenly, Porta pulled the amphi-car to a screaming halt.

'What the bloody hell are you doing?' I cried, clutching at the dashboard with both hands.

In the middle of the road, directly ahead of us, stood an officer. He was holding up a placard on which was written, in capital letters, the one word: STOP. Porta wrenched the wheel round and we went spinning off into some woods at the side of the road.

'What the hell——' I began.

'Russians!' he yelled.

And now I heard them howling behind us.

'Stoi! Stoi!'

Shots cracked all round us as Porta took the amphi-car bouncing in a crazy slalom through the pine trees. A couple of miles further on, he pulled up and turned to the back seat.

'Here!' He tossed a Russian helmet at me, a furry object with a red star on the front. 'Put this on your head and hope for the best. Good thing I spotted that bloke was a Russian, eh?'

I crammed the helmet on and gestured frenziedly at Porta.

'Let's get out of here, for God's sake!'

We folded over the collars of our coats, hugged our Russian MPIs to our chests, peered out from beneath our furry helmets ... and kept a good supply of hand-grenades on the seat between us, just in case ...

Quarter of an hour later we hit the main road again. It was still full of enemy columns on the march.

'Rumanians!' said Porta, and gave a short, cynical laugh.

We reversed, back into the woods, scouted round until we came to a side road, drove a couple of miles and found ourselves brought to a sudden halt. The engine coughed and muttered a few times and faded into an obstinate silence.

'Shit and fucking disaster!' I screamed, diving through the door. 'Let's leave the pissing thing and go on by foot!'

'Don't be a fool,' said Porta, calmly. 'Wouldn't get nowhere if we did that.'

He opened up the bonnet and peered in at the works, while I stood by clutching the MPI and gnawing at the inside of my cheek. A Cossack division appeared and swung past us up the road, horses steaming, hooves clattering, bits and stirrups singing. The soldiers were chanting rhythmically. All very romantic, but I could have done without it just at that moment. I watched impatiently as Porta carefully wiped the sparking plugs, examined the carburettor and the ignition. On a sudden impulse I tugged the death's-head emblem from my lapels and trampled it into the snow. Porta looked at me in a momentary amazement, then shrugged his shoulders and followed suit. Those emblems had caused the death of many a soldier in the tank regiments: we were too often taken for the thugs and sadists who served in Eicke's hated 'murder' division.

'I'm buggered if I know what the point of that was,' reflected Porta. 'They'll shoot us, anyway, if they get their hands on us.'

'I just feel happier without it,' I muttered.

Porta shrugged.

'Can't say it bothers me.'

A corporal from an artillery regiment suddenly stepped towards us from a copse on the other side of the road. I clutched nervously at the MPI, while Porta cotinued his examination under the bonnet.

'Sdrastje!' (Hallo) said the corporal, cheerfully.

'Sdrastje!' we replied, with a great show of bonhomie.

He circled slowly round the vehicle, eyeing it with interest.

'Hitler maschyna,' he told us, with a big grin, and he caught the front wheel an almighty kick and roared with laughter.

'Da,' (Yes) I said, weakly.

'Kharoschyj?'

'Da.'

The corporal laughed again and gave Porta an amiable thump on the back. He leaned over to look at the motor.

'Jalofka,' he commented, straightening up and wiping oily fingers down his coat.

I stared vacantly and nodded my head a few times. I hoped he would take me for an idiot and ignore me. He turned to Porta and began talking at him at great speed, waving his arms up and down and pulling faces. While I watched him closely for signs of aggression, Porta bent over his engine and threw in the odd 'da' or 'niet' at what I could only hope and pray were appropriate intervals. After a bit, Porta put a hand in his pocket and pulled out a packet of grifas.* He offered them to the corporal, whose big pumpkin face split open in a beam of delight.

'Where did you get those?' he asked, in a Russian which I could just about grasp.

'Jenisseisk,' said Porta, promptly.

I wondered if Porta knew where Jenisseisk was, because I certainly didn't, but the reply seemed to satisfy the corporal. He nodded and smiled.

'Jenisseisk, eh? That where you come from?'

'Da,' I said, obediently.

'I wondered what your accent was. I'm from Chita, myself. I don't mind where a man comes from so long as it's not Moscow. If there's one thing I can't stand, it's a Muscovite. Talk like bloody farmyard animals. Can't understand a word they're saying. But Jenisseisk ... I never met anyone from there before. Almost like foreigners!' He grinned at us. 'I'll forgive a man anything as long as he's not from Moscow. We should have killed all the big-headed bastards in the Revolution.'

Porta and I responded to his theory with a positive chorus of 'das', and at that providential moment the engine came to life again. We waved our hands at the corporal, jumped into the car and shot off in a great hurry.

'Thank the Lord we didn't——'

The words were only half out of my mouth, suspended as it were in mid-air, when the car stalled again. Porta flung open

* Opium cigarettes.

114

the door and stepped out.

'We're stuck in a blasted drift!'

The corporal came running up to us, throwing his arms above his head and laughing.

'Horses are better than cars in this weather!' he roared.

He seemed to think he had made a tremendous joke, so Porta and I nodded and grinned and nudged him in the ribs, and he nudged us back, and we all started cackling together. The corporal was the first to recover.

'Come along,' he said, shaking his head severely at us. 'There's work to be done ... Germans to be killed! Let me give you a hand.'

We all three pushed. Straining and heaving and grunting, as the wheels spun round and the car remained still. The corporal suddenly tapped me on the shoulder.

'Wait there! I'll be back!'

He ran away up the road and disappeared into the trees.

'Where's he gone?' I said, nervously.

'He's gone to get help,' said Porta, with a wicked smile of delight at our predicament. 'He's going to bring all his little pals back to give us a shove.'

'Let's leave the bloody thing!' I urged. 'We'll never get it moving before they came back.'

'Don't panic,' said Porta, calmly seating himself behind the wheel. 'Give us another push and see what happens.'

'Did you understand everything he was saying to you?' I panted, as I set my shoulder to the back of the car and heaved.

'Are you kidding?' asked Porta, contemptuously. 'I didn't understand him any more than he understood me ... So what? You don't expect to, in a country this size. Some of 'em practically speak different lingoes ... Mind you, it's just as well I didn't say we came from Chita! I almost did, and then I hit on Jenisseisk instead.'

'Where is Jenisseisk?'

'Haven't the faintest idea,' said Porta, happily.

'Is it a real place?'

'How should I know? It seemed to satisfy him all right.'

From further up the road, I heard the crunching of boots on snow and the corporal's raucous voice.

'Dawai! Dawai!'

'They're coming back!' I yelped. I glanced over my shoulder. 'Dozens of 'em!' I added, as three men emerged from the trees.

At that moment the car shot forward and I fell headlong into the snow. I heard the corporal's merry hoot of laughter. Porta opened the door and shouted at me to get a move on if I didn't want to be left behind. As I flung myself into the moving vehicle, the corporal galloped alongside us.

'Dassvidanja!' he screamed. 'Dassvidanja!' (Goodbye.)

'And you,' I muttered, slamming the door.

A few miles further on we again hit a long column of enemy troops. At one point we were waved aside to let a staff car go past. I sat and jittered while Porta drove steadily onwards. We were approaching a crossroads, where a lieutenant-general was watching the troops march past.

'For God's sake,' I said, 'let's get shot of this bloody thing and carry on by foot. A German vehicle sticks out like a sore thumb.'

'Stick out even more if we suddenly dumped it in the ditch,' said Porta, reasonably. 'Don't worry, they're never think a couple of Jerries would have the nerve to drive around in a VW in the middle of a crowd of enemy troops. They'll just take us for two of their own men what have nicked a Kraut car.'

Porta drove past the lieutenant-general with a defiant flourish. I noticed his head whip round and stare after us, but Porta's optimism proved well-founded and we were allowed to continue without interruption.

About a mile further on we turned off into the Boljov gorge, in an attempt to leave the main road once and for all, but we were waved back again by a couple of furious military police, and we didn't stop to argue.

As we drew near to the Volga, we found the road blocked by two overturned trucks, and we were allowed to make a diversion down a side street. We reached the end of the street, and instead of swinging us back to the main road Porta took the opposite fork. We were pursued by the frenzied shouts and cries of a group of soldiers, and I stared at Porta in horror.

'What are they saying? Are they coming after us?'

'I shouldn't imagine so.' He laughed, removed his Russian helmet and tossed it into the back of the vehicle. 'They were just telling us to be careful ... we're heading towards the German lines!'

Our own side did not exactly welcome us back with open arms. They viewed us with the deepest suspicion and met us with a warning barrage of artillery fire. Even when they had

116

calmed down sufficiently to hear our explanations they seemed not to believe us. They kept saying, 'But where have you COME from?' and, 'How the hell did you get through?' until I began to wonder if it had all been worth it. Finally, and very grudgingly, they took their fingers off the trigger and hauled us along to their company commander, who held us two hours for questioning before giving us permission to rejoin our regiment.

'I should have got us a couple of seats on that plane,' said Porta, bitterly. 'I could have, you know.'

'I don't doubt you,' I said.

'I could have given the two fingers to the lot of 'em. Let 'em stew in their own stinking juice. I could have, if I was that sort of person.'

'Which, of course, you're not,' I said.

Porta glared at me, not sure whether I was being sarcastic.

'I could have,' he said, again, 'I'm telling you!'

'Well, don't pissing well keep on about it!' I snarled. 'I already said I believed you! Just shut up and give your arse a chance!'

We arrived back at our own lines thoroughly disgruntled with each other, and our tempers were made no sweeter by the realisation that we were not even going to receive a heroes' welcome from our own companions. The Regiment was in a panic and no one could be bothered with us. They couldn't have cared less whether we were there or not. Field telephones were buzzing and messengers were running to and fro in all directions.

'What's going on round here?' said Porta, angrily. 'Everything falls to pieces the minute I turn my back. It's always the same.'

The Old Man shrugged.

'Don't see what you could have done if you had been here,' he told him. 'The Russians have broken through in several places and all hell's been let loose.'

Porta turned to look at me.

'See what I mean?' he said, bitterly. 'I should have got a seat in that plane. Left 'em to stew in their own juice...'

Let us seize power now, and let us keep that power no matter what means we must employ to do so.

Joseph Goebbels, Minister of Propaganda
to Ernest Thaelmann—3.1.1932

Two horsemen were trotting briskly down a path in the Tiergarten,* which was deserted at six o'clock in the morning. They were Obergruppenführer Heydrich and Admiral Canaris.

'It is an interesting idea,' said Heydrich, turning to his companion. 'Don't you think so?' He looked straight ahead, between his horse's ears, a smile on his lips. 'Dress up a group of prisoners in Polish uniform and organise an attempt on the radio station at Gleiwitz ... what could be more amusing?' He turned again to Canaris. 'And what could give us a better excuse for launching an attack on Poland?'

Canaris frowned.

'I have my doubts,' he muttered.

'On what grounds?' Heydrich laughed. 'Not moral scruples, I trust?'

Canaris shook his head.

'Moral scuples hardly enter into it, do they? Since no one is in the least likely to accept them as a valid ground for objection.'

'So?'

'So...' Canaris hunched an uneasy shoulder. 'I can't see it coming off, that's all. It doesn't seem to me that you'll be able to keep it a secret for very long. Using prisoners ... they're bound to talk.'

'No need to worry on that score, my friend. None of them will survive the operation.'

Canaris turned to look at him, one eyebrow raised.

'I thought you were calling for volunteers? Promising them their freedom in exchange?'

'Purely as a bait,' murmured Heydrich, in slightly reproachful tones. 'Naturally we can't be expected to keep our promise. It would be the height of folly and sabotage the entire operation ... as you yourself have just pointed out. And in any case, Admiral, I believe I am not wrong in saying that the idea actually originated in your department?'

* Zoological Gardens.

118

'In my department, yes. But not altogether with my approval.'

'Nevertheless, the affair is reverting to you, is it not? It will be carried out under your auspices?'

'No. There you are for once misinformed, Obergruppenführer. My department will have nothing to do with the operation.'

The admiral urged his horse forward into a canter, leaving Heydrich staring thoughtfully after him. For a few moments he continued to trot, rising and falling with the motion of the horse, frowning as he tapped his boot with his riding crop. Canaris slowed down again to a walk, and Heydrich caught up with him at the end of the path.

'May one know why, Admiral? I was under the impression that the Führer himself had already approved the idea?'

'That is so.' Canaris inclined his head. 'However, as I told you just now, the plan was conceived without my knowledge and put forward without my consent. I shall have nothing to do with it.'

'I hardly see that you can avoid it,' said Heydrich, with a slow smile. 'We are all responsible for the actions of our subordinates. I was speaking on that very subject only yesterday to the Reichsführer and the Reichsmarschall, and they were both of the same opinion. This idea originated in your department and it must therefore rest with you to carry it out.'

Canaris slowly lit a cigarette before replying.

'You can't frighten me into it, Obergruppenführer. I'm as well informed as you, and very sure of my facts. I spoke myself with the Führer not long since and explained my position to him. I want nothing to do with the operation.' He blew a thin stream of smoke down his nostrils and glanced sideways at the frozen figure of Heydrich. 'I find the whole concept totally disagreeable. It has nothing whatsoever to do with counterespionage, and I'm warning you now that you'll have the whole Army against you.'

'That's a risk that has to be run. One accepts it.'

Canaris shrugged.

'Sooner you than me.'

They trotted on in silence a while, then Heydrich leaned across to the admiral and lightly flicked his horse's neck.

'Admiral Canaris, I congratulate you! You're a lively old fox and you never miss a trick. But one word of warning: every fox has his day! They all come to a sticky end sooner or later ...'

He pulled his horse round and cantered off towards the large black Mercedes that was waiting for him. Admiral Canaris trotted on by himself.

SEVEN

SUMMARY EXECUTIONS

In the middle of the night, an HE 111 landed in a field near Stalingrad. No one in the Sixth Army knew of its arrival, no one would have guessed the identity of the passenger it had brought. The only men who were present when it landed were a few selected NCOs from the paratroop regiment MATUK. The aircraft was camouflaged the minute it came down, and the paratroopers standing guard had orders to shoot on sight.

The first to leave the plane was Theodor Eicke, the man chiefly responsible for the running of the concentration camps and commander of the Third Panzer Division, the 'murder' squad. The savage brutality of Eicke, and, indeed, of the men under him, had been known to shake even the Führer, and the whole of the division had been deprived of leave for the duration of the war. Keep the animals behind bars and make good use of their particularly revolting talents, but never let them loose amongst the civilian population ...

Behind Eicke came a group of SS men, all specialists in the Nazi art of liqidation. A motorised sledge was waiting for them, provided by the paratroop regiment, but the regular driver was forced to cede his place to Oberscharführer Henzel, known affectionately at Dachau as 'Killer' Henzel.

In a flurry of snow the sledge and its sinister travellers set off towards Stalingrad and the Sixth Army HQ. The air force markings had been removed from the sledge and replaced by the letters 'SS', on the orders of the ever-watchful Eicke. He was a man who paid an almost psychopathic attention to detail and left nothing to chance, as many of his Dachau detainees could testify, from the Austrian chancellor Kurt von Schuschnigg, one of the 'specials', down to the least and most miserable of the Jews who had been dug out of their hiding-places in the slums of Berlin.

The Sixth Army had made its headquarters in an underground bunker which had been previously occupied by the

NKVD. Eicke's unexpected arrival caused an immediate bustle and hubbub. Panic spread rapidly throughout the bunker, even to General Paulus himself. He stood up as Eicke entered his room, and he held out a hand that shook very slightly. Eicke ignored it. He stood at the entrance, legs straddled, eyes flickering with cold contempt as he looked General Paulus up and down. Paulus cut a poor figure of a general at that moment, huddled into two misshapen overcoats, like a small grey creature dragged prematurely out of hibernation. Eicke was wearing the obligatory leather coat, well cut and stylish. He took his time lighting a cigar and spoke only when he was ready.

'Who are you?' he said, in tones of contempt.

'I'm General Paulus.' The general smiled nervously and dropped his hand. 'May I ask to whom I have the honour of speaking?'

'Honour?' Eicke laughed, savouring the word. 'Yes, that's good. I like it.' He strolled into the room, looking disdainfully from side to side. 'You have the honour to be speaking to SS Obergruppenführer Theodor Eicke. I am here on the Führer's behalf. He wishes to know what is going on.'

'What's going——'

'In particular,' continued Eicke, 'whether you're fighting a war or taking a winter sports holiday?'

Paulus began anxiously to massage the fingers of one hand with those of the other. They were long, fine, tapering fingers, made for better things than war. The fingers of a pianist or a surgeon. They had been made to create, never to destroy.

'When I came in just now,' said Eike, mercilessly, 'I quite thought I had been brought to the wrong place. You seemed to me more like a—an aged Bolshevik prisoner warming himself inside a German greatcoat than the Commander in Chief of the Sixth Army! You don't look very much like a general, do you?'

'It's been very hard out here, for all of us,' began Paulus, but Eicke again interrupted him.

'I'm not surprised there's no discipline amongst your troops, General! There's a spirit of defeat in the air ... and it comes straight from the top! It seems I shall have to tell the Führer that one of his generals has given up the fight.'

'That's not true!'

The finely moulded hands began to tremble. The general's protest was that of a man hurt rather than a man insulted, but his Chief of Staff leapt forward in his defence. General Schmidt was the very opposite of Paulus: hard, quick, and very sure of himself.

'SS Obergruppenführer, you have no business speaking like that! I shall put in a complaint!'

'That is your right,' allowed Eicke. 'By all means do so ... To whom should you wish to address it? To the Führer? Because if so, I can save you the trouble: I am his official representative at Stalingrad.'

He pulled a document from his inside pocket and tossed it on to the table. The document gave full powers to Obergruppen-führer Theodor Eicke, in the name of the Führer Adolf Hitler, to hold courts martial and to pass whatever judgements he thought fit.

Paulus pressed his fingers to his forehead in a gesture of despair.

'What does the Führer wish to know? Has he not received my reports on the situation? I've outlined my proposals to him—General Schmidt had an excellent plan which could be put into operation almost immediately. The Führer has only to approve it, and I believe we shall still be able to salvage at least a part of the Sixth Army.'

Eicke looked contemptuously at Paulus.

'The Führer is not interested in salvage operations—only in victory. God knows, he's given you enough time out here! And all you can do is whine to him for more men, more food, more ammunition ... What have you done with all the men you've already had? Where's all your ammuntion gone? Have you been giving firework parties with it?'

'This is preposterous——' began Schmidt, very loudly.

Eicke swung round on him

'All this talk of plans and proposals! Nothing but an attempt to cover up your failure! The Führer instructs me to remind you that the German Army does not turn and run before a horde of Soviet apes! I am told to remind you yet again that what he wants is victory!'

'How?' said Schmidt, dryly.

'How?' screamed Eicke. 'That is not my concern, nor is it the Führer's! How you win the fight is up to you—that's what you were made a general for.' He moved closer to Schmidt, pointing a finger at him. 'But you're asking me! How? All right, I'll tell you how ... Chase the Bolshevics out of Europe, that's how! Good God almighty, you've got twenty-five divisions in this bloody army of yours ... six hundred thousand men and eight

122

hundred tanks ... what more do you want? You could win five world wars with that lot, never mind flushing out a few primitive Soviet peasants!'

General Huber, who had been sitting silent throughout this exchange, nursing his empty right sleeve, could take Eicke's insolent tones no longer. He rose to his feet, his face white with anger.

'Who do you think you're talking to? You're not in your concentration camp now, you know: you're in Stalingrad! And we're not your prisoners, we're officers and soldiers!'

'Ah yes,' said Eicke, turning to him. 'You're General Huber, are you not? I have a message here for you. From General Burghof.'

He handed Huber a slip of paper from the Head of Army Personnel. It was an order for Huber to return to Germany and present himself at the Führer's Headquarters. Huber crumpled up the paper and pushed it into his pocket. He felt instinctively that such an order presaged some ill. It could mean promotion, but he doubted it. A summons to the Führer had always been a doubtful honour at the best of times. His thoughts flew at once to the possibility of his own execution—the firing squad—imprisonment—the liquidation of his family ... He stared across at Eicke, gloatingly regarding him from a cloud of cigar smoke, and he spoke with an effort.

'Thank you,' he said.

He sat down at the table and took no more part in the conversation. It seemed to him now that whatever happened, whether he stayed in Stalingrad and waited for the Russians, or whether he flew back to Germany in answer to the Führer's summons, he was probably a dead man.

General Paulus also remained silent. He was not fitted for war. He wished only to live amongst his books and his art treasures, to read and to think, to be on cordial terms with his neighbours, to interfere with no one and to be left alone to lead a life of peace.

Eicke bowed a slight, ironic bow towards the three generals. Only Schmidt, still hostile, took any notice of him.

'My travels, for the moment,' said Eicke, 'take me elsewhere, but I shall be back very shortly.'

His next call was on the 71st Division at Zaritza. He strode vigorously into the staff bunker, banging on the desk with his baton, a magnificent gold rod bearing the death's-head emblem, which had been a personal present from the Führer. Everyone looked up in alarm at his flamboyant entrance, and the commanding officer, General von Hartmann, rose at once and walked across to him. Eicke and van Hartmann were known to each other of old. There had once been a time when Eicke was an unimportant clerk in the orderly room and von Hartmann his superior officer. It was von Hartmann who had discovered Eicke changing entries in the account books to suit himself and had subsequently had him transferred to a mine-disposal squad. He now faced Eicke in his new role of SS officer, but he gave no obvious signs of apprehension.

'It's a long time since we last met,' he said, coolly.

'Indeed, yes,' agreed Eicke, tucking his gold baton beneath his arm. 'But I haven't forgotten the bad turn you did me!'

He smiled encouragingly at von Hartmann and undid the buttons of his coat, which fell open to reveal a chestful of medals and ribbons.

'Well, General, the Führer's sent me over here to find out exactly what's going on. He's not at all pleased with the progress you've been making. He can't understand why a horde of half-civilised heathens should be giving the German Army so much trouble.'

The general bowed his head and remained silent. Eicke pulled off his gloves and wrapped them round his baton, which he tapped briskly against his calf.

'I should like to inspect your division, if you please.'

'By all means,' agreed von Hartmann, only too anxious to be rid of the man.

He sent him off to look at the 191st, under the command of Captain Weinkopf. Eicke expressed a desire to travel by motorised sledge, but the ordnance officer shook his head.

'I don't advise it, sir. It's not the safest way of going.'

Eicke turned to look at him, eyebrows disdainfully raised.

'Are you scared, Lieutenant? Perhaps I'm already beginning to discover why it is that victory still eludes the Sixth Army...'

The lieutenant shrugged his shoulders and said no more. If Eicke had no regard for his safety, that was his problem: for himself, the lieutenant had long since given up all hope of emerging alive and sane from the horrors of Stalingrad, and whether he died today or tomorrow was no longer a matter of the slightest importance. His entire family had been killed in an air raid on Cologne, and since that time he had ceased to care for his own future.

The sledge had gone no further than a few yards when the

snow all round them began flying in great divots into the air. Despite himself, Eike started.

'Russian mortars,' said the lieutenant, casually. 'Take no notice, they're only small fry. It'll be the field-guns next.'

As if in response, the Russian artillery started up immediately he finished speaking. The lieutenant glanced at Eicke and smiled. Eicke shivered.

'It's certainly very cold,' he muttered, by way of explaining his involuntary tremors.

'Do you find it so?' asked the lieutenant, beginning to enjoy himself. 'I was just thinking how mild it was. We even saw some bullfinches this morning. They're the most fickle of visitors, you never catch a glimpse of them when the weather's bad . . .'

Eicke looked at him suspiciously, but the lieutenant turned blandly away and pointed ahead towards some hills.

'We have to go through a gorge pretty soon. I thought I ought to warn you . . . the Russians have a habit of going mad whenever we appear at the far end of it. It can get rather noisy.'

'That's quite all right,' said Eicke, who was beginning to sweat in spite of the low temperature. 'Carry straight on.'

The sledge disappeared into the hills. It had hardly put its nose out the other side when the ground beneath it seemed to open, a shower of snow enveloped both sledge and occupants, and Eicke flung himself in a panic head first over the side, followed by his fellow SS men. The sledge bucketed to a halt and the lieutenant stepped calmly off and stood looking at Eicke.

'This is it,' he said, simply.

Eicke picked himself up and brushed the snow off his uniform.

'This is what?' he demanded.

'We're here. We can continue on foot.'

They set off together to find Captain Weinkopf, the Russians harassing them all the way. Eicke looked round, irritated.

'What's the matter with them? Do they always carry on like this?'

'Oh, this is nothing!' the lieutenant smilingly assured him. 'A few days ago they wiped out an entire battalion in two minutes flat . . . This way, sir, Captain Weinkopf is expecting us.'

'I'm surprised you have a captain in charge of a regiment,' said Eicke, disapproving

The lieutenant shrugged.

'Needs must, and so and so forth . . . he was the most experienced officer left. The Russians had bagged all the others.'

125

'All of them? You mean——'

'I mean,' said the lieutenant, 'that officers don't last very long in this part of the world ... Here we are, sir.'

They found Captain Weinkopf playing cards with some private soldiers. They were all huddled together beneath three greatcoats, squatting on piles of Russian rifles. They had a couple of petrol cans for a table.

'This is Obergruppenführer Eicke,' said the lieutenant, in a somewhat disparaging tone of voice.

The soldiers looked up. Captain Weinkopf selected a card, placed in on the petrol cans, closed his hand and nodded.

'Ah huh,' he said.

Eicke waited in vain for the group to stand up and salute him. Nothing happened.

'I am here as the representative of the Führer,' he said.

Captain Weinkopf glanced up at him.

'Oh yes?'

'I have come to inspect your regiment.'

'You're welcome,' said the captain. He waved a hand. 'Most of them are out there, in their dug-outs. You can go and look them over any time you like. But I ought to warn you they're all a bit jittery at the moment. They'll shoot at anything that moves, so you'd best watch your step.'

The lieutenant turned away, possibly to hide a grin. Eicke puffed out his cheeks.

'Did you say, watch my step?' he repeated.

'Unless you want your head blown off,' agreed the captain, turning back to his game of cards.

'That is hardly the way to address a superior officer!' snapped Eicke.

Slowly, Captain Weinkopf looked up at him. Slowly, he hunched a shoulder.

'SS,' he said. 'That doesn't count so much out here. We're soldiers.'

'Soldiers!' Eicke made a noise of impatience in the back of his nose. 'You call yourself soldiers, do you? Sitting here playing cards when there's a war to be won! The Führer shall hear about this!'

'Just as you like,' said the captain, indifferently.

Eicke glared down at one of the soldiers.

'What about you?' he demanded. 'What's your job, when you're not gambling your time away?'

'Anti-tank,' said the boy, briefly.

He did not bother to elaborate. He could have told Eicke how only the day before he had destroyed no less than twelve T34s with hand-grenades and mines, but it never occurred to him. He wae barely nineteen years old and already he took his work for granted. He was an expert in the demolition of tanks, but if he ever survived into peacetime he would find there was no demand for his skills.

Eicke grunted and turned away, followed by his silent companions. The lieutenant called out to him.

'Watch out for snipers, Obergruppenführer! A major got his brains blown out yesterday for not keeping his head down!'

Eicke gave him a look of distaste, but he crouched on all fours and crawled ponderously through the snow towards the first line of dug-outs. The watchful Russians at once began firing, Oberscharführer Willmer was the first to suffer, with a bullet between the eyes. Scharführer Dwinge trod on a mine. As the group reached the first of the dug-outs, a soldier gave a shout of amazement as his leg was wrenched off his body by an exploding shell. He seemed in no pain; just sat there staring at the jagged edge of the stump and at the blood spilling out into the snow. A second shell landed near by.

'Christ almighty!' shouted Eicke, throwing himself flat.

The Dachau murderer, the killer of Jews in their thousands, had unthinkingly called upon a Jew to save him, but he saw no anomaly in the fact. He pushed the injured soldier out of the way. A man with one leg was of no further use, let him die quickly and quietly with the snow to cover him as a shroud.

Eicke crawled doggedly onwards and finally jumped down to join a machine-gunner, who looked at him askance.

'Shouldn't hang around here too long if I was you, sir. The Russians seem to be able to spot officers a mile off. We had a general here yesterday what copped it, on account of he went too far forward.'

'Is that so?' said Eicke, nervously.

He left the machine-gunner and moved on, until he was stopped by a young lieutenant with the face of an old man, wanting to know what he thought he was doing.

'Just looking around,' said Eicke, coldly. 'The Führer wishes me to make a report.'

'Good.' The lieutenant grabbed Eicke and unceremoniously pulled him into a dug-out. 'In that case, perhaps you could tell him that my men are trying to fight the enemy on empty bellies. No hot food for over a week! How can men be expected to win victories if they're not given proper rations?'

'That is hardly a matter for the Führer,' said Eicke. 'I'm surprised that an officer of your standing can't deal with it himself. I suggest you take it up with whoever is in charge of your field kitchen. The man's probably stealing.'

'Field kitchen!' The old-faced young lieutenant gave a harsh cackle of laughter. 'My men haven't seen a field kitchen for so long that I doubt if they'd even know what they are!'

Eicke moved his forehead.

'I find that very difficult to credit, Lieutenant. How do you provide for yourselves if you have no field kitchen?'

The lieutenant leaned forward and put his face close to Eicke's. It was grey and lined.

'We forage. We kill. And if there's no time to go out hunting, then we starve.'

'Preposterous!' Eicke turned and snapped his fingers at one of his men. 'Gratwohl! Make a note of it! See that things are put in order round here.' He turned back to the lieutenant. 'Whoever is responsible for this state of affairs will be shot, I can assure you of that.'

'Thank you very much,' said the lieutenant. 'That's a great help.'

At that moment, a sergeant appeared. He jumped into the dug-out, elbowing Eicke out of the way.

'Enemy's attacking, sir!'

The lieutenant at once snatched up his sub-machine-gun and a pile of grenades and dashed off, followed by the sergeant. Eicke and his men were left alone, trembling together in the abandoned dug-out. They had not yet experienced this type of warfare. They crouched with their hands over their heads, listening in horror to the whine of bullets, the shattering of shells, the heavy pounding of the big guns. Above and all round them there was a constant, milling activity. Men ran and ducked and fell. Boots pounded in the crushed snow. Heavy machines were dragged past. Whistles blew, voices cried out. Eicke had no idea what was happening, he could only make himself as small as possible and await the outcome.

The attack was contained. The young lieutenant returned to his dug-out and spread his map across the floor, ignoring Eicke. Eicke cleared his throat, self-importantly.

'Are you able to hold the position, Lieutenant?'

'What?'

The lieutenant looked up, saw Eicke and frowned. It was

plain he had totally forgotten him. Slowly his brow cleared as he remembered.

'I don't really know, Obergruppenführer. Probably not, but we'll hang on as long as we can. The war's already over, of course, but we might as well die fighting as any other way.'

Eicke stiffened.

'I could have you shot for that, Lieutenant! The war is by no means over.'

The lieutenant shrugged.

'That has precisely the same ring about it as the Führer's statement that we were fighting a nation of under-developed savages ... Crap and nonsense! The drivel of a lunatic! Why doesn't he come out here and see for himself?'

Three shots rang out, one after another. The young lieutenant fell like a stone to the ground, crumpling the map beneath him. Eicke put his revolver away and beckoned to his men to follow him. They left the dug-out without a backward glance.

The inspection continued in the direction of the 9th Tank Regiment. Eicke demanded to see the cook.

'Well, Sergeant, I've heard that the men are half starving out here. What do you have to say about that?'

The sergeant shrugged.

'You gimme the grub, sir, and I'll knock something up. Can't do nothing without, can I?'

'What about your field kitchen?' demanded Eicke. 'How can you fight a war without a field kitchen?'

'Search me, sir,' said the sergeant, cheerfully. 'But we haven't got none.'

'So how do you feed the men?'

'Mostly we send out foraging parties, sir. Knocking off horses and such like. Makes quite a nourishing stew, a horse does. That's when you can get hold of one, of course. They're not that easy to come by.'

'And when you can't lay your hands on a horse?' said Eicke, sarcastically. 'What do you eat then? Bullfinches?'

'Not so far, sir. If we can't get hold of nothing else, we usually have a bit of liver.'

'Liver?' said Eicke, startled. 'Where do you get liver from?'

The sergeant looked at him rather pityingly.

'Human liver, sir ... from the corpses. It's quite tasty, you'd be surprised. Nice bit of braised liver ...'

With a handkerchief to his mouth, Eicke stumbled away. He did not mention field kitchens again. The men of Stalingrad had become cannibals ...

'Why aren't you attacking?' he screamed at a middle-aged major, catching him by the arm to gain his attention.

The major looked him up and down out of sad, bloodshot eyes.

'Attacking where?' he said.

'Anywhere, damn you! I'm tired of seeing men hanging around waiting for the Russians to come and get them!'

'What else can they do? We're surrounded ... Besides, we're running out of ammunition and there aren't enough of us to put paid to a flock of sheep.' He laughed, reflectively. 'I'm commanding a battalion that's been reduced to about half the size of a company! And still that maniac in Berlin screams for victory ...'

The major was tied to a tree and shot. Eicke and his party moved onwards in search of fresh victims.

A captain of the engineers was the next to be despatched: he had blown up his equipment rather than leave it for the Russians, but he had not asked permission to do so and was therefore, in Eicke's view, guilty of sabotage. He, too, was summarily shot, and died unrepentant.

The chase continued. Colonel Jenck of the 9th Infantry had ordered a retreat after the majority of his men had been butchered. He was hanged from the sails of a windmill.

They inspected an improved hospital and tore the bandages off two hundred men in order to see the extent of their wounds. Some died under this rough treatment. Others were discovered not to be injured at all, or not to be injured to an extent which Eicke considered valid: one hundred and ninety-seven men were shot, including doctors.

The SS moved inexorably onwards. The crack Italian 'Savoia' Regiment proved an unexpectedly happy hunting ground: the bag was sixty-eight officers, who had authorised the pillaging of German stores in order to keep their own men from starvation.

The hot breath of an inferno was raging over Stalingrad. It was enough to face the Russians without also having to cope with the butcher of Dachau. For many men it was the last straw: they shot themselves without waiting for Eicke to do it.

At the railway station of Zaritza the party came across a crowd of gaunt Rumanian children, with huge eyes and legs like garden canes, begging for bread from the soldiers.

'Get rid of those brats!' said Eicke.

The Rumanian troops themselves undertook the task. They were vicious and untamed, shamefully inadequate in battle, yet wild beasts when confronted by small children. Eicke watched them liquidate their countrymen and then hanged a random fifty per cent of the troops on a collective charge of cowardice in the face of the enemy.

An infantry major had withdrawn his depleted battalion under heavy fire and saved the lives of his remaining men. He himself had lost both legs in doing so and had been flown back home from Gumrak. On hearing all this, Eicke at once made it his business to have the major arrested in Germany and transferred to Torgau, where he was shot on his stretcher a few days later.

A Roman Catholic padre attached to the 44th Division was executed for having preached a sermon on Jesus of Nazareth. As someone slyly pointed out to the greedy Eicke, Jesus of Nazareth was a Jew. In a frenzy of anti-Semitism, Eicke strung the padre up by his feet and had his throat slit. The man remained on the spot for several days, his crucifix on its purple ribbon swinging to and fro. No one thought to cut him down, and men began to use the body as a kind of signpost. Keep straight on until you come to the dead priest. Take the first on your left and you're on the right road . . .

After his orgy of slaughter, Eicke flew back to Germany and delivered his report to the Führer, leaving the Sixth Army to its death agonies, in the crushing embrace of the advancing Soviet troops.

God has sent Adolf Hitler to help the people of Germany restore order to Europe.

August Wilhelm, Prince of Prussia,
at a banquet given by the Officers'
Association—16.6.1936

A few days before Christmas, Privates Wenck and Blatt were sent through a blizzard to Gumrak to pick up the food supplies for their battalion. In the depths of the Russian winter, the allowance for each man was ten grammes of bread, ten grammes of jam and a quarter litre of a watery substance made from horse bones.

Paul Wenck was a well-built boy of eighteen, and even after several months on the Russian front he still had a vast frame and an insatiable appetite. It was the constant hunger that bothered him most. Until a few weeks ago he had been accustomed to exchange his cigarette ration for some extra bread, but such deals were no longer possible at Stalingrad: cigarettes had disappeared from the market and bread was a commodity more precious than gold dust.

The two soldiers were kept waiting for an hour at Gumrak before the rations were handed to them: two hundred and twenty-five for the battalion, plus the jam and the bone soup.

'Two twenty-five,' said Blatt. 'Count it with me and remember it.'

They packed the precious cargo on to their sledge and headed back towards the battalion. It took them eight hours to complete the journey. The weather was appalling and their team of two horses, rib-sharp and broken-down, stumbled and staggered through lack of food. It was dawn when they arrived back at Zaritza.

They delivered the bread to the quartermaster, who insisted they remain while he checked the number of loaves.

'How many?'

'Two twenty-five,' said Blatt.

They counted them three times, but there were only two hundred and twenty-four. Blatt repeated obstinately that there had been two twenty-five; Wenck was not quite so sure. Both soldiers were stripped and searched. Nothing was found on them. But in the sledge, at the bottom of the tool box, wrapped up in a camouflage jacket, was the missing loaf. The jacket belonged to Wenck, and it was Wenck who carried the key of the box.

The court-martial took place in the cellars of a bombed building. Pale and desperate, Paul Wenck faced his judges. His big frame filled his uniform, but his cheeks were sunken and his skin was grey and stretched tight across the bones. He trembled as he stood, through weakness more than fear.

'Why did you steal the loaf?' asked the president of the court.

'I was hungry,' said the prisoner, simply. 'I hadn't eaten for three days and I was hungry.'

The president rolled his eyes in despair.

'Isn't everyone hungry in Stalingrad? Do you think other people besides yourself haven't gone without food for three days? Or even longer? Hunger is no excuse for stealing.'

The court retired to discuss its verdict and decided unanimously that Wenck was guilty under the order of General Paulus dated 9th December 1942, and that he should be sentenced to death in accordance with the provisions of that order. Wenck promptly fainted and had to be hauled to his feet by two guards. It was noticeable that the two guards were sufficiently well fed to have the strength to hold him up quite easily. They slapped his face until he had come to his senses and then dragged him screaming and sobbing from the court. For the theft of a loaf of bread, eighteen-year-old Paul Wenck, thrown into the cauldron of Stalingrad to fight for his country, was sentenced to be shot.

The execution was carried out twenty-four hours later. Private Blatt was a somewhat self-righteous member of the firing squad. The ice was too hard for a grave to be dug, so they covered the body with snow and left it in its frozen tomb.

On Christmas Day it was decided that firing squads were a waste of ammunition: from that time on, offenders would be hanged instead of shot.

EIGHT

GENERALS WE HAVE KNOWN ...

We were sitting in a cellar playing cards, with a pack that belonged to the Old Man. It was black and dog-eared, a veteran of the war, and the pips were sometimes hidden beneath layers of grease, but at least it was honest. You played with Porta's cards at your peril, but everyone knew that the Old Man was straight.

For once, both Porta and the Legionnaire were losing heavily, while Tiny was winning. For some time the Russian artillery had been bombarding us. The light had gone out and we were using candle stubs, and a great split had appeared across the ceiling.

'This is sodding useless!' declared Gregor, throwing in his hand as a new tremor raced across the floor. 'I can't concentrate with this racket going on!'

'Persistent buggers, aren't they?' I said, holding down the table.

We sat back in our chairs and watched another split break out across the ceiling.

'Any minute now,' I said.

'We could always run up a white flag,' suggested Porta. 'Fly a pair of Tiny's knickers from a first-floor window...'

'And get shot for our pains,' said the Old Man. 'Never mind the Russians, we'd be in front of one of our own firing squads so fast we'd never know what hit us.'

'Like yesterday,' said Heide. 'Some yellow-bellied bastard of a general trying to run out with the whole of his company hot on his heels.' He laughed, vindictively. 'They got their just deserts, don't you worry! One of the best executions I've seen since we came to this flaming country. Flags flying, drums beating, they gave 'em the full works ... even had a padre reading out the bible and an Oberleutnant with a sabre to tell 'em when to shoot.'

'What they won't do for a bit of top brass,' I said.

'Top brass!' Gregor snorted. 'They deserve all they get—and more. Bastards, the whole lot of 'em.'

The Old Man raised a remonstrative eyebrow.

'Generalisations,' he murmured.

'Yeah, generalisations!' agreed Gregor, with a venom almost equalling Heide's. 'That's just about it.'

'And just how much do you know about generals, anyway?' mildly inquired the Old Man.

'A hell of a lot, I can tell you! I used to be Field-Marshal von Kluge's driver at one time You know what those bastard generals used to do? Nothing but eat and drink and smoke and copulate for twenty-three hours every day, and plot and plan for the last one.'

'Plot and plan?' said Tiny, at once interested. 'What sort of plot and plan?'

'How to get some bloke in power and push some other bloke out of power ... how to do Hitler in and get away with it ... how to make sure they did all right themselves ... all that sort of thing.'

'And you never denounced them?' demanded Heide, sitting bolt upright on his chair.

'You're dead right I didn't! Let 'em get on with it, that's what I say ... You think I wanted to risk my bleeding neck running off to Adolf with a load of tales?'

'Quite right,' said Porta, nodding his approval. 'Not worth sticking your nose in—unless you stand to gain something by it, of course. Now me'—he puffed out his pigeon chest—'I've had quite a lot of revenue in the past from overhearing other people's plots. High treason, and all that ... they pay very well for keeping your mouth shut.'

'You deserve to be shot, the pair of you!' said Heide, white-lipped.

'Ah, get knotted!' said Porta. 'I'd only been in this lousy bleeding Army two hours before I realised the whole thing was rotten from the arse up. You don't catch me risking my neck to save Adolf Hitler's perishing life!'

'Anyway,' said the Old Man, hoping to avert a vicious scene, 'what happened to von Kluge?'

'Well——' Gregor waited until the sounds of a nearby explosion had died away and the dust had settled and we could check that the roof was still over our heads. 'Well, he and his mates went on with all their plotting and planning—they used to sort of shuffle people about like they was packs of cards. But it was old Adolf they'd really got it in for. All they ever talked about was how to do him in. One day they thought they'd just run up and shoot him, another day they thought they'd shove a grenade under his bum. One chap—some lieutenant-colonel, he was, called von Boselager—he had this crummy notion he could get him with a sabre. Wanted to slice his head off and throw it to the people to kick about the streets. Anyway, what happened in the end was they all got so deep into it they couldn't get themselves out again——'

'Compromised,' said Porta, wisely.

'Yeah, I reckon they was. Well and truly in the shit, up to their rotten bleeding useless necks ... so anyway, this von Kluge, that was a field-marshal, he starts trying to wriggle out of it. Then they all start trying to wriggle out of it. Don't trust each other no more, see? Not one little bit they don't.' Gregor shook his head. 'Next thing I know, they're having dirty great bust-ups with each other all over the place and denouncing each other rotten and Christ knows what all. So then one day old von Kluge's called to this dead secret meeting, and he starts yelling for me to get the car out and off we go in a bloody great hurry with him panting down the back of my neck and banging on the glass with his stick and screaming like a bloody lunatic.' Gregor paused and looked at us. 'It's all very well you lot sitting there grinning, but you want to try having a bleeding nut of a general perched on your shoulder in a fast car ... it ain't funny.'

'You should have denounced him,' said Heide, primly.

Gregor ignored him.

'It was in Kiev, this meeting. You ever driven along that main road they got there?' He sucked in his breath and shook his head. 'One of Uncle Jo's fiascos, that is. More like a switchback than a road. There's one bit—just before you get to some village called Djubendjev, something like that—there's this one bit what goes up like this'—he shot his arm vertically into the air—'round like this'—he wriggled it, rapid and snake-like—'with bloody great ditches on either side of it. They call it Suicide Corner. Every Sunday all the locals go out and wait for the fun to start. It's a sort of traditional pastime with 'em.'

'And I suppose,' said the Old Man, 'you and your general ended up giving them a free show?'

'You've hit the nail on the head,' said Gregor. 'Old von Kluge, he was acting like something out of a Yankee gangster film. Last thing I remember, we was just screaming up to Suicide Corner when he starts banging his stick on the glass and yelling at me to step on the gas ... Next thing I know, I'm waking up in hospital in a sort of plaster coffin. Two months they kept me there. Lying on my back, watching all these sexy birds walking up and down the ward and me not being able to do a damn thing about it!'

'How about von Kluge?' I asked. 'Was he killed?'

'Was he hell!' said Gregor, in disgust. 'Broke his back or something. He's still tucked up in plaster in a hospital bed.'

'Nice cushy way to spend the war,' observed Porta.

'He should have been shot!' said Heide.

There was a pause. Somewhere outside we heard a series of explosions and a cloud of dust drifted slowly down and settled on our heads and shoulders. Tiny heaved a great sigh.

'I worked with a general once,' he informed us.

We looked at him in automatic disbelief.

'Yeah?' said Porta. 'What was you? His right-hand-man?'

'You looking for a bunch of fives?' demanded Tiny.

'Well, go on, then, tell us!' jeered Porta, 'What was this general you worked with?'

'Knochenhauer,' said Tiny. 'In the cavalry, he was. He's dead now—blew his brains out.'

There was a burst of derisive laughter.

'Was that the natural result of having you work with him?' the Old Man wanted to know.

Tiny glowered.

'I was his orderly, I was. We got on very well together. He saved my life, as a matter of fact.' He leaned back, smiling. 'Bet none of you's ever had his life saved by a full-blown general! Old Knochenhauer, he wasn't such a bad sort, really ... See, what happened, I fell out of this tank and got my boot caught in the perishing thing. Nearly had my whole leg wrenched off. Next morning I couldn't hardly walk, so I went off to see the MO. He was a right bastard, like most of 'em are ... you had to have your guts trailing round your feet before he'd believe there was anything wrong with you. Couldn't stand illness, that man couldn't. Funny, when you think of it ... for a doctor ... One chap I knew, he went to see him with appendicitis. This quack said he was pulling a fast one. Stuck thermometers all over him, in his mouth, down his ears, under his arms, up his arse ... even then he didn't believe him. Jesus, everyone else did! Everyone else knew the poor bloke was ill. I went to see him that same night, he was so hot you could've fried an egg on his backside, but all they done was threaten him with a court-martial if he didn't recover within twenty-four hours ... Anyway, he died next morning,' said Tiny, gloating. 'Something went pop inside of him and poisoned his innards. Just goes to show, they don't always know what they're talking about.'

'Natural cynics,' said the Old Man, with a grin. 'Too many people like you knocking around. Makes 'em suspicious!'

'Fell out of a tank!' I said, savouring it. 'That's a good one!'

'I did and all,' said Tiny, aggressively. 'My foot was black and blue, I passed out three times on my way to the quack, and I passed out again when I took my boot off to show him.'

'I hope they cheered,' said Porta.

Tiny shook his head.

'Bastard said I was just trying it on. Seemed to think I'd bashed myself up with a hammer to make it look bad. He couldn't prove it, mind you, but he said there wasn't nothing wrong with me. Next thing I knew I was in the glasshouse peeling spuds. Not that I objected to that,' said Tiny, reasonably. 'It seemed like as good a way of spending the war as any other. Only thing was, my bleeding foot started to get better. By the time the court-martial come round there wasn't hardly nothing wrong with it no more. So when they had the ruddy nerve to accuse me of'—he frowned—'loitering,' he said, dubiously.

'Malingering,' said the Legionnaire.

'Yeah, that's it,' said Tiny. 'That's what it was. Malingering. That carries the death sentence, that does. They packed me off to Torgau and shoved me in the blue wing. It was only a matter of time. I tell you, I thought my number was up ... I was a condemned man,' said Tiny, with melodramatic relish. 'Only I hadn't reckoned on my friend the general.' He nodded and winked at us. 'Saved my life, old Knochenhauer did. Come to Torgau special, like, and had a few words with me. We got on all right, Knochenhauer and me. "So you're the soldier what claims he had a bad foot, are you?" he says to me. "Are you prepared to admit you was having us on or do you still stick to your original story?" So I says I stuck to my original story, and you know what he says to me?' Tiny's face beamed like a beacon in the dimly lit cellar. 'He says, "Soldier," he says, "you're the toughest nut I've ever had to crack. I'm going to send you off for an X-ray. Perhaps that'll knock some of the wind out of your sails ... And when they confirm there ain't nothing wrong with you," he says, "then we're going to shoot you." He couldn't say fairer than that, now, could he?'

'How nice to have a general for a friend,' murmured the Legionnaire.

'So what did the X-ray show?' asked Porta. 'Ingrowing toenails?'

Tiny looked at him in triumph.

'Busted bone,' he said. 'Fractured my foot, hadn't I? That showed 'em a thing or two! That MO what had made the mistake, he wes sent straight off to the front, and General Knochenhauer, he come and apologised to me. All over me, he was. Eating out of the palm of my hand——'

At this high point of Tiny's triumph, we heard the shrill blast of a whistle, the sound of running footsteps, all the signs of a general alert. The door was flung open and a white-faced corporal burst in.

'The Russians have broken through!' he yelled.

There was a moment's pause. The corporal clattered back up the stairs, the Old Man began slowly to gather up his pack of cards. The rest of us stood up and reached for our equipment.

'About time they paid us a visit,' said the Legionnaire. 'I wondered when they'd come.'

The love of liberty is not a highly-developed characteristic of the German people.

Madame de Staël, 1810

On 8th November 1942, the voice of Adolf Hitler rang out across Europe from the Burgerbraukeller in Munich.

'If Stalin was waiting for me to attack in the centre, then he must now be a very disappointed man! I have never been interested in the centre! I have pinned all my hopes on the Volga and now I have the Volga in the palm of my hand! The final battle was fought, by some twist of fate, in a place that bears the name of Stalin himself ...'

Frenzied bursts of 'Sieg Heil! Sieg Heil!' drowned the next two or three sentences.

'All along,' screamed Hitler, 'I have dreamt of conquering that town on the Volga! And now I have it! Now it belongs to us! We have only to overcome one or two minor pockets of resistance and the whole of Russia will be ours!'

Cheers and shouts and wild outbreaks of handclapping, and then the sound of a myriad voices raised in song:

'Deutschland, Deutschland über alles ...'

Ten days after this speech, the Commander in Chief of the Sixth Army received the following telegram from Berlin:

'SIXTH ARMY WITHDRAW STALINGRAD. ESTABLISH AND HOLD NEW POSITIONS. I ORDER YOU FIGHT LAST MAN LAST BULLET. SURRENDER OUT OF QUESTION. ANY ATTEMPTING RETREAT REGARDED AT TRAITORS. I COUNT ON MY GENERALS. FIGHT LIKE CONQUERORS. LIKE WAGNERIAN HEROES.

ADOLF HITLER.'

NINE

TRAITORS

It was a cold, bright January day. Stalingrad, that astonishing city, Oriental–European, swarmed with life beneath cloudless blue skies with a hint of winter sunshine. Its streets were thronged with soldiers, German, Hungarian, Italian, Rumanian,

Slovakian, many of them taking the air with their mistresses on their arm. It might almost have been a garrison town in peacetime. Further north the war was still unfolding, but here in Stalingrad there was a lull.

In a house facing the Isles of Sarpinski, some officers were holding a secret conference. They were all Austrians and belonged to the Viennese Division.

Major-General Lenz held up his tenth glass of champagne and proposed a toast to the vanquished Austro-Hungarian empire. All the officers solemnly drank.

'It was a bad day for Austria when Hitler's soldiers marched into the country.' Lenz shook his head and swallowed the rest of his champagne. 'I never did like the damned Prussians.'

There was a general mumbling and muttering of agreement. Back in 1938 these very same men, in their first mindless enthusiasm, had been only to anxious to throw off their old Austrian uniforms and adopt the grey-green of the Germans. But they had forgotten that now. They had forgotten with what eagerness they had compiled lists of their friends and acquaintances who were not of pure Aryan descent, or who seemed to them to be politically dubious. They had forgotten how readily they had welcomed the chance of becoming a part of Germany. Or, if they had not quite forgotten, they had at any rate modified.

'It was forced upon us,' said Lenz, with a sigh. 'What else could we have done?'

'What else could we have done?' they repeated.

There was a long, reminiscent pause.

'So much for the past, gentlemen! Let us get down to the business of the present.' Colonel Taurog cleared a space amongst the champagne bottles and spread out a map. 'The fact of the matter is, the situation here in Stalingrad is pretty desperate. I don't think anyone would dispute that?' He stared round, but the statement passed unchallenged. 'Hoch got himself butchered at Kotelnikowo, so we needn't expect any help from that quarter. As for all the rumours about an SS division being sent out here, I think we can dismiss those as pure fantasy. We have to face it, gentlemen: in our hour of need, Adolf Hitler has abandoned us.' He looked slowly round the table. 'Are we all in agreement?'

Again, a nodding chorus of heads.

'Our one hope, therefore,' continued Taurog, 'lies in the Russians themselves.' He tapped a document case on the table before him. 'I have here complete details of all our defence positions. Once they are in Russian hands, there should be no difficulty for the enemy in breaking through our lines—with our continued collaboration, of course.'

'Of course, of course,' murmured the collected bunch.

'I think we may safely surmise that such a gesture on our part would not pass unrewarded by our Russian friends. Indeed, I'm sure they could do with the help of people such as ourselves in combating the scourge of Nazism.'

'Quite,' said General Lenz.

It was debatable at what stage General Lenz had actually become a committed anti-Nazi. Possibly only within the last few hours. Or even minutes. Certain it was that the day before he had carried out Nazi orders and condemned to death four young soldiers who had attempted to desert.

'These papers,' he said, indicating the document case. 'They'll have to be handed over to General Rokossovski. He's the one to deal with them. I've already made out a list of all the officers I know who have expressed anti-Russian sentiments. That way he can be assured of whole-hearted collaboration.'

Had it slipped his memory that it was he himself who had been instrumental in arranging the transport of eight thousand Russian women from Sebastopol to the German concentration camps? Had General Taurog forgotten that on his own estate in Austria he had thirty-five Polish slaves, otherwise known as servants? Those slaves had cost fifty marks apiece. The market price was officially thirty-five marks for an able-bodied male, but in practice you always had to include a substantial tip for the supplier and his subordinates in the transit camps. As for the pious, red-faced Colonel Kurz, he had conveniently expunged from his memory the four hundred and seventy-six Russian prisoners in the Karpovka camp whom he had recently shot for the theft of a few kilos of potatoes.

The noble conspirators did not themselves set in motion the wheels of treachery, which were ultimately to crush beneath them several thousands of unsuspecting soldiers. Their rank precluded the actual soiling of hands. They confided the task instead to a Feldwebel of the military police, and this Stalingrad Judas drove off to meet the enemy in a sumptuous Mercedes, waving a special pass which opened all barriers.

A mile or so to the north of Katschlinskaja the big black car was stopped by a Russian reconnaissance group, who, taking no notice whatsoever of the white flag, tore open the doors, pulled out the driver and Feldwebel Bram and proceeded to steal everything they could lay hands on. In vain did Bram protest his mission of treachery: none of the group understood a word of German. It was not until the pair had been stripped of all valuables, watches, rings, cigarette cases and lighters, that a lieutenant appeared and took control of the situation. Bram and the driver were marched off, minus their possessions, to be interrogated by four Russian staff officers. Despite the document case and its valuable information, a trap was suspected. They looked up grimly at Bram.

'A trick like this,' they said, 'will cost your countrymen their lives. Thousands of them will die.'

Bram shrugged his shoulders.

'Thousands must die in order that a handful can go on living,' he said, cynically. 'That's the way it goes. First come, first saved...'

The Russians looked at him with distaste, but with a growing inclination to believe his story. His attitude seemed plausible. They had plenty of Feldwebel Brams amongst their own number.

They checked the papers carefully with the information they already had, and not until they were satisfied it was genuine did they conduct the two men to General Rokossovski and Marshal Jeremenko at Alexandrovna.

The Germans had suggested that by way of signifying their agreement the Russians should drop green flares from an aeroplane at a given time and place; the conspirators would then give the go-ahead by replying with red and yellow rockets. Not until then would Bram and his driver be allowed back through the German lines to make their report to General Taurog.

The following day, at five o'clock in the afternoon, an Ilyushin set off with a supply of green flares, and two days later the Russians began a massive build-up of troops outside Dubowka, where General Vasilevski was in command of three thousand tanks and sixty thousand Cossacks, the ordinary infantry regiments having been judged too slow for the anticipated attack. Six infantry divisions and one armoured division were also moved into the area. It made a total of a hundred thousand men, and, in addition, motorised divisions of the Third Army were called up to halt the movements of German troops along the length of the Volga.

Meanwhile, the conspirators put the finishing touches to their plans. Taurog organised his military police, the prison staff, the hygiene personnel and the engineers and armed them against the day when they would be shooting their fellow-countrymen in the back and moving over to the other side.

It was Lieutenant-Colonel Hinze, of the 100th Rifles, who proved the weak link in the chain. Having plotted and planned with the best of them, he now attempted to solace his own conscience by pouring out the whole miserable story in what he thought was the inviolable secrecy of the confessional. Unfortunately for the conspirators, Hinze's confessor was a Nazi soldier first and a Roman Catholic priest second, and he lost no time in running off to General Lattmann, the officer commanding the 14th Panzer Division, and passing on the news. Hinze was arrested within the hour and betrayed his fellow-conspirators during the course of his first interrogation.

Generals Taurog and Lenz were hanged in the Alexandra Basilika. The others were shot in the streets and their bodies kicked into the gutter with large placards round the neck: I AM A TRAITOR WHO SOLD MY COUNTRY TO THE ENEMY.

The following day, the Russian offensive began. The massed hordes of troops and vehicles burst upon us like waters from a broken dam, swarming down upon us, crushing us beneath them, pouring onwards, wave after wave after wave. In most cases, there was no opportunity to fight back. One entire division was wiped out of existence in less than an hour. The carnage was swift and terrible. It came upon you, sweeping out of nowhere, and had gone almost before you had time to draw breath. And in its wake it left a rolling sea of fire and a patchword of bodies and blood, stray limbs and pieces of machinery. Those few who survived an attack frequently lost their sanity and went howling and raging into the engulfing flames.

Porta, Tiny and myself were buried at the bottom of a pit beneath a mass of dead men. What had happened to the rest of the Company, we had no idea: we did not dare to stick our heads out and see.

A couple of hours after the Russians had swept over us, we heard approaching tanks and recognised them by the sound of their engines as Tigers. But still we remained hidden. We were taking no chances, not even with our own side ... The tanks ground onwards, shaking the earth and dislodging several bodies. We rearranged ourselves in our ditch, with corpses beneath us and all round us and a narrow channel of air for breathing. We stayed there all through the night. The stench was atrocious and the touch of the cold, lifeless limbs was a constant reminder that one false step on our part and we should soon be in that state ourselves.

Early in the morning, we crept cautiously out of our stinking trench and took a look round. Not a sign of life. We didn't hang about in search of familiar faces, we left the graveyard behind us and set off towards Stalingrad, in the hope that the Russians had been kept out by the 16th Division and that we should meet up with our own regiment—or the tattered remnants of it.

On the road, we were joined by a solitary, downcast Russian. He had been taken prisoner a few days before and had survived the previous day's massacre but was now too scared to make his way back to his own side. It was the old story: to be taken prisoner was a disgrace punishable by death.

'How would they know you'd been with us?' I said.

'They'd know,' he assured us. 'And Tovaritch Stalin himself forbade anyone to become a prisoner.'

'Stalin is a turd,' said Porta.

The man looked up, inquiringly. We graphically explained the word to him and he hunched his shoulders in silent acquiescence.

All along the road the bodies were piled high, their limbs frozen into grotesque shapes. The snow was spotted crimson with the spilt blood of the dead, and black with the leaking oil from overturned vehicles. We saw the charred wrecks of cars and tanks, a trail of abandoned weapons, helmets without heads, heads without bodies, mutilated stumps of arms and legs. We helped ourselves as the fancy took us to spare clothing, a new pair of boots here, a fur coat there, until we looked quite uncommonly presentable. The Russian stood by and watched. It seemed to be his morale rather than his morals which prevented him joining in the pillage. It had reached such a low ebb that warm clothes and comfortable footwear held no further attractions for him.

Towards dusk we came upon a German field hospital. It was a shambles, filled to overflowing with the sick, the wounded and the totally diorientated. Food was scarce, medicine almost non-existent. Even the doctors were thin on the ground. Nevertheless, it was a sort of haven and we found it easy enough to mingle with the crowd. We stayed there for three days, enjoying the rest. After the nightmare of twenty-four hours spent in a ditch full of dead bodies, that verminous, stinking hole of a so-called hospital was as good as a luxury hotel. The Russian silently disappeared. We invited him to stay—the chances are that no one would ever have noticed him—but he was uneasy in company and he wondered off alone into the dusk.

Unfortunately, on our third day Porta disgraced himself. He was caught in the act of eating a dying man's rations and was promptly dragged down to a cellar and held there pending a court-martial. As he indignantly pointed out to us, there was no room for sentiment in the middle of a war; the dying man had had no further use for his rations, while he, Porta, desperately needed them to keep his strength up, so that he could go on fighting for the Führer. It was surely more logical to sustain a fit man than one whose hours were numbered? But indignation was hot against him and Porta was shut away.

'What'll we do?' said Tiny. 'Leave the stupid bastard to stew in his own juice?'

'They'll shoot him,' I said.

Tiny shrugged, his shoulders.

'They'll shoot us if they catch us trying to spring him. And why go and piss on your kipper? It's quite a cushy number here, I wouldn't mind staying on.'

'But it can't last,' I said. 'The Russians will be arriving any day now. We'll have to get out sooner or later.'

In fact, the place was in such chaos that it proved simple enough to free Porta from his cellar. Tiny put the guard out of commission—no very difficult task, since the man was on crutches—and the three of us fled into the comforting darkness of the surrounding woods.

Towards dawn we were offered a lift by a passing padre driving an amphibious VW. We had not even the time to ask him where he was going before three enemy aircraft swooped low out of the clouds and raced along the road strafing everything within sight. The car blew up and we saw the obliging padre no more.

From that moment on, luck was against us. About a mile further down the road we were surprised by a patrol of motorised MPs, who promptly arrested us as deserters.

'Deserters, my fanny!' said Porta, indignantly. 'We're looking for our regiment!'

This, it seemed, was exactly what everyone else claimed to be doing. We were thrown into the attics of a nearby farmhouse, where we found ourselves locked up in the company of fifty other unfortunates. They, too, had been picked up off the roads. Some were in a genuinely dazed condition; some had been wandering aimlessly about the countryside, some had been caught pillaging, while others undoubtedly had been in search of their own companies. It appeared that we were all indiscriminately condemned to death.

'Bloody greased lightning,' said one man, bitterly. 'Don't stop to ask you no questions, they just stick a bleeding label on you and that's your lot, you've had it, mate.'

He was quite correct. Only a couple of minutes after our arrival, a Feldwebel appeared and solemnly pinned pieces of card to our chests.

'What's all this?' said Tiny, indignantly.

Our informant waved a hand.

'Death, that's what that is ... Don't worry, we've all got 'em.'

The door opened and a couple of constables came in. They glanced round the room and beckoned to a man sitting by himself in a corner.

'Come on! We'll have you next, you look pretty knackered.'

The man was dragged out, we heard the sound of shots, the sound of tramping feet, and the constables returned. This time they went off with a loudly protesting sergeant. We found we could count up to fifty-three before the shots were fired, and up to a hundred before they came back for their next victim. Occasionally the proceedings were interrupted by the delivery of a fresh prisoner. One Oberfeldwebel succeeded in killing a guard and throwing another down the staircase, but he himself was so seriously wounded they had to take him out on a plank of wood to be shot.

'Us soon,' I said.

'Bet they do me last,' said Tiny, with simple pride, as he flexed his gigantic muscles.

We both turned to look at Porta, but for once he remained silent.

'Are you thinking of something?' I inquired, hopefully.

'What is there to think about?' he retorted.

I shrugged my shoulders.

'I somehow never pictured it like this,' I said. 'I always fancied I should be killed outright ... step on a mine, something like that ... Funny how it turns out, isn't it?'

'Bloody funny,' said Tiny.

At that moment the two constables returned. They looked round the room and their glance flickered over me, passed on, returned briefly to me and finally settled on someone else.

'That was a close shave,' I said, as they bundled their victim through the door.

'Your turn next,' suggested Tiny.

'Take a bet?' I said.

Suddenly, from somewhere outside, we heard the familiar sound of tank tracks. We stampeded to the window, but before we could reach it there was the thunderous crash of cannon fire, followed by the rapid typewriter clacking of a machine-gun. We could see nothing through the window, it was too high and too small. Tiny hoisted himself up into the rafters, kicked a hole through the thatch roof and pushed his head out.

'What's going on?'

'What's happening?'

'What is it?'

We all clamoured round him, demanding information.

'It's the bleeding Russians!' said Tiny. 'Bleeding Cossacks galloping all over the place ... couple of tanks just gone through—whole village is on fire——'

'Let's make a break for it!' shouted Porta, hurling himself at the door.

Tiny and a large Feldwebel set their shoulders to it and went crashing through. At the foot of the stairs lay a constable with a bullet through his head. Tiny snatched up his sub-machine-gun and we poured through the door. It was the Feldwebel who called us back.

'How the hell far do you think you're going to get without your papers?' he yelled after us. 'No papers and red labels pinned on your chest ... you must be raving bloody mad!'

The rest of the crowd went streaming off, pell-mell in a panic. Only the three of us turned and hesitated.

'All very well to talk,' said Porta, pulling off his condemned label and throwing it into the trampled snow, which had been churned up by the tanks and the Cossack horses. 'They took our papers off us when they brought us in.'

'Well, you're buggered without 'em, that's for sure. No papers and you're a goner in this war.'

'You got yours?' demanded Tiny, aggressively.

'No...' The Feldwebel stood frowning, then suddenly snapped his fingers. 'Hang on a minute! Give me that thing!'

He grabbed the gun from Tiny, moved back into the house with the three of us close on his heels, walked down the passage and pointed silently to a closed door.

'In there,' he mouthed. 'I reckon that's where they've put 'em.'

A burst from the sub-machine-gun and the door crashed

open. Another burst, and three astonished constables fell open-mouthed from their chairs. We found a whole stack of papers in a drawer. Our own were fortunately near the top of the pile.

'Best set fire to the place,' advised the Feldwebel. 'Just in case . . .'

'In case what?' said Tiny, looking vacant.

'In case some nosey parker comes along and sees our names on one of their lousy lists! You want to be picked up and shot in six months' time, all because we didn't finish the job properly?'

We left the farmhouse in flames and set off along the street, now deserted.

'You coming our way?' said Porta.

'Which way's that?'

'Back to our company, if we can find it.'

'Oh no! No more war for me, thank you very much. I've been in this business a hell of a long time—too bloody long, I sometimes think. I used to be with the SA in the old days . . .' He shook his head. 'I've had a belly full, I don't mind telling you. This little lot's just about finished me.'

'So what'll you do?' I said.

'Go over to the other side, I reckon. Find the Russians and give myself up. I'd sooner see out the war in a prison camp than go on like this.'

'They don't take prisoners,' said Porta. 'They'll shoot you.'

'Or drag you along behind a horse,' added Tiny, eagerly. 'I seen 'em do that to a chap one time.'

The Feldwebel shrugged.

'I'll have to take my chance.'

'Well, all the best,' said Porta, without much hope in his voice. 'I'm as sick of it as you are, but I don't fancy a prison camp. Leastways, not a Russian one . . . Now, an opportunity to get across the Don, I wouldn't say no to that!'

'Get across the Don?' The Feldwebel laughed. 'You'd never make it. You'd freeze to death on the steppe before you'd even been gone twenty-four hours. Even the wolves can't survive out there. They come down into the villages and scavenge for food. And if you think it's cold now, you just wait until the temperature drops to fifty degrees below zero and see how you like it! Enough to freeze the balls off a brass monkey! You'll be thinking of me in my prison camp . . .'

'With a bullet through your head,' said Porta.

We shook hands and went our separate ways. We never did

learn what happened to the Feldwebel, though we often had cause to remember his words.

About half a mile out of the village we caught up with a small group of wounded men crawling back to find their regiments. We stayed with them and were joined later, at varying intervals along the road, by other stragglers, until we became quite a sizeable group.

Some hours later, at a place called Rotokina, we fell upon familiar faces. The Company was there but they had no time to welcome us back for our arrival was the signal for the Russians to launch yet another attack, and almost immediately orders came through that we were to withdraw to new positions further south.

A government must take care that its people are not irrevocably swept away in the drunken delirium of heroics.

Adolf Hitler, *Mein Kampf*

The commanding officer of the 71st Infantry Division, General von Hartmann, had given the order for a subterranean village to be constructed near Zaritza. The task was entrusted to the 578th Engineers, and they in their turn enlisted the help of the two thousand Russian civilians who were held prisoner in that area. They were put to work as slave labour, women and children, old men and idiots, the sick and the dying. Seventy-five per cent never survived to see the result of their efforts.

The village was called 'Hartmannsdorf', and extravagant rumours were rife throughout the whole of the Sixth Army. The general's bunker, it was said, had four rooms and a bath and had been furnished with articles stolen from the museums of Stalingrad. There was a chandelier and a four-poster bed, thick carpets and rugs on the floor, oil paintings and crystal vases and a whole library of precious books. The general's Division had been the first to enter Stalingrad, and it was naturally assumed they had laid hands on all the valuables they could find.

In addition, the village was reputed to have its own flour mill and two silos full of grain; a poultry farm with six thousand chickens; a herd of over a thousand cows; stables containing one hundred and thirty-eight thoroughbred horses; a dairy and a bakery.

Certain it was that the general and his staff could be seen most mornings enjoying themselves on horseback in the countryside surrounding Zaritza. It was a bewildering sight for the soldiers who made their painful way back into the town from distant battlefields. Men weak with hunger, men gravely wounded, men half dead with typhus, looked upon the well-fed general and his plump and healthy staff and wondered if they were ghosts from the past.

Hartmannsdorf flourished until the middle of January 1943, but the 71st Infantry Division was wiped out of all practical existence some time previously. It was in January that von Hartmann called up the remnants, gathered them together and marched bravely out of his village to launch a last desperate attack upon the enemy. It had not been the general's idea to

151

make heroes of the remaining few. The orders had come from Berlin.

'We are but pawns,' said von Hartmann, grandly. 'The Führer disposes of us as he will.'

TEN

GENERALS' CAKE-WALK

A portly Russian general, flanked by two sergeants, came towards us bearing a flag of truce. Our orders were to shoot all envoys on sight, but after a second's hesitation Captain Glaser told us to hold our fire. The Russian general moved closer. He was a big man, over six feet tall with powerful chest and shoulders, hanging belly and sturdy legs. His face was harsh and furrowed, his small blue eyes pitiless as the Russian winter.

As they approached, one of the sergeants tossed across a white sack. We picked it up gingerly and looked inside ... Food!

'A present from the Soviet people,' said the general, in good German. 'I am instructed to offer you terms for a capitulation. The offer to remain open until 1800 hours, after which time I am instructed to inform you that we shall launch a massed attack of tanks and artillery. You understand, of course, what that would mean, Captain?'

Not only the captain: we all understood. A massed Russian attack would completely annihilate us.

'From midnight onwards,' pursued the general, with a bland smile of anticipation, 'we shall take no prisoners and accept no surrender.'

Captain Glaser bowed his head in silent acceptance. Whichever way you looked at it, it was the end of the great German victory in Russia.

'On the other hand,' said the general, replacing his smile by a severe frown of discouragement, 'if the offer is accepted then each of your soldiers will be given the same ration of food as is given to our own troops. Your sick and your wounded will receive the necessary treatment.' He smiled again, showing a row of needle-sharp teeth. 'We know that you are short of food and medicine.'

Already, from the corner of my eye, I could see Porta conducting his own brand of negotiations with the enemy. I saw

152

Porta take out a packet of opium cigarettes and I saw one of the Russian sergeants hand over a packet of photographs. I wondered what thrills Porta could experience from pornographic photographs when we all stood to be wiped out of existence in less than twelve hours' time.

'Accept the offer and you will be treated honourably, as soldiers. Decline, and——'

The general made a brief gesture. Captain Glaser very slightly hunched his shoulders.

'I shall pass on your terms to General von Hartmann.'

'Let us hope he will prove a reasonable man. All this continued bloodshed can profit neither side.'

In a bunker near the railway line at Orlovka, a group of officers were seated in solemn conference round an old plank table. General von Hartmann of the 71st; General Stempel, commanding officer of the 176th Infantry Division; General Pfeffer, Colonel Crome and General Wultz.

'In my opinion,' von Hartmann was saying, 'we have no option but to fight until the last man goes down, and then to kill ourselves rather than fall into the hands of the enemy.' He looked round at his fellows. 'It is up to us to set an example.'

'I agree,' said Wultz. 'It would be a fine end.'

'And the men?' asked Colonel Crome.

The question fell heavily into the sudden silence. The generals looked covertly at Crome. He had been promoted to lieutenant when in command of assault troops at Arras. He had the Cross of Merit round his neck and his tunic was heavy beneath the weight of his other decorations. He was still absurdly young to be a colonel.

Crome cleared his throat and spoke again.

'What about the men?' he said.

'Colonel Crome,' said Pfeffer, 'never mind about the men. Our duty is quite clear. Our first thoughts now must be for Germany. However'—he turned to von Hartmann—'I cannot agree that we should kill ourselves. We must die, yes! But not by our own hands ... What I propose,' he said, his eyes gleaming with an almost childlike pleasure, 'is that we ourselves should lead the men into battle ... March at their head with bayonets fixed! What a way to go, gentlemen! What a way to be remembered!'

'Splendid! Splendid!' cried Stempel, quite carried away by the glory of it all. 'Drums and trumpets! What a spectacle! I find it most edifying!'

'Think,' urged Pfeffer, 'of the monuments they would erect to our memory. Never before, in the history of our nation, has such an attack taken place! They were led by their generals, bayonets gleaming in the sunlight ...'

'Beautiful!' sighed Stempel. 'I can see it all ... I only wish I could be there when they describe the scene to the Führer ...'

'Never mind all that,' said von Hartmann, irritably. 'What about the details?'

'Ah yes!' Pfeffer leaned forward, eyes eagerly gleaming. 'I have it all planned. I have it all worked out. I thought we should honour the occasion by wearing our dress uniforms——'

'The ones we brought with us to celebrate our victory,' said von Hartmann, dryly.

'And this, too, will be a victory in its own way!' cried Pfeffer. 'How glorious, how honourable, how——'

He broke off in annoyance as a Feldwebel arrived, followed by Captain Glaser. They saluted. The Feldwebel laid a white sack on the table and took a respectful pace backwards.

'What is this?' asked von Hartmann, distastefully.

'Bread and sausages, sir.'

'Bread and sausages?' Von Hartmann looked round rather wildly at his colleagues. 'Bread and *sausages*, Captain? Have you lost your head?'

'No, sir. It's a gesture from the Russians. I have to report that General Woronow of the Third Armoured Division has offered us favourable terms for capitulation. The offer is open until 1800 hours. If we don't accept it by then they're going to fling all they've got into one final attack.'

The generals remained silent and stunned. Only Colonel Crome seemed capable of speech.

'And if we do accept?' he said.

'General Woronow assures me that we shall be treated with honour. The officers can retain their arms and the men will be issued with rations of food. Our sick and wounded will be taken care of.'

Colonel Crome raised an eyebrow and glanced at his colleagues.

'The Russians,' pursued Captain Glaser, 'are as anxious as we to bring the hostilities to an end.'

This remark brought the generals' heads up in one sharp movement. General Pfeffer banged on the table with his hand.

'How dare you come to us with such disgraceful propositions! How dare you hold converse with the enemy! Even to

154

contemplate surrender makes my blood run cold with shame! Has not the Führer said he expects each man to fight to the very end, no matter what the final outcome?' He lifted his head, proudly. 'For my part, I intend not to disappoint him. Others, of course, may do as they like. I shall stand firm.'

'We have already agreed on a course of action!' snapped von Hartmann. 'Pray let us have no more histrionics!' He turned back to Captain Glaser. 'As for you, I wonder you have the effrontery to show yourself before us. Surrender to these half-baked barbarians——'

'Out of the question!' cried Stempel, hearing his drums and trumpets pounding in his ears. 'A Prussian officer would sooner die!' He leaned across the table and stared penetratingly at Captain Glaser. 'In any case, what were you doing parleying with the Russians? You know the orders! Why didn't you shoot the bastards?'

'It was difficult, sir. On the spur of the moment, like that . . . it was difficult to make up one's mind. I thought perhaps——'

'You *thought*?' broke in Stempel, incredulously. 'Hell and damnation, it's not your duty to *think*, Captain! It's your duty to carry out orders!'

'A clear case of contempt,' said von Hartmann.

General Pfeffer nodded. He picked up his gaily decorated helmet and settled it on his head: a judge about to pronounce the death sentence.

'You know what this means, Captain?' He began solemnly to intone. 'In the name of the Führer and of the German people you are hereby condemned to face death by a firing squad for failure to carry out orders . . .'

Pfeffer and von Hartmann nodded their agreement. They were Prussian officers. Iron discipline, head before heart. It was the spirit of the old days under Frederick the Great.

The Feldwebel disarmed the captain, the guard was called up. They led him outside, into the snow. Minutes later and the German Army was another officer short. The firing squad left him where he fell, too weak to waste their energies digging a grave, too indifferent to death to feel any respect for the man they had shot.

Down in the depth of the bunker, the officers still sat round the table. Pfeffer still wore his golden helmet.

'All the same,' Colonel Crome was saying, 'we can hardly just ignore it. We shall have to take some sort of action . . .'

'Of course,' said von Hartmann, in quelling tones.

'So——'

General Stempel suddenly interrupted with a short cry of hysteria and snatched up the telephone. The others turned to watch. They listened in silence as he called up his division and crisply gave the order to attack the Russians immediately with every man they had. But they were unable to catch the reply:

'If you want to attack the bleeding Russians,' snarled a voice from the other end of the line, 'then get out there and attack them your bleeding self, you stupid old cunt!'

There was a click, and the line went dead. Stempel sat back, pale and gasping. He had not yet been able to grasp the fact that his division had for some forty-eight hours consisted of no more than sixty men under the command of a lieutenant. In his swiftly deteriorating mind he still saw himself at the head of a great body of men.

Von Hartmann leaned forward.

'Do you think that was quite wise?' he inquired.

Stempel made a strangulated choking noise and abruptly left the room.

'How very odd,' said Pfeffer.

Back in his own quarters, Stempel screamed for his batman.

'Get me out of this and into my dress uniform!'

'Your—*dress* uniform, sir?'

'Do what I say!' shrieked Stempel.

Five minutes later, arrayed in his pearl-grey trousers with the red stripe, in his green tunic with the gold braid, Stempel called his two ordnance officers to hear his last words.

'The men have betrayed me,' he said, in low, shaking accents. 'I have no alternative but to take my life. And so I bid you farewell, gentlemen. We shall not have died in vain at Stalingrad. History will remember us ... Heil Hitler!'

He picked up his revolver, closed his mouth round the barrel and pulled the trigger. The two officers stood frozen in a stiff salute, the tears rolling unchecked down their faces.

Two hours after Captain Glaser had been shot and General Stempel had committed suicide, a trio of generals stepped out on to the snow-covered steppe. They were dressed up as if for a parade. Their gold trappings glittered and winked, the red stripe on their trousers shone abroad like a beacon.

'Hallo, hallo!' said Porta, as he caught sight of them. 'Here comes the reserve ...'

'What're they poncing about like that for?' demanded Tiny. 'Might just as well get a loudspeaker and tell the flaming Russians they're on their way.'

The Old Man gravely shook his head.

'Something funny's up,' he said. 'When you get the brass hats strolling about on the battlefield like that, you can bet your life they're going to make a mess of things.'

The generals trod solemnly towards us. They looked like something out of a light opera, we could hardly take our eyes off them. Lieutenant Keit, still young enough and inexperienced enough to be impressed by the sight of a bit of gold trimming, stepped smartly forward and saluted.

'Seventy-first Infantry Division, sir! Three officers, eighteen NCOs and two hundred and nine men.'

'Thank you, Lieutenant.' Von Hartmann raised a hand in the manner of one about to bestow a holy blessing. 'The time has come for you and your men to show that you are worthy of the great trust that the Führer has placed in you.'

'Sir!'

Lieutenant Keit sprang into the air, his arm flying up into another salute.

'We are all about to die, Lieutenant. True patriots and brave soldiers. History demands that we should be heroes. Let us not fail in our destiny.'

'Whatever you say, General.'

The lieutenant gave a nervous half grin of pride, quite overwhelmed that such an honour should befall him. Von Hartmann and the others then turned and began casually to stroll out into the middle of no-man's-land. We were so amazed that it was several seconds before even Porta found his tongue.

'Well, God rot my perishing toe-nails!' he exclaimed. 'You ever seen the like of that before?'

'They've lost their bleeding marbles,' said Tiny, staring with mouth agape. 'Dressed up like a dog's dinner ... they don't stand a chance, they'll be picked off in no time ...'

'What's the point of it all?' I demanded.

As we watched, von Hartmann nonchalantly unslung his rifle from his shoulder. His companions followed suit. They moved with the same air of alert precaution as men on safari; no more, no less. They seemed blissfully unaware that Russian snipers lurked along the borders of their territory ...

Von Hartmann's rifle suddenly cracked. A Russian soldier catapulted into the air. Back in our dug-out, we gave a suppressed cheer. A German general stepping it out towards the enemy lines and actually firing a rifle!

'Must have been a fluke,' hissed Porta, jealously.

Seconds later, von Hartmann bagged another Russian. Within the space of the next five minutes he had accounted for three more. All this with a common rifle, such as we suspected he had not handled for a good many years! Porta became so enthusiastic he began shouting aloud.

The generals went on their way, strung out in a line. Pfeffer and von Hartmann and Wultz. They seemed to be enjoying themselves. They were firing indiscriminately at everything that moved, shadows, snowflakes, trees and Russians, and Wultz laughed aloud every time he squeezed the trigger.

But such sport could not last indefinitely. The odds were outrageous, and already the smooth surface of the snow was being churned into divots by enemy gunfire. The three generals prowled on regardless, amiably boasting of their individual scores. Back in the dug-out, we laid bets on the winner. Pfeffer was in the lead at the moment, with von Hartmann a decent second. Wultz was trailing a little. His enthusiasm was boundless, but his aim was poor.

'Who'd have thought it?' muttered Porta, at my side. 'Who'd have bloody thought it?'

For months, now, the German radio had been claiming that the generals were fighting side by side with the men. Until this moment we had always regarded it as a master-stroke of comedy, designed to give the troops a good belly laugh. But the laugh, so to speak, was now very much on the other cheek.

General von Hartmann was the first to succumb to the inevitable. We saw him sink groaning to his knees, a hand pressed into his side. He raised his rifle, attempted a final gesture of defiance, but before he could fire he was blown into the air by an exploding shell.

General Pfeffer was the next to go. He suddenly plummeted forward, headfirst in a straight line to the ground. His helmet, with its gold tracery, fell off his head and rolled a few yards into a snowdrift. We saw a Russian soldier crawl out of his hole, snatch it up on the end of his bayonet and covetously withdraw. A general's helmet was a precious prize indeed and would doubtless make its new owner a rich man before the day was out.

General Wultz was shot in the back and lay screaming and writhing on the ground. Two men were sent out to retrieve him. One of them was killed outright, the other received a bullet in the hip on the way back. The general died within seconds of being rescued.

Lieutenant Keit, in a burst of naïve enthusiasm, called for volunteers to recover the bodies of Pfeffer and von Hartmann. Not a man stepped forward. Who cared about a couple of dead generals? We listened dispassionately while the lieutenant abused us for traitors and cowards, and we watched without very much interest as he and a fool of a sergeant-major crawled out into no-man's-land. The sergeant-major caught a bullet in the head before he had gone more than a few yards. The lieutenant came back alone in a furious temper.

At dawn came the promised attack. In the vanguard were a solid mass of T34s; forbidding, prehistoric shapes, like an army of mechanised dinosaurs. We were powerless against them. We had nothing left to fiight them with and they ran straight over the top of us, crushing men and equipment as they came, meeting no resistance.

After the tanks came the infantrymen with sub-machine-guns and rifles. Row upon row of them, elbow to elbow, running towards us. They had no need to break their tight-packed formation, they met with none but the most fragmentary opposition.

The few of us who had survived the first onslaught leapt in terror from one hole to the next, sweating, slipping, gasping, faint with fear and hunger, panic-stricken and helpless. I tripped and fell, and lay sobbing with fright in the snow. The straps of my pack were cutting into my shoulders, rubbing them raw, and I had lost my helmet as I scrambled out of the path of an oncoming tank. We were the hunted now, a few frightened sheep pursued by a massive pack of howling wolves, and nowhere we could run.

Gregor leapt out of a nearby shell hole and gave me a vicious kick in the ribs as he dived past me.

'Get up, you lousy swine! Get up and fight!'

My muscles responded instinctively to the command, without my mind or my will having anything to do with it. They sprang up with a strength I never suspected them of possessing, and they carried me fast in Gregor's wake.

I crouched panting at his side, in a slight dip in the ground. Over the top of a snowdrift we fired into the midst of some oncoming Siberians. The recoil of the heavy guns pounded against our shoulders, bruising the muscles, but we went on firing and hardly noticed it. Sheer desperation gave us some sort of manic strength, and for a moment the Siberians hesitated and fell back. Gregor jerked his head.

'Let's get out of here!'

Bent double, we fled across the snow-covered ground, straight into the path of some approaching tanks. We flung ourselves into a shell hole and crouched there, praying we had not been spotted. The firing of the heavy cannons chewed up the ground on either side of us. One of the tanks was making straight for our puny sanctuary.

'Down!'

Gregor gave me a tug and we clung together in the bottom of the shallow pit. They must have seen us, they were aiming right at us. The first shot flew over our heads, the second was so close we could feel the wind as it zipped past. And all the time the great white monster was coming nearer. The ground was shaking beneath its twenty-six tons of steel.

'Jump!' I shouted.

But we didn't jump. We just caught each other's hands and held on tight like children, crouching paralysed in our hole as we waited for death.

From a short way ahead we heard the chilling shrieks of men in agony as the T34 claimed its first victim. I saw the barrel of the cannon, and then the belly of the tank itself, rearing upwards and over us, poised to strike. In that second, without even thinking, I snatched up a magnetic mine and hurled it under the body of the creature. Gregor and I flung ourselves flat with our hands pressed over our ears. There was no time to speculate whether the mine would stick: it either did or it didn't, and if it didn't we should probably never know about it.

With a great roar, the tank exploded. Flames shot over our heads, flying debris filled the air and rained down upon us. We rolled ourselves in the snow, and Gregor peered over the top of the hole and fell back again in a fresh spasm of terror. A second tank passed by, so close we could have reached out and patted it. After the tank came running feet and swiftly moving khaki legs. Russian infantry. We remained where we were. There was really nothing else we could do.

One pair of feet stopped running. Their owner had evidently spotted our bodies. We held our breath and lay still. I received a vicious blow in the kidneys; Gregor's head was trodden down deep into the snow. We bit our lips until they bled, but we made no sound. I could hear the heavy breathing of the soldier, and I expected that at any moment he would use his bayonet, just to make sure. But no, thank God, he was in too much of a hurry to catch up with his companions. He turned and ran off.

'Tschort wosmy!' he remarked, in some scorn, as he departed.

Painfully, Gregor and I screwed ourselves out of the snow. Gregor was red in the face and half suffocated. I felt that at least one of my kidneys was probably ruptured.

We remained crouched in our foxhole. It was dangerous even to raise your head, and quite useless to contemplate surrender. The Russians were remaining true to their threat and taking no prisoners. The generals who could have saved our lives had indulged in a form of ostentatious suicide, and left the rest of us to fight it out. Those generals had never known what it was to suffer. They had never known the gnawing, gut-twisting agonies of constant hunger; they had never been cornered in a shallow shell hole with the belly of an enemy tank poised over their heads; they had never been exposed twenty-four hours on end, in thin summer uniforms and sheets of newspaper, to wind and snow and air so cold that it cut deep into your lungs with a sharp, knife-edge pain every time you drew breath. They had gone plump and padded to meet their fate, and even in death they had been cushioned from the real horrors of warfare.

Gregor suddenly nudged me.

'Siberians,' he mouthed.

I turned and saw them coming. Our most dreaded enemies. They ran heavily, clumsily, through the snow, their sturdy bodies bloated like waterlogged bread rolls in their quilted uniforms, their faces blue with cold beneath their thick fur helmets. One would have said, at first glance, a band of jolly farmers out for a cross-country run ... only their walking sticks were rifles, and their rallying cries were, 'Kill! Kill! Kill!'

No German is an innocent German; neither those who are on the point of death nor those about to be born. The master race must be exterminated. We must be fanatical in order to kill the fanatics. Kill, kill, kill ...

Gregor and I turned and fired. We stood no chance, but years of experience imposed their will upon us. And for one moment the Siberians hesitated. They stopped in their tracks as we stood and fired. They had not expected to meet death in their moment of triumph ...

Hitler's worst enemies could scarcely dispute the advantages already gained from a restored civilisation.

The Times, London, 24.7.1933

Seen from behind, the lieutenant-colonel looked to be drunk. He staggered and rolled, his shoulders slumped forward, his head hung down, his gait was slurred and uncertain. Only those who watched his approach could see that his wrists were tied in front of him and that he was evidently still dizzy from a fierce blow on the head, which had torn open part of his scalp and caused the blood to run down into his eyes. His sparse grey hair was matted. His uniform was torn and filthy.

After the lieutenant-colonel came three other officers: the colonel's adjutant, a major and a paymaster-general. They were all in a similarly distressed condition, and they all had their wrists tied together with pieces of barbed wire.

A group of SS men, rifles tucked beneath their arms, hustled the condemned men into position. The clear moonlight illuminated the scene and picked out the sinister death's-head emblems in a tracery of silver.

In the centre of the square was an oak tree. Beneath the oak tree had been placed four chairs. A few sleepy soldiers, pulled from their beds and bidden to attend, stood shivering, yawning round the gallows.

A Stumbannführer strutted self-importantly before the doomed officers.

'Well, you bunch of yellow-bellied traitors! If you've anything to say, you'd better hurry up and say it. Now's the time, because you won't be given another chance in this world ... And make it brief, nobody's interested in it but you.'

The lieutenant-colonel pulled himself tremblingly to his full height and raised his bloodied head.

'I am innocent of all the charges,' he said, in tones that indicated it was not the first time he had made the protestation. 'I have always done my duty. I have never asked for anything for myself. I should not have——'

'Enough!' barked the Sturmbannführer. 'We're not here to listen to your lies!' He turned, sneering, to the others. 'Well? What about you? You want to add your bleats to his?'

The major looked across boldly at him, with clear blue eyes that seemed indecently naked in their hostility.

'A band of perverts and sadists is running this country! Sick men, the lot of you ... emotionally retarded and mentally degraded, with twisted minds and filthy habits. Under anyone else but Hitler you'd all be locked up in a lunatic asylum, where you belong.'

'That's enough of that drivel!' The Sturmbannführer, visibly shaken by the major's words, snapped his fingers at an Oberscharführer. 'Get them ready.'

The four officers were hoisted on to the chairs. Expert hands slipped lengths of rope round their necks, tied the knots, fixed the slack to a branch of the tree. The Oberscharführer stepped forward, a smile of anticipation on his face. Gustav Kleinkamp was an SS executioner of distinction. He claimed to be holder of the world record in hangings, and no one disputed his right to the title. The Sturmbannführer nodded, and Kleinkamp, with a fine precision and an almost theatrical sense of timing, swept away the chairs with a neat movement of the foot and bowed his head to some imaginary applause that seemed to ring in his ears.

The SS men stood watching as the bodies twitched and jerked at the ends of the rope. The soldiers went on yawning. They had seen it all before.

A few yards away, in the background, Theodor Eicke sat watching the scene through the window of a truck. The moon lit up his profile and he was seen to be smiling.

Gruppenführer Eicke enjoyed doing his duty. He could easily have surpassed Kleinkamp's record, had he not felt that the physical act of hanging a man was somewhat beneath an officer's dignity. Nevertheless, he could appreciate such zeal in an inferior. It was Eicke who had caused to be painted on the side of all vehicles in his division the words, 'WE WANT CORPSES NOT PRISONERS!' until General Model, his C-in-C, had indignantly ordered their removal.

Model was the only general of whom Eicke was reputed to stand in awe. He held all the others in cold contempt, which perhaps was not to be wondered at since he had early in his SS career crossed swords with no less a personage than General Field-Marshal Busch and gained the better of him. It was on 26th May 1940, and Eicke had committed the first of his many war crimes: he had enclosed a hundred British prisoners of war in a Belgian farmhouse and shot them one by one. Busch, almost as outraged as the British themselves must have been, had threatened a court-martial, and it was Himmler who had intervened on Eicke's behalf. Himmler had no particular wish to save Eicke's skin, but he felt the honour of the SS to be at stake and his own powers to be challenged.

'In any case,' he had scoffed, 'what's all the fuss about a few dead Englishmen? Who asked them to interfere in the first place? Why couldn't they have stayed at home in their miserable little island and leave us alone?'

From that day on, Eicke had felt himself to be a person apart. It seemed to him that by his intervention Himmler had given him carte blanche to carry out what atrocities he would. He was not bound by the general laws of humanity as others were.

ELEVEN

CHRISTMAS ON THE STEPPE

For five days a snowstorm had blown and howled over the Volga. It came to us all the way from Kazakhstan and it whipped itself up into a fury as it raged across the steppe. The Russians were accustomed to it and equipped to deal with it, and the wind blew in their favour. We Germans were terrorised by it and it left in its wake a long trail of corpses with every fresh gust that hit us.

The few survivors from the massive Russian attack had crawled for comfort into a bunker near the banks of the Volga, and there we huddled day after day, listening to the wind and the rumbling of our empty bellies. Faces were stark and grey beneath their helmets; uniforms hung in limp rags from skeletal frames. We had discovered that hunger was more demoralising than either fear or defeat.

Reichsmarschal Goering had promised Hitler to send his aeroplanes over to the stranded Sixth Army and drop food supplies to us, but Hitler had not thought to ask him where the aeroplanes were to be found. Even we, isolated as we were, knew that Goering could not keep his promise. There were no aeroplanes. So what was Hitler counting on? Goering and his non-existent aircraft? Or God and his angels? Either way, it seemed as if we were doomed. Goering was fallible and God was no longer with us. For many weeks past he had been on the side of the enemy. Even that rabid anti-Communist in London, Winston Churchill, was lending his aid to the Soviets. Nobody loved the Russians, but everybody hated the Germans.

All along the front the enemy loudspeakers shouted their defiance:

'Stalingrad has become a German graveyard! A German death every minute!'

For once, propaganda was the voice of truth. But it was not the Russians who were killing us, it was the weather and the lack of food. Men dropped dead in their tracks. Literally dropped dead. One minute you would be talking to someone, the next minute he could be lifeless at your feet. Men dug themselves holes in the snow, seeking for warmth, and were discovered stiff and frozen next morning. We found tanks which had run out of petrol, with their crews dead inside them. Officers leaned against the parapet of trenches, giving orders to their men, and faded away to death in mid-sentence. Men died overnight inside the bunker and no one realised that the brittle, twiglike heap beneath the threadbare blanket was now a corpse.

'Stalingrad a German graveyard ... a German death every minute ...'

Our little group was probably luckier than other isolated bodies of survivors in that we had two excellent foragers and scroungers in the person of Tiny and Porta. Whenever we were on the point of foundering, that redoubtable pair would pick up their rifles and an old jute sack and slip off into the night on a food-hunting mission. They never once came back empty-handed. Sometimes it was only the putrefying bones of a dead horse, but with careful preparation even they made enough soup to preserve us for another few days. On one occasion they turned up with thirty-seven tins of assorted food and half a duck which they had stolen from beneath the noses of the enemy. They had not set out with the intention of stealing from the Russians, not even Tiny and Porta were as outrageous as that; but they had lost their way in the dark and ended up behind Russian lines, and while they were there it had seemed silly not to take advantage of the situation. Unfortunately, two of our men died as a result of over-eating ...

'Bloody gluttons!' grumbled Tiny, as we slung their bodies outside.

The whole of the German front line, such as it now was, was perpetually bathed in flames. Our bunker trembled beneath the constant pounding of heavy fire, and those survivors who were still existing in scattered trenches and dug-outs found themselves literally blown from their shelters like dead leaves in a high wind. Occasionally men lost their minds and could be seen galloping along in a hail of shells and machine-gun fire, waving their arms in the air and laughing happily like children.

We were no longer a regiment, scarcely even a company; simply a gathering of remnants brought together for the final days of Stalingrad.

After a while we were joined by an SS Unterscharführer. He staggered exhausted into the bunker and promptly took possession of Porta's camp-bed. That bed was now Porta's most-prized belonging. He had picked it up from an abandoned farmhouse on one of his foraging trips, and when he was not using it himself he was in the habit of letting it out at so much per hour. The sight of a stranger, and an SS man at that, lying on his bed without paying the fee, was altogether too much for Porta. He turned to Tiny.

'Get him off,' he said.

Tiny shambled amiably across the room, lifted the man bodily and dropped him to the floor, where, to everyone's intense astonishment, he continued to sleep and to snore as if nothing had happened.

The district was populous that day. Only minutes after the Unterscharführer's arrival, the door was kicked open by a booted foot and an SS general stormed in, sub-machine-gun held at the ready. He stood in our midst like the Colossus of Rhodes, glaring down upon us, his face blue with cold beneath his fur bonnet.

'Well? Lost your tongues, have you? Who's in command here? Who's the most senior?'

'I am, sir.'

The Old Man stepped forward.

The Colossus looked him up and down and his lip rose into a sneer.

'And who are you?' he asked.

'Feldwebel Beier, sir.'

'Which regiment?'

'Twenty-seventh Panzers.'

'How many men have you got here?'

'Seven NCOs, forty-three men ... We've also got one bazooka, two sub-machine-guns, six light machine-guns and one flame-thrower.'

'Ammunition?'

'Yes, sir.'

'Well? How much?'

The Old Man just perceptibly shrugged his shoulders.

'I couldn't say exactly, sir.'

He might have added, and what the hell does it matter, anyway? If the Russians attacked us, we certainly had not enough to defend ourselves for more than a few minutes. The general kicked a tin helmet across the floor, and the sleeping Unterscharführer awoke with a resentful start.

'Hell's bells, Feldwebel! We're still fighting a war, you know!'

'If that's what you call it, sir,' said the Old Man, respectfully.

The general changed his tack.

'What are you doing here, anyway? Why aren't you with your regiment? You're not serving any useful purpose skulking here like this.'

'The regiment doesn't exist any more, sir. We're all that's left.'

The general made an impatient noise with his tongue and turned to stare rather piercingly at the Unterscharführer, who had risen to his feet and was hovering at the back of the group.

'What's that man doing here?' He pointed a finger. 'You! Unterscharführer! Get back to your own battalion! You have no place here!'

The Unterscharführer smiled rather slyly.

'Haven't got a battalion, sir. We were surrounded at Rynok.' He drew a finger across his throat. 'Only lasted half an hour. I was buried under a load of corpses, they didn't spot me.'

The general raised an eyebrow.

'That's your story, Unterscharführer. It remains to be seen what a court-martial will make of it. To me it sounds suspiciously like desertion.'

He unbuttoned a top pocket and pulled out a large black cigar. Julius Heide at once rushed forward with a light and received a kick in the shins on his return.

'Arse-licker!' hissed Tiny, venomously.

The general walked over to Porta's bed and began to spread out a map. He beckoned towards the Old Man as he did so.

'Where was your last position, Feldwebel?'

'Near Kotluban, sir.'

'Kotluban, eh?' The general found it on the map. 'Thirty-three miles ... hm ...' He frowned, pulled out a pencil and began making a series of marks. And then looked up gloatingly at the Old Man. 'Feldwebel, perhaps you will kindly clarify something for me. Here is Kotluban'—he pointed to it—'and here'—he pointed again—'is a Soviet Guards regiment. Show me exactly where your positions were, if you please.'

'Here, sir. Near this wood. Facing away from the Volga ... We were part of the 16th Panzer Division.'

'That is as may be, Feldwebel! But it hardly explains to me how you succeeded in crossing the enemy lines in order to get from Kotluban to your present position!' He swung round on the Old Man. 'Am I to infer that you were issued with special passes signed by the Soviets?'

The Old Man pinched his lips disapprovingly together.

'If you mean, sir, that any of my men collaborated with the enemy or deserted their posts or anything of that nature, then I hope you'll pardon me saying that you're talking through the top of your brass hat! We leave that sort of behaviour to the officers, sir. The only man who went over to the Russians was Lieutenant Reiniger of the 79th Infantry Division. He was put in charge of the regiment, but he deserted before he'd been with us twenty-four hours. He not only gave away our positions he also——'

'That's quite enough, Feldwebel! Hold your tongue!'

The general slapped the Old Man hard across the face with his leather gauntlets. The Old Man breathed very deeply and remained where he was, but to everyone's surprise the Unter-scharführer suddenly bounded forward with a cry of rage and made straight for the general. He can hardly have been avenging the Old Man. We could only assume that his mind had snapped, and with it his instinct for self-preservation. Before he had even reached his intended victim, the general had snatched up his sub-machine-gun and pumped him full of bullets.

'Pity,' observed Porta. 'We'd hardly got to know him.'

The general glared across at us, eyes snapping in his hawk face.

'Well? Is there anyone else here who's tired of life? Because if there is, just let him step forward! I'll be happy to deal with him.'

We stood looking back at him; hating him, despising him, with murder in our hearts and our hands meekly by our sides. We had been too well trained. We had been Prussian slaves for too many years to break the habit of blind obedience. The idea of raising one's hand against a general was not one that came readily to mind.

'Very well!' He moved to the door, breathing heavily through dilated nostrils. 'Pick up your arms and follow me. You're under my command from now on.'

We left the bunker and took up positions along the Stalingrad–Pitomnok railway. On our way there we stumbled across the remains of a battery of howitzers, now half-heartedly manned by the only three survivors from the original group. The general swept them into our midst and commandeered the howitzers. We set them up and dug ourselves in, then settled down to wait. For what, we hardly knew. But the general had said wait, and so we waited. He was huddled into his greatcoat and had let down the flaps of his fur cap to cover his ears. The rest of us shivered with rattling teeth and frozen limbs in our holes in the snow.

At dawn, the enemy arrived. A convoy of T34s in search of trouble. We saw them breast the slope, hang for an instant in space, then come thundering down towards the railway line. They crossed over with no opposition. Our infantrymen fled from their holes before the great white monsters, and a few of them escaped. The tanks pounded after them, caught up with them, tossed them into the air, ground them into the snow, moved on implacably. Mounds of pulped and bloody flesh lay strewn in their wake.

Behind our camouflaged howitzers we crouched and waited. A man needed nerves of steel to sit tight while a row of monstrous great tanks bore down on him. My own nerves were of a pretty mediocre variety, and had it not been for the dogged presence of my companions on either side of me I should almost certainly have fled before the tanks were within striking distance. They rumbled on towards us. Nine hundred yards ... eight hundred ... seven hundred ... If we missed at the first opportunity, we should not be given a second. We should join our infantry companions as mutilated heaps of raw flesh in the snow.

The tanks seemed almost on top of us. They were gathering speed, evidently not yet suspecting our hidden presence.

'Fire!' shouted the Old Man.

The four big guns roared together. The moment had come, and we had not failed. The leading T34s were thrown into the air in a flaming mass of debris, and our fear abruptly left us. We even knew a certain exaltation. We had it in our power even now to destroy the enemy! We no longer noticed the cold, our nerve ends no longer trembled, our muscles no longer twitched with the tension of waiting. The oft-repeated gestures, loading and firing and loading and firing, were so familiar as to be part of us and to dispel our momentary terrors. The guns roared, the tanks drew back; torrents of flame burst out of the turrets, balls of burning metal were thrown after them and tossed up and down on jets of scorchingly hot air. Men were quickly reduced to blackened corpses, their mouths drawn back over their teeth in hideous charred grins. Nineteen tanks fell prey to our guns and the sky was hidden behind a great black umbrella of smoke.

There was a moment's respite. We were running dangerously short of ammunition, but the general had no intention of pulling out. We remained at our posts, waiting for the next onslaught.

They came straight at us this time. They had obviously spotted our position, and they rolled majestically forward in a hail of shells, in no particular hurry. No matter how many we wiped out, another always moved in to fill the gap.

Those infantrymen who had survived the first attack now came scurrying towards us from their shallow holes in the snow, taking shelter behind us as if some measure of safety lay in the big guns. But once the ammunition had gone we were as powerless as they, and the poor fellows were merely exchanging one hell for another.

I saw a young boy in twisted agony with a broken back. His tortured screams rose even above the roaring of the guns, temporarily blotting out all other sounds, but there was nothing we could do for him. There was no time to take out a revolver and put a bullet through him.

Russian shells were landing amongst us with increasing accuracy. The cries and yells of the wounded men were growing slowly to a nightmarish cacophany. I saw Big Paul from Cologne crumple up with his breast bone smashed and his ribs crushed in; I saw Corporal Duval from Sauerland collapse with his left arm hanging in shreds from a shattered shoulder; Sergeant Scheibe from Wupperthal had had both legs neatly severed below the knee; a shell exploded beneath the feet of Private Weiss from Breslau and reduced him immediately to a shapeless phantom of crushed bones and blood-splattered flesh.

The tanks continued relentlessly to stagger up the slope and tumble down towards us on the other side. How many more of them lay beyond the slope, we could only guess. In my imagination, I saw an endless line.

A shell scored a direct hit on Gregor's gun. The long cannon slewed round and had smashed off the head of his loader before the boy had time to duck. The body remained standing a few seconds with a fountain of blood spurting into the air. Gregor escaped injury but lost control of his nerves. He threw back his head and laughed and laughed, while the blood cascaded down his uniform. I had no time to slap him out of it, I was far too busy with my own affairs. When I glanced at him seconds later he was on his knees in the snow, his whole body shaken with sobs.

The attack stopped quite suddenly. The T34s veered round in the opposite direction and ploughed off through the snow. No more came over the ridge towards us. For several minutes we stood gaping, staring after them in imbecilic disbelief. Their victory had been assured, we could not possibly have held out for more than another quarter of an hour at the very most. And there they were, moving off into the snow, leaving us shaken but alive in the midst of our fallen companions, whose bodies were already growing stiff.

All round was the acrid smell of cordite, which burnt the throat and the lungs and made the eyes water and smart. I saw Gregor staggering to his feet and the Legionnaire grimacing with pain as the Old Man dressed a deep gash in his forehead. For once in his life he had been wearing his helmet. Without it he would certainly have been scalped. Across the sullied snow towards us came the general, followed by a group of silent, brooding soldiers. He waved an impatient hand towards the guns.

'Blow those things up, they're no more use to us! Reassemble down there, in the gorge.'

He strode off, leaving Porta and me to dispose of the howitzers. We set the charges, Porta lit the fuse and we ran off towards the assembly point in the gorge. Just as we reached it there was an almighty explosion and our anti-tank battery was no more. In a few hours all traces would have been covered by a fresh fall of snow.

It was thirty-eight degrees below zero. The wind, as usual, was howling across the steppe and blowing icy crystal chips into our raw faces. Whichever way you looked you encountered the glassy stare of a corpse, saw a stray arm or leg protruding from a drift, saw a trail of red over the snow. It seemed that the whole of the vast steppe had been turned into a graveyard.

At the head of the straggling column marched our SS general. His long coat was whipped about his legs by the wind, but his neck was protected by the upturned collar, his head was snug in its fur bonnet and his feet encased in stout leather boots. The man was, of course, quite mad. We had realised that almost straight away. He was a cold-blooded fanatic bent on fighting his way single-handed across Russia, and we poor fools were to be dragged at his heels as convenient, transportable fodder for the enemy guns.

We dug ourselves in again by the side of the Volga, at the foot of a triangle of steep hills. From there, we could see long columns of enemy troops on the march, crossing the frozen river, and the next day the heavy artillery opened up and the bombardment began. Four times I was blown from the shallow trench by the force of the blast. On the last occasion I had to be rescued by Porta, who made a quick sortie and hauled me back again. I was in such a state of shock that it was several minutes before I could manage to stand unaided.

The section in the neighbouring trenches were subjected to a barrage of napalm grenades. A long line of fire ran through the ranks and men clawed their way screaming out of the trenches with their hair and their clothes alight. The very snow itself seemed to be on fire. The smell of burning flesh filled our nostrils, impregnated our clothes and our skin, until the stench turned our stomachs and made us vomit.

I had succeeded in wedging myself beneath some blocks of concrete, and I set up my sub-machine-gun so that it pointed through a narrow fissure. Porta and Tiny were on either side of me, and we crouched together at the bottom of the trench chewing hungrily at a few hunks of dry bread, of the consistency of brick. The thought of ordinary bread, even stale, plain, mildewed bread, was an almost unbearable luxury.

As the enemy poured in to attack, the mists from the Volga came rolling towards us, shrouding the landscape in a chill, damp haze. For a few moments the panic and confusion were such that we fired blindly, not knowing whether it was friend or foe. And then, looming up out of the mist, came the squat, bloated forms of the Siberians, animated snowmen in their thick, white, padded costumes. We heard their raucous yells of encouragement, of death to the Germans and glory be to Stalin!

We beat off the first wave of the attack, but our fanatical general would give us no respite. With a wild shout, he was down the hill and chasing after the withdrawing enemy, and we had no option but to go running along with him like a stampede of silly frightened horses. The Siberians had evidently not expected such an act of madness on our part. They were taken off guard. Some stopped and fought, others scuttled back to their own lines, where their officers, demented like the general, promptly turned them round and sent them back again into our midst.

It was a chaotic skirmish in which I, for one, had very little idea what was happening. In the desperate, hand-to-hand crush, we swayed and fought over the bodies of the wounded, grinding them beneath our boots, drunk with blood, drunk with exhaustion, drunk with fear, strangling, clubbing and bayonetting.

We finally put them to flight and took possession of their bunker, although we were well aware that such possession could be purely temporary. We had not the strength to hold it against a full attack, and the Siberians would surely come back in force.

Meanwhile, we made the most of our stay by raiding the larder. The Siberians had left a fair supply of rations behind them and we descended like a horde of deprived vultures. I saw Tiny tearing with his front teeth at a lump of fatty bacon, while Porta raced about like a madman, hands flying in all directions, cramming as much as he could into his mouth until it bulged in two great pouches and he was hardly able to swallow; after which he began cramming his pockets, instead.

It was with the greatest reluctance, and only under severe pressure, that we consented to move out. The enemy were already closing in on us and we finally fled in a shower of shells.

From the far side of the Volga the heavy batteries opened up. The ground was trembling as if about to split open. The general bawled at us to keep moving, but we had more sense. All round us were exploding the dreaded napalm grenades, which tore a man's very lungs from his body, and we went to earth instantly. No use trying to run through such a storm. All you could do was find a hole and stay put, curled up at the bottom of it with your head well down. Anything on the surface was swiftly devoured by the engulfing sea of flame that swept the earth in the wake of the explosions.

I leaped with a shout of terror into a dug-out and landed on top of Porta. I knocked him off balance and we fell down together as the hot blast of the furnace blew over our heads.

The barrage lasted all night long, and all night long we remained crouched in our holes with our heads buried deep in the snow. Not even the calls of nature took men into the open.

Better a pair of sodden trousers than a mouthful of that killing air that hung overhead.

Strange that although we all knew the war was lost, we still never spoke of defeat. We never spoke of the past, and we rarely mentioned the present. It was always the future. Even now, deep in this well of seemingly endless misery, we clung stubbornly to life. Cold and starving, stinking, filthy and terrified, hounded aimlessly from one point to another across the bloodied steppe, scarcely any longer human, we nevertheless still believed ourselves to be men, and fought for our right to existence.

Towards morning, the firing quietened down and we began slowly to relax. Once or twice we cautiously raised our heads and sniffed the air. It smelt bad, but it would clear.

With the coming of dawn, three JU 52s suddenly appeared on the horizon. We turned our eyes up towards them and watched in disbelief as they came steadily nearer. They swooped down from the clouds, flying in wide circles, indifferent to the Russian anti-aircraft batteries or the possibility of enemy planes in the neighbourhood. They were evidently searching for us.

Whether they spotted us or whether they simply decided to jettison their load and return home, we neither knew nor cared. But the sky was suddenly full of parachutes, floating down like great yellow mushrooms before us, and at the end of each parachute was a large container. We became almost hysterical as we watched the slow descent. We danced up and down in the trenches, singing and shouting and hugging each other.

'Food!' roared Porta, at the top of his voice.

Before the general could make any attempt to stop us, we were over the parapet and racing towards those precious containers. We thought nothing of personal danger in that moment. Let the enemy hurl at us what they would, we were going to pick up our ration of food even if we died as we ate it! Each container should hold sufficient to feed an entire company. For the first time in weeks we were faced with the prospect of full bellies.

The anticipation was almost unbearable. It was as much as we could do to detach the containers and drag them back with us, instead of tearing them open on the spot.

'Nosh,' blubbered Porta, falling down into the trench.

His mouth was full of saliva, bubbling in tiny globules round his lips.

'Never again,' vowed Gregor, 'will I say a word against the

174

Air Force! God bless 'em!'

With one voice, we sent up a cheer for the brave pilots of those JU 52s. May they reach base safely, they deserved it! And three cheers for Himmler, too! Maybe the bastard wasn't as bad as he was painted.

Like children tearing open their Christmas stockings, we ripped apart the containers. My head was full of visions. Bright, mouth-watering visions in the garish colours of cheap comics. There were crudely pink sausages, great bloated things oozing fat and straining to bursting point in their glistening skins. There was a plump and succulent chicken, basted brown with a crackling skin. There were potatoes and milk, and bacon and bread, and cheese and biscuits and fresh fruit and lightly boiled eggs and coffee and caviar and——

The container fell open. The contents spilled out. There was a moment's shocked silence.

No sausages. No chicken. No bread, no milk, no bacon. Only a quantity of flea powder, a few sheets of notepaper and a vast stack of coloured photographs. Hitler and Himmler, Goering and Goebbels and all the rest of the trashy band.

The trenches rang with howls of rage and despair. Men wept and cursed and beat their heads in a frenzy against the hard-packed snow. We became violent in our disappointment, and we called upon a God we no longer believed in to strike Adolf Hitler dead for the trick he had played upon us.

The coloured photographs were scattered to the winds and carried on towards the Russian lines.

'Wipe your arse on Adolf Hitler!' bellowed Porta. 'That's all the swine's fit for!'

What the SS general made of it, we never even attempted to imagine. He watched us in grim-faced and tight-lipped silence and made no attempt to quell our jeers and catcalls. He was perhaps aware that to have done so would merely have incited us to revolt. We were in no mood to tolerate the prating of one of Hitler's officers.

We left our positions under cover of a snowstorm. With any luck, it would be several hours before the enemy discovered we had withdrawn.

On the road to Olowka, we began running into the occasional group of fugitives, fleeing from the tractor factory which was still somewhat precariously held in German hands. The general forced us to another halt and set up a barricade. We spent the next twenty-four hours shooting deserters. Those who gave in without a struggle were co-opted into our group. Any who attempted argument or excuses were despatched forthwith. All officers were shot on the spot and no questions asked.

We set off again at dawn the following day, our numbers swelled into quite a respectable column. A few miles further on, in a fold in the landscape, we came across a regiment of corpses. They were buried beneath a carpet of snow, but a myriad of bones, frozen into position, still appeared above the surface and pointed the way to the communal grave. We paused only long enough to check that they were German bones, then made our way to the great stone bunker, carved deep into the rocky face of the hillside, which had obviously served as the last refuge of the slaughtered regiment.

A carbide lamp still remained on a table and by its light we saw that we had entered into a house of the dead. The corpses were piled high round the walls, stretched out on the floor, propped up against tables and chairs, lying over and across each other. In a high-backed chair sat a lieutenant-colonel with his head thrown back. Upon examination he was found to have a bullet hole in the base of his skull. We looked significantly at one another: the NKVD had passed this way. On an operating table lay a doctor with his throat cut. Flung into a corner were two nurses. Porta looked at them regretfully and shook his head.

'Pity about that,' he said.

Exhausted, we flung ourselves to the ground, wherever we could squeeze ourselves in between a couple of corpses, and fell asleep, regardless of the filth and the stench. Even the general permitted himself the human weakness of closing his eyes.

Whether we slept five minutes or five hours, I never discovered. We were woken very suddenly by the trembling of the ground beneath us and the well-known sounds of tanks on the move. The Old Man reached out and extinguished the lamp, which we had left burning as we slept. For half an hour we crouched, silent and terrified amongst the corpses, while the tanks rolled past. They were very close to the bunker, travelling in the direction of Gumrak.

When it seemed that the last one had passed, and there had been no movement for almost fifteen minutes, the general stood up and jerked his head at us.

'All right! You've had your rest ... Pick up your weapons and follow me.'

We took with us all the food we could lay hands on, all the mangy, mouldering crusts of bread, all the rotting bits and pieces of unknown vegetable matter, all the putrefying scraps of meat, including a hunk that was strangely white and bloodless. The Old Man said it was human flesh, and looking at the hideous anaemic thing I was quite willing to believe him; but Porta, totally undaunted, tore off a mouthful and chewed it, savouring its flavour.

'What's it like?' I said, curiously.

Porta licked his lips.

'Not half bad! I reckon it must be topside of general ...' He turned and dug the Old Man in the ribs. 'If this is human flesh, mate, than all I can say is hold on to your skins when I get hungry again!'

The general impatiently motioned us forward. We marched, unmolested by Russians, until we came to a spot north-west of the railway line and a mile or so from Pestjanka. There, for no very apparent reason—except, perhaps, a manic desire on the general's part to meet up with he enemy—we dug ourselves in again.

Inevitably, before we had been there very long, the Russians discovered us and moved in to dislodge us. They came swinging towards us in tight ranks, stepping it out as if they were on the parade ground. They were easy enough to pick off, but the minute one man fell another came forward to take his place. They simply ignored the bodies, marching right over them. Sometimes they built them up into ramparts, sometimes they flung them as convenient bridges across the barbed wire, but however many we killed they still came on in vast numbers.

I was crouched in my snowhole beneath the remains of an American bulldozer. As I peered out, I saw a Siberian soldier running towards me. He was still some distance away, he didn't even know I was there, but I had him in my sights, I was aiming at the spot directly beneath the red star on his helmet ... I squeezed the trigger. On the soldier's chubby face appeared an expression of anguish and surprise. I could almost hear the thoughts running through his poor, stupid, confused head, in the seconds before he died. Had he been shot? Had he really been shot? Is that what it felt like? Was that his lot? Why was he here, what was he fighting for? What was he doing with a bullet through his brain, dying by the side of a strange river in a land that was not his own? Where were his wife and his children, his cows and his horses? Why was he lying spreadeagled in the snow, so far from home?

In the spring, when the snows melted and released him from

his frozen shroud, he would be piled into a great communal burial pit with a hundred thousand others. For the moment, he remained where he had fallen, trampled underfoot by his comrades.

We retreated along the side of the railway line. From a shell hole, a weak voice called out to me. I hesitated. A face was peering over the top, a crooked finger was beckoning. The face looked like a mask of badly applied rubber solution. It bulged and it wrinkled and it sagged. It was gunmetal in colour, except round the eyes, which were sunk deep inside great black holes. It was the face of a young officer. Cautiously, I approached him. He was almost up to his waist in what seemed a pool of blood. It was blood: as I stared down, I realised that both his legs had been crushed into a thick red purée. There was nothing I could do for him. I thrust a revolver into his outstretched hand and ran on. His voice came shrieking after me.

'Help me, soldier! Please help me! For God's sake, don't leave me here to die ...'

Perhaps I should have shot him myself. But it was already too late. From behind the cover of a bush, I watched, appalled, as a wandering Russian tank suddenly caught sight of the terrified man, trapped in his legless, dying body. It paused, very deliberately changed direction and went out of its way to demolish the shell hole. It turned once on its axis, slowly, savouring the sensation, and then continued on its interrupted path. Another filthy Fascist out of the way! Another Russian hero! If only Stalin could have been there to see how valiantly his troops were fighting.

Porta and I sprang at the same moment on to a slowly lumbering T34, which was flying a red flag from its aerial. We wrenched it off and hung it over the forward observation slit to obstruct the driver's vision, then clamped a couple of magnetic mines on the side of the tank and hurled ourselves into the snow.

Stalingrad, the communal grave ... Stalingrad, where one German soldier died every minute, while back in Germany a madman strutted and pranced and screamed himself hoarse ... FIGHT LAST MAN, LAST BULLET ... Unhappily for us, there were still enough fanatics willing to obey the manic injunction.

The 24th December found us outside the town of Dinitrijevka. It was Christmas Eve, and we received our present in advance: a mass infantry attack from the Russians. They came screaming across at seven o'clock in the morning and the struggle continued until three in the afternoon. It would hardly be true to say we repulsed them, we were barely holding our own, when for some reason they decided to withdraw. Doubtless they knew they had us in their grasp. They could afford to tease us a little, to play cat and mouse with us. We were theirs for the asking and they could move in at virtually any given moment and mop us up.

The sudden silence was unnerving. We felt instinctively that the abrupt withdrawal was merely a refinement of torture and presaged some new horrors for the morn. Our lunatic general refused to withdraw and we could do nothing better than huddle in our dug-outs and wait helplessly for the next attack.

On Christmas Day, at three o'clock—precisely the same time as they had withdrawn the previous day—the enemy returned. But not in force. Five T34s were all they sent. Five T34s in a line, moving across the snow towards us. From a loudspeaker on the leading vehicle came the stirring sound of a march. The five tanks proceeded in perfect formation towards the Third Section. There was nothing we could do to halt their advance. We were powerless, we had almost nothing left to fight with. No anti-tank guns, no flame-throwers, no heavy artillery, not even grenades.

At the last moment, the T34s turned in their tracks and set off at a tangent, away from the Third Section and towards the hitherto unsuspecting Second. From the loudspeaker came the strains of the Radetzky March. Solemnly, ponderously, deliberately, each tank came to a halt before a dug-out. Terrified men stared up at them, some too scared to move, some already scrambling out. The tanks rose up, came crashing down into the snow, pulping and pulverising, each tank turning slowly on its axis. That done, they casually mopped up the one or two who had escaped and went back the way they had come, soon disappearing in a cloud of snow.

We watched in silence. The silence of death. Not a voice spoke, not a shot was fired. The Second Section was no more, but twelve bloody heaps lay in the snow. And we sat back and waited.

The next day, at three o'clock, they returned. The same formation, the same music, the same cold precision. Another section disappeared. We buried our heads ostrich-like in the snow to muffle the sound of our companions' unearthly shrieks and to shield our eyes from the sight of their mangled corpses.

The long winter night was silent and full of terror. We thought we still heard the screams of the dying men, but it was only the wind howling across the steppe.

Towards dawn, a few random shells landed on the snow-covered slope behind us, presumably to make sure we were awake and ready to receive their propaganda outburst, which came booming across from their loudspeakers:

'German fascists! Capitalist swine! We'll be over again today ... round about three o'clock ... the same as yesterday ...'

'Capitalists!' jeered Porta. 'Gregor, fetch my Cadillac, I feel like taking a trip to the Côte de bleeding Azur!'

The loudspeaker crackled again, and a different voice was heard. It spoke better German than the last one, and it was altogether more agreeable and more persuasive in tone.

'Comrades!' it cried beseechingly to us. 'This is Sergeant Buchner of the 23rd Panzer Division speaking to you ...'

We looked at each other, wonderingly.

'Why don't you come across and join us? Show yourselves to be friends of the people! Throw off your bondage! Break out of your chains! Spit on your capitalist masters!'

Sergeant Buchner promised us all manner of earthly rewards, including a supply of women, if we would only surrender ourselves to the delights of the Soviet Union, that proletariat paradise where working men were free and happy.

'All very well,' said Porta, 'but what's the point of exchanging a capitalist master for a Communist one?'

Two men made a desperate bid to gain the proletariat paradise, but their capitalist master, in the shape of our rabid SS general, gunned them down before they had covered more than a few yards.

The Russians returned as they had promised, at three o'clock in the afternoon. We crouched paralysed with fear in our holes. Whose turn today?

The usual five tanks moved slowly across a field of fresh snow, to the usual accompaniment of martial music. Porta defiantly took out his flute and began playing in competition. The rest of us sat and stared. Our holes were as deep as we could possibly dig them. We had no tools at our disposal and the ground underneath the snow was hard as granite.

One or two men bounded out and began loping across the field away from the tanks. They were shot by their own officers. Desertion in the face of the enemy ...

Through a small hole which I had bored through the wall of packed snow which surrounded me, I watched the approaching tanks. There was nothing to do save wait. I had nothing with which to defend myself. Not even a grenade to throw. Not even a bullet to put through my head.

A tank passed within a few yards. I crouched even smaller in my hole. The tank moved on. It chose our neighbours for its target. I heard them screaming as they died. We knew them well, they had been our companions for some time, and I tried to shut out the sounds of their agony and to close my mind to the pictures that were flooding it. But I couldn't help hearing, and I couldn't help seeing . . .

I saw Sergeant Wilmer, the cheerful little shopkeeper from Düsseldorf. I saw his face as he died. I remember how he told us he had joined up in 1936 for four years, and how he had written personally to Hitler in 1940 asking that he should now be allowed to go back to Düsseldorf. Hitler had never replied, and Wilmer had never understood. And now he never would understand. Poor Wilmer! Nothing but a heap of blood and crushed bones in the snow. What a way to go . . . God, what a way to go!

The screams continued. It was important, for one's own precarious sanity, not to attach the sounds to any particular face, but visions swam before men's eyes whether they would or no. Was it Böhmer, bit fat Böhmer, the machine-gunner from Cologne? Or was it his assistant, that skinny little fellow from Lübeck? Or was it that other chap—what was his name? That little dark chap who came from Hamburg and was obsessed by railways? Well, whatever his name was, he had seen his last train go by . . .

Their faces lingered before my unwilling eyes. Their screams tore through my head.

'Stop that noise!' shouted Heide, hysterically. 'Stop that bloody awful noise, for God's sake!'

He crammed his fingers into his ears, but nothing kept out the sound of those screams. Only God seemed deaf to them. Gott mit uns, it said on our belts, but we all knew it for a lie. God was not only not with us, he was nowhere near us on that day. Perhaps he never had been near us. Perhaps it had always been a lie.

They came again, the following day. The same music, the same slow advance. And still we remained helpless at our posts and waited for death.

This time, they settled on the Fourth Group. As we watched, a sergeant of the Marines jumped from his hole and began tunnelling away from them through the soft top layer of snow,

181

burrowing underneath it like a giant mole. He crawled so fast he seemed almost to be swimming, his arms and legs flailing before and behind, pushing the snow out of his way.

His comrade was not so ingenious. Left alone in the hole they had been sharing, he panicked, shot out at the last moment and tried to run. The leading tank lumbered after him. I saw it rear up, catch the man by one arm and toss him into the air. As the body came down, they began to play with it, worrying it, pushing it about, tearing off first one arm and then the other, finally crushing the mutilated corpse deep into the snow. They had no pity, these Russians. They could hear the shrieks of the poor wretch as they ground him beneath them, but they went on with their sport until he was no more than a red splat in the snow.

The slaughter was over for another day. There was always a chance that something would happen in the next twenty-four hours to save us from our fate. The general might come to his senses and pull out; the Russians might disappear in the night; the war might even come to an end ...

It was a shock when the familiar row of T34s appeared on the horizon for the second time that day. We were scarcely able to believe it, it was going against all the rules of the game. Once a day, at three o'clock. That was the routine. They had imposed it themselves and they had no right to break it. The unfairness of it all filled me with bitter resentment and brought me close to angry tears. I was momentarily more concerned at the Russians' lack of honour than at my own imminent and agonising death.

The first tank had already found its prey. A lieutenant, a middle-aged professor from Munich, who threw up his arms in a futile gesture, attempting to ward off the blow. But human arms are a fragile defence against thirty tons of metal, and the T34 smashed them contemptuously aside and went on to claim the rest of its victim.

And now, at last, it was our turn. They came at us in a line, music blaring. For the first time, the general himself was directly threatened. He shouted ferociously at us to remain at our posts, but Porta, pausing only to give him the two fingers, leapt from his hole and went bounding away through the snow, followed by his black cat, who had stuck to Porta like a leech through all our various vicissitudes. I held my breath, my head moving in a panic from side to side as I tried to watch the approaching tanks and the receding Porta at one and the same moment. We waited for the general to open fire. The officers waited for the general to open fire. Now that he himself was facing death, would his fanatical principles still hold good?

Apparently not. With a sudden agile bound, the general was up and away, running after Porta as fast as his legs would carry him through the deep snow. That was the signal for the rest of us. Heads down, lungs heaving, we deserted our posts and fled in the face of the enemy. It was blatant disobedience of the Führer's orders. The last man, the last bullet ...

The tanks came after us, mechanical monsters in pursuit of men. Anyone who stumbled or tripped, anyone who lagged behind, was caught up and crushed, while the rest of us ploughed on without a backward glance, only too thankful that a comrade's torture and death was giving us a few seconds' respite. I didn't care who they caught, so long as it wasn't me. My terror was too great to permit the luxury of caring for anyone else's skin.

Gasping, panting, sobbing, I stumbled onwards through the snow. It was impossible to keep up a fast pace for very long, the snow was too deep, it clung round your legs and it was like trying to flounder through sand dunes. The air was so cold that it burnt your throat and tore your lungs apart. My nose had started to pour blood, and between sobbing and panting and bleeding I began first to choke and then to suffocate. I suddenly tripped and fell headlong into a deep drift. It was rather like falling into a hot bath. Or a feather bed. Or a blast furnace. I shrieked in agony as the boiling cauldron of the snow took hold of me in its grip of fire. The pain was ecstatic. It was beautiful. It consumed me and it lulled me and I wanted it to go on for ever ...

A large hand suddenly gripped me by the shoulder and hauled me out of my hypnotic shroud. I dangled helpless with my feet off the ground as Tiny shook me like a rat.

'What's the matter with you?' he demanded, roughly.

He set me down and slapped me hard round the face. A spurt of blood from my nose splashed into the ground at my feet. Behind us lurched a T34, its flame-thrower reaching out for us across the snow.

'Get a move on!' roared Tiny.

He caught my hand and bounded off through the snow, towing me behind him. Some way in front I saw Porta and the general, running neck and neck with the black cat springing at their heels.

We eventually reached a narrow gorge in a range of high hills.

The T34s had fallen back and seemed to have abandoned the chase, and we threw ourselves down in exhausted heaps with glazed eyes and hunched shoulders.

The gorge appeared to be a military dumping ground. It was full of wrecked vehicles, empty crates and cans, unidentifiable chunks of twisted metal. We lay about uncaring in the rubbish, while the Legionnaire sat cross-legged and cleaned his sub-machine-gun.

'Army shit-heap,' he said, nodding round at the gorge. 'Saw something very like it at Sidi-bel-Abbès.'

There was scarcely any French colony where the Legionnaire had not done battle. He was a born soldier. Less fanatical than Heide, but tougher and more instinctive in his reactions. He didn't care where he fought or who he fought. Fighting was his job and he carried it out with the same dour efficiency wherever he was. His heart was still in France, with the Legion, but he saw nothing anomalous in fighting at Stalingrad for Hitler. He was reserved and independent, unemotional but not insensitive, ruthless and reliable. While Heide straightened his uniform, the Legionnaire checked his sub-machine-gun. The rest of us lay inert and vacant amongst the abandoned ironmongery in the gorge.

The general suddenly appeared and strode angrily amongst us.

'On your feet! What are you lounging about for? Who gave you permission to relax?' He swung round and glared at Porta. 'You needn't think I've forgotten your behaviour ... desertion in the face of the enemy! I shall deal with you later.' He took a pace backwards. 'And that goes for the rest of you, as well!' he shouted. 'A more disgraceful exhibition of collective cowardice I have yet to see. It shall not go unpunished!'

The T34s had disappeared, and the rising wind howled about our ears and drowned the noise of their distant departing engines. The general chivvied us to our feet. We distributed what weapons we had and stood about wearily on aching legs. The general yelled for us to fall into line and for all section chiefs to step forward. From somewhere amongst us came a loud snort of derision.

'Section chiefs! How many of those does he think we've got left? Bloody butcher!'

There was a moment's silence. I felt a nervous desire to start braying like a donkey. Tiny opened his mouth and guffawed, and the general at once moved forward and grabbed him by the collar.

'You! Was it you who said that?' He pulled out his pistol and jabbed it into Tiny's ribs. 'Admit it or I shall shoot! You have three seconds ... one—two——'

'Leave him alone! It was me!'

A man stepped out of the ranks and came up to the infuriated general. He was a sergeant. His head and neck were swathed in bloody, off-white bandages. One of his hands was a withered stump, the bones of the fingers curled in upon themselves, the flesh burnt away. The sergeant was the sole survivor of a section that had been destroyed by Russian flame-throwers. He stood defiant before the general.

'Bloody butcher,' he repeated, stolidly. 'You're all butchers, all you generals——'

He was knocked off balance by a hard hit across the mouth. He staggered, and with his good hand snatched at his revolver, but before he could draw it the general had put a bullet through his temple.

'Let that be a lesson!' He whipped round again on Tiny. 'As for you, I shall deal with you later. I've had my eye on you for a long time. You're a trouble-maker and a coward and you're not fit to be a soldier.' He glared at Tiny, daring him to open his mouth, and Tiny stared straight ahead with an expression of abstract imbecility on his face. 'All right!' The general put away his revolver. 'Find a volunteer and go back and see if there are any survivors. Rejoin us at Gumrak. And make sure you do the job properly ... Remember, I shall have my eye on you from now on!'

The general walked away. Tiny at once turned to me.

'You're the volunteer,' he said.

I swung round, indignant.

'Get knotted! I never opened my mouth!'

'What's that got to do with it? He said to find a volunteer, you heard him——'

'Well, I'm not the man you want!' I snapped.

Tiny looked at me with narrowed eyes.

'You refusing to obey orders?'

'I'm refusing to volunteer,' I said.

There was a moment's pause. Tiny tried again.

'I'm *ordering* you to volunteer,' he told me.

'All right,' I said. 'So I'm refusing to obey orders.'

Tiny drew a deep breath.

'I shall tell the general. I shall tell him I found a volunteer

185

and the volunteer refused to do it and that's refusing to obey orders, I don't care how you look at it, it's a downright refusal ... You saw what happened to that bloke just now, didn't you? That's what'll happen to you when I tell the general about you refusing to be a volunteer when I told you you'd got to be a volunteer and when he'd just told me to find a volunteer and when——'

'Oh, all *right*!' I shouted. 'I'll be a bloody volunteer!'

Tiny hesitated.

'You mean you're offering to come with me and see if there's any survivors?'

'Only under pressure.'

'That's OK. Just so long as you're doing it of your own free will ... Come on, let's get going.'

Porta, who had been hovering near by, awaiting the outcome, now introduced himself into the conversation.

'Just bring my bed back with you, will you?' he said, casually. 'We got out in such a hurry I left it behind. I reckon it should still be there.'

Porta had made everyone's life a misery, carrying his camp-bed round with him. Even the general had been unable to separate them.

'For my part,' I said, with dignity, 'I have no intention whatsoever of dragging a bed all the way to Gumrak. You and your bed can go and get stuffed.'

'Yeah, I'm with you,' said Tiny. 'You Berliners,' he told Porta, with distaste, 'you got your arses too high off the ground. A damn sight too high. You want to come down to earth a bit and join the rest of us.'

'I can't break the habits of a lifetime,' protested Porta. 'We're used to sleeping in beds, where I come from. I don't know what you people in the provinces do, but in Berlin we're accustomed to all the refinements of life.'

'Provinces?' repeated Tiny, in outrage. 'I don't live in the provinces! I'll have you know we've even got an opera house in my town!'

'Opera house!' jeered Porta. 'More like a mud hut for the peasantry!'

We parted on very bad terms. Tiny went charging off into the snow, yelling at me to follow him. He went so fast that I couldn't keep up, but each time I stopped to draw breath he yanked me forward by the shoulder and gave me a kick up the backside.

'Get a move on, you stupid sodding Swede!'

'Dane!' I roared.

'What's the bleeding difference?'

There wasn't any difference, as far as he was concerned. Swedish, Danish, it was all the same. And in the circumstances in which we found ourselves, it seemed hardly worth arguing.

There were, of course, no survivors. We found one or two bloodied heaps still dotted about in the churned-up snow, but nothing that was even remotely recognisable as a human being. Even the famous bed was in pieces.

'Let's get back,' I said, anxiously. 'Before the Russians spot us nosing about.'

'All right, all right, don't be so bleeding impatient! I've not come all this way for nothing. I'm not going back empty-handed.'

'But there's bugger all here!' I said.

'I'm not going back without nothing,' he replied, stubbornly. 'He wanted his bed, so he's going to have his bed.'

'Christ almighty!' I snapped. 'What's the use of a bed in a flaming thousand pieces?'

Tiny crawled about the ground collecting the bits, deaf to all appeals, ignoring all threats. A Russian machine-gunner started up and I dived into the nearest hole and cowered. Tiny calmly carried on with his task. The machine-gun stopped, and I was about to stick my head out and tell Tiny to get a move on when a searchlight was turned on us and Tiny and his pieces of bed were revealed in all their idiocy. From the Russian lines came loud shouts and bursts of laughter. I fell back into my hole and Tiny raised a clenched fist and shook it above his head.

'Turn that light off, you stupid bastards, you're blinding me!'

To my astonishment, they switched the searchlight off without a murmur.

'I'm getting out of here!' I yelped, and I bounded out of the snowhole and set off at a run before the Russians had time to come to their senses.

I could hear great roars of merriment coming from their lines, but I felt their sense of humour was probably fickle and could change at any moment to violence.

We reached Gumrak without further incident, and Tiny gloatingly handed Porta a neat pile of iron fragments and strips of canvas.

'Here you are,' he said.

Porta looked at them a moment.

'What's all this, then?'

'The old wanking chariot,' said Tiny, gleefully. 'Your bed what you asked for ... Risked my neck getting that for you. Bleeding Russians tried to shoot me up, didn't they, Sven?'

'I wouldn't put it as strongly as that,' I said, sourly. 'I think they were all roaring drunk.'

SS Brigadenführer Paul Augsberg presented himself at the Sixth Army Headquarters and demanded to see General Paulus.

'Sir!' He began respectfully enough, but in tones that indicated he had come for a purpose and had no time to waste. 'I consider it absolutely essential that the order be given immediately to break through the Russian lines. Trying to carry on the fight like this is sheer lunacy and everyone knows it. As things stand at present, we've got just about enough tanks and heavy artillery to get through. Only give me the word and I'll prove it to you! But leave matters as they are and before many more days are past we shan't have a cat in hell's chance of getting out ... Look!' He jabbed a finger vehemently on the Brigadenführer's wall map. 'This is where we should make the attempt ... here, near Kaslanowska. The enemy lines are stretched pretty thin at that point. We'd stand an excellent chance of breaking through.'

'General Augsberg,' said Paulus, with a smile, 'you know perfectly well you're asking the impossible. The Führer has stated his orders quite clearly: we are to maintain our position here and fight it out.'

'Fight it out? Fight it out? What the hell with? Dead men and snowballs?'

Paulus lightly hunched a shoulder. General Augsberg leaned across the desk towards him.

'Well, all right, then! If Hitler says we've got to stay here, we've got to stay here ... but at least let's tell the Russians we're willing to come to terms!'

Paulus shook his head.

'No terms, General Augsberg. The Führer was quite categorical. We stay here and we fight.'

Augsberg straightened up. He stared down at Paulus with pinched nostrils and raised eyebrows.

'To what purpose, may I ask Are we deliberately trying to push the men over the edge? Do we really want them to turn against us and get rid of us that way?'

'No fear of that, General. German soldiers would never rise up against their officers, the habit of obedience is far too deeply ingrained in them. The whole of our country's fortunes are based upon an unbroken chain of obedience, from the lowest link to the highest——'

'Blind obedience!' snapped Augsberg. 'Unthinking and unreasoning——'

'Perhaps so, but that is, nevertheless, the quality that will finally carry us through to victory. Things may look black at the moment, but don't allow a minor setback to demoralise you, General Augsberg. We shall triumph in the end. The German nation never does anything by halves.'

'It would appear not,' said Augsberg, bitterly. 'Certainly nobody could ever accuse us of being defeated by halves at Stalingrad ... a good full-blooded no-nonsense massacre!'

He turned abruptly and left the room, striding angrily along the great wide corridors of the GPU building. Round the area that housed General Paulus and his staff were stacked the bodies of German soldiers. Frozen corpses, piled high against the walls in the manner of sandbags. Good soldiers of the Fatherland even in death.

General Augsberg walked on, through passages where the sick and wounded lay dying side by side on the stone floors. He passed through the room next to the operating theatre. It was full of corpses and amputated limbs, tossed carelessly about the floor. There were one or two bodies that might or might not have been still alive, but had been abandoned by the surgeons as being hopeless cases. In a corner, huddled into himself, his gaze vacant and his eyes full of tears, was General von Daniels. His lips moved silently, his lower lip trembled. General von Daniels had lost a whole division. The 176th Infantry, all seventeen thousand men, had been wiped out by the Russians, and their commanding officer now sat weeping for his dead men and his vanished hopes, with a mind that was shattered beyond repair. General Augsberg paused a moment to regard him, then shook his head and walked on.

Other officers he passed, sliding along in the shadow of the walls, guilty faces over guilty shoulders ... high-ranking officers who had obeyed the command to fight to the last man and the last bullet, who had sent their military police even into the hospitals, dragging out the wounded to fight for the Fatherland, and who now, having thrown away many thousands of other men's lives, were bent on saving their own. Their sights were set upon the distant Volga, upon escape at all costs from the last-ditch fighting and the growing mounds of bodies.

General Augsberg crossed a courtyard and continued across a pile of black and still smouldering ruins. Below him, in a long, thin, straggling line, was a reluctant column of soldiers. They were dressed in rags, their heads sunk low on their chests, their feet dragging, their shoulders hunched. General Augsberg stood watching them. The German Army, *en route* to God knows where to do God knows what. They would simply fling themselves into the snow and fire haphazard until their ammunition ran out. Their deaths would be inevitable and pointless.

The last man trailed out of sight. General Augsberg seemed suddenly to make up his mind. He walked onwards with determined tread across the rubble.

TWELVE

RETREAT

It was early in the morning when General Augsberg appeared in our midst. He tossed a bag of provisions at us without a word, then very deliberately began clearing his pockets of all personal papers and setting light to them. We watched him wonderingly. His face was set hard, his lips pursed together. Not until he had set fire to the last of his papers did he turn and address us.

'Right!' His eyes flickered over us, resting on a man here, a man there, as if trying to gauge our possible reactions. 'I have a simple proposition to put to you: either you can stay here and wait for the Russians, or you can come with me and try to fight your way through to our front line. The choice is yours. If you stay here you'll almost certainly die. On the other hand, if you come with me, the prospects are scarcely any brighter. If you do decide to come, you travel light. We carry nothing but arms and ammunition. It'll be hard going and we probably shan't make it. You might prefer to stay here and take your chance with the Russians. If so, I shan't blame you. I'm not offering anyone a joy ride—just a fighting chance. And some may not even call it that. Some may call it suicide. I don't know until I'm out there.' He paused. 'All right,' he said. 'That's all. I'm on my way.'

He turned and walked out, into the first red-gold rays of the rising sun. There was a moment's silence, and then the Old Man slowly stood us, stretched, pressed his hands into the small of his back, picked up his sub-machine-gun and ambled off with easy, bow-legged gait in the wake of the general. One after another, the rest of us followed, until we stretched out in a column, about eight hundred men, the remnants of many different regiments. We even had a couple of pilots with us. Their Condor had been shot down but they had landed behind German lines, and they now joined us in our bid for life. They were marching just in front of me, and I looked with continuing and increasing envy at their fur-lined flying jackets and their sealskin boots. I was wearing a variety of rags, like everyone else, and I had forgotten how it was to feel warm and comfortable. In addition, I was carrying a machine-gun and its tripod over my shoulder, and it was carving into my thin flesh and protruding bones. After a few miles, I gave an impatient cry and tossed the tripod into the snow. The Legionnaire chidingly shook his head.

'Silly thing to do,' he said. 'You'll be feeling the need of that sooner or later.'

I shrugged my shoulders and ignored his warning. The tripod remained in the snow.

We reached the main Stalingrad–Kalatsch road, where vast columns of tanks were *en route* to Stalingrad. Their observation panels were open, and their crews were singing and shouting like over-excited schoolboys on a coach trip.

There had obviously been an accident on the railway line. It was blocked by a string of overturned carriages. One entire coach was crushed, two were rammed into each other, one was standing on end. Some way off from the track lay the burnt-out wreckage of the engine.

We stopped to survey the scene, and Augsberg called the Old Man across to him.

'Take your group across first. We'll give you covering fire if it really becomes necessary, but try to get over without being seen, it's probably our only chance. Once you're over, don't wait for the rest of us. Carry on to Jlarionovskij, we'll meet up there.'

The Old Man came back to us, waved a hand and pointed. We negotiated the road successfully and ran like hares across the plain. Twice I fell under the weight of the machine-gun, and twice it needed all my willpower to stagger upright and carry on. The third time it happened I just lay in the snow and moaned, but the Legionnaire kicked me to my feet and pushed me ahead of him, running after me and thumping me viciously in the small of the back whenever I showed signs of slowing down. He himself was unbreakable, he had been schooled in exile in the deserts of the Foreign Legion, and all my tears, my curses, my threats, left him quite unmoved.

192

We reached another road. It was flanked on either side by overturned vehicles, German ambulances which had been shot up by Russian machine-gunners, and, as we passed them, great black crows rose flapping and croaking into the air. Inside the vehicles were piles of frozen corpses. Some of the bodies had had their skulls broken open, or neatly sliced off like coconut shells. We knew what that signified: when men are dying of hunger, when rations have been cut to two grammes of bread per day, and even that is not always forthcoming, then it is possible to fill an aching belly with human brains. A doctor had told us long ago, before we dreamt that we should ever suffer the pangs of starvation, that brains are extremely nourishing. Tiny was the only one of us who had ever sampled them. He dipped one day into a dead colonel's skull, but was unable to keep the meal inside him for long enough to derive any nourishment from it. We found rat quite palatable, but brains we could not fancy. Perhaps we had not yet suffered sufficiently.

We reached Jlarionovskij at last, but were moved on almost at once by General Augsberg.

'No time to hang around admiring the scenery,' he said, briskly. 'We've a long journey ahead of us.' He took the Old Man to one side and showed him the map. 'We'll go as far as Peskowtka, then turn off at right angles towards the Don. I think with any luck we should be able to make it, but it's there, of course, that the problems really begin: somehow or other, we've got to get across that river . . .'

The plain seemed to be endless. We traipsed across it, mile after mile, with a hard blue frosty sky above us and crisp white snow all round. Nothing but snow and sky. Not a tree, not a bush, not even a withered shrub. The dazzling whiteness began to hurt my eyes. No matter in which direction I looked, I could find no comfort from the glare. If I closed them, the pain was so intense I had to open them again after only a few seconds; but keeping them open only intensified the constant throbbing ache. I began soon to see bright silver flashes and whirling patterns of purple spots. Daggers plunged deep into my pupils. Burning tears spilled out and coursed down my cheeks. A mile or so further on, and I could hardly see at all. I began staggering and stumbling, and the vague black blur of the boots of the man marching in front of me made me dizzy and sick. I snatched up a handful of snow and crushed it against my eyelids, hoping for some relief, but it felt like burning embers.

My senses began to swim away from me. I lurched onwards

after the black boots, which trod regularly up and down in the snow, luring me after them, but my brain was in a delirium inside my head. I saw myself marching to my death. I saw myself as one of those who perished somewhere between the Volga and the Don, lying in my silver silken shroud between the Volga and the Don ... What a fascinating name that was! The Don. The Don. The Volga and the Don. The words began to beat out a rhythm to the pounding of those big black boots. The Don, the Don, the Volga and the Don. The Don, the Don, the Volga and the Don. The Don, the Don ...

I became slowly aware that the Old Man and Tiny were hoisting me up between them. My body felt heavy and stupid. My eyes were still paining ne.

'What's the matter, Sven?'

It was the Old Man speaking; calm and kind, as always. I pressed a hand against my eyes.

'It's this damned snow! Nothing but snow wherever you look ... Why does it have to be so bloody white all the time?'

'What colour would you like it to be?' said Tiny, by way of a joke. 'Black?'

'Black would be beautiful,' I said.

Tiny guffawed. The Old Man held out a hand to Porta, who passed over a bottle.

'Here,' he said. 'Have a drink. That'll do the trick.'

'We're nearly there now, anyway,' added Porta, trying to be helpful.

I knew he was lying, but by the time I had swallowed several mouthfuls of vodka I no longer cared quite so much.

We reached a village of dilapidated huts, and the Legionnaire was sent off in command of a small group to reconnoitre, while the rest of us sank gratefully into the welcoming snow to await their return.

The Legionnaire reappeared half an hour later and beckoned us to follow him. The village showed all the signs of having been abandoned in a hurry, and the sole remaining inhabitant was a thin white cat, which made the mistake of rubbing against Porta's legs and whining for food. Unfortunately, the great black feline monster that had adopted Porta as its owner was of a jealous disposition, and was, moreover, growing daily more aware of the demands of its own deprived belly. It was bigger and stronger than the white cat, and it leapt on it with howls of fury and tore it apart. Before Porta could bag it for his own, the black cat had carried it off in triumph and was later seen to be licking its lips and preening itself in a corner.

We made out way through the village, examining each of the huts. In one we found an overturned table, ruined food and a collection of toys. We ate the food and went out to the stable, where five bodies, frozen stiff and obviously dead for some time, were dumped unceremoniously on top of one another. Porta bent down to examine them.

'Shot through the back of the head,' he told us. He looked more closely. 'With a nagan,' he added.

We all knew what that meant: the NKVD had been at work again.

In the pantry of another cottage we found an entire family hanging from a row of hooks in the ceiling. We didn't trouble to cut them down, there seemed little point. We merely pushed them to one side like a bead curtain and walked through in search of food. There was nothing to eat, but Porta discovered a wooden cask in the corner. He cautiously sniffed at it before raising it to his lips and swallowing several mouthfuls.

'Well? What is it?' asked Heide, curiously.

'Have a go and see for yourself.'

Porta handed it to him, belched loudly and wiped his mouth across his sleeve. Heide looked suspiciously from the cask to Porta and back again to the cask. He took a mouthful and swallowed it, then let out his breath on a long, wheezing cough and turned red in the face.

'Bloody hellfire! That's enough to burn a hole in your guts!' He looked indignantly at Porta. 'Are you sure it's not sulphuric acid?'

The cask was passed round. We all suffered the same interesting reaction as Heide.

'What the devil is it?' demanded the Old Man, pressing a clenched fist hard into the middle of his chest and gasping. 'I feel as if my lungs are on fire!'

Porta grinned.

'I reckon it's samorchonka ... Uncle Jo Stalin's special pick-me-up for tired troops. Two casks like this are reputed to be enough for a whole company.'

'I believe you,' I said, staggering out of the pantry, through the hanging bodies, in search of a chair.

'Couple of mouthfuls of this stuff,' said Porta, 'and a man's willing to wrestle barehanded with a sixty-ton tank.'

'It's not quite as bad as I thought,' admitted Heide, rather sheepishly propping himself against the wall. 'Now that it's gone, it's really quite pleasant.'

'What's it made of?' I asked. 'Red peppers?'

'Maize, potatoes, beetroots——' began Porta, who always had the recipes for such things.

'What sort of beetroots?' demanded the Old Man, already intoxicated. He wagged a wise, farming finger at Porta. 'There's more than one, you know. Just like potatoes. There's more than one variety. Which one are you talking about?'

'Any one,' said Porta, firmly. 'Maize, potatoes, beetroots—any variety'll do. They're all as good as each other. And you just shove 'em in a barrel and let 'em rot for a few weeks. They reckon it takes about a month. All the scum and stuff, you can take that off and put it in the pig swill. Does 'em a world of good.'

'Does me a world of good,' said Gregor, snatching back the cask.

'Samorchonka,' went on Porta, 'is Stalin's secret weapon ... What they say about faith, hope and love, and all the rest of the balls ... all this crap about Gott mit uns ... well, the Russians don't give a damn for any of it. They chucked faith, hope and love into the dustbin, and they got rid of God, and they invented samorchonka instead ... leastways, Uncle Jo invented it. Trust a Jew to know what's what!'

'Stalin's not a Jew,' protested Heide, reaching out for the cask.

'Who says he ain't? Joseph's a Jewish name, ain't it?'

'In that case,' cried Heide, 'you ought to be ashamed of yourself, Joseph Porta! You know bloody well the Führer said anyone with a Yid name had got to change it!'

'It's not the name that makes you a Jew,' said Gregor, with an air of owlish sagacity. 'In any case, Stalin doesn't like 'em any more than Goebbels ... and he's called Joseph, too,' he added, as one making the discovery of the century.

He raised the cask to his lips, but the Legionnaire removed it just in time.

'Thing about Stalin,' he said, 'I grant you he's got the same bee in his bonnet as Adolf, only he goes about things in a far more sensible way. Like he feeds his Jews to enemy artillery rather than Dutch ovens ...'

'Nobody loves the Jews,' said Gregor, mournfully.

'Not out here, they don't,' agreed the Legionnaire, 'You remember that crazy Pole we saw that time? The one that kept a Jew chained up in his back yard in place of a guard-dog?'

'So what the hell are we all fighting about?' shouted Heide, in a sudden burst of rage. 'Stalin hates the Jews, Hitler hates the Jews, I hate the Jews, everybody hates the Jews! Why don't we all turn round and *fight* the Jews?'

'Seems to me,' said the Old Man, glumly, 'Hitler's made a right cock-up. Sticking them in gas chambers and that. It's just plain daft.'

'Whaddya mean by that?' shouted Heide.

The Old Man belched.

'It's just plain daft,' he repeated, forming each word with the tender care of the almost completely intoxicated. 'Who's going to love us when we've slaughtered all the Jews? Who's going to love us when we've lost the war? Who's going to——'

'That's anti-Nazi talk!' screamed Heide. 'That's defeatist!' He had had several more mouthfuls of Stalin's secret weapon and was even more intoxicated than the Old Man. 'I could have you arrested for that! I could have you shot! I could tell Hitler! I could——'

He suddenly lost his balance and fell sideways, collapsing in a heap on to the stove, where he at once set up a fearful wailing and shrieking, pleading with us to fetch an ambulance.

'I'm burning!' he moaned. 'I'm on fire! Can't you see the flames?'

Since the stove was unlighted, and had evidently not been used for several weeks, we ignored his shouts and turned contemptuously away. All except Tiny, who obligingly urinated over him and quenched the supposed flames.

'Thank you, thank you,' murmured Heide. 'That's much bette⁻ ... lovely cool rain ... lovely raindrops ... all over me ...'

His voice trailed away and he fell into a loud, snoring sleep. We turned our backs on him and set about finishing off the samorchonka. We had quite forgotten where we were, or what we were doing there. Half an hour later and I doubt if any of us could even have remembered that we were in Russia, let alone several miles behind the enemy lines. By the time we followed Heide's example and fell into a communal stupor, I don't believe we were even aware of our own identities.

We were wakened at dawn by General Augsberg kicking open the door of the cottage and shouting at us to get to our feet. I opened my eyes rather painfully and looked about me through the swirling red mists of hangover. Hammers and sickles were hard at work inside my head. My mouth was dry, my throat was raw, and in the depths of my stomach a thick and savage sea was heaving to and fro. I staggered upright and watched the walls come and go as the floor undulated into the distance. At my side, the Old Man stood swaying with a hand waving in uncertain salute somewhere towards the ceiling.

'What the devil's been going on in here?' roared the general. 'It looks like a bloody thieves' kitchen!'

I did wish the man had the common courtesy to keep his voice down at that hour of the morning. It was really more than I could stand. With my stomach contracting and my throat gasping, I sank slowly back to the floor level.

'Get that man on his feet!' screamed the general.

Porta and the Legionnaire hauled me up and we staggered together across the room and fetched up against the wall, where we lay panting and perspiring with our tongues lolling out and our eyeballs rolling.

'All present and correct, sir.'

The Old Man spoke slowly and earnestly and with an obvious effort. As he did so, Heide turned round and vomited.

I suppose the only reason Augsberg didn't shoot us on the spot was because he was in no position to suffer the loss of seven experienced soldiers.

'He'd never get home to Hitler without us,' declared Tiny, as we stood shivering outside in the snow.

As the black skies of night turned slowly into the dismal grey of a Russian dawn, we prepared to set off once again. The bitter shock of the knife-edge wind and the hard-packed snow beneath our tattered boots had quickly sobered us up, and we stepped out fairly briskly behind the general. Very few of us possessed suitable footwear for the time of year. Most of us were marching with rags and newspapers wrapped round our feet. Porta (of course) was one of half a dozen who had managed to equip themselves with skis, and it was in fact Porta who was the first to reach the Don. We saw him hesitate at the top of a slope, then turn and come racing back to us in a cloud of sparkling silver droplets.

'The Don!' He swept round the general in a wide circle and came to an ostentatious halt before him. 'Just the other side of the hill!'

The general frowned, already uneasy.

'The Don? Are you sure?'

'Positive, sir.'

There was a sudden silence. The column shuffled to a halt

and men stood listening with their heads to one side. Not a sound. No gunfire, no shells, no rattle of machine-guns, no tanks. Only the rushing winds from Kazakhstan howling their enmity across the endless plains.

The general looked heavily at Porta.

'You saw no sign of troops?'

Slowly, Porta shook his head.

'Nothing, sir. There's nothing out there.'

The silence continued. We went on listening, unable to believe that all this long time we had been marching towards emptiness. What had happened to our army on the Don? Where was it? Had it ever really been there? Or was that, too, another of the lies they had been telling us?

The general turned back to look at his long column of men. They were sullen, now, with disappointment and despair. Sooner have stayed in Stalingrad than march all this way to join an army that no longer existed.

'Let's press on!' Augsberg waved his hand in a circular motion and pointed ahead, up the slope. 'See what we can find.'

All we came across was one abandoned P4, camouflaged by great drifts of snow. It had obviously belonged to the armoured division of Mannstein, which had failed to get through with our supplies at Christmas.

'Don't see why they left it here,' said Porta, as we brushed off the top layers of snow and examined the vehicle. 'Seems to be in perfectly good condition. It's the tracks that are buggered up, that's all. Get them in working order and I reckon we could make use of it.'

A section of sappers were called up and the problem put to them. Their young lieutenant shook his head, dubiously.

'Could be done, sir, but it would take time.'

'How much time?' demanded the general.

'Hard to tell ... six hours, perhaps. Maybe a bit longer. We've got no proper tools, we'll have to improvise.'

'Well, give it a go. We could do with some transport.'

It took them eight hours, in the end. Eight hours of hard slog, reconstructing the shattered tracks. And then, with Porta at the wheel and a crowd of men pushing, the heavy vehicle heaved itself slowly out of its bed of ice and nosed forward across the snow. The general turned to the one MO we had with us.

'Dr Heim, it's up to you to decide which men need to be transported and which are still capable of walking. Any who try to swing the lead can stay here and rot, I'm not carrying passengers. Only the worst cases of frostbite and other injuries are to be allowed into that vehicle ... Do I make myself clear?'

'Perfectly, sir. But there'll be more genuine claims than there are places.'

'I leave it to you.'

The doctor turned away to select his chosen few, and the general called up the Old Man.

'Feldwebel Beier, I'm putting you in charge of the vehicle. Anyone who tries to climb aboard without authorisation, I give you my full permission to shoot. Corporal Porta can be your driver, Sergeant Heide can man the cannon and the radio ... Sergeant Martin'—he beckoned to Gregor—'take the machine-gun.' His gaze wandered round and came to rest on a badly wounded sergeant-major, whose feet were no more than two raw and shapeless masses. 'Do you have any experience of tank armaments?'

'Yes, sir.'

The sergeant-major hobbled hopefully forward on the rifles he was using as crutches. The general regarded him with narrowed eyes, then nodded.

'All right. In you get.'

We set off down the other side of the steep slope towards the frozen river. The tank was skidding so badly we thought the improvised tracks must surely break, but Porta was an experienced driver and handled tanks with the same love and care as a man might give his horse.

The main body of us crossed the river and turned to watch the halting progress of the P4. The danger now was that the ice would crack under the three tons of steel, for the Don never froze right down to the bottom. Everyone except Porta had left the vehicle. He pushed it forward slowly, slipping now and again on the glassy surface, and we heard the warning groans and then the sharp retorts of the ice splintering beneath the weight. At last he reached the great misshapen blocks that lay between the frozen water and the river bank. The tank ground its way over the top of them and fell to the other side in a shower of crystal sparks. A great cheer went up and the privileged few climbed back into their seats. We had crossed the Don.

My eyes were paining me again, aching and throbbing in spite of the few precious drops of medicine the doctor had given me. If only we had had some Alpine troops amongst us, Porta would almost certainly have been able to beg, borrow, steal or extort a pair of dark glasses for me. But the High Command had not seen fit to issue such luxuries for ordinary troops.

'Bloody lunatics!' snapped the Legionnaire, putting out a hand to steady me as I tried to stagger along with my eyes closed. 'Send an army into the depths of Russia dressed in their ruddy nightgowns and expect them to fight a battle! Murdering bloody swine!'

It was rare for the Legionnaire to be moved to such invective, but he was perfectly correct. They had sent over a whole army totally ill-equipped to deal with the prevailing weather conditions, and they had not even the dubious excuse of ignorance. For ten years, German officers had taught in Russian military academies and had actually helped the Russians evolve the best equipment for troops fighting through the hard Soviet winters!

We marched for six hours before we were allowed a rest, and we fell about in the snow, exhausted and almost beyond caring.

'What what you're doing with that thing,' warned Tiny, as I threw the machine-gun carelessly away from me. 'We could be in need of that sooner than what you think.'

'Sod the thing,' I muttered. 'It's like a bloody incubus.'

'I dunno about that,' said Tiny, doubtfully. 'But what about anti-freeze? You got any of that for it, have you? The Legionnaire's got a whole can of it, I saw him nick it out of the P4.'

'He wouldn't let me have any,' I said, too lazy to make the effort of finding the Legionnaire and requesting some.

'You asked him?' demanded Tiny.

'No, I haven't,' I said. 'I don't care about anti-freeze. I don't care if the sodding thing gives up the ghost. I only wish it would, and then maybe I could stop lugging it about with me everywhere I go.'

'I'll ask him,' said Tiny, equably. 'You stay there. I'll go and get some. Don't want it to seize up on you, do you?'

I felt quite guilty when he returned a few minutes later, cheerfully swinging a can of anti-freeze.

'Gave it me without a murmur,' he told me. 'I thought I'd have to twist his arm, but——'

He broke off, listening. I sat up and shaded my eyes, squinting into the sky.

'An aircraft!'

'One of ours!'

It was a Focke-Wulf. We scrambled to our feet, aching limbs forgotten, and began waving and shouting. Gregor let off a flare, and the Focke-Wulf banked slightly, circled round us and flew over our heads at a height of six hundred feet or so. We could see the crew signalling to us. We could see the black crosses on the wings. We threw our arms round each other and danced mad waltzes of triumph in the snow.

A steel helmet was tossed out of the plane. The pilot gave us the thumbs-up, circled again and flew off towards the west. We made a dive for the helmet. Inside, a hasty message had been scrawled:

'Hold tight, we'll be back! Keep an eye open for us. Good luck!'

'They're coming to fetch us!' screeched Gregor, leaping into the air and throwing his arms wide.

One of the pilots from the Condor shook his head, rather sadly and scornfully.

'No such luck! They might just about be able to land here, with an empty crate, but they'd never be able to take off again. Not in a month of bloody Sundays. Not even empty, let alone with a full load.'

'He's right,' said the Old Man, reluctantly. 'We're not going to get much help from that direction.' He jabbed his finger into the air. 'Not from God or from aeroplanes ... There's only one way we'll get out, and that's by using our feet.'

'Using our feet?' moaned Porta. 'How much longer we got to go on using 'em, then? We got as far as the Don and didn't find nothing. How much further we got to go? Next stop the Rhine? Jesus God, I'll never make it!' He suddenly clapped a hand against the right side of his chest. 'I'm not a fit man, I shouldn't be here, I've had a heart murmur since I was six——'

'Not surprising,' muttered the Legionnaire. 'Seeing as you've got a misplaced heart ...'

Porta glared briefly at him and moved his hand over to the left.

'I had rheumatic fever when I was seven. I've had pneumonia three times. I didn't ought to get wet and cold like this. I didn't ought to be here in the first place. I can't go on marching all the way to Germany!' His voice rose to a pitying shriek of quite alarmingly shrill pitch. 'I've got a bad heart, I tell you! I need help! I need a doctor! I can't go on like this!'

He gave a loud shout of pain, doubled over, staggered a few paces in convoluted fashion, then collapsed moaning into the snow.

'What is it? What's happening?' The MO, alerted by Porta's

melodramatic shrieks, came rushing up to us. 'What's the matter with this man?'

We stood round in a circle, staring down at the writhing Porta. The doctor spoke impatiently.

'What's wrong with you? Why are you making all that noise?'

'He's a sick man,' said Tiny. 'Got a bad heart. Ever since he was six.' He cocked a hopeful eyebrow. 'Alcohol, sir?'

'What do you mean, alcohol?'

'That's what he always takes when he comes over bad. It sort of stimulates the action of his heart, if you see what I mean.'

The doctor looked uncertainly from Tiny to Porta.

'Has he really got a weak heart?' he said. 'Or is he putting it on?'

'Putting it ON?' repeated Tiny.

'Putting it ON?' said Gregor.

'That's a sick man,' said the Legionnaire. 'He's had pneumonia three times.'

The doctor was fresh out of medical school. He had come straight to Stalingrad full of good intentions, and it was a hard training ground. He knelt dubiously by Porta's side, while Porta gave a fair imitation of a man on the point of agonising death.

The crowd now parted to allow the general and the young lieutenant a ringside seat. They looked at the badly over-acting Porta.

'All right, all right!' said the general, irritably. 'That's enough of that. This is no time for histrionics.'

Porta opened his eyes and rolled them in the general's direction.

'Vodka...' he mouthed, pitifully.

'Pull yourself together, man!'

The general turned and walked away. The lieutenant grinned.

'Vodka...' moaned Porta, transferring his attentions from one man to the other. 'Vodka, for the love of God...'

'The love of God be damned!' said the lieutenant, holding out his flask.

Porta snatched it eagerly from him and fell back. He drank greedily, with his mouth wide open and the flask upended.

'You've saved my life, sir. How can I ever thank you? Shall I ask the Führer to give you a medal? I reckon you deserve one. I reckon you——'

'Spare me my blushes! Just give me back the rest of my vodka!'

The lieutenant walked off laughing, in the wake of the general. The doctor shook his head, doubtfully.

'They shouldn't be sending men with weak hearts into the front line,' he said. 'You ought to be demobilised...'

We dug ourselves in and prepared to spend the night in the same spot, just in case the Focke-Wulf returned. In the distance we heard the roar of engines.

'Heavy lorries,' said the Legionnaire. 'If we could only nick a handful, we'd soon be home.'

Away to the east, the night was lit up with a red glow. It was Stalingrad, still burning. To the north, flashing streaks of light darted across the sky, striping it black and white like a monstrous zebra.

'Artillery,' said Heide.

'Balls!' Gregor turned challengingly upon him. 'There's nobody left to fight up that way!'

Heide shrugged his shoulders.

'Can't help that. It's still artillery. It might be ghosts using it, but if so, they've got bloody big guns for ghosts ... Come on, stop arguing and get those perishing cards dealt!'

'You'd do better to sleep,' advised the lieutenant, as he walked past.

'I can never get to sleep with the light on,' said Porta, jabbing his thumb in the direction of the glowing red sky.

The lieutenant smiled.

'Well, I'm sorry. I can't put out the flames of Stalingrad for you...'

We played cards throughout the night. The fever of gambling was upon us. Safe in the knowledge that nobody had more than a few coppers on him, we were able to win and lose vast sums without a qualm. All amounts were solemnly entered in Porta's little black book, but so what if you did finish the night owing a small fortune? The final reckoning was never likely to come.

'We shall all be dead before then,' comfortably remarked the Legionnaire, who had gambled away his entire earnings for the next five years.

The morning saw us red-eyed and foul-tempered. Porta took his seat in the P4 and drove off at the head of the column. The rest of us followed on foot.

'How far do you reckon it is to Germany?' asked Tiny, in tones that confidently expected me to know the answer down to the last few inches.

'A good long way yet,' I said, sourly.

We had done about an hour's marching when the promised aeroplane appeared in the skies. Not the Focke-Wulf this time. A Heinkel 111. We sent up flares and waited patiently until it was overhead. We were too tired, now, to sing and dance; and some of us could remember that other occasion, when they had sent us pictures of Hitler and tins of flea powder ... But not this time! This time it was for real. The canisters that floated down to us beneath their parachutes contained sausages, ham, bread, sardines ...

'Collect it up!' bawled the general, over the noise of the stampede, as men seized on the canisters and tore them open with bayonets. 'Collect it all up! Everything must be rationed out! Don't eat it all at once!'

'A message, sir.'

The Old Man handed him a note that had been found in one of the canisters.

'Strong concentration of cavalry seven miles to the north-west of the Nich–Tschirskaja–Thernys railway line. Proceed with caution. Kamenski–Stalingrad line in enemy hands. Bridges patrolled by tanks. Heavy formations advancing west to south. Kalitwa occupied by enemy troops. Bridges impassable without artillery support. Heavy fighting near Aidar. Nearest enemy position, thirty miles to the north of you.'

'Bunch of morons!' snarled the general. 'We don't want to know where the enemy are, we'll find that out soon enough for ourselves! More to the point if they told us where to find our own damned troops!'

The Old Man was staring into the distance, where the departing Heinkel was now no more than a dot in the clouds. His face looked shrivelled and shrunken, and he shook his head in despair, as if the aircraft's departure spelt the end of our hopes of survival.

'I reckon they've already crossed our names off,' he murmured. 'That's the last time they'll bother with us.'

The general glared at him. He shouldered his rifle and stalked on, shouting at us to follow.

The retreat continued, deeper and deeper into the frozen plains. The vicious east wind cut through our clothes, through our skin, into our very bones, blowing and howling with all its spiteful might, as if trying to sweep us away. We were the hated enemy, invaders of another people's land, and we felt the hostility all round us.

Suddenly, from a fold in the ground, appeared a Russian

supply column. Porta swung the tank sharp left and pulled up behind a solid wall of snow, but the Russians had seen us. Their cries came sharp and clear across the plain.

'Stoi! Idi soda!'*

And then, gaining courage, they suddenly came at us with bayonets fixed. It could not have been every day they met up with stray German troops, and it seemed to over-excite them. An officer ran ahead, waving a revolver.

'Ruki werch! Ruki werch!'†

'Bloody nerve,' growled Tiny.

He raised his rifle and fired. The foolhardy officer crumpled up, and his men, rather taken aback, stopped short and looked at us with new respect.

'Spread out!'

We scattered instantly, and within seconds our machine-guns were sending the enemy racing backwards. Porta was crouched behind the P4, steadily firing with a long-range rifle which used explosive bullets. One had only to bury itself in a man's shoulder for his entire arm to be wrenched off his body.

The Russians retreated busily, leaving several of their number behind, but they were turned round and sent straight back again by their commissars, who seemed to wield the power of the devil himself over their men.

'Cover me!'

A sergeant rose from beside me and moved out into the open with a flame-thrower. A long red tongue went snaking towards the Russians and engulfed them in a sea of fire. The sergeant laughed happily as he saw them burn. He turned and gave me a quick salute and a mischievous grin before running off to set light to a few more people. He obviously loved his job. It was not one that I myself particularly envied, but it takes all sorts to make a war.

We outnumbered the enemy and they eventually gave up the fight and withdrew to discuss their next move. It was already growing dusk, and the steppe soon became thick with darkness and with silence.

General Augsberg threw himself down beside us, his frozen lips cracked and bleeding.

'At 2300 hours we move out. Meet up again at the Tschir. It's about forty miles west of here.'

He moved on to the next group, leaving us flabbergasted.

* Come here!
† Hands up!

'Forty miles!' I said. 'Only forty miles ... Why not make it New York while he's about it? Who's going to last another forty miles, for God's sake?'

The Russians came at us again, tearing across the snow in the blackness. My machine-gun was still in working order, thanks to the Legionnaire's anti-freeze, but it was difficult to control without the tripod and I kept firing short. In the end, Tiny snatched it away from me, slipped the strap over his neck and, disdaining the enemy guns, stood in the midst of flying shrapnel and fired rapidly from the hip. I watched him in awed wonderment, until he jerked me back to reality with a kick that sent me flying.

'I want another magazine! Don't just stand there gawping! Go and get me one!'

I crawled away through the snow, ran back through a shower of bullets, grabbed the machine-gun and in my panic jammed the loading mechanism. Tiny gave me another kick. I accepted the blow meekly and wished I possessed his thick skin and brutish lack of fear. I always imagined Tiny as having nerve fibres the size of tree-trunks.

Again the Russians fell back. A couple of infantymen came across and set up their machine-gun in position near by. We learned that they had fought at Moscow and we accepted their presence with grudging respect.

From afar off, in the darkness, we heard men shouting for stretcher-bearers. In the confusion, there was little that could be done. Germans and Russians lay side by side, bleeding to death. We had no stretchers, we had only one doctor, and already the general was passing along the same order as before: reassemble at the Tschir.

'Where IS Tschir?' demanded Tiny, in fretful tones.

Nobody answered him.

'Well, all right,' he said. 'If you don't know where it is, you might at least know WHAT it is.'

'It's a bloody town!' snarled Porta.

'A river,' said the Old Man, with an air of slightly weary apology. 'It's a river.'

'ANOTHER river?' said Tiny. 'Stone me, that's all you ever bleeding do in this country ... march from one bit of flaming water to the next ...'

We lay back in the snow, listening to the silence, waiting for the next attack. Near by, a man had unwrapped a filthy rag and a package of old newspaper from his arm, revealing a hole the

207

size of a small pudding basin. The skin round the edges was deep purple, almost black. The hole itself was full of mouldy yellow pus. I caught the Legionnaire's eye and we both looked away, as if we had found each other out in the act of some obscenity. The man with the pus-filled crater tore a strip off the edge of his shirt and began solemnly binding it round his arm.

'Could have been worse,' he said, cheerfully. 'Could have been blown right off, I suppose.'

I said nothing. I knew, and the Legionnaire knew, and the man himself probably knew, that before very long the arm would have to come off in any case.

In the distance we heard a long-drawn-out howl. One of the infantrymen looked up.

'Wolves,' he said, briefly.

The Russian horses began to join in, whinnying and tossing their heads. They hated the wolves as much as we did.

A rocket flared into the sky, and at the same moment there was a shout from the other end of the lines.

'They're moving across from the road!'

An artillery sergeant came running up to us, waving an arm over his head.

'We're pulling out! Abandon all heavy arms! You two'—he pointed at random, catching Tiny and me—'cover the retreat!'

He galloped off, and everyone else followed—except Tiny and me. We stayed behind to face the new horde of Russians. The two infantrymen sprang up, Porta, Gregor, the Old Man, the Legionnaire, Heide, they all went rushing off behind the sergeant. Even the man with the bandage took to his heels, still trying to tie a knot with one hand and his teeth. Tiny and I grimaced at each other and crouched for comfort behind the machine-gun.

The minutes passed. I looked repeatedly at my watch, but the hands seemed not to be moving. It must have been broken in the last skirmish. I decided to count the seconds instead. Half an hour later, I glanced at Tiny.

'How the hell long have we been here?'

Tiny glanced at his own watch.

'Nearly ten minutes,' he said.

'Ten minutes?' I said. 'Is that all?'

He looked at me.

'Whaddya mean, is that all? It's long enough, ain't it?'

'Too long, ' I said. 'Why don't we pull out? They must have got clear by now?'

'I reckon you're right,' agreed Tiny. 'It's time we pushed off.'

We looked at each other, licking our lips and not moving.

'Better a live coward than a dead hero,' said Tiny.

'Too damn right,' I agreed.

'So let's go, eh?'

'Why not? What are we waiting for?'

I slipped back the safety catch on my sub-machine-gun and prepared to move, but as I did so Tiny stretched out a hand and held me back. He put a warning finger to his lips and then cupped a hand behind his ear. Tiny could pick up the smallest sound, he could have heard a sparrow breathing half a mile away, but I listened and could hear nothing. He held up a finger, his head to one side. And then I heard it myself, and I looked in astonishment at Tiny, who had had several seconds' start on me and should by now have interpreted the sound. He had.

'The buggers are digging a tunnel over here . . .'

Rapidly, he tied three grenades together and crept over the ridge. Seconds later, there was a violent explosion. Tiny came running back, waving at me to follow him.

'Let's get out of it!'

I needed no second invitation, I was after him like a shot. We caught up with the rest of the company trudging through the snow by the side of a frozen stream. As we approached them, a line of enemy fire broke out and a stray shell exploded almost in our faces. It caught hold of the man with the bandage and tossed him high into the air. He screamed hideously as he went up, but he was already dead by the time he came down. Tiny and I were splashed with his blood, great streaks of it down our faces and tunics.

We began running. It was difficult in the snow, it caught at our feet and dragged us down, but we kept it up mile after mile until we could run no longer and the men at the head of the column collapsed in exhaustion, their hands pressed to their sides, their breath steaming out into the cold air.

In the far distance, away across the endless plains, we heard the sound of gunshots.

'That's Ivan, clearing the place up,' said Porta. 'I'd recognise the voice of a nagan anywhere.'

We rested for ten minutes, and then went on again. Throughout the night we marched. Some men fell out and we left them huddled in grey heaps in the snow. By morning they would be dead. Already, some of those who had dropped by the wayside from the head of the column were on the point of death as we passed them.

'Victorious Sixth Army on the retreat,' said the Legionnaire, in his dry way. 'What a heroic sight . . .'

I looked ahead at the straggling column; I looked back at the men strung out behind. Grey-faced and stoop-shouldered, the sick and the starved and the crippled. Scarcely three hundred left, and many of those would be gone before the night was out.

'They do tell me,' said Porta, glancing at my face, 'that it's quite cosy, freezing to death.'

'They, of course, have already tried it?' I said.

Porta shrugged.

'I'd as soon go that way as be shot through the back of the head.'

'Or crucified on a door-frame,' said the Legionnaire.

'Or castrated,' added Gregor. 'They do it with blacksmith's tongs, did you know?'

'That's not the worst,' said Tiny, eagerly. 'I met a chap who they'd——'

'Pack it in!' roared the Old Man.

Tiny looked at him, quite hurt.

'I was only going to tell you about the things they'd do if they ever got their hands on us . . .'

Already an old soldier at the age of twenty, I knew only too well what they were likely to do. I didn't need Tiny to tell me. I'd heard the tales of castration and crucifixion. That was why I was marching through the night with a sub-machine-gun slung over my shoulder and a couple of grenades on my belt.

'In actual fact,' said the Legionnaire, 'never mind they cut your balls off and stick dirty great nails through your hands and feet, I don't believe they treat criminals like us nearly as badly as they do the PU boys.'*

'Everyone treats the PUs like shit,' said Porta. 'Both us and the Russians. It don't seem to matter whether they're wearing a bloody swastika or a red star, nobody can't stand the sight of 'em.'

'That's because the Nazis and the Communists both have the same mentality as each other,' explained the Old Man. 'They're

* PU regiments – those classified as 'politically doubtful'. The Legionnaire and the rest belong to a disciplinary battalion, drawn from the ranks of military and civilian prisoners of various kinds.

blood brothers under the skin. If the Nazis label someone as politically undesirable, then the Commies do the same, and vice versa.'

'I reckon that's about the size of it,' said Porta.

We marched on a while in a brooding silence, and then Tiny, who seemed to have something on his mind, turned in puzzlement to the Old Man.

'Look here, I don't get it,' he said. 'If they're what you said they are and they're all the same under the skin and they all hate Jews and they all do the same as each other, then what the bleeding hell are they fighting about?'

The Old Man shrugged.

'Who cares? What difference does it make to you and me what they're fighting for?'

'This Adolf Hitler is a curious phenomenon. He'll certainly never become Chancellor. Postmaster-General, possibly—although even that I very much doubt—but Chancellor, never! Why people should go round in fear of him is more than I can understand ... What is he, when all's said and done, but some jumped-up provincial? Some raw Bohemian house painter with an over-developed sense of his own importance? I warrant you, gentlemen, that within a year or two the man will be forgotten, and his party of young hooligans along with him.'

President Hindenburg, during a conversation with General Schleicher and the Bishop of Munster—14.2.1931

On 1st October 1933, SS Standartenführer Theodor Eicke, inspector-general of the concentration camps, made the following speech to his famous Tod* Regiment:

'Tolerance and humanity are signs of weakness. The man who feels himself incapable of cutting his mother's throat or castrating his father, should he be called upon to do so in the course of duty, is of no use to me. And, by the same token, of no use to Germany ... By the oath we take, we render ourselves strong in mind and body. We shall not flinch, no matter what the task! We shall employ without hesitation and without qualms the most brutal methods available to us, if by so doing we shall achieve our ends. Better to kill a dozen innocent men than let one guilty man go free!

'We cannot expect the ordinary citizen, leading his ordinary bourgeois life, to understand or to sympathise with us: his imagination cannot go that far. He must therefore be protected from knowledge that would be both distressing and dangerous for him. The work that we do here, in our camps, amongst the sub-humanity and the politically undesirable, must be kept strictly secret. You—my soldiers—my own Tod Division—you amongst all men must be hard! Hard as granite! For you the sight of blood must be no more disturbing than the sight of water running from a tap! For you the screams of our enemies must sound no different from the screams of a pig when its throat is cut ... Learn to enjoy your work! Destroy the traitors! Burn their anti-social books, nip their reactionary

* Death.

212

daydreams in the bud, crush them beneath you and learn to laugh as you do it! And always remember, National-Socialism has three sworn enemies: the priests, the Jews and the intellectuals. Be always on the look-out for them. If you can find no other justification for arresting them, then arrest them simply for what they are—and take care to plant your own evidence as you do so. It is as well to be in the habit of carrying proscribed literature with you as you go about. That way, you can always be sure of having something to pin on the bastards ... Never forget that the end justifies the means!

'I regret to say that there are those, even high up in the ranks of the Gestapo, who have still failed to grasp that we have entered upon an era of bloodshed. These are the imbeciles who would retard progress by making rules and regulations under the headings of humanity and justice. I say to you now, ignore them! They will be dealt with when the time is ripe ...

'One last word, and that is, Patience! The day will come when we shall have all the traitors in Germany locked behind bars, and then I promise you a free hand ... Soldiers of death, you shall have your hour of glory!'

THIRTEEN

DINNER AND DANCE WITH THE KALMUCKS

For five days we had been pushing forward in the face of a swirling tempest of snow and wind. Vision was restricted to a few yards and progress was slow and tedious.

We discovered the village entirely by accident, when Porta almost drove the P4 straight into a vague grey shape which turned out to be a hut. He gave a shout of indignant amazement, and we at once moved forward in support with our arms at the ready. We mistrusted all abandoned dwelling-places. More often than not they were stacked from floor to ceiling with enemy troops.

Porta pulled the P4 back into a firing position. The Legionnaire stepped forward and kicked open the door of the hut. A wave of heat at once rushed upon us.

Through the narrow entrance we saw a dim, smoke-filled room and a huddled group of civilians, who regarded us with a faint anxiety. In the centre sat an old crone on a milking stool,

213

nursing an earthenware bowl full of what looked like sunflower seeds. From behind the large stove we saw the frightened faces of children. Experience had already taught them that soldiers of either side were liable to bring destruction and death.

'Ruki werch!'* I cried, none too certainly, to a young man wearing a torn sheepskin coat and German Army trousers. 'Ruki werch!' I told him, waving my sub-machine-gun under his nose and picking on him for the simple reason that he was the nearest to us.

He rose slowly from his chair, his hands behind his head. Gregor stepped forward and patted him up and down for weapons. He had none. The Legionnaire took a look behind the stove, but there was no one else there: only the children, their heads full of fleas and their faces full of tears.

An old man stretched out his hands towards us, an amiable smile of welcome on his face.

'God be praised, Germans! I thought you'd never come back! It's been a long time, and Babushka is dead...'

'Who the blazes is Babushka?' demanded Tiny. 'What's he raving on about? Have we been here before?'

'God knows,' said Gregor, helplessly. 'All these bloody peasants look alike to me.'

'Let's shoot the old goat and be done with it,' urged Tiny. 'I don't like people who want to shake hands with you. It's what the Gestapo always do before they lock you up and start pulling your finger-nails out.'

'Let him be,' said the Old Man. 'He'll die soon enough without you giving him a helping hand.'

The village was small and we rapidly searched it from one end to the other. No Soviet soldiers; only simple Kalmucks, mostly old men, and women and children. Those in the first hut had set lighted lamps before the icons and were pressing glasses of tea upon us. The samovar was singing in the corner and it was all very cosy and tea-shoppy and just a bit unnerving.

'Doesn't taste too bad,' said Tiny, gulping down his tea and smacking his lips. 'For hot water, that is ... Could do with a bit of rum to liven it up, but I've tasted worse.'

He looked round hopefully in search of hard liquor, and the Legionnaire closed steely fingers over his wrist.

'Drink your tea as it is and don't abuse people's hospitality,' he said, between his teeth.

Tiny blinked, and said no more. The Legionnaire was very

* Hands up!

hot on matters of etiquette, and I felt suddenly ashamed of the sub-machine-gun beneath my arm. How could I stand there pouring their tea ration down my throat and threatening them with firearms? Awkwardly, I propped it against the wall. Seconds later an old woman shuffled across, gave me a toothless grin and removed the weapon to the other side of the room, where she set it down with great care by the stove. She then sat beaming and nodding at me across the room, while I frantically tried to attract the Old Man's attention to my plight and wondered if the Legionnaire would bawl me out for abuse of hospitality if I were to go across and retrieve my property. I felt naked without it. I felt I should rather stand there without my trousers than without my sub-machine-gun.

'Gospodin,' said Porta, deferentially inclining his head towards the old man who had first addressed us, 'we are your servants.'

'You what?' said Tiny.

He stood goggle-eyed as the oldest of the Kalmucks began to gather about Porta, pressing little presents upon him, little oddments, bits and pieces, food and drink, which he graciously accepted in his bad Russian. He then, to my horrified astonishment, offered them his sub-machine-gun in return.

'Here, what're you doing that for?' demanded Tiny, his jaw dropping on to his chest.

'Shut your bleeding mouth and let me get on with it!' hissed Porta. 'I know the habits of these people. Keep 'em happy and we'll all get along fine.'

Porta certainly seemed to be getting along fine. The Old Man watched him in some amusement, and shook his head wonderingly.

'What a country! What a daft bloody country! One minute they're putting bullets through the back of your neck, the next minute they're treating you like royalty ... And this,' he said, turning to the Legionnaire, 'is the simple land that the Austrian peasant sent us out to conquer! Adolf doesn't know the half of it. He just doesn't know the half of it ...'

The Legionnaire slowly nodded his agreement.

'Come to that,' he muttered, 'I'm not sure that I do, either. They're all right at the moment, gentle as lambs ... but you rub 'em up the wrong way and they'll be at your throat within seconds ...'

After the tea-drinking ritual, the women cleared the great wooden table and spread across it an embroidered cloth with elaborate lace edging. From the reverent way they handled it, I gathered it was some sort of ceremonial cloth which had probably been in the village for centuries, handed down from generation to generation. We were served with the local wine in shapely earthenware goblets, and a whole sheep roasted on a spit was brought into the hut by two girls. They set it before the starosta, the village elder, and he took down from the wall a great Cossack sabre, sharp and gleaming, and raised it above his head. Tiny, growing ever more anxious, began to finger his revolver and glaring across the room at Porta. I confess I was none too happy myself. I had my back to the stove and had to keep twisting my head round every few seconds to see if the sub-machine-gun was still there.

The starosta brought his sabre whistling down through the air and sliced the head clean off the sheep. Then, holding it aloft, he paced solemnly round the table and deposited it in front of Porta. The rest of us were seated on the bare floor, but Porta, who had earned for himself a position of privilege, was cross-legged on a fat silk cushion. He smugly regarded the sheep's head and poured out a flow of nonsensical and ingratiating Russian to mark his appreciation of the honour.

Before we could eat, we were entertained with dancing. Four young girls appeared in the doorway. They were wearing flowing white robes, which apparently represented winter, and behind them came four more dressed in blue, which stood for spring. The room rang with the sound of twanging balalaikas, and at the sight of the dancing girls Tiny stopped glaring at Porta and suddenly lost all interest in his revolver. He let his hand fall to his side and sat forward eagerly, with his tongue sticking out of his mouth and his face puckered up in a gorilla grin of delight.

'For God's sake!' said the Legionnaire, restraining him. 'This isn't a brothel!'

Tiny spared him a fleeting glance.

'What're they carrying on like that for, then?'

'They're entertaining us,' said the Legionnaire. 'It's just for watching. Strictly hands off.'

Tiny made a noise of contempt and turned back to the alluring spectacle of four winter girls and four spring girls disporting themselves before him. Tiny had no appreciation of the dance as anything other than a gymnastic prelude to bed, and I could see he genuinely believed the Legionnaire was pulling his leg.

Porta, meanwhile, always more interested in practicalities than in daydreams, had dug out the sheep's brains, divided them in two and offered half to the starosta and half to his eldest son, thus causing a murmur of admiration and respect to run round the room. This German was obviously a man of high breeding and exquisite manners!

The wine jug passed busily back and forth. It was, fortunately, considered the height of politeness to belch in Kalmuck society, and Porta went from strength to strength, farting loudly and cutting off the right ear of the unfortunate sheep and handing it with exquisite good taste to the starosta's eldest daughter. It appeared that he had now scaled the very summit of Kalmuck etiquette. Porta had at last found his rightful position in society.

The old woman with the sunflower seeds inserted herself between the Legionnaire and me and began telling us what had happened in the village before our arrival. It seemed that a section of Russian cavalry had passed through, and the first sight to meet their eyes had been a brown shirt hanging on a line to dry outside one of the huts.

'Babushka's hut,' said the old woman, mournfully. 'It was her lover's shirt. Her lover was a German.'

The Legionnaire pulled a face.

'SS, by the sound of things.'

The commissar in charge of the group had slashed the shirt with his sabre and had his horse trample upon it until it was in shreds, and had then followed this burst of petty contempt by sending two of his NKVD men into the hut in search of Babushka, who was taking temporary refuge in the stove. Seventeen years before, Trotskyite soldiers had hidden in that very same stove. Babushka was discovered and hanged, just as the Trotskyite soldiers had been before her. Just as several other villagers were, including the old woman's only son. Their bodies had been flung into the snow and their relatives forbidden to give them a decent burial. The Legionnaire and I listened with wavering interest to the tale. We had heard of too many similar incidents to be very much moved.

While Porta and Tiny, glutted with roast mutton and wine, lay back with silly smiles on their faces and dancing girls on their knees, I rested my head against the Legionnaire's shoulder and closed my eyes. The atmosphere was thick with smoke and with sweat and the wine had been stronger than I knew. Half asleep as I was, I felt the old woman creep closer to me. I felt her hand on my brow, sweeping back my hair, and I heard her thin, cracked voice crooning over me. I was just like her son, her only son whom the NKVD had murdered. We were the same age as each other, I looked just like him ... I fell asleep with the gentle touch of her old calloused hand stroking lightly back and forth across my brow, and for the first time in many months I dreamt that the war was over.

The next morning, when we took our departure, the old woman pressed a leg of mutton into my hand.

'For you,' she whispered. 'No one else, mind ... just you! May God protect you, my son ...'

The whole village turned out to say farewell. Some of them even accompanied us as far as the river, but none would dare to cross it. On the other side there were NKVD men, roaming the countryside with their nagans. The Kalmucks hated and feared the NKVD more than anything else on earth.

'Same thing in Indochina,' mused the Legionnaire. 'You could be at home amongst your enemies and killed by your friends ... God help those poor devils if the commissars ever find out we were there.'

The retreat continued. The snowstorm continued. Lost in the middle of a forest, we encountered some stray Cossacks. They were as surprised to see us as we to see them, but we stopped half-heartedly to do battle with each other. It seemed the height of lunacy to stand fighting in a snowstorm in the middle of a forest. I believe both sides would far have preferred to pass on without exchanging blows, but there was always some fanatic like Heide who wanted to kill.

We moved on from the forest, out into the open. The wind was so strong we were scarcely able to make any headway. Hour after hour we marched onwards in search of the front line, bent double, our feet shuffling through the heavy drifts. Days merged into nights; nights, for all I knew, into weeks; weeks into months, into years, into decades ... It seemed we had spent all our lives stumbling across Russia.

'Never mind! Wait till we get to the Tschir——'

'We'll find our troops at the Tschir——'

'We'll be OK when we reach the Tschir ...'

And so at last we reached the Tschir, and the snow was still falling and the landscape was still bare, and where the German front line was to be found was anyone's guess.

'They're not here!'

The cry went up; astounded, incredulous, stunned.

'They're not here!'

A hundred or more chapped lips mouthed the words, as men floundered forward in the snow, unable to believe that after all this while we were still on our own.

We could take no more. Even the most foolhardy of optimists had reached the end. Even the redoubtable General Augsberg fell on to his knees and buried his head in his hands.

'Oh God! My God! For pity's sake...'

He seemed momentarily to have forgotten that the SS were strictly forbidden to believe in God.

There was no sound save the howling of the wind, and to that we were so accustomed that we hardly noticed it. No gunfire, no shells, not even the faint rumbling of distant artillery. No signs of the front line for hundreds of miles in every direction.

'Brigadenführer!' The young lieutenant, who had grown visibly older since I first saw him, hurried forward and knelt in the snow by the general's side. 'You can't give up! You can't abandon us now!'

'Let me alone! Go away and leave me in peace! I'm not going any further...'

'But, sir—all these men—all of us here—we've all put our faith in you. You've brought us this far, for God's sake don't give up now!'

The general looked up at the young lieutenant. His grey eyes were bleak. The usual lunatic SS fire had died out, and he looked almost human.

'What is the point of carrying on?' he asked, simply.

Behind him, we stood in a cluster, waiting to be told what to do. The lieutenant rose to his feet. Round his neck he was wearing a blue woollen muffler. I wondered who had knitted it for him. Mother, wife or sweetheart? Growing maudlin, I imagined the loving hands settling it about his neck as they saw him off for the very last time at the station, and I felt suddenly sorry for the young lieutenant who was going to die. No older than I was, and he was going to die ... we were all going to die...

Somewhere behind me, a man burst into anguished sobs. General Augsberg settled his monocle into his eye, adjusted his face into its normal hard lines and stood up.

'All right! What are we waiting for? Let's press on!'

We crossed the Tschir as we had crossed the Don. Another river behind us.

'The next one's the Kalitva,' said the Old Man. 'Somehow, I

don't reckon we're going to find anything there.'

'Don't worry,' said the Legionnaire, with a hard smile. 'There's always another after that ... the Oskol, if I remember rightly. And from the Oskol to the Donetz it can't be more than seventy or eighty miles ...'

'And what happens after that?' I asked, bitterly. 'What happens if we still haven't found them?'

The Old Man shrugged.

'I suppose we just go straight on until we come to the Dnieper.'

'The Dnieper!' I snorted. 'Who the hell do you think's going to get that far?'

'No one, but it gives you something to think about,' said the Legionnaire, amiably.

Not far away, limping badly and in obvious pain, was a sergeant-major from one of the crack units of the German Army. He was their last survivor. Shortly before the battle of Krasnij Okjabre, their padre had delivered a sermon in which he had stated very firmly that whatever happened, it would be the will of God. The padre himself had not survived to explain to the sergeant-major why it was that God had willed the whole of the unit to be wiped out by Russian flame-throwers. The sergeant-major had been a gloomy, introspective fellow ever since.

Behind us, small but determined, trotting through the snow with his head down, came the paymaster from the 'Greater Germany' Division. Back home in Vienne, the paymaster owned a hotel, and there had been a time when he was far too proud to speak to his inferiors unless it were to give an order. Since Stalingrad, however, he had been only too pleased to talk to anyone who was left, to anyone who would stop and listen to him, and he had even been known to hold long conversations with Porta, who was anxious to discover why he did not abandon the idea of a conventional hotel and set up a high-class brothel instead. The paymaster was himself growing quite interested in the idea. He would walk for miles lost in silent daydreams of the girls he would have and the services he would offer.

We spent a few hours at night resting in a deserted village, where the huts were no more than blackened ruins. In the charred remains of a stable, we found a dead horse. The flesh had been preserved by the low temperature, and when Porta had defrosted it and sliced it up, we cooked it over an open fire and dished it out as beefsteaks. One man declared it was the juiciest and most tender meat he had ever tasted.

'They do say,' remarked Gregor, thoughtfully sucking the blood off his fingers, 'that human flesh is the best of the lot.'

'Some people swear by it,' agreed Porta, cheerfully. 'In the Russian prison camp near Paderborn you used to be able to get human liver on the black market.'

'You ever try it?' I asked.

'No, but I reckon I would have, if I'd been starving enough ... And if nobody didn't tell you what it was, where's the objection to it?'

We set off again at dawn, on our long march to nowhere, but now the P4 was playing up and refused to start. The engine was iced up and we had to abandon it in the village. Some of us were secretly and jealously rather glad that Porta now had to join the rest of us on foot, but it was the end of the road for those who were too badly wounded to walk.

As we marched, we strained our ears for the sound of battle, but all we heard was the whining of the wind and the crunching of boots in the snow. Porta gave it as his opinion that the front had moved from Russia and that the last battle was now being fought on the Rhine itself. He could well have been right, but no one really cared any more.

And so the weary retreat continued, mile after desperate mile across the howling steppe. We were less than three hundred now. Behind us lay the stiffened remains of over five hundred men, dead from frostbite, typhus, dysentery, exhaustion and despair.

We stopped for another rest. We were able to cover less ground each day. Our resistance was very low and we could no longer cope with the bitter Russian winter. Defying any NKVD who might be within striking distance, we lit a fire and huddled round it, holding out our hands to the blaze and feeling the warmth of the flames as they flickered over our feeble bodies. Porta lit an opium cigarette, but it had barely gone once round the group when the familiar order to be on our way was shouted across to us. One of the baggage-masters, an elderly sergeant who had already been through the First World War, remained on the ground, crumpled up with his hands pressed hard into his guts.

'Come on!' I said, putting a hand beneath his elbow. 'Time to go ... you can't stay there like that.'

'Leave me be,' he muttered. 'Just leave me be.'

'Get up and march, Grandad!' Gregor dug him none too gently in the ribs with his rifle. 'We can't afford to lose any more men.'

'You surely haven't come all this way just to lie down and die in the snow?' I said. 'Not now, when we're almost there?'

'Where?' He looked up at me, his face grey and leathery. 'Where are we?'

I shrugged a shoulder.

'There,' I said, helplessly. 'Can't you hear the guns?'

'No. I can't hear any guns.' He drew his legs up to his chin, sweating with the agony of some tearing internal pain. 'Go away, boy, and let me be. I've had my day. You're young enough to make it, but I'm not ... I'm old and tired and I'm going to die.'

'What are you men still doing here?' The lieutenant came running up to us. He jerked a thumb over his shoulder. 'Fall in with the rest of the column!'

Gregor moved off. I pointed silently at the old man, doubled up in the snow. The lieutenant looked at him.

'Dysentery,' he said. 'Leave him, he wouldn't last out the day even if we took him with us. He should never have come in the first place. He should have stayed in Stalingrad and waited for the Russians.'

He took out his revolver, levelled it, hesitated a moment, then swore and pushed it back into its holster.

'Get a move on!' he shouted, as he ran after the column.

I took one last look at the old man. He turned his face up to me, and with a shaking, clawlike hand he held out a dog-eared envelope.

'If you get through ... if ever you get home ... send this to my wife, and tell her—tell her I couldn't help it. Tell her how they betrayed us. I didn't mean to die, but I—couldn't help it ...'

I took the envelope from him and put it in my pocket.

'I'll tell her,' I said. 'I'll tell everyone, don't you worry! I'll tell the whole damn world what the bastards have done to us——'

'Sven!' It was Heide's voice. He was running towards me across the snow. 'What the flaming hell are you doing? I've been sent back to look for you.'

I gestured towards the old fellow.

'He's on his last legs.'

'So what? There's nothing you can do about it.' Heide

scarcely glanced at him. 'He's not the first and he won't be the last. What's the matter with you? Got bitten by the religious bug? Christ almighty, you're a soldier, not a bleeding priest! Take this and come on!'

He picked up my sub-machine-gun and thrust it at me. He was right, of course: there was nothing I could do about it. I couldn't sit by the old boy's side and wait for him to die. I couldn't carry him on my back for the next thousand miles. I bent down and whispered in his ear.

'Don't worry, Grandad ... I'll get through! I'll deliver your letter for you ...'

We marched all through the night, with only a couple of short rests. We marched all through the next day, and the day after that. Our numbers thinned out still further. Only the toughest and the most determined were now left to carry on with the retreat. We floundered through the snow, fought against the tearing wind, crossed innumerable rivers, lost our way in immense forests.

At one point I was marching behind a man who quite suddenly collapsed at my feet. He was a tall man, he swayed forward like a felled pine tree, stiff and straight, but as he hit the ground he crumpled up and lay in a heap. I had been marching behind him for several hours and he had given no signs of an impending collapse, but now he came crashing down so fast I had no time to avoid him, and I tripped headlong and fell into the snow at his side. I turned him over and saw his face: it was red and feverish, and the throat was covered in pink spots. His breath was foul-smelling. I shook him by the shoulder, but he only moaned and writhed.

'So what?' echoed Heide's voice in my memory. 'There's nothing you can do about it ...'

There wasn't. Out here, on the frozen steppe, with no medicines and no possibility of rest or treatment, typhus was a death sentence. I took the man's revolver from his holster and put it into his hand, closing the fingers round it. I had scarcely regained my place in the column when a shot rang out.

That night, we bivouacked in a wood. All the others dug themselves deep into the snow, curled up and fell into an exhausted sleep, but our group lit a fire and sat round it, cooking the remains of the frozen horse meat, which we had carried with us. The Old Man produced some soft and wrinkled potatoes from the depths of his pack, and Gregor had a twist of salt. Grilled steak and roast potatoes, a few drags of an opium

cigarette and the leaping flames of a camp-fire ... it was almost
enough to make a man believe he was at peace with the world.

We lay in a circle, our feet upturned to the glowing embers.
The soles of Porta's boots began to smell of burning, and he sat
up and took the boots off, and then removed his socks for the
first time in weeks. The big toe on his right foot was turning
blue. It served as a warning to the rest of us. We tore off our
own boots and socks and examined ourselves carefully, and
wherever we suspected trouble we rubbed the affected spot with
snow. The pain was agonising, but it brought back the circulation and restored life to flesh that would otherwise have died.
Nothing is so treacherous as a frozen limb. Porta could have
walked round for days, never knowing anything was wrong,
until gangrene had set in and it was too late.

Next morning, shortly before dawn, we reported our finds to
the doctor and he at once ordered a general inspection of hands
and feet. One man was found to have a leg that was blue almost
as far as the knee. He could feel no pain and had never suspected what was happening, not having had cause to look at his
legs for many weeks past. The doctor took General Augsberg to
one side and told him the news.

'There's only one way to save him, and that's to take the leg
off ... But how the devil do we transport him after that?'

'We don't,' said Augsberg, shortly.

Before the doctor could protest at this only possible answer,
Tiny came bounding across to us from the trees.

'Something's moving over there!'

Everyone fell silent. We stood listening, frozen limbs and
gangrene forgotten.

'Can't hear a bloody thing,' said Porta. 'I reckon you're
imagining it.'

Nevertheless, he stamped on the fire. It never did to take
Tiny's warnings lightly. His brain may not have been too sharp,
but his hearing was more acute than anyone's.

And now we heard it ourselves. A faint cracking and crackling,
as of twigs being snapped underfoot. Tiny was already flat on
the ground, with the MPI ready to fire. The rest of us scattered,
crouched in dug-outs and behind trees and bushes, straining
our eyes in the darkness of the wood. Again we heard the sound
of twigs, the sound of rustling undergrowth. It was quite clear
now, and it was almost certainly a man, or men. Animals moved
silently through the dark forest.

'It's Ivan!'

The word was passed swiftly, in a whisper, from hole to hole, from tree to tree. Everywhere, men stiffened and pressed their fingers against the trigger. Those of us who seconds before had been doubled up with the pangs of dysentery, those of us who had lain exhausted in the snow, those of us who thought they no longer cared for life, were suddenly reunited in tacit agreement that whatever else befell us we were not going to be taken alive by the NKVD. We had seen the tortured corpses of too many German soldiers to expect any mercy at their hands.

The noise grew sharper in outline. And then we heard voices, rough and coarse, conversing in undertones.

'Germanskij . . .'

'Job Tvojemad . . .'

I guessed they were Siberians. They must have picked up our traces a long way back and been following us ever since. They were known for their tenacity, they would stay on the trail for thousands of miles and never give up.

'NKVD,' hissed Tiny, making a preliminary movement. 'Let's get the hell out!'

'Too late.' The Legionnaire stretched across a restraining hand and pressed him down again. 'Now they've got wind of us they'll never let go.'

We had no alternative but to stay and fight. Out of the trees glided a line of white phantoms. We could hear the faint swish of their skis in the snow. Behind their white masks, we knew that glittering dark eyes were peering through the gloom in search of us. We lay hidden, watching as they moved forward. My throat contracted with terror, and only the habit of years, the hard habit of Prussian discipline, kept me hidden in my snow dug-out. At the head of the group was a commissar. I saw the hammer and sickle and the red star on his helmet. He pointed forward, in our direction. Straight at us, it seemed to me.

'Over there!'

From his position behind the MPI, Tiny turned and rolled despairing eyes at me. I caught his panic and made a slight, involuntary movement. Quick as lightning, the Legionnaire reached out and laid his hand over mine. He winked at me, warning, reproving, encouraging. I swallowed a mouthful of air and my panic subsided.

A sudden shot rang out. The commissar clutched both hands to his heart and slowly collapsed into the snow. Someone else had lost his head and had not had the comforting pressure of the Legionnaire's steady hand to reassure him. Thank God, at

225

least, he had not lost his aim as well as his head.

I heard the general's whistle blow. There was a sound as of thunder, and a billowing sea of flame swept forward and engulfed the six white phantoms. The lieutenant crawled towards the Old Man.

'Feldwebel, take your men and get out there after the rest of 'em!'

'Us again,' grumbled Porta. 'I tell you, if it weren't for mugs like us we'd have lost this perishing war years ago!'

'Then why, I wonder, do we prolong the agony?' murmured the Legionnaire, already slipping a knife between his teeth and moving forward after the Old Man.

We made our way through the trees, sweeping round in a semicircle to come out on the far side of the Russians. Tiny suddenly held up a hand and pointed ahead. How he knew they were there, I haven't the faintest idea. He claimed afterwards that he had heard a Russian fart, and with Tiny's strange gift that could well have been true. At all events, we caught them in the middle of a clearing, only a few yards away from us. Their attention was still turned in the opposite direction, where we had left the main body of the troops.

Silently, with infinite care, I fitted my bayonet to my rifle. The Legionnaire was the first to move. He darted forward through the bushes, caught the sentry round the neck with one arm and plunged his knife deep into the man's back. The sentry fell forward with a grunt of surprise, and his companions turned in stupefaction as the rest of us charged in.

We slaughtered them mercilessly, as they would have slaughtered us had not Tiny's sharp ears caught them out in their first stealthy approach. Two of them attempted to surrender, their brawny arms held high above their heads, almond eyes imploring in big, shapeless faces.

'Sorry, chum,' said Porta. 'Didn't no one ever tell you there was a war on?'

He shot them both, quite calmly and with no emotion. Tiny, meanwhile, was jubilantly capering about the clearing with a fistful of gold teeth and gold fillings. He had a little leather bag which he kept about his person. It was bulging with plundered teeth, and every now and again he would bring it out and send the tiny pieces of gold winking and flashing across the palm of his hand, much as a jeweller pours out his diamonds and rubies for approval.

We rejoined the rest of the column and moved onwards

across the steppe. The wind had died down and the mid-morning sky was a piercing blue against the dazzling white expanse of snow. The sun hung in a great blood-red ball high above our heads. It had not much warmth, but it spread a little optimism amongst us and it caught the crystals of snow for miles around and made a thousand winking pinpoints of light. Porta brought out his flute and we marched quite jauntily as he played.

Before we had gone more than a mile or so, my eyes began paining me again. I suffered from them some part of every day, but when the skies were grey and overcast the pain was bearable, only a dull ache and the occasional sharp stab, to which I had grown almost reconciled. But today, with the piercing azure sky and the dazzling crystals, it became a tormenting agony. Red-hot needles plunged through my retina and carried straight up into my head. The clear blinding white of the snow was gradually blurred into a grey mass of cotton wool. Black circles began dancing before me. My head was full of bright flashes and sparks and my footsteps began wandering.

'Don't do that,' I heard the Legionnaire saying. 'You'll only make it worse.'

And I felt my mittened hands being firmly removed from my eyes, where they had been vigorously attempting to knead my eyeballs out of their sockets. I turned my head blindly towards the sound of the voice. The Legionnaire was no more than a shadow. I began shambling and stumbling, and the Old Man put an arm round my shoulders to keep me from falling. I moved along in a delirium of pain, muttering and moaning to myself, and when we stopped for the first short break I was quite willing for them to shoot me on the spot as we had shot so many others who were suffering.

I lay with my head cradled in my arms, neither knowing nor caring what was going on around me. I heard Tiny say, 'Kill him! Finish him off! What's it matter? He's on his last legs, anyway! So what if we hurry him along a bit?' I thought he was talking about me, and had I had the strength I would have lifted up my head and screamed, 'Yes, yes, I'm on my last legs, get on with it!' But as it turned out, they were not discussing me but the sole survivor of the First Cavalry Division, who had been racked with dysentery for several days past and was now slowly dying in the snow only a few yards away from me. On his nose were a pair of dark glasses. Special glasses, designed to cut out the penetrating ultra-violet rays of the snow.

'They'd do Sven a treat,' said Gregor.

I rolled over and half opened an eye.

'What would?' I demanded, feebly. 'What's going on?'

There was a pause.

'If he doesn't kick the bucket before we move on,' said Tiny, 'I'm going to shoot the bastard.'

There was another pause. I believe I must have lost consciousness, because the next thing I remember they were hauling me to my feet and pushing a pair of dark glasses on my nose. The relief was immediate. The mists cleared, the stabbing pains began to recede, I was able to stand up unaided.

'Did he——' I turned to look at the body of the dead cavalryman. 'What happened to him?'

'He died,' said the Old Man, grimly.

'Just in time,' added Tiny.

We went off in search of the MO, who, according to the regulations, had to approve the issue of the glasses and record his approval in my passbook. It was purely a formality, but regulations being regulations, and the German Army still being the German Army, even if it were torn to shreds, it seemed wise to be on the safe side.

It was such a relief to be able to look the world in the face again that I felt capable of marching another thousand miles. It was a shock when the doctor refused to approve my wearing the glasses.

'More than my life's worth,' he said. 'Special glasses are only issued after a rigorous examination of the eyes.'

'Then examine his flaming eyes!' cried the lieutenant, testily.

'I can't do that,' said the doctor. 'I'm not an eye specialist ... besides, I don't have the proper instruments. I'm sorry, I'm afraid I can't possibly approve the issue of dark glasses to this man.'

'For crying out loud!' exclaimed the lieutenant. 'He's as blind as a bat without them! Any fool can see that, it doesn't require a specialist!'

'I can't help what any fool can see,' said the doctor, growing angry in his turn. 'I'm only going according to regulations.'

'Regulations! Regulations!' The lieutenant strode up and down in the snow in a fine rage. I stood gratefully watching him with my new eyes. 'God help the German nation if it can't do anything without regulations! Here's a man who's suffering, and there's a pair of dark glasses that no one else wants, and here's a bloody quack saying he can't approve of it because of the regulations ... regulations, my arse! What do you suggest

we do with the perishing glasses? Carry them all the way back
to Germany in a waterproof bag?' He suddenly pulled out his
revolver and faced the trembling doctor. 'You just sign that
man's papers or we'll be going on without you!'

The doctor signed; I wore my dark glasses; the column
moved on and the body of my dead benefactor from the First
Cavalry Division was left behind in the snow. I had never
known his name and I had already forgotten him.

If a stone should fall on the jug, that's unfortunate for the jug. If the jug should fall on a stone, that's unfortunate for the jug. It's always unfortunate for the jug.

The Talmud

Order of the day sent to all divisions by the Commander in Chief of the Sixth Army, Generaloberst Friedrich Paulus:

'As a soldier, I wish to remind all other soldiers that it is an act of dishonour to fall into the hands of the enemy. It is therefore the duty of an officer to take his own life rather than suffer such a fate. If he allows himself to be taken prisoner, he is no longer worthy of the uniform he wears. He will be considered as a deserter and a traitor to his country and will be tried as such when the hostilities are at an end.

'The above should be taken to apply equally to non-commissioned officers and other ranks. To surrender is an act of cowardice! Our Führer Adolf Hitler demands of us that we fight to the last man, the last bullet. Be worthy of his trust!

'Heil Hitler!'

On the same day as this order was issued, four high-ranking officers left Stalingrad. General Jaenecke had had his skull cracked open by a falling roof beam and was evacuated by aeroplane. Generals Pitkert and Hube were flown back to Germany on the orders of Army Personnel. Major-General Berger left on his own initiative. He was arrested on the airfield at Warnapol and was shot behind the hangars two hours later.

Just outside Stalingrad, a quartermaster-general blew up himself and his staff shortly before Russian troops overran their position.

In the hospital of Baburkin, a surgeon and his four assistants were preparing to operate when a column of T34s appeared in the road outside. The surgeon had just sufficient time to snatch up a handful of grenades before the Russians walked in. The hospital was largely destroyed, and not a single living person was found inside.

Near Katlowska, four hundred Russian tanks crushed the tattered remnants of a German division. A lieutenant and five of his men succeeded in escaping the carnage, but they were picked up by a police patrol less than an hour later and shot for having sabotaged the Führer's orders.

The last man, the last bullet ... Be worthy of his trust!

FOURTEEN

PRISONERS OF THE NKVD

A new and even more violent tempest was now blowing up from the Siberian deeps. It battered relentlessly against us, day and night. It was almost impossible to walk upright and we staggered along with hunched shoulders and drooping arms and now and again dropped on to all fours like animals. Sometimes an extra strong blast would pick a man up and carry him several yards before dumping him disdainfully into the snow like a discarded package. The cold had also intensified. The temperature had sunk to such depths that the constant tears which streamed from men's eyes were at once transformed into hard crystal droplets.

It became at last impossible to go on, and we dug ourselves into the snow and stayed buried for four days while the tempest raged all about us and whipped the drifts into great shining mountains. Struggling trees and bushes were torn from the ground and borne past us on invisible currents. On two occasions we saw wolf packs running before the wind, streaming past our snowholes with their scrawny necks extended and their yellow eyes gleaming. They took no notice of us, nor we of them. We were all too much occupied keeping ourselves alive.

We grew so accustomed to the whining and the moaning of the wind that during the rare intervals of peace we were frightened by the unnatural silence and dared scarcely breathe for fear of giving away our positions to the enemy.

The Russians could have been sheltering only half a mile away, in the next dip of the landscape, and we should never have known. The falling snowflakes were so thick, and were whipped into such patterns of frenzy, that visibility was cut to a few yards.

On the morning of the fifth day the wind had subsided to its normal pre-tempest level, which now, in comparison, seemed like a mild spring zephyr. We dug ourselves out of our icy prisons and fought our way through the drifts in the wake of General Augsberg. After his one unguarded moment of human weakness when we had crossed the Tschir, he had closed in again upon himself and was once more the SS man-machine, grimly leading a pack of terrified and half-starved men across the Russian wastes in search of a phantom German Army.

'Ivan,' said the Old Man, suddenly, as we marched.

He raised an arm and pointed across the plain. Far off, in the distance, we could see a long column of heavy tanks moving across the landscape.

'They're heading west,' said Heide. 'That's where the front is.'

'That's where Germany is,' I said.

'Germany!' cried Gregor, with angry scorn. 'Why not France? Why not America? You could even get all the way to Japan and back if you kept on long enough ... Why Germany? Why not the bloody moon?'

'If that's the way you feel about it,' I said, indifferently.

'Don't you kid yourself we're ever going to get back to Germany, mate! You'll be lucky if you reach the next perishing river!'

'That's defeatist talk!' screamed Heide, snatching out his revolver. 'You could be shot for that!'

Within seconds, the two of them were rolling about in the snow with their hands round each other's throats. I distinctly heard Gregor threaten to bite Heide's head off. Heide's one aim was to blow Gregor's brains out. To such a pass had we come, and not even the Old Man or the Legionnaire could be bothered to put a stop to it. They spared one disinterested glance for the fighting pair, shrugged their shoulders and walked on. Tiny and Porta stood half-heartedly cheering, and I found myself thinking, 'If they kill each other, it'll be more rations for the rest of us ...'

In the end, the lieutenant appeared and clobbered them both, and they staggered back into the column bow-legged and dazed.

We had been on the march for fifty-six days now and we were scarcely recognisable as civilised human beings. We had far more in common with the wolf packs we had seen.

The retreat continued. Early one morning we reached the next river, the Oskol. No sign of German troops, but the last faint flicker of hope had long since burnt itself out and we felt no pangs of disappointment. On the opposite bank of the river was the small market town of Kubjansk. There we should find the rest and the warmth and the fresh supplies of food we so badly needed; but there, also, we might find the enemy.

'Oberfeldwebel!'

The general came striding up to the Old Man, and I saw

Porta catch Tiny's eye. Here we go again ... always us! Take your section and go and have a scout round...

For once, Porta was wrong. It was General Augsberg who was going to lead the column across the river and into Kubjansk, while the Old Man and the rest of us were to stay behind and await the outcome.

'We'll give you the OK when we've cleaned the place up—if it needs cleaning up. If they start firing on us before we get there, just stay put and wait to see what happens.'

'Only too pleased,' muttered Tiny, as we watched the general sliding down the bank followed by the lieutenant and the rest of the men. Suddenly, as they approached the village, a volley of shots rang out.

'Ivan!'

Porta flung himself behind the machine-gun. The opposite bank of the river became in an instant a struggling mass of men, as the Russians swarmed out of the village and clashed with the general and his advancing troops. Within a matter of minutes, we saw our companions disarmed and led away, prisoners of the enemy. The Old Man sat back and calmly lit his pipe.

'Only to be expected,' he remarked. 'A place like that ... it was bound to be occupied.'

'There was nothing we could do,' said Gregor, virtuously. 'He told us to sit tight and wait.'

'Quite so.' The Old Man puffed out a thick cloud of stinking smoke. God knows what he'd put into that pipe in place of tobacco! 'Stay put and see what happens. And now we've seen, and it's up to us to go and get them out of it.'

'Get them out of it?' snapped Heide. 'You must be joking! Get us out of it, more like ... Any minute now and we'll probably hear the firing squads start up.'

'When I want your advice I'll remember to ask you for it,' the Old Man equably assured him. 'And until we know for certain that they're dead, we shall assume that they're alive.'

'So what's the plan?' asked the Legionnaire, quietly.

The Old Man pointed across the river with the stem of his pipe.

'Go over there and get them out. Attack the enemy when they're not expecting it. It's the least we can do for Augsberg. If it weren't for him, we'd never have got this far.'

'I agree,' said the Legionnaire. 'We owe him that much.'

'We don't owe anybody anything!' snarled Heide. 'He couldn't have got this far without us, don't you kid yourself!'

The Legionnaire looked at him, cold and contemptuous, then slowly turned away. The Old Man stood up; sturdy, immovable, unquenchably loyal.

'Can I have two volunteers to go across and reconnoître?'

Tiny and Porta were on their feet before anyone else.

'One thing I've always wanted to find out,' said Tiny, as they set off together, 'and that's what Ivan gets up to when he thinks he's all alone . . .'

They were gone two hours. It was mid-morning when they returned. Tiny was carrying a large bundle over his shoulders, wrapped round his neck in the manner of a fox fur. It turned out to be a pig, half-roasted with the spit still in place.

'Just picked it up in passing,' said Tiny, casually letting it fall at the Old Man's feet. 'It's not quite finished cooking, but we didn't have time to hang around.'

'What about the general and the rest? Did you find out what's happened to them?'

'They're in an empty pigsty,' said Porta. 'All herded in together with two sentries guarding them.'

'And how about the Russians? What strength are they? A company? A battalion?'

'A battalion, I should say.'

'A battalion of women,' added Tiny, in disgust. 'More women than men, and so sodding ugly, not even a gorilla would fancy 'em.'

'Seem to be part of a supply section,' explained Porta. 'They've got lorries full of grenades parked under the trees.'

'Amateurs!' said Tiny, still brooding over the general lack of sex appeal. 'They haven't even stood a proper guard.'

'They're probably not expecting any more German troops to be in the vicinity.' The Old Man put away his pipe and nodded, thoughtfully. 'An attack is the last thing they'll be waiting for.'

He divided us into groups and Gregor and I set off with Porta towards the cover of some woods. The trees were so thick they cut out all the light and it took our eyes a while to grow accustomed to the darkness. Gregor hated woods at the best of times. He stuck close to my heels, almost treading on me, breathing heavily and anxiously down my neck.

'Don't shit your knickers before the show's even started,' protested Porta.

'It's these bloody trees,' muttered Gregor. 'I keep seeing things in them.'

'Nothing like a good tree,' said Porta, cheerfully. 'You can climb up 'em, piss up 'em, hide up 'em——'

'I wish you'd climb up one and stay there,' I hissed, almost as nervous as Gregor. 'All this flaming racket ... they'll hear us coming miles away.'

'Bugger me!' said Porta, in disgust. 'It's like taking two maiden aunties out for a stroll!'

We moved on in silence and darkness. Twig-fingers with thorny nails reached out and clawed at our uniforms. Behind every bush lurked an enormous, fur-clad Mongoloid figure, waiting to jump out upon us. We trod cautiously onwards, feeling the ground with our feet. Porta tripped in the tangled undergrowth and fell sprawling. His sub-machine-gun landed in some bushes, and he was so furious he picked himself up and began kicking a tree-trunk. Gregor and I stood silently watching in the gloom, far too scared to laugh or jeer.

We retrieved the weapon and pressed onwards. Suddenly, overhead, there was a loud burst of wing-claps and a vast crowd of crows rose flapping and clacking from the trees.

'That's fucked it,' said Porta. 'That'll bring the whole Red Army out to investigate.'

We reached the edge of the wood and stood in the shadow of the trees, waiting for the Old Man's signal. Kubjansk was spread out before us. The sky had darkened and the snow was beginning to fall again. It was good weather for launching a surprise attack. Our group was to move out under cover of a protective smoke screen, and Gregor and I were to make our way to the pigsty and deal with the sentries.

The whistle blew, and we moved in on our rescue mission. Shells and grenades rocked the buildings on their foundations and set the very streets afire. Machine-guns clattered, women ran shrieking out of houses, dogs and children were everywhere under your feet. Gregor and I charged along the main street and dived for cover behind an American threshing machine, a goodwill present from the United States to the Soviet Union, as a nearby house collapsed with a roar and a wall of bricks came tumbling down. In one of the neighbouring streets a shell scored a direct hit on a lorry loaded with grenades.

By the time we reached the pigsty, the panic was such that we found the prisoners had already dealt with their guards and were streaming out into the streets. The lieutenant caught sight of Gregor and me and grabbed us by the shoulder.

'What the devil's going on? Have the Americans arrived?'

235

'It's all right!' I yelled, above the general uproar. 'It's only us!'

We made our way out of the burning town, meeting more resistance from the smoke and the flames and the falling buildings than from the enemy. We had lost fourteen men and had nine wounded, of whom seven we were forced to abandon. They would have died sooner or later on the march, and there was no possibility of carrying them with us. General Augsberg, his uniform blackened and torn, and his face covered in angry burn marks, lost no time in driving us forward again, away from the village and on towards the west. The sight of the flames would be certain to bring other enemy units to investigate, and we were in no condition to face full-scale combat. Our task now was to dodge the enemy where ever we could.

Somewhere ahead of us, somewhere over the hundreds of miles of snow-covered steppe, lay the Donetz. We had made that our goal.

'As far as the Donetz and no further,' we said. 'When we get there, that's our lot.'

But we had said that about the Don, and we were still marching ... Our spirits were low, and falling lower every day. We grumbled incessantly, and orders were carried out with provoking slowness. Even the equable lieutenant lost his temper and began threatening us. Not until General Augsberg, choosing the right psychological moment, gave a blast on his whistle and called us to order did we regain at least the rudimentary aspects of an army on the march.

The general knew well the power of a whistle, and he used it sparingly and to good effect. The Germans are a nation of natural slaves. They respond to the crack of the whip and the threat of the jackboot; to the shrill blast of the whistle and the hectoring shouts of their superiors.

The whistle is one of the most powerful instruments in all Germany. It controls the nation's life, from the kindergarten through to the army. At school, children fall obediently into line at the call of the whistle; in the street, traffic comes to a halt when the policeman puts his whistle to his mouth; in the barracks, men are marched and drilled and trained by the whistle. Conquerors can cause oceans of German blood to be spilt, and whole seas of tears to be shed; they can take away their uniforms and take away their weapons and forbid them their armies ... but only let them take away their whistles and Germany would fall to its knees and never rise again!

Shouting is not so ingrained in civilian life as in military, but for a soldier it is as much to be feared as the ubiquitous whistle. At Breslau, I remember, we attacked Polish tanks with bare fists and bayonets, all because a quartermaster-sergeant shouted at us. Another time, I and a comrade bodily picked up and supported a huge brute of a horse that refused to be shod—all because a sergeant-major bawled at us. We then spent two months in hospital with torn tendons, but although the doctors were doubtful whether we should be fit for continued military service, they changed their minds pretty quickly when the CO screamed at them.

Perplexing people! Wild beasts that have to be tamed by the whip. Led not by persuasion but by brute force. Broken in, but never completely broken down. And I had chosen to become one of them . . .

The general brought the column to a halt at the edge of a wood which was not marked on his map. Most German maps of Russia seemed to have been inspired by lunatic guesswork. The general angrily folded it up and crammed it into his pocket, then picked out Gregor and me as a couple of unwilling volunteers to explore the wretched wood.

We had penetrated about a mile inside it when suddenly and silently, from the trees and the undergrowth, rose a party of men in a variety of different uniforms. There was no opportunity to turn and fight. They were on us before we realised it.

'Who are you? Where have you come from?'

The spokesman was wearing a faded Russian uniform. As Gregor and I stood staring with our hands held above our heads, he clouted us both in the face and repeated his question.

We had fallen into the hands of the Vlassov Army, a group of partisans who worked behind the Russian lines and were noted for their savagery. Having no very strong aspirations towards martyrdom, Gregor and I opened our mouths and talked. We explained how we had marched out of Stalingrad and how our numbers had steadily dwindled. We impressed upon them that after the fracas at Kubjansk we were the only two to have escaped. They were obviously suspicious, but for the moment they decided to believe us and to keep us alive for further questioning when we reached their headquarters.

With hands secured with barbed wire, we shuffled along in the midst of our captors. For three days and nights we marched, mainly through the forests. At one point we trekked across the snowy wastes in order to collect some supplies that had been parachuted into the void by German aircraft. I wondered how many other supplies had fallen into enemy hands because the pilots had been unwilling or unable to pinpoint their targets.

On the evening of the third day we reached a village and came to a halt. At the entrance to the village, a Russian lieutenant and a German sergeant hung side by side high up in a pine tree. The partisans waged war on everyone.

We stayed twelve hours in the village and then moved on, but not before our captors had filled a sledge high with provisions and laid a charge of explosives in every one of the mean little huts. The village was burning fiercely as we left it.

We took to the forest again, with Gregor and I pulling the loaded sledge behind us. We had no idea where we were going and we never did find out, for only a couple of hours after we had left the village we were overrun by a group of Russian soldiers, and after a short skirmish the partisans were disposed of, leaving Gregor and me alone to face the enemy. A sergeant came towards us. He had a large red face covered in blisters and patches of rough skin, and he was wearing a forage cap with the light blue cross of the Service Corps. It could have been worse, it could have been the NKVD; but at that moment one Russian seemed every bit as bad as another. The sergeant searched us both and gloatingly removed Gregor's tiny pocket knife, only an inch long and quite useless.

'Hitler's secret weapon?' He wagged it under our faces, then threw back his head and guffawed. All his men stood and guffawed, as well. 'Hitler kaput!' he merrily informed us. 'All Germanskij are vermin! Long live Stalin!'

He wasn't a bad bloke, really. Apart from prodding and poking us in the back as we stumbled through the trees, he used us quite decently. He laughed a great deal and tried to hold conversations with us, but neither his German nor our Russian was up to the task. As we reached the village where his division had set up its quarters, he rearranged his face into a hideous mask of ferocity, began jabbing us with his rifle and driving us before him, shouting at the top of his voice.

'Dawaï, dawaï!' he screamed, flashing his eyes about to see if his superiors were watching. 'Hitler kaput! Long live Stalin!'

He marched us triumphantly along the main street and stopped before a two-storey, brick-built house. The door was flung open and we were kicked inside and pushed at gun point along the passage to a room at the far end, where we were confronted by an elderly adjutant and several officers, all wearing the blue epaulettes of the Service Corps. The adjutant stood up and strutted over to examine us. Quite gratuitously, he struck us both very hard across the cheek with the back of his hand.

'Tschort!' he cried, contemptuously.

They were all the same. German or Russian, the only difference lay in the uniform, although the Russians were perhaps a little less refined in their methods. The adjutant's behaviour would certainly have done credit to an SS sergeant. He screamed till he was purple in the face, and he then drew breath and spat at us. As his spittle dribbled uncomfortably down my cheek, I instinctively raised my hand to wipe it away and was knocked almost senseless by the blow he gave me.

'Woenna plennys,* kaput!' he screeched, tearing the eagles off our uniforms. 'Here! You eat!'

He thrust them at us, and obediently we put them into our mouths and chewed our way through them. It was not, after all, so very terrible to eat a piece of cloth. There were plenty of worse fates that could befall us; and probably would, given time. For the moment, they contented themselves with throwing us into a small, damp, airless cellar, used as a store for potatoes. The place smelt unimaginably foul, and all the potatoes were rotten. We gnawed our way through one or two, because Gregor swore they were more nourishing when rotten than in any other state, but really it was as much as we could do to keep them down. Our stomachs rebelled even as we ate them.

Some time later, it seemed like days, but it could have been only a few hours, the door was opened and a soldier came in bearing a bowl of some turgid and evil-smelling liquid.

'Job Tvojemadj!' he said, cheerfully.

He raised the bowl to his lips and spat into it, then looked down at us and laughed. He seemed to be inviting us to laugh with him. The Russians certainly have a sense of humour.

'Fish soup,' said the soldier, and he laughed again. He banged the bowl before us, slopping most of the contents over the side. 'Very good. You eat.' He closed one eye in a clumsy wink. 'You shot tomorrow,' he promised.

He walked out, locking the door behind him. Gregor and I stared down at the fish soup with the great glistening glob floating on the top.

'Somehow,' I said, 'I don't quite fancy it.'

* Prisoners of war.

239

'I'd sooner have a spud,' said Gregor, reaching out for one.

I lay on my back and thought of General Paulus. I wondered if he was eating fish soup, and if so whether some repulsive verminous soldier had hawked into it. I thought it unlikely, on both counts. No fish soup for General Paulus. Even in the midst of defeat, his table would be plentifully supplied.

The hours passed. We had no means of telling whether it was day or night, but we thought it must be day when they brought us another bowl of the fish soup. They had thought up a new refinement this time: they not only spilt the stuff on the floor, they forced us to go down on our knees and lick it up. Left alone with the unpalatable remainder, our hunger was now such that we fell upon it and drained it to the last drop, only to find the corpse of a mouse lying at the bottom of the bowl. It crossed my mind that if Porta had been there he would have found some way of cooking the creature and making it eatable. Gregor and I just flung it into the furthest corner of the cellar and tried to forget it had ever been there.

'Bloody swine!' said Gregor, shaking all over. 'Filthy bloody swine ... we could get food poisoning from eating that rotten stuff!'

I shrugged an indifferent shoulder.

'They're all the same ... Do you remember that time at Kiev when the SS lined up those women along the ditches and made them unpick the yellow stars from their clothes before they shot them?'

'So what?' grumbled Gregor. 'That's hardly the same as putting mice in people's nosh, is it?'

'Why not?' I said. 'It's just a refinement ... people take pleasure from torturing other people.'

'That was the SS, it's nothing to do with us.'

'That's what you think,' I said, grimly. 'What the SS does, it does in the name of Germany. And if we lose the war ...' I nodded at him in the gloom. 'If we lose the war, it'll be you and me that'll pay for it.'

The door was suddenly thrown open and two NKVD men marched in. Without a word, they dragged us to our feet and up the steps. Had it not been for the green crosses they wore, they might almost have been our own SS moving in for the kill.

'Dawaï, dawaï!'

We were thrown into the back of a lorry loaded with munitions, and we sat down on a couple of cases of grenades and wrapped our arms round ourselves. It had been damp and cold down in the cellar, and the frosty open air was putting the finishing touches to our chilled bones. Just before we drove off, another NKVD man appeared and held out an imperative hand.

'Give me all your valuabls—watches, pens, lighters, rings, cigarette cases——' He snapped his fingers. 'Anything like that, hand it over! You won't be needing finery at Kolyma.'

Gregor and I had not a single valuable between us, they had long ago been lost or stolen. The man paused only to beat us into semi-consciousness and then closed the doors on us. They were all the same. Green cross or death's head, what difference did it make? I remembered a day when the SS had set fire to an old Jew's beard because he, too, had no valuables to hand over. Communist or Nazi, hammer and sickle or swastika, what difference did it make?

The lorry moved slowly along the icy roads. Gregor and I eventually returned to life and crawled back on to our grenade boxes, where we sat shivering and complaining for mile after mile. At last we reached a town, fair-sized from what we could see of it, and were handed over, like a couple of parcels, to our new captors.

Towards the evening, we were taken for interrogation by a half-drunk lieutenant-colonel of the NKVD, supported by a shapeless woman interpreter in the uniform of a captain. Gregor and I stood side by side and took it in turns to answer, like some ridiculous double act.

'Where have you come from?'

'Stalingrad,' I said.

'Stalingrad? You take us for imbeciles? All Germans at Stalingrad were killed, it says so in *Pravda*. Try again, please! Where have you come from?'

'Stalingrad,' said Gregor.

The captain swelled out the area of her bosom and exchanged glances with the lieutenant-colonel.

'That's quite impossible!' she snapped. 'Stalingrad is over four hundred miles from here and we have patrols everywhere.'

This time, Gregor and I exchanged glances.

'I can't help that,' I said. 'We've still come from Stalingrad. Maybe *Pravda* made a mistake.'

She turned on me, whip in hand, and sent the thong lashing across my face.

'Speak when you're spoken to! Enough of your lies!'

She cracked her whip again, lit a cigarette and stuck it between her thick red lips. To say she had no sex appeal at all would have been an understatement. She was scarcely even humanoid, let alone female. She stepped back a pace and stood regarding us with glittering eyes. The lieutenant-colonel spoke, and she relayed it to us.

'So! You persist you were at Stalingrad! Which division?'

'The 16th Panzer.'

'Who was your commanding officer?'

'Lieutenant-General Angern.'

'Rubbish! You're talking rubbish!'

She turned and muttered at the lieutenant-colonel, who heaved himself up, staggered round the desk and prodded me hard in the stomach with the butt of his revolver. I wondered why it was they seemed to dislike me so much more than Gregor.

'Liar!' he shouted.

The captain's great red upper lip curled a sneer.

'We know you're spies,' she said. 'Why not admit straight away that you never were at Stalingrad? Why not admit that you are Fascist agents?'

Gregor let his head droop to one side.

'Because we've come from Stalingrad,' he muttered.

'So ... very well! Stick to your lies! We shall unmask you as we go along ... Where was your division fighting, at Stalingrad?'

'Which army does the 16th Panzer Division belong to?'

'Who were the Russian troops opposing you?'

'Who was their commanding officer?'

'Give me again the name of your own commanding officer!'

The questions went on, rapped out one after another, tossed back and forth in translation from the captain to the lieutenant-colonel, who both seemed increasingly uneasy at the accuracy of all our answers.

'This is not possible!' shouted the captain, at last; and to my secret satisfaction, she lashed out with her whip at Gregor. 'How could you come all the way from Stalingrad? The NKVD have arrested all the Fascist pigs who managed to break through our lines! No one was able to escape! How did you manage it?'

'We were part of a combat group led by an SS general,' explained Gregor, very patiently, for the ninth or tenth time.

The lieutenant-colonel gave a furious roar and reached out

for his bottle of vodka. I could quite understand his displeasure. If Gregor and I had indeed come all the way from Stalingrad, then it meant that certain officials and certain officers—such as very likely himself—were in for a rough passage. When Moscow came to hear of the inefficiency which had allowed a group of German soldiers to slip through the net, there was bound to be a general inquiry and a consequent reshuffling of ranks, with a number of immediate transfers to the front line.

'What happened to the rest of you?' asked the Captain, sullenly.

'We're the only two left,' said Gregor. He waved a vague hand in the direction of the windows. 'The others are somewhere out there, on the steppe. You'll find them soon enough when the snow melts.'

'You mean they died?'

'That's about the size of it.'

'Where? How?'

'On the Don, on the Tschir——' Gregor hunched a shoulder. 'We ran out of food, we didn't have any winter clothing or medicines. Men got sick with typhus and dysentery. Some of them got frostbite.'

The captain nodded as she translated this to the lieutenant-colonel. She seemed satisfied with the answer.

'Of course, you couldn't hope to survive a Russian winter,' she said, contemptuously. 'You should have stayed at Stalingrad with the rest of your troops. You've had a long journey all for nothing.'

'That's all right,' I said, risking another punch in the face. 'We enjoyed it.'

She gave me a repulsive smile.

'All good things come to an end. You are now under arrest and regarded as criminals. You crossed our borders with intent to kill, and for that you can be shot. Even if you are spared the ultimate penalty, the least you can expect is twenty-five years' hard labour.'

They made us sign our names to a document declaring that we had attacked the Soviet Union. Being in the uniform of German soldiers, we could scarcely deny it. Tomorrow, the captain informed us, we should be photographed and have our fingerprints taken. We should then be recognised officially as criminals.

'Nice to think we shall have some sort of status,' I remarked to Gregor.

Gregor made no reply. He seemed temporarily to have lost all interest in life.

We were taken outside and thrown into the back of an American jeep. Next to the driver was an ancient sergeant with First World War medals on his chest. We were guarded by a corporal, who sat with his MPI across his knees and a cigarette stuck between his lips. It was not the usual cheap machorka, all smoke and smell, but a Red Star, the special brand reserved for members of the NKVD and other important Soviet citizens.

We were in no doubt that our fate would be decided before the night was out, and we had no doubt, either, that we should be shot. Our crime was not so much having entered Russia in the first place as having broken out of Stalingrad when *Pravda* had already declared this to be an impossibility. If the news ever leaked out, Stalin himself would lose face, and this was the really unpardonable aspect of the whole affair.

The stinging wind whipped across our faces and through our thin uniforms. It was even colder sitting still in an open jeep than marching across the steppe. The three Russians were decked out in fur caps and boots and thick greatcoats, but Gregor and I were very ill-protected. And after all, if the German Army could not provide its soldiers with proper clothing, why should the Russians bother to do it for them? Especially as we were already condemned to die.

We drove for hours along the Moscow–Orel–Kharkov road. No one spoke. The old sergeant sank deep into his coat and closed his eyes; the corporal went on smoking; Gregor stared vacantly into space out of dim eyes set in deep violet hollows. To the north-west the horizon was shot through with streaks of crimson, and I could hear the muted roar of artillery. I nudged Gregor.

'The front,' I said.

'So what?' retorted Gregor, through clenched teeth and barely opened lips.

Towards dawn we left the main highway and turned off down a B road, narrow and winding. The old sergeant was snoring in the front seat. The corporal's head was sunk on to his chest and his mouth had fallen open. Even I was only semi-conscious, in spite of the cold. Gregor suddenly nudged me in the ribs. I jerked my head up and he put a finger to his lips and let his eyes slide sideways towards the sleeping corporal. I followed his glance. The MPI had fallen out of his grasp, although the sling was still over his arm. As I sat looking at it, the vehicle bounced in a pot-hole, the corporal's arm fell off his lap and dangled into space and the MPI slipped down towards the ground. Gregor bent forward and caught it neatly as it fell. The corporal slapped his tongue across his lips as he slept and heaved himself into a more comfortable position. We were moving along the edge of a wood. Gregor settled the MPI under his arm and silently released the safety catch. We looked at each other and nodded ...

I jumped at the same moment as Gregor opened fire. I fell into a deep snowdrift, and as I clawed my way out I saw the vehicle crash headlong into a tree and buckle like a concertina. Gregor came running up the road towards me, waving the MPI above his head.

'Let's get out of here!'

'Hang on,' I said. 'Why not nick a couple of their nice fur caps before we go.'

We walked back down the road. All three of the Russians were dead. I snatched off two of their caps and we pulled them on, letting down the flaps over our ears.

'They'll murder us for sure if they catch us like this,' said Gregor.

'They were going to murder us anyway, remember?' I struggled with two of the corpses and wrenched off their jackets. 'Here!' I thrust one at Gregor. 'Might as well do the job properly while we're about it. At least we look like Russians ... So long as no one actually speaks to us, we might even manage to get away with it.'

'It's asking for trouble,' moaned Gregor. 'We'll be shot as spies.'

We pushed our way into the forest, through the tangled undergrowth. Thorns caught at our legs, tearing through our clothes and digging into our flesh. Overhanging branches clawed and scratched at our faces until we were streaming with blood. We reached a clearing and ran like stags, back into the shelter of the trees, back into the clinging briars, on and on with panting breath and trembling legs, until at last we came out of the forest and back on to the familiar snow-covered carpet of the open countryside. We flung ourselves down, gasping and heaving. I stayed on all fours like an animal. My chest was full of knots and my eyes were hurting me again. My precious glasses had been taken from me long ago by the partisans.

Some way ahead of us lay the main Kharkov–Moscow road. And far off on the horizon we could see the smoke and flames of the front. On the road were long columns of lorries and trucks moving westwards; dancing pinpoints of light in the semi-darkness. Gregor handed me a cigarette. It was a Red Star, out of a packet he had taken from the dead corporal. The first few puffs made me feel weak and sick, but I persevered and the fierce pangs of hunger which had been gripping my belly began gradually to subside.

'That must be the road that leads to the front,' I told Gregor.

'So what? You're not suggesting we take it?'

'Why not? Who's going to take any notice of a couple of NKVD men?' I patted the green cross on my fur bonnet. 'They'll pick us up for sure if we go skulking across the fields. They'll never think of searching for us down there on the road.'

Gregor looked at me.

'You mean, walk along as bold as brass in the middle of 'em?'

'Can you think of anything better?'

We walked down to the road and took our place in the slow-moving stream of traffic, Russian cars and lorries mixed up with American Willys and Studebakers, their white US stars painted out and replaced by the hammer and sickle. For a couple of miles we marched along quite boldly. Faces peered out at us and looked the other way again as soon as they saw our green crosses. We were in danger of growing over-confident, and it pulled us up with a nasty jolt as we realised we were approaching a genuine NKVD checkpoint.

'What'll we do?' hissed Gregor. 'We haven't any papers!'

Within seconds, we had disappeared into the ditch behind the shelter of some bushes. We lay there shivering in the icy wind, watching as the trucks were allowed past after a brief check, while the soldiers on foot were called to a halt.

'Probably looking for us,' said Gregor, glumly.

'What are we going to do?'

I stared helplessly at him. It had been my idea to join the Russian columns, not his, but now we were here I felt suddenly exhausted, unable to think the most elementary thoughts or perform the simplest of actions for myself. I wished Porta or the Legionnaire were with us. They always knew what to do. I had never seen either of them at a loss. I needed someone to guide me gently but firmly by the hand and tell me where to go.

I glanced at Gregor. He was white-faced, chewing at his lower lip, staring at the passing column like a frightened rabbit. Perhaps he, too, wished Porta and the Legionnaire were with us? Or Tiny or the Old Man, or anyone but me?

'Well, we can't sit dithering in a ditch for the rest of the war.'

I tried to speak firmly, to convince myself that I was making some sort of practical suggestion. Gregor looked round at me. He seemed to gain a new strength from my feebleness.

'We'll have to get a lift ... climb into the back of a passing truck.'

'The passing trucks,' I said, 'are practically nose to tail. The chap in the one behind would be bound to spot us.'

'Very likely,' said Gregor, with cold indifference. 'But unless you've anything better to suggest ...'

His tone implied, you got us into this mess, don't start whining when I'm trying to get us out of it. And in any case, I couldn't think of anything better.

We remained crouched in the ditch, almost frozen into position, for nearly an hour, watching the column as it passed and watching for an opportunity to steal a free ride. Suddenly, bumping and jolting over the icy ground, a Molotov came full speed ahead along the road. The column creaked to a halt and vehices obediently pulled in to one side for the Molotov to pass. It was on our side of the column. We nudged each other into action, judged our moment, darted out into the road and hurled ourselves at the tailboard. For a few yards we were dragged along behind it, and then Gregor managed to heave himself inside. He held out a hand to me. I felt as if all the muscles in my body were being wrenched apart. Gregor pulled and I strained. The Molotov raced onwards. At last I succeeded in gaining a foothold, Gregor gave an extra tug and I fell into the back of the vehicle, tied into a thousand knots of agony.

We were fast approaching the checkpoint, Gregor rolled us both under a pile of sacks as the heavy lorry shuddered to a halt. We heard shouts, heavy boots crunching across the snow, doors slamming. Gregor seized his MPI, and in terror I pulled it away from him. One shot in a moment of panic and we should have the whole pack at our heels. We lay side by side under our protective covering, not daring to breathe too deeply for fear the rise and fall of our bodies would be noticed.

Someone looked into the back of the vehicle. He moved a crate of grenades to one side, he prodded about a bit with a rifle. Gregor and I stopped breathing altogether for the duration. It could have been only a few minutes before the Molotov set off again, but minutes can seem like hours in certain situations.

We cautiously raised our heads. Following the Molotov was a Studebaker, driven by a shifty-eyed Mongol. The long column stretched out for miles. And all the time the familiar sounds of the front were growing closer. We had crossed hundreds of miles in a vain search for that front, and now here we were being taken straight to it in a Russian vehicle!

After another hour or so we stopped for petrol. Gregor and I ducked back beneath our sacks as a shower of empty jerrycans were tossed in upon us. The sharp edge of one caught me a blow on the head and I lost consciousness for a while. How long I was out, I don't know, but I was jerked back to wakefulness by the sound of explosions. I sat up in a panic and looked round for Gregor.

'German artillery,' he told me. 'We've just come into their firing range.'

'That's all it needs,' I said, bitterly. 'Blown up by our own bloody guns...'

The Molotov began swaying from side to side as the driver, plainly unnerved, increased his speed. I don't blame him: anyone driving round with twenty tons of grenades behind them would be unnerved in such a situation. Gregor and I certainly were. We crept shivering under our sacks and lay there with our hands over our heads.

The column slowed to another halt. We heard running footsteps and men shouting. We peered out into the night and saw that several vehicles were on fire.

'Shall we go?' suggested Gregor. 'Before the balloon goes up?'

And he nodded significantly at the grenades.

'What about him?' I said, jerking my thumb towards the Mongol driver of the Studebaker.

Gregor shrugged.

'Take a chance ... He might not notice us. Even if he does, he'll only take us for NKVD.'

We crawled out of our sacks and jumped over the tailboard, almost straight into the arms of a stupified infantryman. He pointed ahead at the burning vehicle and began jabbering at us. Gregor and I nodded vigorously.

'Job Tvojemadj!' I responded, feeling the need for some comment.

The man appeared quite satisfied with this observation. He chuckled throatily and ran off into the darkness. Behind us, the Molotov started up again and pulled slowly away. Officers were shouting orders, men were milling about in confusion, it was the ideal moment to make our escape.

We crawled out of our sacks and jumped over the tailboard. Calmly, we began to walk away from the turmoil and the sound of the pounding German batteries. We passed a Russian officer, who hurried by without so much as a glance. Seconds later, a monstrous explosion lifted him off his feet, flung Gregor and I to the ground and sent up a whirlwind of debris, both human and mechanical. A gust of scorching air blew over us. The first explosion was succeeded by a whole series of others. Gregor and I staggered to our feet and dived headfirst into the nearest snowdrift to escape the suffocating heat.

Slowly and painfully, we moved through the mounting chaos. Shells were bursting all round us. The air was full of flying lead. And now it was nearly morning again and we were approaching one of the worst of our trials: the zone that lay between the artillery and the HKL, patrolled by field police, those jackals ever on the prowl for fresh prey.

We decided to go to ground. We dug ourselves into the snow, Gregor using his MPI, while I attacked it with a rifle I had purloined. The Russian day is very short in winter, but to us it seemed an eternity as we lay buried in the snow and anxiously awaited the night.

A patrol passed close by. We heard the creaking of boots and the clanking of helmets against gas-masks. I felt they surely must discover us, but they marched past without sparing a glance in our direction.

As soon as it was dark, we crept out of our hiding place and looked round; smoked our last cigarettes, stamped our feet and swung our arms to restore the circulation, then set off on the last lap of our journey.

One behind the other, we crawled on hands and knees through the scenes of carnage and destruction. Bodies freshly dead and dying; bodies stiff and frozen, corpses for over a week. Burnt-out tanks, overturned trucks, debris of all descriptions.

The whole of the front was alive and simmering. The big guns were silent, but every now and again came the faint, distant crackle of machine-gun fire, or we saw the flare of a magnesium grenade. Tracer bullets lit up the darkness, occasionally a single cannon roared its defiance. And then again, an uneasy silence would fall upon the uneasy night. The two sides were preparing to come to grips at dawn, growling at each other, making their little warning noises. All about us we felt it, the air was thick with the signs of the coming clash.

A Russian patrol came by ... so close I could have reached out and touched them. A great ball of fear rose into my throat and almost choked me. I could feel myself on the edge of breaking, I knew my nerves could not take much more. I wanted to open my mouth and scream aloud into the night, scream and scream and keep on screaming until I had screamed it all out of me ...

The patrol passed on. Gregor jumped into the shell hole beside me, dislodging a corpse. It fell down on to my feet. I gave a shrill yelp of terror as I felt its clammy weight upon me, and Gregor closed a hand over my mouth.

'Sh! Take a look over there!'

He pointed ahead. I could see nothing but darkness. I felt he was probably trying to lure me on with promises of false visions. And then, by the swift light of a flare, I saw it ... the first of the barbed wire!

We crawled on towards it, jumping from hole to hole, from corpse to corpse. The wire had been destroyed in several places and the ground was thoroughly trampled. Any mines must have long since been exploded. Now and again hung the tattered corpse of a man. Now and again a naked bone protruded from the earth.

Once safely under the wire, we moved stealthily on towards our own lines. It was a temptation to start running, but they would only have taken us for Russians and opened fire; it was a temptation to call out in German, but they would almost certainly think it was a trick. In neither case would they stop to ask questions. When in doubt, fire: that was the rule of the front line.

We reached the first of the trenches and stumbled down into it, rolling joyously on top of each other. I fell into the snow and began kissing it in sheer gratitude for our deliverance. Gregor beat upon it with his hands in a frenzy of triumph. And then we heard approaching footsteps and the clicking of a safety catch, and I saw Gregor open his mouth to shout, and this time it was I who silenced him and put a cautious finger to my mouth ... just in case. And just as well: the voices were those of Russians.

We lay still at the bottom of the trench and waited a long, long time before we dared move. Even now our trials were far from over, it seemed.

The first streaks of dawn found us still out in the open. We discovered we were sharing a hole with an unexploded shell. One of those that was capable of tearing the very flesh off your bones. We looked at it askance.

'Spit on it,' I said. 'Porta always does ... he says it brings you luck.'

'God knows, we need it,' muttered Gregor.

We duly performed our act of obeisance, then crawled out of the crater and began running across the black and pitted wastes towards our own lines. They could surely not now be far away, and it was essential we reached them before the morning attack began.

Suddenly, emerging wraithlike from a fold in the landscape, rising up in the pale light of dawn, came a tank. As it grew nearer, it grew less wraithlike and more unpleasantly realistic; huge and menacing, black cross on dirty white turret, the long cannon stretched out towards us like the accusing finger of death ... It was a Tiger! It was one of ours!

'Nicht schiessen! Nicht schiessen! Wir sind Deutsch!'*

We stood shouting at them, waving our hands in the air. All our screaming was quite useless, for they couldn't have heard us. On the other hand, if we turned and ran they would open fire immediately. We could only stand, waiting, with our hands behind our heads, while the heavy tank came onwards. The long finger of the cannon remained pointing directly at us. The Tiger rolled majestically over the top of a broken field-gun, crushing it beneath its grinding tracks. We stood our ground as it approached. The least movement on our part and they would certainly shoot.

The tank was now almost upon us. The hatch was flung open with a harsh metallic clang, and a heavily perspiring face looked out at us from beneath a grey helmet. I saw the death's-head insignia on the lapels. It was an officer, a member of Eicke's SS Tod Division. Even more surprising that they had not shot us on sight.

'Heil, Ivan! Where are you off to, ape-men?'

He pointed his pistol at us. We saw his lips drawn back over sharp teeth, gleaming white against the grime of his face. Without waiting for our reply, he beckoned us over to him.

'Come aboard, Soviet swine! And no funny business, or you'll go straight off again ... feet first!'

We scrambled up into the tank, still clasping our hands behind our necks. The hatch clanged shut and the vehicle

* Don't shoot! Don't shoot! We're German!

lurched forward. Three other Tigers appeared, and we fell in behind them. Gregor and I sat sullen and silent beneath the watchful eyes of the SS officer. We felt he was not sure what to make of us. He was plainly itching to shoot us on the spot, yet military discipline told him that a couple of stray Russians wandering about near German lines might well be more valuable alive than dead. Gregor and I kept our mouths shut and our hands up.

The four Tigers reached base and we were ordered outside. The SS surrounded us, jeering, sneering, prodding and poking at us. Live Russian soldiers seemed to be somewhat of a rarity amongst them.

'All right!' snapped the officer. 'Talk fast if you want to keep a head on your shoulders ... Where have you come from? What were you doing near our lines?'

'Bloody hellfire!' burst out Gregor, suddenly unable to restrain himself. 'Here've we been searching for the flaming lines ever since we left Stalingrad, and now he has the nerve to ask us what we're doing here!'

The man was too taken aback at the sound of Gregor's homely German accent and the mention of the word Stalingrad to upbraid him for showing lack of respect towards an officer. He looked disbelievingly from one to the other of us.

'Stalingrad?' he repeated. 'You've come from Stalingrad?'

'Part of the Sixth Army,' I said. 'We came out with General Augsberg.'

There was silence. They stood staring at us as if we were a couple of dodos returned from extinction.

'Why the hell are you wearing that crap?' demanded one of them, pointing at our Russian caps and tunics.

Gregor shrugged.

'When in Rome ...' he said.

'We marched here with the NKVD,' I explained.

'A likely story!'

It was plain they still lusted after blood, and plain that they now dared not take a chance and kill us, just in case we really had come from Stalingrad. In the end, they found a compromise: they ripped off our enemy uniforms, hurled them to the ground and riddled them with bullets. It seemed an acceptable substitute for shooting flesh and blood Russians.

'I don't give a damn how many Russian and Polish women have to die, those anti-tank trenches must be dug! Let them die in their thousands! What does it matter to me? Not a fig, except insofar as their deaths will hold up the completion of the trenches...'

Heinrich Himmler, during a secret conversation
with SS officers at Posen.

General Roske, commanding officer of the Fourteenth Armoured Corps, confronted General Paulus in his office. General Paulus was pale and ill at ease. He was smoking one cigarette after another and his forehead was damp with perspiration. The left side of his face jumped and twitched as a nervous tic took control of his muscles.

'Roske, my dear fellow! I can't tell you how pleased I am to see you! They told me you were dead...'

'Not yet,' said Roske, grimly.

Paulus gave him an agitated smile.

'The casualty rate amongst our generals is alarmingly high ... Did you know we've lost seven, to date? No other army has had such misfortune. By the time the fighting comes to an end, I sometimes wonder if we shall have a single general left.' He shook his head, and the left side of his mouth twitched rapidly in and out. 'Errors have been made, in all honesty one is forced to admit it ... but the important thing is to learn from one's experience! Those same errors will not be made again.'

'General, have you heard what's happening amongst the troops?' broke in Roske, impatiently. 'They're living more like wild beasts than human beings. They're having to eat corpses to keep themselves alive ... men are dying of quite simple injuries because the doctors have nothing to treat them with ... they don't have so much as an aspirin to give them! There's no order, no discipline, no food, no ammunition ... what are we doing? What the hell are we doing? What are we supposed to be waiting for?'

'For a miracle, perhaps...' Paulus crushed out a cigarette stub with one trembling hand and clawed up a fresh packet with the other. 'It's no use asking me, my friend. I didn't give the order, it came from the Führer. You and I are soldiers, we can only obey ... Fight to the last man, the last bullet.' He shook his head and hunched, tortoise-like, into his collar. 'There can be no question of surrender.'

'Then we shall die!' said Roske, shortly.

Paulus slowly looked up, his eyes haggard. Almost imperceptibly, he shrugged his shoulders.

'We have no choice ... Give your men my warmest regards.
Tell them, we are all in this together. And if there is anything I
can do for you, anything at all, you will of course let me know.'

Two hours later, General Paulus sent a telegram to Berlin:

'On the anniversary of his rise to power, the Sixth Army
salutes its Führer. The swastika still flies over Stalingrad.
May our fight give heart to future generations. May it ever be
said that in their most desperate hour they did not give in.
We believe in victory and in our Führer. Heil Hitler!

'Stalingrad, 29th January 1943.'

FIFTEEN

BACK IN GERMAN LINES

We were taken to Kharkov in an amphi-car and handed over
to a battalion stationed in the Djinski barracks on the slopes of
Nova Bavaria. A quartermaster-sergeant sent us off straight
away to the stores to collect some new kit and some weapons,
where they told us that anyone arriving from Stalingrad was
automatically sent on to Djinski.

'Anyone?' queried Gregor. 'You mean, there are quite a few?'

'A small trickle. One or two turn up each week.'

We asked him about our own group, but either they had
genuinely not passed through the barracks or else the man had
been told to keep his mouth shut, for he denied all knowledge of
them. Even had he seen them, the chances were he would not
have talked, for immediately after our visit to the stores we had
to report to the secret police for a detailed interrogation. It was
like being with the NKVD all over again. No one seemed
willing to believe that we could possibly be telling the truth.

'So! You say you came out of Stalingrad?' asked a young
and cocksure captain, with a faintly sardonic smile on his
lips.

'We did come out of Stalingrad,' said Gregor.

'How?'

'An SS general took us out. There was a whole group of us, about eight hundred men.'

'The name of this general?'

'Augsberg. General Augsberg.'

The captain rustled importantly amongst some papers on his desk.

'When was this? What was the date?'

Gregor and I looked at each other and shrugged.

'About the 26th or 27th January,' I guessed.

'I see.' He looked up at us. 'So the fighting was still going on at Stalingrad when General Augsberg led you out?'

'Yes—in one or two places,' I said, innocently. 'The Russians were on the point of attacking our position near the New Theatre and the Place of the Dead.'

The captain smiled at this. He made a note on a clean sheet of paper and then amiably offered us his cigarettes.

'When the general led you out, did no one raise any objections? None of the officers?'

Gregor shook his head.

'No. It was pointless staying in Stalingrad, the Russians were walking all over us. We couldn't possibly have held the place. The game was over, we just wanted to get out.'

'And continue the fight elsewhere,' I added, with a vague premonition of danger. 'Somewhere more useful.'

'Stalingrad was lost months ago,' said Gregor, contemptuously.

'Of course, of course,' murmured the captain, leaning back in his chair and playing with his cigarette lighter. 'So General Augsberg formed a combat group and led you out ... and none of your officers raised his voice in protest?'

'Not as far as I know,' said Gregor, vaguely.

'And yet General Augsberg was a stranger to you? He was not your commanding officer?'

'Ah well——' Gregor shrugged. 'It was all a bit of a mess. We were just the remnants, like. A few men from this division, a few men from that ... Nobody wasn't properly in command until General Augsberg came along and took over.'

'He was the sort of man,' I said, 'you did what he told you to do. You didn't stop and argue.'

'But did you not realise he was ordering you to desert?' murmured the captain, very smooth. 'Surely you must have done? You had weapons, you had ammunition, there were eight hundred of you ... quite a powerful group! Why did you not stay behind and fight the enemy?'

'Fight the enemy?' repeated Gregor, looking rather blank. 'There wasn't any point, they were clobbering us from all directions ... in any case, we just did what we were told.'

'As always,' I added.

The captain stood up. He walked round the desk, flexing his legs and creaking his high leather boots. He gazed sternly upon us.

'It was your duty to oppose this man! You should have spoken out against him——'

'Sir,' I protested, 'have you ever heard of an ordinary soldier speaking out against a general?'

He obviously hadn't. He walked back round the desk, picked up his riding crop and began thoughtfully beating himself with it.

'You were up against the Russians at Gumrak, were you not?' He evidently knew the answer to the question already. 'What happened when the fighting was over? What did you do?'

Gregor gave a short laugh.

'Scarpered!'

'We made for the Don,' I said, quietly.

'It seems to me,' remarked the captain, 'that after deserting from Stalingrad, the whole of your march was one disordered flight towards the west.'

'Towards the German front line,' I said.

The captain ignored me.

'Did the general never order you to attack the Russian positions? Did he never organise acts of sabotage against the enemy? Did you never blow up their arms dumps, sever their supply lines?'

'What with?' said Gregor. 'We just pushed on as fast as we could.'

'We were looking for the German front line,' I repeated.

Again, the captain ignored me and concentrated on Gregor.

'You had a medical officer with you ... What role did he play? Did he arrange transport for your sick and wounded? Did he perform any operations?'

Gregor laughed again.

'In that weather?' he said.

'We couldn't possibly arrange transport,' I explained. 'We didn't have any. And it simply wasn't possible to operate in those conditions. In any case, we had no medical supplies.'

'So you abandoned your wounded in the steppe?' The captain narrowed his eyes to slits, then opened them wide in accusation. You left them to die? And no one spoke out against it? Not even your general?'

'There was nothing we could do! Men were dying like flies ... we had no food, no winter clothing, no bandages ... almost everyone had dysentery or frostbite or both together ... or typhus, that was even worse ... it was as much as we could do to drag ourselves along, let alone carry sick men with us.'

'So you left them to die?'

'It was impossible to do anything else!'

The captain and I stood glaring at each other.

'Impossible, eh?' He savoured the word, gently beating the back of his legs with his crop. 'Impossible ... Well, we shall let others be the judge of that. Let us press on with your story. During your flight from Stalingrad, did anyone ever speak out against the Party? Against the Führer? Did anyone ever criticise the way the war was being fought?'

Gregor and I firmly shook our heads.

'No?' said the captain, with a faintly ironic smile.

'No,' I said.

'You seem almost indecently sure of yourself?'

'I am sure. Very sure.'

'Hm ...' He turned back to his desk, gathered up the various sheets of paper and placed them neatly in a folder. 'If you have any letters to deliver, any personal effects belonging to dead men, you can give them to me.'

'We haven't,' said Gregor. 'The Russians took everything off us.'

'How much did you tell the Russians?'

'Nothing. Only our names and our units.'

'Oh? And the NKVD was quite happy with that?' He smiled another of his ironic smiles, then nodded to us that we could leave. 'Speak to no one of this interview. Keep your mouths shut about Stalingrad. If anyone asks you any questions, they must be reported immediately to the GEFEPO.'

An hour later, we were reunited with our own company, where our arrival caused a minor chaos.

'Look who it bleeding well isn't!' yelled Tiny, lumbering across to us.

'We thought you must be dead!' declared the Old Man, trying to fling his arms round both of us at the same time.

'Where the hell did you get to?' grumbled Porta. 'We waited two flaming hours on the edge of that wood. I said to the general, I said, the mean bastards have stumbled on a pack of Russians and don't want to share the caviar with us . . .'

They were all there, the Old Man, Porta, Tiny, the Legionnaire and Heide. Even Barcelona had turned up to greet us! Thrown out of hospital and declared fit to die for his country, he had had the great good fortune to be sent back to his old company.

'They're re-forming the Sixth Army,' he told us. 'Christ only knows where they're going to get the extra men . . . they must be going through the whole of Germany with a fine tooth-comb.'

'What's happened to Augsberg?' Gregor wanted to know.

'And the lieutenant and the doctor?' I added, anxiously.

The Old Man shrugged.

'Do you have to ask? Weren't you put through your paces by the Secret Police?'

'You mean they've arrested them?'

'What else could they do? An army's not an army without discipline. And Augsberg left Stalingrad against Hitler's orders. Technically he's a deserter. And he knew what he was doing.'

'But that's lunacy!' protested Gregor. 'Anyone who stayed behind to die in Stalingrad when he could have got out, needs his head examined! In any case, it wasn't desertion. We weren't running away from the front line, we were trying to find the perishing thing!'

Life for the next few days was more bearable than it had been for a good long while. We were forbidden to speak of our exploits, but everyone knew where we had come from and we were regarded with some awe . . . to have survived the renowned hell of Stalingrad! To have crossed the Don! To have outwitted the Russians! We were fêted and celebrated and regarded, in our apparent indestructability, as minor deities.

One day, as Porta and I were strolling peaceably together, enjoying a sudden burst of sunshine, a gross quartermaster-sergeant came tumbling out of a hut and made straight for us. He seized Porta by the shoulders and shook him.

'Hauber! Where the hell have you been for these past five hours? I've looked everywhere for you!'

Porta, admirably restraining his normal impulse to shout obscenities, stepped back a pace and regarded the man. He was wearing spectacles with lenses about an inch thick, and it was plain that he was still unable to see more than a yard in front of him.

'What do you want me for?' demanded Porta/Hauber, playing for time before deciding whether or not his new role was worth it.

'What do I want you for? Good God in heaven, there's a war on, man! There's work to be done, supplies to be fetched, men's bellies to be filled . . .'

I stood watching as he dragged Porta away with him. For a while I leaned with my back against a tree trunk, drinking in the sun and wondering how long I should bother to wait, and then Porta reappeared, grinning, and waving a sheet of paper at me.

'Come on!'

'What for?' I said, not willing to move from my tree trunk without good cause.

'Going to pick up a load of provisions for the fat fool in glasses.'

'Why do him a good turn?' I grumbled, peeling myself away and joining Porta in the cab of a large lorry.

'Why not?' said Porta, winking roguishly at me. 'Might just do ourselves one at the same time, eh?'

We reached the depot and Porta handed in his requisition.

'Who are you?' demanded the sergeant in charge. 'Where's Hauber?'

'Sick. He was taken bad very sudden in the night.'

'Poor old Hauber! What is it, do you know?'

'Liver trouble,' said Porta, without turning a hair.

The sergeant rubber-stamped and signed the requisition and asked no more questions, and we took the lorry round to pick up the goods. For a start, we had a load of uniforms dumped on us. That was followed by five hundred rifles. My spirits began to fall, and Porta's face turned slowly red with rage.

'Bloody sod!' he shouted. 'If I'd known it was going to be this kind of trash . . .'

But then we picked up some crates of tinned food and we began to grow more cheerful, and when we finally stowed away ten crates of vodka Porta's pride and self-importance knew no bounds.

'Just leave it all to me,' he said, climbing back into the cab. 'I know how to manage these things.'

We pulled up in a narrow street, where, with the help of a Russian deserter, a new-found crony of Porta's, we stacked all the food and drink in a cellar beneath a bombed building. As for the lorry, we simply drove it out of the village and blew it up with grenades.

'Let 'em think the partisans nobbled all the stuff,' said Porta. 'Or the Russians, if they prefer ... just so long as it gets 'em off of our backs!'

We enjoyed our ill-gotten gains at leisure and never heard any more about the incident. All manner of wild rumours were flying about the town just at this time, and possibly everyone was too concerned trying to disentangle truth from fiction to pay any attention to a lost lorry. It was said that the Russians had broken through on the north front and that fighting was now taking place on former German territory. It was also said that there had been a 'strategic withdrawal'—which in any language can be taken to mean a headlong retreat from the enemy. Something, certainly, was in the wind, for day and night there was a constant traffic along the Bjelgorod and Orel roads.

Before we had quite finished our secret supply of vodka, we were sent off on a training course: how to demolish tanks ... We, the experts!

'Bloody nerve!' grumbled Porta. 'I've demolished more tanks than they've had hot dinners ...'

On our return to the barracks, we found the place in a state of upheaval. Everywhere, gangs of men were hard at work scrubbing, painting, pulling down, putting up, removing, replacing, stealing and secreting. Rumour now had it that we were to be sent back to Berlin.

'It could be true,' said Gregor, doubtfully.

'So what's the point of all the spring-cleaning?' I demanded.

'And all the exercises and courses and lectures?' added Tiny.

'Tell you what!' said Porta. 'Bet you a pound to a pinch of pigshit we're going to surrender ... They're trying to lick the barracks into shape so's we'll all look like real Prussian soldiers when Stalin comes marching in!'

'Someone told me the other day,' put in Barcelona, eagerly, 'that we're no longer at war with the West, and President Roosevelt and the King of England's coming to visit us ...'

A couple of months ago he would have been too ashamed to repeat such a blatantly ridiculous rumour; and if he had, we should have laughed him to scorn. But now, such was the atmosphere, so full of hopes and fears and general expectation, that some of us even began rather covertly to learn a few words of basic English.

Only one story was dismissed out of hand, and that was the rumour that Hitler was going to pay us a visit. President Roosevelt, yes; the King of England, yes; but Hitler, no. After a moment's stupefaction that anyone—even Heide, who had brought us the news—could be gullible enough to believe such rubbish, we broke into great gusts of delighted laughter.

'What a load of bollocks!' shouted Tiny.

'Perhaps he wants to see the ghosts of Stalingrad?' suggested the Old Man.

'All right,' said Heide, tight-lipped. 'All right, have a good laugh. Make fools of yourselves. You'll see ...'

And, God help us, we did!

Two days later, the rumour was confirmed. Hitler in person was said to be walking round the barracks ... he was here! He had come! He was amongst us! Our Führer, which art in Nova Bavaria ...

Panic broke out and spread like wildfire. Officers ran in circles issuing lunatic commands; NCOs ran after them, issuing contradictory commands. Men grew irritable and fought each other as the confusion and uncertainty increased. He was not actually *in* the barracks ... he was on his way to the barracks ... he was approaching the barracks ... he would be with us by midnight, he would be with us tomorrow, he would be with us next week ... he had been and he had gone, he wasn't really coming ...

Shortly before midnight, we were all neatly lined up and waiting for something to happen. We were clean and attentive and polished to a high gloss. Two sergeants had been posted at the far end of the street to act as watchouts and sound the alarm.

Three hours later, wilting slightly, we were still at our posts. The officers were growing nervous, we were growing bored and several men had taken the easy way out and collapsed.

And then the sergeants came running back with the news that he was coming, and seconds later three Hoesch trucks rattled into the courtyard and disgorged a horde of SS officers. The SS officers jumped out and ran about a bit and finally formed themselves into a cordon, pistols in hand. We watched their antics with some interest. At least they relieved the monotony.

After the trucks came the lorries, four of them, full to the brim with LSSAH* men. They tumbled out after the SS officers and ranged themselves in two rows, with the MPIs held triumphantly before them. It was such a smart manoeuvre I felt like applauding or throwing buns, but I stood like a statue and

* Hitler's Personal Guard.

merely swivelled my eyes to the right and met Porta's swivelling to the left. We exchanged glances of silent contempt.

After the lorries came a long line of vehicles containing yet more SS men. These began running in all directions about the courtyard, waving and screaming and making a great deal of noise. They charged up and down between our ranks, threatening us indiscriminately, as the fancy took them, with the Field Police, the Gestapo, Torgau, the gallows and the firing squad. We stared stonily ahead and did not flinch.

When they had calmed down and restored a sense of order amongst themselves, we were treated to a few moments' very pregnant silence. We all stood, waiting. From afar off we heard a warning fanfare on a trumpet. One of the guard dropped his MPI with a tremendous clatter, and there was a ripple of smothered laughter. The SS men tightened their grip on their pistols. High up on the wall, a cat yowled loudly into the night.

Two special Mercedes bowled through the gates and drove up to our commanding officer in a crescent of flying snow. From the first car stepped General Field-Marshal von Mannstein, followed by what seemed to be his entire staff. The number of medals on display was positively dazzling. Gold epaulettes were two a penny, monocles were so plentiful I thought some people must be wearing one in each eye, and the rattling of spurs and sabres sounded like an entire cavalry charge. From the second car stepped General Guderian, who was suffering from a severe head cold and had to keep touching the end of his nose with his handkerchief.

The CO presented the regiment to him. He inspected us carefully, slowly, rather sorrowfully, with his great baglike eyes staring at us over his drooping jowls and his nose for ever dripping.

General Guderian presented the regiment to General Field-Marshal von Mannstein. He, in his turn, prowled up and down and looked us over. I wondered if they would remove anyone who was too offensive to the eye, and if so, why was it that Porta was allowed to remain.

We went on standing, and waiting. No one would dare to collapse at this stage in the proceedings.

Outside in the street we heard a Russian woman crying her wares. She had fish for sale. Everyone, from von Mannstein downwards, instinctively stiffened: the Führer hated fish ... Four SS men rushed outside and bundled the old crone off.

Possibly they killed her. What did it matter, so long as the Führer's sensitive nostrils were not assailed by the loathsome smell of fish?

More crowded SS vehicles drove into the courtyard, and there in their midst, was the big black Mercedes in which Adolf Hitler sat enthroned. He stepped slowly out, flexing his legs and drawing his knees rather high as he walked. He always did that when he inspected the troops. It was like some weird ritual dance. Of his face, all that could be seen were his nose and his moustache: the rest was masked by the shadow of his helmet and the collar of his greatcoat.

'Men of the Second Tank Regiment,' he began—we weren't the Second Tanks at all, but naturally no one dared to put him right. 'Men of the Second Tank Regiment, I thank you from the very bottom of my heart for all your courage and your gallantry! You are the pride of Germany! When the war is over and we are victorious, your country will reward you! In the meantime, be patient and loyal! Heil!'

'Heil Hitler!' we bellowed.

It was a relief to open one's mouth after such a time. We roared from the very bottom of our lungs.

Hitler walked round examining us, with his curious elevated leg movements. The generals followed behind. Now and again the Führer stopped to pass a comment or to hold brief converse with some honoured soldier. He didn't speak to any of our company, but he did pause before Porta and silently stare at him for several seconds. He seemed to find Porta morbidly fascinating. I wished I knew why. I felt an almost overpowering desire to join him in his contemplation of Porta's face, and I hoped to God Porta wouldn't forget himself and open his mouth.

In seven minutes precisely it was all over, and without shaking anyone's hand Hitler climbed back into his Mercedes and was driven away. Three minutes later, the courtyard was clear once again. The entire visit had lasted no more than ten minutes.

Not long after the Führer had left us, we assembled in the pisshouse for a game of cards. We were all feeling disgruntled and in some way cheated. We had waited so long and seen so little! And what we had seen had been such a clown, such a dwarf, such a parody of what we had been expecting!

'Was that really him?' asked Tiny, doubtfully. 'Was it really him, do you reckon, or do they send someone else dressed up like him?'

'It was him, all right,' said the Old Man.

'Jesus!' said Tiny, picking up his hand. 'He's such a weedy little bastard, ain't he?'

'Those who survived the fighting of the front line have no call to congratulate themselves. The real heroes are those who fell.'

Adolf Hitler—19 March 1945

On the morning of 1st February 1943, the following telegram arrived in Berlin from General Paulus in Stalingrad:

'Mein Führer! The Sixth Army has kept faith. We have fought to the last man, the last bullet, as you ordered. We have no more arms, no more ammunition, no more food. The following divisions have been totally wiped out: 14th, 16th and 24th Panzer Divisions; 9th FLAK Division; 30th MOT Division; 44th, 71st and 176th Divisions; 100th Rifle Division. Heil Hitler! Long live Germany!'

At five-thirty on the same day, the Sixth Army sent its last radio message:

'The Russians have penetrated the bunkers.'

Lieutenant Wultz, the radio officer, then sent out the internation signal EL: there would be no more transmissions from that station. With a spade, he destroyed the equipment; with a pistol, he blew his brains out.

General Paulus, the reluctant soldier who had all along declared, 'I have been given my orders, I can but obey!' now sought to dissociate himself entirely from current events.

'I want nothing to do with any of it,' he told his Chief of Staff, who had come to him with the news that the Russians had once more offered terms for an honourable capitulation. 'I wash my hands of the whole business. The idea of capitulation is repugnant to me and I shall accept no responsibility for such a course of action. I wish only to be treated as a private person. You may take over command of the Army and pursue what actions you think fit ... And you may tell the Russians from me that I have no intention of crossing the town on foot! If they wish us to co-operate, let them behave like gentlemen. Let them provide transport for the use of myself and all my generals ... But I leave it to you, Schmidt. I shall have nothing to do with any of it.'

SIXTEEN

THE TRAIN

The station was like a thousand others in Russia. At the entrance, a few faded spring flowers wilted in the pale sunshine. Outside the station master's office lay a pile of horse dung. Everyone cursed it and everyone elaborately walked round it, but no one took the trouble to fetch a bucket and spade and remove it. It would probably stay there until it rotted away.

The platforms were full of peasants and chickens. Some had been waiting more than two days for their train, and to prevent the chickens wandering away they had broken their feet. One man had a pig on a dog-lead. It was a fine pig, fat and white, with a distinctive black head. It was called Tanja, and it occasionally answered to its name. We cast many covetous glances towards it, but not even Porta dared raise a hand against such an animal.

There was no shortage of trains, they arrived and departed ceaselessly, but hardly any of them carried passengers. By far the greater number were munitions trains travelling towards the east. They were powered by two engines, one at the front, one at the rear; immense steam locomotives belching out clouds of grey smoke, and their drivers and stokers black and sweating. Those railwaymen were almost as familiar with violent death as we ourselves. The accident and sabotage rate was high and their work perilous in the extreme. Round every bend death could be lying in wait for them.

Occasionally a goods wagon was reserved for the transport of corpses, but the main priority was being given to the carriage of damaged field-guns and other equipment back to Germany to be repaired by prisoners of war. One special track was reserved for Red Cross trains. They passed non-stop through the station every twenty minutes, filled with injured men.

We ourselves were *en route* to a convalescent centre on the Black Sea. Porta told us it was the ante-chamber to paradise and kept up a mouth-watering description of the meals we should eat and girls we should sleep with. According to him, the streets were thronging with half-naked whores, and you had only to stroll about and make your selection. We were by no means sure that Porta had ever actually been to this resort, or, indeed, that he had ever even heard of it before; but we liked the vision he conjured up too much to risk premature disappointment by questioning him over closely.

There was, of course, no home leave for men serving at the front. We had to make do with a few days in a recuperation centre as a sop to keep us quiet. The least that would get you home was to have both arms or legs blown off.

A hospital train chugged through. The crowds turned towards it and stood watching until it was out of sight and only a few wisps of smoke could be seen. A peasant standing near by sighed deeply and consulted the timetable for the hundredth time. It was dated 1940 and bore no relevance whatsoever to present conditions. The man shook his head and began grumbling at us.

'Three hours late, it's disgusting what things are coming to in this country ... They get on to the wrong line, you know. They send them off willy-nilly anywhere they choose, never mind the people waiting to get on them. It's high time something was done about it.' He looked us over rather critically, taking in the details of our uniforms. 'I don't suppose it's like that in Germany,' he said. 'Why can't you people do something about it, now that you're here? You're meant to be the efficiency experts, aren't you?'

At this, a whole knot of peasants turned towards us and began clamouring.

'It wouldn't be allowed in Germany!'

'No sense of duty, that's what the trouble is ...'

'I've been waiting here twenty-four hours——'

'All I want to do is get to Nikopol. It says in the timetable it was due yesterday morning. But where is it?' A stout man with a chicken tucked under each arm nudged Porta in the ribs and looked trustfully up at him. 'Where's it got to, eh?'

'It's been delayed,' said Porta. 'That's what it is, it's been delayed ... It's the war, tovaritch. The war delays everything.'

'But when's it going to come, that's what I want to know?'

'Give it time,' said Porta, looking very wise. 'Be patient, comrade! You can't hurry these things.'

Half an hour later, an engine pulling both goods and passenger wagons puffed into the station and groaned to a halt. A great shout of joy burst forth from the crowd. Chickens, baskets, pigs and children were swept up and crammed towards the train. Dogs ran about barking, and wetting themselves and

267

everybody else with excitement. The station was too small to accommodate such a long train and the last two coaches extended beyond the platform. We all tumbled pell mell on to the railways tracks and surged towards them. The man with the black and white pig became stuck in a door. People pulled from in front and pushed from behind, and both man and pig set up a terrified squealing. The guard blew his whistle and shouted. He ran up and down the platform in a frenzy and finally drew his pistol and fired several shots into the air.

'Sabotage!' he screamed.

The crowd ignored him. No one knew where the train was going, it was not to be found in any timetable and there was no indication, either on the train or on the platform, but everyone, nevertheless, was hell bent on climbing aboard. Porta wriggled through a window and fell into a carriage headfirst. I saw Tiny fighting his way through a mass of clucking chickens. A Rumanian sergeant pulled out his sabre and attempted to decapitate Barcelona, but a fat woman elbowed her way between them and knocked the sabre to the ground. Military police appeared and began hitting out indiscriminately. A sergeant pulled out his revolver and fired a shot into the crowd. The bullet whistled past the head of the black and white pig, who promptly leapt out of its owner's arms and went howling through the train like a hand-grenade. Instantly, all those who had succeeded in climbing aboard set off in chase of it.

At last the platform was empty and the train was full. People were sitting in the luggage racks and standing in serried ranks in the corridors. The black and white pig had been recaptured and locked into one of the lavatories along with a calf and six self-important geese. Chickens were everywhere, under the seats, on the seats, perched on people's heads and laps. The police were pushed off bodily and the train started up, without bothering to wait for the guard to blow his whistle. He galloped along the platform beside it, red in the face and bellowing, while we hung from the windows and shouted obscenities. Ultimately, some kindly peasant flung open the door of the last carriage and hauled him up.

'Pity about that,' remarked Barcelona, closing the window. 'I was quite enjoying it.'

Porta looked across at him.

'Ever hear of a bloke called Manfried Katzenmeyer?' he asked, pushing a cackling hen off his lap.

'No,' said Barcelona. 'Should I have?'

'Not necessarily. It just reminded me of him ... that fool of a guard getting left behind like that.'

'Why? Is that what happened to Manfried Katzenmeyer?'

'Yeah, he's a kind of legend,' said Porta. 'He started off in the last war as a captain in the artillery, only he pissed his kipper good and proper by mixing up one box of grenades with another and causing bleeding chaos when they tried to fire on the Froggies. So they took him out of that and put him in charge of transport. They reckoned he couldn't do much harm there.'

'They'd have shot him today,' I observed.

'Ah, very likely,' agreed Porta. 'Well, they did, in the end ... When Adolf came along, they started screaming for manpower, and they was willing to use any bleeding nut what volunteered —including Katzenmeyer. Well, that was asking for trouble, that was. He'd already proved he was an imbecile ... Anyway, they gave him this train to look after. He didn't know the first thing about trains, but they reckoned as he didn't actually have to drive the flaming thing, it didn't really matter. All the stations he stopped at, they used to hate his guts. Always bawling everyone out and finding fault. Niggly, if you know what I mean ... When I first come across him, he looked like a field of blinking dandelions. He'd togged himself up with this special uniform, covered all over in bits of yellow braid ... They used to call him the Shit House King, in them days. He had this rule, see, about opening your bowels at set hours. Twice a day, once after breakfast and once before kip. Officers and men, he treated 'em all the same. He used to send 'em off, regular as clockwork, and then stand there timing 'em. Three minutes thirty seconds and two bits of bog paper, and God help anyone what had the runs——'

'And what about the train?' said Barcelona, smothering a yawn.

'What about the train?'

'I thought you were telling us about it, that's all.'

'All right, all right, I'm coming to it,' said Porta, irritable as ever when someone tried to rush him. 'Give me time.'

'So what happened?' said Barcelona.

'So he got left behind one day. It was his own stupid fault. They'd stopped at some crummy little station the other side of the Donetz. Dunno what its name was, it doesn't matter. It was some one-horse place where nothing ever happened ... Well, there was an old boy of about ninety-eight used to stand there leaning on his broom and watching the trains go past. Someone had given him this broom back in 1922 and told him to hold on to it—just to give him something useful to do. Know what I mean? In a country like Russia, you can't have people just standing about doing sweet bugger all. So ever since 1922 this old boy had leaned on his broom and not done no one no harm. He'd seen 'em all come and go—he'd seen Wrangle's cavalry and Trotzky's marines, he'd seen the Cossacks when they had their little revolution, he'd seen the Germans back in 1914 ... he'd got to the stage where he didn't give two damns for no one in authority. He knew they was all the same underneath, just wearing different uniforms. He'd heard 'em all shouting and bawling in his time ... Long live the Tsar! Long live Lenin! Long live Russia! Long live the Kaiser! Long live Germany! Up with the Revolution! Down with the Revolution! Up with——'

'So the train went off without him, did it?' said Barcelona.

Porta glared at him.

'Not him! Katzenmeyer!'

'Ah yes.' Barcelona nodded. 'Of course.'

'Katzenmeyer got out of the train to boss people around like he usually done, and he saw this old geezer leaning on his broom. So of course he bawls him out and asks him what the hell he's doing just standing there. So the old geezer tells him about this commissar back in 1922, giving him the broom and telling him to keep hold of it. So then Katzenmeyer gets mad and starts shooting his mouth off and asking him if he's opened his bowels recently and how long it takes him to shit and all the rest of it, and while he's doing this his train suddenly ups and offs without him. So he goes tearing up the line behind it, waving his arms about and screaming like a bleeding nutter, trips over the points and knocks himself doolally. And meanwhile,' said Porta, with relish, 'the poor bastard train goes roaring off along the track without a guard and nobody knows where the hell it's meant to be going, so every station it gets to they just shove it off on to whatever line happens to be free and send it on its way.' Porta's eyes gleamed. 'It went all round Europe!' he told us. 'It passed through Kiev no less than fifteen times. Berlin saw it three times. It even got as far as Paris, and the Frogs didn't know what to do with it so they sent it on to Amsterdam and Brussels. After that it got lost and wasn't seen again for nearly two months. It turned up at last at Munich, full steam ahead from Rome. Even then the fools didn't recognise it in time. They got in a panic and changed the points and sent it off to Frankfurt. The railway officials were going berserk. They simply never knew where it was going to turn up next. People standing on little country platforms used to be frightened out of their lives by this bloody great train suddenly surging up out of nowhere. The driver couldn't pull up, you see. They reckon he'd have gone all the way to Pekin in the lights had stayed on green. It was lucky for him someone turned 'em on red and stopped him just in time, otherwise he might still be whistling round Europe in the middle of the war.'

Porta leaned back in his seat, looking very well pleased with himself. There was a short silence. Gregor, the Legionnaire and the Old Man were all asleep. Heide had found a magazine and was reading it. The Old Man suddenly snored.

'What happened to this Katzenmeyer fellow, then?' asked Barcelona.

'They shot 'im,' said Porta.

'Ah!'

Barcelona turned and looked out of the grimy window. Tiny suddenly leaned forward.

'What about the people in the train?' he said, aggressively. 'I don't see how they could have still been alive after all that time. What did they eat? And what about the train? How did they run it? Where'd they get the——'

Fortunately, mid-way through the sentence, there was a frantic squeal of terror and the black and white pig came charging through the compartment chased by the six geese. Tiny was so entranced by the sight that he forgot all about his awkward questions.

We reached a station called Winnitza and had to change. We waited all night on the platform and not until the following afternoon did the next train arrive. It was called an express but it stopped every half an hour at the most obscure stations on the line, and we had to travel in open trucks. We were not even able to obtain any food during the interminable waits, because the authorities had neglected to put the proper stamps on our cards.

At Novojovsk we parted company with the express and were hitched on to a smaller and somewhat dubious locomotive which pulled us very slowly along a narrow branch line. The branch line ended suddenly at a place called Slin. It appeared that it had been laid at the start of the war and then abandoned, and no one now knew where it had been ultimately intended to go.

From Slin we had to walk across some marshes towards the

271

main line, where we waited several hours before succeeding in scrambling on board a munitions train. We had an uncomfortable journey sitting on boxes of grenades, and three times the train came to a halt and we had to hide under the wagons while enemy aircraft attacked us.

At Krivy Rog two sappers came aboard carrying a fire extinguisher. They sat on the grenades with us and we learnt that one of them had been posted missing, believed dead, over a year ago, while the other had escaped from a transport train six months earlier. Their pockets were crammed with forged passes and travel documents, and it appeared that they spent their time moving freely about Europe under the noses of the field police.

'What's the fire extinguisher for?' I asked, politely.

They looked at me and frowned.

'You could be very glad of it,' they said, 'travelling on a munitions train . . .'

Four days later, we arrived at our ante-chamber to paradise. Stiff and sore, and cynically prepared to be disillusioned, we climbed off the train and waved goodbye to our two friends.

'So where are the whores?' Tiny wanted to know, as we stared across the platform and saw nothing more appetising than a policeman dozing in the sun with his MPI across his knees.

'Never mind the whores!' The Old Man threw down his kitbag, stretched his arms high above his head and took in a deep breath of air. 'I smell spring! The lilac must be in bloom!'

It was true. It hung everywhere in great purple bunches, and its fragrant scent was almost unbearably sweet after the sweat and the filth of the trenches.

The policeman woke up and broke the spell which had momentarily descended upon us. He jerked his MPI towards us and roughly demanded our papers. They were all in order, but he had to take out a fat file of photographs and go through them in detail, carefully checking them against us in the hope of making an arrest. It was with sullen reluctance that he finally allowed us to leave the station.

We walked out into the town. Rows of pretty little white houses with tiny gardens. The hot noon sun riding high in the sky. We kept close to each other, elbow to elbow, and our boots rang out indecently loud in the quiet street.

'Why's it like this?' hissed Tiny.

'Like what?' said the Old Man.

'So quiet . . . nobody about . . . I don't like it. Something's

272

wrong.'

'Nonsense!'

The Old Man smiled and walked on, but the rest of us agreed with Tiny: such unaccustomed silence was unnerving.

'Look!'

The Old Man was standing at the top of the slope, pointing ahead. Anxiously, we ran up to him.

'What is it? What's the matter?'

Porta fingered his revolver. The Legionnaire had a hand on his knife. Tiny kept glancing nervously over his shoulder.

'Just take a look!' roared the Old Man.

We looked. There, spread out below us, dazzling in the sunshine, was the sea. A great blue lake of water fringed with palm trees. Further along the coast were cypresses and scented bushes and glowing crimson flowers the size of soup plates.

Staring hypnotically, we moved towards it.

'Is it real?' Tiny kept asking; and he seemed to be serious. 'Is it really real?'

Keeping to the left, as do all soldiers in unknown territories, we walked slowly down the steps towards the beach. At the foot of the steps we met a guard, who pointed out the Army convalescent home. The light breeze was full of the salt scent of the sea, and the waves made a gentle hissing sound as they dribbled up the beach and rolled back again.

Porta suddenly nudged Tiny in the ribs.

'Get an eyeful of that,' he muttered, nodding his head towards a couple of girls stepping across the sand towards us on their way to the sea.

They were young and well formed, with great pneumatic breasts bulging out of their skimpy bathing suits. Barcelona whooped, and Tiny gave a loud catcall.

'Holy Mother of Kazan!' whimpered Gregor. 'I'd almost forgotten what they looked like ...'

Porta went plunging off towards them, followed eagerly by the rest of us. Only the Old Man and the Legionnaire remained aloof and amused on the outskirts. The girls fluttered and screamed as Tiny's great paw groped at their bottoms, and Porta propositioned them outright with bottles of vodka as a bait. They escaped from us and ran shrieking down to the sea. and a barrel-chested sergeant suddenly accosted us with a shout of rage.

'What the hell do you think this is? A cattle market? Keep your hands off my girls or I'll have you sent to Torgau!'

'*Your* girls?' queried Porta eagerly. 'You mean, you let them out on hire?'

'I mean they're two of my nurses!' he roared. 'You keep your filthy hands to yourself! This is a respectable garrison, we don't have to put up with you people behaving like pigs the minute they let you out of the trenches!'

The Old Man stepped forward, looking the sergeant coldly up and down. The man's uniform was flamboyantly new and smart.

'Have you ever been to the front line?' asked the Old Man, quietly.

'Of course I haven't! I work in the infirmary. What do you take me for?'

Porta lifted one leg off the ground and let out a resounding burst of wind. It smelt like a gas attack, and it blew straight into the sergeant's face. He choked and staggered backwards.

'All right!' He pointed a finger at Porta. 'You've asked for it! You came here in search of trouble and by Christ you're going to get it!' He took out a notebook. 'Name and number!' he snapped.

'Don't be a fool,' said the Old Man.

He pulled open his coat and revealed his rank of sergeant-major, together with the various decorations he had gained during his years at the front. The sergeant swallowed rather resentfully.

'You want to watch your language in future,' jibed Porta. 'Might find yourself trying to nobble a colonel one day.'

'Shut up,' said the Old Man.

'I don't see why I should,' began Porta, aggrieved.

'Well, just do!'

The sergeant had recovered himself.

'You stick to the rules,' he said, 'and you'll enjoy yourself in Zatoka. We got discipline, but we're democratic. If everyone behaves himself, we all get along fine. You're here for a rest, but you still got to have discipline. Like in a barracks. Law and order ... You'll find a list of the rules pinned up in the bed-rooms and the recreation rooms. And don't try tearing them down!'

He marched off chest first along the beach. Tiny and Porta disappeared into the town in search of girls. Gregor pulled me to one side.

'I don't know how you feel,' he murmured, 'but I rather fancy one of those nurses myself ...'

274

There was one small problem: how to get at them! It was against the rules for them to visit us in our bedrooms, and it went without saying that it was also against the rules for us to visit them in their bedrooms.

Their quarters were on the fourth floor of the adjoining house. It was impossible to use the front door, there were spies lurking in every corner. We slipped outside under cover of darkness and I climbed on to Gregor's shoulders and hauled myself on to the first floor balcony, then gave Gregor a hand up. We looked apprehensively at the drainpipes.

'You reckon it'll take our weight?' I said.

'Try it and see,' said Gregor. 'If it takes you, it'll take me. You're the heaviest.'

'I beg your pardon,' I retorted, outraged, 'that is a palpable untruth!'

'Stop bleeding moaning!' he said, giving me a shove towards the suspect drainpipe. 'Either you want it or you don't, and this is the only way you're likely to get it!'

We reached the roof and clambered over the guttering, cold sweat breaking out between our shoulders. Far, far away below us lay the sea and the rocks. I stared down at them and shivered.

'It's a funny thing,' I said, 'but I can't stand heights. It's one of my weaknesses.'

'And nurses are one of mine!' replied Gregor, with an evil grin.

We crept along the roof to their room, then leaned over the edge of the guttering and threw pebbles at them through the open windows. They looked out and saw us, twisting their heads round, pulling faces and pretending to be shocked.

'We're coming down!' hissed Gregor.

They made no attempt to stop us. Indeed, their room was so tidy, so seductively arranged, so softly lit, that I was tempted to believe they had anticipated a visit.

'Look,' said Gregor, suddenly stiff and foolish in their presence, 'we've brought you something.'

And he thrust a large bottle of vodka and a tin of caviar at them, while I, equally maladroit, handed over my own contribution: a watch and a bracelet that I had stolen from Tiny, who in his turn had stolen them from someone else. I was still waiting for him to discover his loss.

The girls received their gifts with little squeaks of glee. We all sat down together in the dim light and regarded one another.

The vodka was passed round; we ate the caviar and some minced meat and red cabbage. The girls giggled a great deal and eyed us up and down, trying to assess our likely performances. One of them was big and blonde, the other was small and dark. Truth to tell, I was scared stiff of both of them!

The brunette finally attached herself to me, slipping on to my lap and putting an arm round my neck as we sipped our vodka. I felt myself beginning to sweat. I wondered why on earth I had come. It was worse than waiting in the trenches for the enemy to launch an attack ... It was so long since I had had a woman. Suppose I made a fool of myself? She would be insulted and I should be shamed. And the word would spread round the company and my life would be a misery. I should never have come. Let Gregor have both of them. He was welcome.

The girl rubbed her face close against mine. I felt her lips, half open, brush across my mouth. Next moment, it seemed as if she was devouring me. I stopped feeling scared and began to feel rather cautiously excited. I let an exploratory hand crawl spider-like up her leg, and she wriggled with pleasure. I began to grow more bold.

Gregor was more forward than I. He had already taken possession of the blonde and laid her flat out on one of the beds. A pair of pants came flapping across the room like a frightened pigeon, followed by a stocking. The blonde giggled rather shrilly but made no attempt at resistance.

I found myself being pushed backwards, off the chair and on to the bed. My companion launched herself after me, lying on top of me, her lips nuzzling the base of my neck.

'What's your name?' she murmured. 'Mine's Gertrude.'

'Gertrude ... I'm Sven.'

'German?'

'Danish.'

'Ah! Danish!' I felt her fingers plucking at me, slowly removing my clothes. 'I've been married twice,' she chattily informed me. 'My first husband was killed in Poland and the other worked at the Ortskommandantur. The English blew it up. The whole road was gone within ten minutes. Incendiary bombs,' she explained.

'Oh yes?'

I was not interested in the English and their incendiary bombs. My temperature had rocketed so high I felt quite dizzy. I pulled her to me, pressing her against me, and she wound her legs about me and rubbed herself up and down.

'It's been such a long time,' she whispered.

'Me too,' I said.

We were silent a while.

'Have you had many women?' she asked.

'I don't know ... How can I remember?'

'How can you forget?' she chided.

'It was all so long ago ... we've just come from Stalingrad ... I can't remember all the things that happened to me before that.'

'Stalingrad!' She gave an ecstatic shudder and pressed herself even harder against me. 'That must have been terrible ...'

'Very nasty,' I agreed, and I began sweating profusely.

'It's a wonder a man can live through it——'

'Don't worry,' I murmured, 'this makes up for it all ...'

And it did, at the time. We spent the whole night making love. We passed through the *Kama Sutra* from cover to cover and were ready to begin all over again with the dawn. But time was up, and Gregor and I had to make our way back across the rooftops.

'Watch how you go!' said the girls, hanging out of the window and giggling. 'It won't be as easy as when you came!'

As we slipped unsteadily down the drainpipe to the first floor balcony, we saw two dim figures galloping homewards with bottles tucked under their arms. Tiny and Porta.

'Where have they been?' I demanded.

'Dunno,' said Gregor, 'but they're breaking the rules: no drink allowed on the premises ...'

'No sex allowed on the premises,' I said, owlishly.

Gregor and I sniggered happily as we clambered over the balcony.

For four days we continued to play in the ante-chamber to paradise. Each night Gregor and I mountaineered across the rooftops and each morning we stumbled back again, exhausted. We were drunk with the fresnly discovered delights of sex, and perhaps it was as well that we were called back to the front before the pleasure began to grow stale. The Legionnaire looked at us and laughed softly to himself.

'You look worse than when you came,' he remarked.

'A change is as good as a rest,' said Gregor, with all the solemnity of one who is expounding an original theory.

'Just as well!' retorted the Legionnaire. 'You two haven't had a moment's rest since you arrived! On the job morning, noon and night ...'

We travelled back in a train that was full of horses. We stretched out in the feeding troughs that were fixed to the walls, and Gregor and I fell asleep almost immediately. But this time we were woken not by soft lips and gentle caresses, but by the insistent nuzzling of the horses and the hot blowing of their sweet, hay-smelling breath on our cheeks. We and the poor beasts were going back together to the horrors of war.

'We shall be ruthless in our fight against the opponents of the Confederation of the German Peoples. All those who cannot integrate into our society must be exterminated, regardless of race or religion.'

General Goering, during a talk given
to the police—12.12.1934

A section of blood-spattered T34s nosed their way slowly down the centre of the road, between the serried ranks of corpses which lined the pavements and even spilled over into the gutters. In the leading tank, Lieutenant Jevtjenko gazed with complete indifference at the gaunt grey shadows that came crawling out of the sewers and the cellars, out of the ruins and the bomb craters. They were men, these furtive shadows; starving, withered and broken. But to Lieutenant Jevtjenko they were merely the scum of a defeated army.

A German colonel suddenly ran into the road and flung wide his arms.

'Heil Hitler!' he shouted, as Lieutenant Jevtjenko's tank approached him; and, 'Heil Hitler!' he cried, as it crushed him beneath its tracks.

The colonel had lost his mind. Many men had lost their minds at Stalingrad. Amongst them was General Lange, who, at the last moment, as the victorious Russians marched back to claim their property, seized hold of a machine-gun and turned on his own men. He killed several hundreds before he ran out of ammunition.

Behind the column of T34s came a low black car. It hooted impatiently as it forced its way through the crowds of soldiers that were now milling about in the street. It gradually moved up the column and overtook the leading tank. Inside, reclining in the back seat, were two generals. One was in khaki. That was General Pölkownik, a Russian staff officer, The other was in grey, with scarlet lapels and a baton in his hand. That was the newly promoted Field-Marshal Friedrich Paulus. He glanced now and again through the windows, staring unseeing at the ragged soldiers who lined the street and patiently awaited their fate at the hands of the Russians. Prison camp, or maybe worse. Field-Marshal Paulus smiled at a comment of General Pölkownik's, and the two men laughed together. Paulus never once referred to his starving troops; he never once made

279

mention of the 285,000 corpses that lay scattered over the steppe, or the 10,000 execution orders which he himself had signed during the last forty-eight days of the battle for Stalingrad. All that was over and done with. He could look out of the window at the grey-faced men and be unmoved by their suffering. The battle was over, they were no longer his concern.

Meanwhile, one of his generals was caught trying to steal a hunk of horsemeat from a wounded lieutenant and was battered almost to death for his pains. Yelling and raving, he was dragged away by three Russian officers and thrown into a prison camp in one of the Red Army buildings. Not all generals could be promoted to field-marshal and be driven through the streets of Stalingrad in a big black car.

Down in a cellar, beneath the blackened ruins of a factory, a field hospital had been set up. And in one corner of the cellar crouched a small group of men from the 44th MOT Division. They were gnawing at things that came out of a bucket. The bucket had been taken from the operating theatre, and the things they were eating were amputated limbs. It was the first square meal they had had for more than three months.

SEVENTEEN

EXECUTIONS

The truck turned in at the prison gates and we were enveloped in a great cloud of choking dust blown up by the wind. As it slowly cleared, we were able to look about us and see what kind of place they had sent us to.

The central prison at Charkov was something of a showpiece. We were connoisseurs of prisons, and we recognised a bit of quality when we saw it! At Charkov, all the buildings were painted an ostentatious white for purity. They were scrubbed clean and shining with virtue, and were as yet unmarked by graffiti. They were laid out in the shape of a star, and the whole prison did its best to look like public pleasure gardens.

In the courtyard of Block 4 it was exercise time, and the prisoners were running in circles with their hands anxiously holding up their trousers. No belts or braces are allowed in military prisons: governors live in perpetual terror lest some cunning fiend in a condemned cell should manage to hang himself before the firing squad can get at him.

The truck came to a halt and we reluctantly jumped out. Twelve men in battle-dress; twelve rifles and twenty-five bullets per man ... We knew what it meant. We had all of us been through it before. We were the firing squad, come to murder some poor bastard.

'Why can't the sodding SS do their own dirty work?' grumbled Porta.

'They can't stand the sight of blood,' explained the Legionnaire, solemnly.

Nobody laughed. We were in no mood for laughing. Not even Heide really enjoyed being a member of a firing squad.

'Wonder who's going to cop it this time?' speculated Tiny.

'Whoever it is, I hope to God they don't start screaming and wailing,' I muttered. 'I can't stand it when they do that.'

'Quite right,' said the Legionnaire. 'They should go bravely to their death and let us gun them down with clear consciences.'

I looked at him suspiciously. He grinned at me.

'The self-pitying bastards!' he said. 'When my turn comes to die, I shall think of the poor firing squad ...'

'It's all very well,' I said, heatedly. 'It's not as if we asked for the bloody job——'

'Eh, what about that bird we had to do in that time?' interrupted Tiny. 'That telephone bird? Remember how she yelled and fought——'

'Will you for Christ's sake shut up!' The Old Man turned on us, his forehead gathered into deep frown lines. 'Let's get the job over with and stop belly-aching about it!'

We marched through the prison and came to a stop in the small patch of garden behind the governor's quarters. A large red star still stood guard over the door, and the letters NKVD still stared out at us; but the flag that flapped above our heads in the breeze was the Nazi one. Swastika and red star together. Both brought me out in cold beads of fear.

In the middle of a flat patch of dry earth stood a wooden post, newly erected and creosoted. Leather thongs were attached to it; one to bind the ankles, one for the hips, one for the arms and the shoulders. For the moment they hung limp, awaiting their first victim. The previous post and set of thongs had probably been shattered by flying bullets. It was said that they would last for about four hundred executions, but after that they had to be replaced.

A major was waiting for us, and saw fit to deliver himself of a pep talk.

'You men have been specially chosen for this task—hand-picked, as you might say. I know it's not everyone's idea of fun, being in a firing squad, but we all have unpleasant duties to perform at one time or another and it's up to us, as soldiers, to carry them out to the best of our ability.'

'We have been through it before,' murmured the Old Man.

The major stared at him.

'Precisely! That's why you've been picked for the job. It is, in its way, something of an honour.'

'I see,' said the Old Man.

The major squared his shoulders.

'Just remember, when the time comes, that these swine are deserters. They let the side down and they deserve to be shot. Don't go feeling sorry for them. They ran out and left their men to die ... Not only that, but any one of you caught firing wide, and believe me, you'll be the next ones out there, tied up at that post ... Aim for the heart and don't try any funny business. Are you with me?'

'I catch the general drift of it, sir,' said the Old Man.

'Yes, well you just remember what I told you ... no funny business!'

He turned and walked away, across the dusty brown earth towards a sweet-scented lilac tree, where he was joined by two priests, one RC and one Protestant. We watched him until he was out of earshot.

'Big deal,' said Barcelona, sourly. 'What's he think we are? Greenhorns?'

'We've been specially hand-picked,' Porta reminded him. 'It is, in its way something of an honour ...'

'An honour I could do without,' grumbled Barcelona.

'I don't like it,' said the Old Man. He shook his head. 'I don't like the look of it ... something funny's going on ...'

A lieutenant came across and inspected our weapons and supply of ammunition. He put us through our paces, seemed satisfied, walked off and left us waiting.

We waited for almost an hour. Somewhere nearby, way up in a poplar tree, a woodpecker was industriously drilling a hole. The execution yard gradually filled with officers, who stood in little groups, smoking and talking, pacing up and down and tapping their feet. They seemed on edge and apprehensive, there was an air of uneasy anticipation in the governor's neat little garden.

The woodpecker completed his work and flew away. Two large black crows flapped slowly towards the abandoned tree, the frayed edges of their wings splayed out like fingers. They perched on the topmost branch and sat hunched up, side by side, waiting for the show to begin.

From the condemned block came four police constables. In their midst was the prisoner. His hands were tied before him, and he was wearing a threadbare greatcoat. As we watched, the group disappeared behind a clump of lilacs and we lost sight of them for a few seconds. They came back into our field of vision, and we saw that the prisoner was a tall and imposing man, walking with an air of upright dignity despite his tied hands. As they came nearer, we were able to recognise him. A horrified murmur ran round the twelve of us.

'Augsberg . . .'

'General Augsberg!'

'The shits!' muttered Porta, by my side. 'The filthy dirty sodding lousy shits!'

The group came to a halt before the major who had lectured us. They exchanged salutes. The major faced the condemned officer.

'SS Brigandenführer Paul Augsberg, it is my duty to tell you that your appeal has been turned down by the Commander-in-Chief of the Fourth Army. You are therefore condemned to death for having left the combat zone at Stalingrad, and for having taken with you a body of men, all of whom were fit and able to face the enemy, and thus deprived the Sixth Army of troops needed for the defence of Stalingrad. Have you anything to say before you are executed?'

The general looked down at the major.

'You poor naïve fool!' he said, contemptuously.

The major swallowed. He beckoned to the priests, but Augsberg waved them away.

'None of that mumbo jumbo!'

The general was led to the execution post. Expert hands secured the leather thongs.

'They can all go and get stuffed,' whispered Tiny. 'I shall fire wide.'

'So shall I,' I hissed back.

'Me too,' agreed Porta.

The major faced the firing squad.

'Take aim ... fire!'

Twelve shots rang our simultaneously. General Augsberg's head fell forward on to his chest, but we could not see where he had been hit. The doctor, his stethoscope dangling round his neck, stubbed out a cigarette and walked forward. We saw him lift up the general's head. We saw his expression change. He didn't even trouble to use his stethoscope.

'The prisoner's still alive! The bullets didn't touch him!'

The major's jaw fell open.

'Would you mind repeating that?'

'Certainly.' The doctor straightened up. 'I said, the prisoner is still alive. The bullets didn't touch him ... I suggest you try again.'

The major's tongue flickered snakelike over his lips. He turned furiously upon us. We could tell he was displeased by the way he spoke.

'Listen to me, you filthy swine! Any more of that and you'll be for the firing squad yourselves! And I mean that!' He drew in a deep breath, evidently controlling a wild impulse to lash out at us there and then. 'Now, get on and do the job properly and don't waste any more time!'

Once again, he gave the order to fire. His voice was high and hysterical.

This time, twelve rifles were aimed directly at the square of red material pinned over the heart. We had made our futile protest, there was no point in prolonging the general's agony. If we didn't shoot him, others would; and would then shoot us, in our turn.

Two stretcher-bearers ran up with a pine coffin. They untied the dead body and dumped it inside, scattered sawdust over the bloody earth, picked up the coffin and disappeared behind the lilacs.

We were ready for the second execution. The group was already waiting in the shadow of the trees. Four guards and a lieutenant. Our lieutenant. Our young lieutenant with the woolly muffler, who had come all the way from Stalingrad with us.

This time, the major dispensed with his monologue and came straight to the point.

'You know what you're here for. Have you anything to say?'

The lieutenant shook his head.

'Do you want the services of a priest?'

'I want nothing ... Just get on with it and let it be over quickly, that's all I ask.'

The major waved him onwards to the execution post. He turned and glanced malevolently in our direction, as if to make sure we had heard the lieutenant's last wishes and would honour them. The lieutenant himself looked across at us and smiled. His eyes travelled round the group, resting briefly on each one of us. I felt terribly ashamed. There was nothing we could any of us do, yet I felt so ashamed.

'Prepare to fire!'

I was trembling almost too much to take a steady aim. I closed my eyes. I didn't want to see where I was shooting. I had a faint hope I might hit the major.

'Fire!'

Twelve loud cracks, and then silence. And then, from a long way off, the voice of the doctor, pronouncing the lieutenant dead. I opened my eyes and saw the two stretcher-bearers galloping off with their second coffin. Over by the wall, beyond the lilac trees, was a freshly dug ditch. In the ditch was General Augsberg, already covered in earth. The lieutenant now joined him, and they lay buried together, the latest in a long line of unnamed graves.

We had one more execution to face. We knew who it must be, even before we heard his frenzied screams of protest. He didn't want to die ... But out on the steppe lay the bodies of five hundred men whom he had been unable to save. That was his crime, and for that he must pay with his life.

They dragged him kicking and fighting to the post. The major was having a bad day of it. These executions were a tricky business, and men like the doctor made no attempt to co-operate. Why couldn't the wretched fellow go off quietly, without all this fuss and bother?

The black cowl was handed over. The doctor's head was pushed into it and his accusing cries were muffled.

One of the execution squad suddenly fell forward in a faint, leaving only eleven of us to murder the doctor.

The Roman Catholic padre walked up to the faceless being in the black mask and attempted to soothe him with a prayer. The doctor now began weeping.

'Fire!'

Eleven shots, and this time we made very sure we did not miss our mark. Since the doctor had to die, let it be over quickly.

Afterwards, we were free for the rest of the day. They gave us a litre of vodka each and sent us off to drink ourselves into oblivion and forget the deeds they had forced us to do. But there are some deeds one cannot forget, some memories one cannot wipe out, and that day has remained with us ever since, violent and vivid in our minds. There are some things a man feels too guilty to forget . . .

We didn't know at the time, but found out much later, that even as we were shooting her husband, Frau Elizabeth Augsberg was opening and reading a telegram in Berlin:

'Berlin–Charlottenbourg . . .

'If you wish to see the soldier Paul Augsberg for the last time before his execution, which is due to take place on 6th May 1943 at 800 hours, you should present yourself at the Military Prison of Kharkov, in the Ukraine, on 5th May at 1900 hours. A visit of ten minutes' duration will be allowed. You should bring this telegram with you.

'(Sgd) Mannstein—Generalfeldmarschall
'OB4—Panzer Armee.'

General Augsberg would have been dead and buried by the time his wife had finished reading the telegram.

THE END

BLITZFREEZE by SVEN HASSEL

The Führer's commands were simple – forward to Moscow! And so the mighty Panzer regiments thundered into action – killing, raping, burning their way across the great wastes of Russia . . .

But this was to be the bloodiest of all Hitler's wars – a war where Russian infantrymen threw themselves before the oncoming tanks, where women fought as savagely as men, where German guns killed Germans and Russians alike, mangling them indiscriminately into tattered hunks of meat . . .

And finally Porta, Tiny, Barcelona, all of them – caring nothing for who should win the war – began the long retreat – back through the corpse-littered plains where blood and bodies were already frozen beneath the winter ice . . .

0 552 09761 6

ASSIGNMENT GESTAPO by SVEN HASSEL

Their more unorthodox weapons were lengths of steel wire and knives with double-edged blades, and some of their most prized possessions were gold teeth snatched from corpses . . .

The 'Disciplinary Regiment', a tank company in Hitler's army – without a tank to its name – was fighting a brutal war against the Russians. A bunch of hardened criminals in filthy rags, stinking to high heaven, this company was worth an entire regiment of freshly laundered troops from Breslau. Guerrilla warfare on the Eastern front was for them a prelude to the bloody massacre of Russia troops who'd attacked the German reserves and occupied their head-quarters. Then the 'Disciplinary Regiment' was sent to Hamburg where their next assignment was guard duty for the bestial Gestapo . . .

0 552 08779 3

A SELECTED LIST OF WAR BOOKS
PUBLISHED BY CORGI

THE PRICES SHOWN BELOW WERE CORRECT AT THE TIME OF
GOING TO PRESS. HOWEVER TRANSWORLD PUBLISHERS
RESERVE THE RIGHT TO SHOW NEW RETAIL PRICES ON COVERS
WHICH MAY DIFFER FROM THOSE PREVIOUSLY ADVERTISED IN
THE TEXT OR ELSEWHERE.

☐ 10808 1	THE WILD GEESE	*Daniel Carney*	£1.95
☐ 10807 3	FIREPOWER	*Chris Dempster & Dave Tomkins*	£2.95
☐ 11168 6	COURT MARTIAL	*Sven Hassel*	£2.50
☐ 10400 0	THE BLOODY ROAD TO DEATH	*Sven Hassel*	£2.95
☐ 09761 6	BLITZFREEZE	*Sven Hassel*	£2.50
☐ 09178 2	REIGN OF HELL	*Sven Hassel*	£2.95
☐ 28779 3	ASSIGNMENT GESTAPO	*Sven Hassel*	£2.50
☐ 08603 7	LIQUIDATE PARIS	*Sven Hassel*	£2.50
☐ 08528 6	MARCH BATTALION	*Sven Hassel*	£2.50
☐ 08168 X	MONTE CASSINO	*Sven Hassel*	£2.50
☐ 07871 9	COMRADES OF WAR	*Sven Hassel*	£2.95
☐ 07242 7	WHEELS OF TERROR	*Sven Hassel*	£2.95
☐ 11417 0	THE LEGION OF THE DAMNED	*Sven Hassel*	£2.50
☐ 07935 9	MERCENARY	*Mike Hoare*	£1.95
☐ 12419 2	CHICKENHAWK	*Robert C. Mason*	£3.95
☐ 11030 2	VICTIMS OF YALTA	*Count Nikolai Tolstoy*	£3.95
☐ 10499 X	THE GLORY HOLE	*T. Jeff Williams*	£2.50

All Corgi/Bantam Books are available at your bookshop or newsagent, or can be ordered from the following address:

Corgi/Bantam Books,
Cash Sales Department,
P.O. Box 11, Falmouth, Cornwall TR10 9EN

Please send a cheque or postal order (no currency) and allow 60p for postage and packing for the first book plus 25p for the second book and 15p for each additional book ordered up to a maximum charge of £1.90 in UK.

B.F.P.O. customers please allow 60p for the first book, 25p for the second book plus 15p per copy for the next 7 books, thereafter 9p per book.

Overseas customers, including Eire, please allow £1.25 for postage and packing for the first book, 75p for the second book, and 28p for each subsequent title ordered.